NEIL LANCASTER is the No. 1 digital bestselling author of both the Tom Novak and Max Craigie series. His first Craigie novel, *Dead Man's Grave*, was longlisted for the 2021 McIlvanney Prize for Best Scottish Crime Book of the Year. The second Craigie novel is *The Blood Tide*, which has topped several e-book and audio charts, and was also longlisted for the McIlvanney Prize and shortlisted for the Dead Good Readers Award. He served as a military policeman and worked for the Metropolitan Police as a detective, investigating serious crimes in the capital and beyond. As a covert policing and surveillance specialist he utilised all manner of techniques to investigate and disrupt major crime and criminals.

He now lives in the Scottish Highlands, writes crime and thriller novels, and works as a broadcaster and commentator on true crime documentaries. He is a key expert on two Sky Crime TV series, *Meet, Marry, Murder* and *Made for Murder*, and appeared on a BBC true crime show, *Big Little Crimes*.

✖ @neillancaster66
🅕 @NeilLancasterCrime
www.neillancastercrime.co.uk

Also by Neil Lancaster

The Max Craigie Novels
Dead Man's Grave
The Blood Tide
The Night Watch
Blood Runs Cold
The Devil You Know

The Tom Novak Novels
Going Dark
Going Rogue
Going Back

NEIL LANCASTER

WHEN SHADOWS FALL

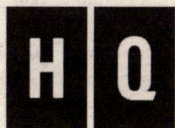

ONE PLACE. MANY STORIES

HQ
An imprint of HarperCollins*Publishers* Ltd
1 London Bridge Street
London SE1 9GF

www.harpercollins.co.uk

HarperCollins*Publishers*
Macken House, 39/40 Mayor Street Upper
Dublin 1, D01 C9W8, Ireland

This edition 2025

1
First published in Great Britain by HQ,
an imprint of HarperCollins*Publishers* Ltd 2025

ISBN: 9780008551391

Typeset in Sabon LT Pro by HarperCollins*Publishers* India

Printed and bound in the UK using 100%
Renewable Electricity at CPI Group (UK) Ltd

FSC
www.fsc.org

MIX
Paper
FSC™ C007454

For more information visit: www.harpercollins.co.uk/green

Dedicated with my deepest respect to all the men and women in the Mountain Rescue Teams, Coastguard search-and-rescue helicopter crews and members of Police Scotland who keep people safe on the Munros of Scotland.

Your bravery never ceases to astound me.

Max Craigie CV

Military Service

Craigie Joined the Army as a junior leader, on 12/09/1999, passed infantry training with distinction and was posted to 3rd Bn, The Black Watch. Notable operations listed below.

2003 Operation Telic 1 (Invasion of Iraq) Initial attack on Basra. No incidents of note. Received Brigade Commanders Commendation for leadership, and restraint under fire during a live contact.

2004 Undertakes selection for ████████████

2005 Successful completion of selection to ████████████ *posted to* ████████████ *at* ████████████ *deployments to* ████████████ *on covert operations*

2009 deployed Operation Herrick. Engaged in operations against the Taliban, including Operation Panther's Claw. Awarded a "mention in despatches," for bravery (citation available)

2010 Discharged from army at conclusion of contract. Conduct certified as "exemplary."

Metropolitan Police History.

2010- Joins Metropolitan Police (MPS) and undertakes training at MPS Training establishment.

2010 -Brent Borough response policing. Undertakes training towards specialising in criminal investigations.

2014- passes national investigators exam, completes, and passes Detective Foundation Course.

2015-Undertakes and passes training for deployment as ████████████ Successfully entered onto the ████████████████████████ DS Craigie undertakes a number of successful deployments targeting the most serious of criminality. Examples include Operation ████████████████████████, ████████████████████.

Awarded Commissioner's High Commendation for exceptional bravery disarming, and arresting a gunman who, seconds before fatally shot a drug rival. Operation Maximus.

2020 Selected for SC07, Serious and Organised Crime Command. Successfully targeted a number of criminal networks, disrupting major crime, and being responsible for managing proactive operations such as ████████, ████████, and ████████.

Proactive operation (Operation ████████████████████ ████████████████████)

2021-Operation Lucrative. Investigation of an armed network targeting commercial premises. Engagement with an armed suspect during which Craigie engaged with, and fatally shot a suspect who was in the process of robbing a commercial premises. Shooting was judged to be justified by IOPC, and Coroner recorded a verdict of lawful killing. *Family continues to push for a reinvestigation.*

2021-Craigie transfers to Police Scotland.

WHEN SHADOWS FALL

1

LEANNE WILSON COULD barely contain her excitement as she looked out of the window of her room at the Cluanie Inn, a steaming cup of tea in her hand. The summer sun was only just emerging over the horizon, painting the sky a vivid crimson. The weather had been stunning all week, and today looked like it was going to be no different.

She picked up her phone, opened the camera and took a selfie, her thumb extended as she grinned widely. She posted the picture on her Facebook page. *Final cuppa before big ascent of A' Chralaig and Mullach Fraoch-choire.*

This would be the seventh and final day of her Munro-bagging holiday in the Highlands of Scotland, and she was looking forward to it hugely. It was a big day of climbing, including a difficult ridgeline, but the weather was looking utterly beautiful again with a forecast of clear skies and light winds. The sunrise was quickly fading, as usual this far north, to be replaced with an ice-blue sky, and just a couple of lenticular clouds that hung like woolly flying saucers.

Her phone beeped with a notification from Facebook. It was David reacting to the post with a heart. A second later a response flashed up. *Have fun, babe.* Leanne frowned and minimised the app, having no intention of reacting to her recently ex-boyfriend. Even now, at 5 a.m., he was trying to get inside her head, which was why she was here, ready to climb two Munros while he was no doubt about to get on a train for a day in London. She shook her head, realising that she was well rid of him; he was a manipulative bastard, and this trip was her way of saying, 'Fuck you, David. I don't need you.'

She checked the rucksack she'd packed the night before, as she had done every night on this trip, which she'd planned like a military expedition. Then she pulled on her worn and scratched Meindl walking boots and laced them up, the leather almost caressing her feet, so perfectly worn in were they. She stood up, feeling a swirl in her head as the blood whooshed.

A final check of her gear and she studied herself in the full-length mirror. In her expensive climbing gear and bandanna-covered honey-blonde hair she looked tanned, lean and fit and much younger than her forty years. 'All the gear, no idea,' David would have scoffed. Well, she was showing him, right now. She was out here, on her own and conquering Scotland.

She gave herself a reassuring nod as she passed the mirror, picked up her walking poles, and set off out of the comfortable room, determination coursing through her veins. Then she headed towards the steep incline that led to the summit, over a thousand metres up. Two more Munros, then it would be back down to Glasgow to her new life in her new home away from David. No more sarcastic, sneering boyfriend controlling her every move.

*

The climb had been brutal. A straight-up slog on a grassy slope at a vicious incline for an unrelenting 750 metres until she hit the ridgeline of A' Chralaig. As the incline levelled off, she stopped, breathing hard, legs burning, and looked around her. The scenery was just breathtaking. There was no other word for it. A massive vista stretched away in all directions, stark against the cobalt sky. A mix of jagged grey peaks, rolling green hills and glens everywhere she looked. Behind her was the long, thin flash of water of Loch Alsh sparkling as the sun hit its smooth surface. It felt like she was on top of the world. She breathed in deeply, drinking in the clear air that was scented with grass and the faintly organic smell of the soft peat beneath her boots. She was more content than she'd been in many years, knowing that she was here, on her own, seizing life as a single woman. She needed no man in her life, and certainly not that bastard David. She carried on, picking up her pace on the gentler slope towards the ridgeline, taking in the scenery with a continuing wonder.

A prickle of sweat had broken out on her back, as the early morning sun had now fully cleared the horizon and was beating down with unusual summer warmth for this part of the country. Very soon, she'd ascended the incline that led to the huge cairn of stones that marked the thousand-plus-metre summit of A' Chralaig.

Breathing heavily, she wiped the film of sweat from her forehead and pulled the cap from her head. She was far too warm. She removed her rucksack, leant it against the cairn and pulled off her jacket, stuffing it inside the pack. She took out the steel insulated water bottle and took a deep draught, relishing the cooling Highland water. Her phone buzzed in her pocket; it was a message from David.

Miss you, hun. Be careful on the hill, you're not used to the exercise x 😊

Leanne frowned, irritation flushing her already pink cheeks at the passive-aggressive message.

'Fuck you, David,' she muttered to herself, as she opened the camera app and took another snap of herself, thumb extended with the vast and spectacular scenery behind her, the blue of Loch Carron juxtaposed against the deep green of the lush grass. She'd fucking prove him wrong. Within a second, she'd uploaded the photograph onto her Facebook feed.

Boom! Summit of A' Chralaig done. Now on to Mullach Fraoch-choire. No stopping this girl! 😊

She pocketed her phone and heaved her rucksack on her back and set off again, turning onto the rocky, precarious ridgeline that snaked towards the distant peak of her next destination. The terrain was severe, sloping steeply away on both sides of her, and she kept to the narrow but firm footpath where thousands of boots had tramped before her.

A speck of blue flashed two hundred metres ahead of her, and she realised she wasn't alone on the hill, despite how early it was. Her intention had been to experience the solitude of climbing the Munros alone, but it looked like someone had beat her to it. She picked her way along the sharp ridgeline, keeping up a steady pace. Despite the sheer nature of the terrain she was totally relaxed and was thankful that she had absolutely no fear of heights.

The path descended a little, taking her away from the worst of the terrain, which seemed to be almost impassable. As she rounded the corner, she saw a baseball-capped man, wearing mirrored shades and a blue windproof, sitting on a rock on the narrow path. He had a mug in his hand and a cigarette in his mouth, a cloud of smoke hanging around him. He didn't look at her, just stared out at the stunning view that was laid out in front of them.

'Braw morning,' he said, raising his tin mug, but still not looking at her.

Leanne smiled. 'Morning, yes, it's lovely. Are you local?'

'Kind of,' he said, taking a long drag on his cigarette with obvious pleasure, but he still didn't turn to face her. Leanne wrinkled her nose as the acrid cloud reached her. She hesitated, a niggle of discomfort in her stomach. She'd have to almost squeeze past him as he leant against the jagged stone of the steep ridge.

4

'Mind if I pass? It's a bit tight,' she said, trying to keep her voice light.

'Aye, dinnae mind me,' he said, still not turning to face her. He just raised his mug to his mouth, once more. Leanne looked at him a little more closely, as he stared out into the broad vista that seemed to stretch out to the very ends of the planet. He was lean and fit-looking, with tanned and lined skin that spoke of a life outside. She breathed and relaxed a little. He was just like her, another person on the side of a Munro enjoying the sun.

'Right, best be cracking on then. Still a long way to go,' said Leanne, moving off.

The man smiled and pressed his back against the rock face, flicking the end from his half-smoked cigarette and tucking it into his chest pocket.

As Leanne approached him, she turned away from the rock face to allow enough room to pass without making contact with the stranger. She had just passed him and was beginning to step up her pace when he spoke again, his voice colder and harder.

'Mind how you go, Leanne.'

As if shot, Leanne spun to face him. His warm smile was gone, and the sunglasses suddenly made him look more like a predatory insect. What was visible of his face had changed. His expression had morphed from an easy smile to a blank mask, utterly devoid of expression, his lips pursed and jaw firm.

'H . . . how do you know my name?' she said, the words catching in her throat, and the blood in her veins suddenly icy.

'Oh, Leanne. I know more than you can imagine.' He smiled.

Leanne screamed. A piercing shriek that echoed in the vast, open space.

2

DS MAX CRAIGIE was standing on the beach at Chanonry Point, the long, thin and narrow peninsula punctuated by a white lighthouse that jutted out into the Moray Firth from the seaside village of Fortrose on the Black Isle.

He was standing next to a small, bird-like elderly woman with a cloud of grey hair who had binoculars pressed to her face as she looked out into the sparkling blue water. She wore a blue windcheater, despite the stunning weather, which was emblazoned with 'Whale and Dolphin Conservation'.

She gasped, and her trim body tensed. 'Max, look, it's Flake. I've not seen him for fucking ages, looks like the Bad Boys are returning,' she said, handing the binoculars over to Max, her eyes shining.

'Language, Auntie Elspeth. I've no idea who the Bad Boys are, and no idea who Flake is,' said Max, accepting the binoculars, making sure he was facing her when he spoke. Elspeth was profoundly deaf but an expert lip-reader.

'Och, don't be such a bloody prude. You hear ten times worse every minute of every day with that potty-mouthed boss of yours. Now look at them.' Elspeth pointed, her finger quivering with excitement. 'That's definitely Flake. I can tell from the nicks in his dorsal fin; how exciting, this will mean a real stramash in the pod,' she said, hopping from foot to foot. Aunt Elspeth was Max Craigie's closest and only living relative, his parents having died in a car crash many years ago. She was a real force of nature, with a diverse range of interests, lots of friends and a curiously foul mouth. She was heavily involved in local conservation and was an active volunteer with the wildlife charity that monitored whale and dolphin populations.

She turned to look at him, her fierce eyes sparkling in the bright sunshine. 'Well, that's true, and I'll be back there tomorrow. I've already had an expletive-laden message from him today accusing me of being a shirker.'

'Aye, well, he can take a running, bastarding jump. You need to get back because that lovely lassie you're married to must be about ready to drop my great niece or nephew any time. How long now?'

'Another fortnight, we're told.'

'And you didn't ask what sex?'

'No, Auntie E. Not enough surprises nowadays, are there?' Max turned back to the view, just as a bottle-nosed dolphin broke the surface of the glittering sea, a massive salmon in its mouth, which it tossed into the air almost playfully. There was a gasp from the thronging crowd that was on the shoreline watching the display.

'Oooh, that was Charlie. I've not seen him around for a while, either.' Elspeth's face was alive, and Max could almost feel the waves of happiness wafting from his beloved aunt.

Max felt a buzzing in his pocket, and he plucked his phone out and looked at the screen, a flicker of surprise when he saw who was calling.

'Shay Hammond, long time no hear, mate. What's up?'

Elspeth stared intently at Max and spoke in a hoarse whisper. 'Tell Shay I said hi.' She nodded, grinning widely.

'Shippers, it's been way too long. How you been?' The voice was bouncy and full of energy, as was always the case with the caller. Shay Hammond had been a schoolfriend of Max's many years ago. Max had left to join the Army at sixteen but Shay had stayed on at school, later joining the Navy where he'd served as a helicopter pilot. He was now working for the Coastguard as a search-and-rescue helicopter pilot out of Inverness Airport.

'I'm good, pal. In fact, I'm up on the Black Isle, at the point. Popped up to see Elspeth, who says hi by the way.'

'You come to the Highlands and don't mention it to me? You're a scumbag, Craigie. Hi, Auntie Elspeth.'

'Shay says hi back, Auntie E.' Max nodded at Elspeth before continuing. 'Sorry, mate, a flying visit. Need to get back in case Katie drops.'

'Blimey, is that soon?'

'Very. She's huge, uncomfortable, grumpy, and it's all apparently my fault,' said Max, chuckling.

'That sounds familiar. Wait till she's in pain and pushing, she'll definitely blame you then. When are you heading back down the Central Belt?'

'Later today.'

'Can you pop by the base at the airport? We had a death on a hill recently, and I'm not happy about it. Something doesn't feel right.' Shay's normal chirpy voice was instantly more serious.

'Did local cops come?' asked Max, frowning.

'Yeah, but how can I put this generously . . .' He paused a moment. 'They didn't seem that arsed. Can you pop by? I can tell you all about it and show you the video. We recovered the climber to the base, and the undertakers have just picked her up. Something feels off, shippers.' Shay's use of the term 'shippers' for 'shipmate' was typical for an ex-Navy man.

'When are you on till?' said Max, feeling the familiar tingle in his stomach at the prospect of something new.

'Here all night until 1300 tomorrow. We've been caning the flying hours so won't be heading out unless there's a shout, but let me know when you're coming, yeah?'

Max looked at his watch; it was almost 2 p.m. 'I probably need to make tracks, anyway. I'll be there in an hour.'

'Awesome, I'll have the kettle on.' Shay hung up.

'Something serious?' asked Elspeth, her eyes questioning.

'Who knows, Auntie E? A death on the hill that Shay's not happy about. I'm gonna go and have a chat, and then I'd best head off. I don't want to cop too much flak when I get home.' Max hugged his aunt tightly, and she returned his embrace.

'You look after that wee girly, Max, she's way too good for you. And call me the second you have news, okay?'

'I promise, Auntie E.'

3

'HOOFING TO SEE you, shippers,' said Shay in his soft Black Isle brogue. He was a tall man, the same age as Max, with short salt-and-pepper hair, and a permanent smile on his dimple-cheeked face. He was dressed in a bright orange flight suit, and his handshake was firm.

'Been too long, pal. How've you been keeping?' asked Max, clapping him on the shoulder.

'Awesome, mate. Come up to the crew room for a cuppa, kettle's permanently on,' he said, turning and setting off up the stairs, two at a time.

'How're you liking it back in Scotland? Big change from London, right?' asked Shay, as he made the tea in two cracked mugs.

'It's different, for sure.'

'A big move – what prompted it?' Shay handed Max a steaming cup.

'You heard about the shooting, right?' Max said, referring to an incident where he'd been forced to shoot an armed robber. It had been a clean shot, and Max had been fully exonerated, but the IOPC inquiry had been brutal.

'I did hear, aye. Nasty business.'

Max shrugged. 'Left a sour taste, and it was made clear that my career was possibly not going to progress as I'd hoped. I was a bit controversial, shall we say, and as always, the senior officers closed ranks.'

'So, you moved four hundred miles north to escape the Sassenachs. Is it working out?'

Max smiled. 'Aye, Katie was reluctant at first, but she moved up, and now all's well. Culross is nice, you should come and visit soon.'

'Job good? Anti-corruption, I heard. Well, that's what Katie told my missus. She's a big fan of *Line of Duty*, so she was terribly excited about you going after bent coppers.'

Max snorted with laughter. 'Hardly *LOD*, but we're a small team that works direct for the Chief Constable, and we do whatever we're asked. It's just turned out that anti-corruption always seems to be the big deal. It's a good job, although it's a bit full-on, and the hours can be a bit tricky. Katie's already grumbling about the hours for when the bairn arrives.'

'I'm mostly fuming that you've been up here a few years, and this is the first time we've been in touch, you shite.' Shay grinned, and lightly punched Max's shoulder.

'So, what's this case all about?'

'A shout a week ago, that made me think, and the more I thought about it, the less I liked it.'

'I don't like it when ex-matelots think. Always a bad sign,' Max said with a half-smile.

'This is true, but this was a bad shout.'

'Well, your shouts are never about good stuff, are they?' Max paused. 'Go on, then.'

'We were called after sightings of an injured person at the bottom of the ridge on A' Chralaig, which the caller didn't want to attempt to get to. Don't blame them, mate. It's bloody treacherous once you're off the track, it's hellish steep.'

'Where's that?'

Shay sprang to his feet and tapped his finger on a large wall map at a point on the northwest of Scotland. 'A' Chralaig is north of Loch Cluanie in the Glen Affric to Glenmoriston range. You not bagged it?'

'Can't say I have.'

'Mate, it's a good hill. It's off the main tourist trail, so even in summer you can almost have it to yourself if you leave early enough. I'll take you up there one day.'

'Can we get to the point, Shay?'

'Fine, fine. Well, anyway, I put the helo down and we yomped to the casualty, with Chas and Jimbo, the winch paramedics, and there was nothing we could do for her. She was well gone, terrible head injuries and multiple fractures. Dead as a dodo, mate.'

'So why aren't you happy about this one?'

Shay sighed, and sipped at his tea before continuing. 'Look, we don't normally go out for corpses, we tend to leave it for the Mountain Rescue Teams to go in on foot, but we had no confirmation that she was dead, so we flew in anyway. It didn't feel right from first glance. She was on the hill on her own, which isn't unusual.' He placed his mug down on the coffee table and reached for his phone. He flicked and swiped at the screen before handing it to Max. A high-resolution video filled the screen of the top of a narrow-looking ridgeline, which then focused on a bright-red-jacketed and crumpled-looking body a good distance down from the apex. The track looked clear, and the weather was stunning.

'I see what you mean about steep, but it looks a decent track,' said Max, handing the phone back to Shay.

'That's part of my problem with the whole thing. She was properly dressed with good boots, decent kit, walking poles and a proper rucksack. The contents had spilled everywhere – she had emergency food, warmers kit, lightweight crampons. She even had an OS map around her neck and a Silva compass.'

'So, an experienced climber?'

'I'd say so. The going was perfect and dry, the wind negligible, and the track we think she fell from was decent and sound.'

'And?' said Max, knowing the answer already.

'There was no bloody reason for her to fall from that track. Unless she had a major medical event that made her stagger off the path, just how the bloody hell did she fall?' Shay sat back in his nylon-covered armchair and scratched at his grizzled hair.

'And what did the local cops say?' said Max, feeling his stomach tighten.

'Just asked us if there were any suspicious circumstances. They searched the body and found her phone and purse with driving licence in it. Her name was Leanne Wilson, forty years old, from Glasgow.'

'And?'

'And then nothing, they just shrugged and said they'd send an undertaker for the body, inform the family and get the Procurator Fiscal on it. That was it. I don't like to point fingers, but it seemed like they didn't give a toss. It felt distinctly half-arsed.'

Max paused a moment, his mind turning over. A lone, experienced walker falling from a dangerous ridge was not entirely unheard of, and the investigative options were limited in the absence of any witnesses or person with a serious motive to cause harm, but Max sensed that Shay had more.

'Shay, why do I get the impression that you haven't said everything that's on your mind?' asked Max, one eyebrow raised questioningly.

'Well . . .'

'Well, what? Spit it out, man.' Max's voice hardened a little.

'Well, idle hands and all that. I was bored and decided to google Leanne Wilson to see if that threw anything up.'

'And did it?'

'Not as such, but . . .' He paused to sip his tea and grimaced.

'Shay, I have a pregnant wife at home, who is going to give me pelters if I don't get back at a reasonable time,' Max said, folding his arms with a smile.

Shay reached for his phone again and swiped before handing it to Max. It was a Facebook profile for Leanne Wilson. There was a photograph of an attractive blonde woman, wearing Oakley sunglasses, smiling widely while standing on top of a stone cairn that was clearly at the top of a mountain.

'What am I looking at?' said Max.

'A selfie that Leanne took on top of the hill. Look at her last entry.'

Max scrolled down the feed to the first photograph. Leanne was beaming with her thumb extended and the status read, *Boom! Summit of A' Chralaig done. Now on to Mullach Fraoch-choire. No stopping this girl!* 😊

'You're obviously interpreting something from this?' said Max.

'Scroll down, shippers.'

Max looked to the previous photo of Leanne in her hotel room, beaming at the camera, her thumb extended again. The post bore the caption, *Final cuppa before big ascent of A' Chralaig and Mullach Fraoch-choire.*

'Yeah, she's really putting herself on the map, right, and she also put a picture on earlier in her hotel just before she started the climb. My point is, that any bugger could see this, being an open profile.'

'Are you thinking that this level of sharing on a non-private account may have made her vulnerable?'

'Look, I've had this situation multiple times, and I've never been happy with the police response, so I checked back on the recent deaths, and I'm concerned with what I found.' Shay sat back in his chair and rubbed his face.

'Go on.'

'I went back and checked and in the last year four of them were lone female walkers who fell for no apparent reason.'

Max shrugged. 'Munros are dangerous places.'

'That they are, but women hardly ever die on the hills, it's almost always men. I looked at the stats and in the previous ten years, of the 114 fatalities on the hills, only ten were women. Always been the case, blokes are stupid and reckless, and women are more sensible. And now we have four in a matter of months, all without any reasonable explanation as to why they fell. All well-prepared, decent weather, firm tracks and no sign of any daft behaviour.'

Max felt a fluttering in his stomach. 'I'm sensing there's more?'

'What if someone is targeting lone women climbers, and shoving them off cliffs?'

4

Warriston Crematorium, Edinburgh, 1982

HAMISH REMAINED SITTING *in his pew as the curtains closed, slowly, and with as little ceremony as when his mother used to close the curtains in their flat in Leith. The image in his mind of his Maw was as vivid and intense as the cartoons she'd let him watch on the rented TV that sat in the corner of the small room.*

Except on this occasion, it wasn't his mother; instead the curtains slowly closed as if by magic, only the soft whirring of some unseen machinery giving any indication as to what was happening. He continued to stare, as the heavy, faded brocaded curtain stuttered as the machines stopped. His eyes remained fixed, wide and blue as the fabric fell still.

Everyone else in the chapel began to stand up and leave, talking in whispers. No one was talking to him, but there were kind eyes in familiar and unfamiliar faces as they looked at him. Uncle James reached across and took hold of Hamish's hand. His hand was big, smooth and dry.

Now he couldn't see it anymore, and he didn't know whether to be happy or sad.

The coffin that is. He couldn't see the coffin anymore.

The coffin in which his dead mother lay. Or at least that's what he'd been told. That Maw was in the coffin, and now she was going to be burned in the oven, and her 'essence' would go up into the sky, where Jesus would take care of her. That was what his Uncle James had said, anyway. He'd asked his Auntie Eunice if this was true, and she hadn't answered, but simply shook her head, her eyes almost slits as the smoke from the long cigarette pursed between her scarlet lips drifted upwards. Her eyes were cruel and pale, like those of the snake that Hamish saw when he watched Animal Magic on their little telly. It had mean eyes that almost seemed to hypnotise the wee mouse, just at the point before it struck. Maw had switched the TV off, saying, 'Now, Hamish, pet, I don't like you watching this,' her eyes kind, but blurred, and sad, because of the gin that she didn't know he knew about. Or maybe the tablets that made her sleep for a long time.

He didn't really like Auntie Eunice at all. She pretended to be nice, sometimes, but he had heard her saying to Uncle James, 'Why us, James? Why do we have to have your sister's little shit live with us?' Her voice was as cruel as her eyes, and even though she was supposed to be beautiful, with her blonde hair piled on top of her head, her pretty dresses and lots of make-up, to Hamish she just looked ugly. She reminded him of Agatha Hannigan, the cruel owner of the orphanage in the film Annie, which Maw had taken him to see a while ago. Agatha Hannigan drank too much, too. Same as Maw, and same as Auntie Eunice. He wondered, not for the first time, why grown-ups drank so much. He was never going to drink alcohol.

Uncle James turned to him, his eyes damp with tears. He was kind and nice, and his eyes were like Maw's, but he was always away on oil rigs where he made lots of money. At least, Hamish assumed he made lots of money, because their house in Stockbridge was massive and posh, with a long staircase and big banister rail that swished around the swirling stairs that were hard and shiny because the cleaner was always polishing them.

'Come on, lad, it's time to go home,' said Uncle James, his crooked teeth showing in a grin. He reached his arm around Hamish's bony shoulders and hugged him tight. He smelled of tobacco and whisky, but on him it was somehow comforting.

'Is Maw gone forever, Uncle James?' he said, feeling a cold sensation begin to seep into his bones.

'Aye, son. You'll come to live with us, and we'll look after you, eh, Auntie Eunice?' His smile widened, and his eyes sparkled behind the sadness as he glanced at her.

Auntie Eunice smiled, her teeth big, white and straight, but her eyes didn't change at all. In fact, they looked cross. 'Of course, darling. We'll look after you now that your mummy has gone. We're just so happy you're coming.' Her voice sounded like the Queen's when she gave her speech on Christmas Day, and Hamish could tell that she really didn't mean it.

'Sarcastic' was a word that his English teacher had told the class about recently, and Hamish was pretty sure that Auntie Eunice was being sarcastic. His stomach flipped and flopped, and he began to feel the tears well up in his eyes, and his jaw wobble.

Uncle James pulled him in tighter, but Auntie Eunice just raised her eyebrows and shook her head.

'Come on, lad. Let's go home,' said Uncle James.

5

KATIE WAS SITTING on the bench at the front of their cottage in Culross when Max arrived home, pulling his helmet from his head and placing his big KTM motorcycle on its side-stand. The late-afternoon sun was balmy and warming, and Katie's face was tanned and clear, a testament to the long, unusually warm summer that they'd been experiencing. She was wearing shorts and a vest top that had ridden up exposing her midriff.

'How was Auntie E?' said Katie, as Max fussed the irrepressible blonde, shaggy-coated Nutmeg, who was currently trying to leap into his arms, her pink tongue flicking out at his sweaty face.

'As foul-mouthed and bouncy as usual. She sends her love, by the way,' Max said, kissing his wife. She wrinkled her nose and shoved him away.

'You're stinking, man, you need a shower before you kiss me. All that time in the saddle while wearing that heavy gear, not sure why you didn't drive in the air-conditioned car we own.' Her words were softened with the tones of her Yorkshire heritage.

'Perfect biking weather, babe. How you feeling?' he said, placing his hand on her swollen stomach.

'My ankles should now be more accurately described as "cankles", my back is sore, my right hip is aching where the little sod keeps punching me, and I'm too bloody hot. When I moved to Scotland, I thought it'd be bloody freezing all the time,' she said, ruffling Max's sweaty buzzcut scalp. 'Ew,' she added, grimacing and wiping her hand on his jacket. Nutmeg suddenly decided that she'd had enough of fussing Max, and settled down next to Katie, her muzzle resting on her bump. This had become the norm ever since Katie became pregnant; Nutmeg had transferred ninety per cent of her affections to Katie and had assumed the role of her protector. Max grinned and sat down on the bench, pulling his bike jacket off as he did.

Katie wrinkled her nose again. 'What took you so long?'

'I dropped into the airport to see Shay. He wanted a chat about a death on a Munro he wasn't happy with.' Max pulled out his phone and checked it. There was a message from Ross, his DI on the small Policing Standards Reassurance team at Tulliallan Castle. As usual DI Ross Fraser didn't mince his words.

Are you gracing us with your fucking presence tomorrow you workshy, idle fud? This was a typical message from his boss, which hid the truth that he was, in fact, a kind and considerate man who cared deeply for his staff. He just didn't like to show it too much.

Max sniggered as he tapped at his keys. *Aye, I'll be in early. Something I want to run past you.*

'Ross?' said Katie, peering at Max's phone.

'Aye. His usual charming self,' he said, grinning and holding the phone up, which buzzed again. Katie giggled at the message that flashed up on the screen.

Oh fuck, I hate it when you want to run something past me. Someone always ends up dead in a bastard ditch, and I don't get home to Mrs F for a week.

'I'm taking it that whatever Shay told you is the thing that's come up?' said Katie, eyeing her husband suspiciously.

'It's nothing. I just want the team's opinion.' Max shrugged and ran his hand over Katie's bump. There was a sudden twitch, and her belly rippled, and Max could almost see the shifting of a foot inside his wife's body. Katie winced. He lightly stroked the taut skin.

'Little bugger is lively. He's gonna be like you, isn't he? Never bloody sitting still.' She frowned, but her eyes sparkled with amusement.

Another shift in Katie's midriff caused a sudden jolt in Max's stomach at the prospect of his child, almost ready to make an appearance. This was getting increasingly real. A whole brand-new human, just a few inches away. His son, or daughter. The same thoughts that had been growing in his mind over the last few weeks surged again. Max had been close to his own parents, and he wondered, could he be as good as them? How could he balance the demands of his job – a job that had come to define him – with that of being a good dad?

'Max?' Katie's voice penetrated his reverie and dragged him back into the present.

'Sorry, what?

'I said I'm hungry, and you said you were cooking?'

'Pasta?' said Max, getting to his feet and stretching his back.

'Fine. And Ben and Jerry's Caramel Chew Chew for dessert,' she said, breaking out into a smile. Ever since becoming pregnant Katie's love for that particular brand and flavour of ice cream had grown to almost an obsession.

'Of course, madam. Good job I stocked up,' said Max, heading for the house.

'You'd be making a trip out to get some if there wasn't any. That's your only responsibility in this pregnancy, apart from the obvious,' she said.

Max headed through the house and into the kitchen, where he put a pan of water on the stove to boil. His phone buzzed again in his pocket. It was Shay.

I was wrong. It wasn't four deaths. It was five. Attached to the message was a newspaper link about a death on Beinn Eighe, just over a year ago.

Experienced climber Tracy Sweeney dies in horror 200ft fall from Beinn Eighe. Police mystified as to cause.

Max's stomach began to churn as he read the report. Five deaths in just over a year. Almost half the amount of the previous ten years, in good conditions and with no obvious cause. Something was wrong. Something was very wrong. He looked at the photograph attached to the article of the dead woman that was in lurid colour. A woman was grinning widely in a blue North Face peaked cap with tendrils of glossy blonde hair poking out. She looked tanned, fit and healthy. Max sighed.

He looked back through the house, at Katie sitting staring at the stunning panoramic view across the landscape to the Firth of Forth. She shifted uncomfortably on the bench, and he decided then and there to not discuss the case with her. The baby was due soon, and he needed to be here for her.

He tapped a reply to Shay. *Cheers, I'm discussing with my team tomorrow, and I'll get back to you.*

He sent the message and then composed another to the team's WhatsApp group. *We may have a problem. Meet in the office at 9?*

The phone buzzed; it was Norma replying immediately. *Anything you need your most talented ninja analyst to get moving on?*

Max's brow furrowed. It sounded really thin, but getting Norma ahead of the game would be valuable. He tapped at the keys. *I'll send you something direct, see what you can do?*

6

'WHAT THE HELL is going on in here?' said Max as he opened the door to the team's office in the bowels of Tulliallan Police HQ. As always, he tried to straighten the permanently askew and dog-eared laminated A4 sign on the door that proclaimed POLICING STANDARDS REASSURANCE. There was plaster dust everywhere below a hole in the ceiling where a couple of plasterboard tiles had apparently collapsed inwards and were currently lying in a soggy heap on Ross's desk.

'Aye, you might ask, and you'd know if you'd seen fit to grace us with your presence a bit earlier. I thought you said nine o-shiting-clock?' said DI Ross Fraser, his face an even deeper shade of its normal red. There was a white powdery stain all over his misshapen suit jacket, which he was frantically brushing at with a big, meaty hand.

'I am asking, and it's five minutes past and the traffic was crap.' Max entered the room and was immediately assaulted by the fusty smell of damp. He wrinkled his nose. 'Phew, it stinks in here,' he said, as he rounded a pile of ceiling tiles.

'I'm just amazed you turned up at all. Gonna start calling you Part-Time Craigie, soon.' Ross continued to wipe his desk down, flicking stray pieces of sodden plaster off the stacks of documents.

There was a snort of laughter in the corner of the room, and the team's analyst, Norma, popped up from behind her bank of computer monitors.

'According to building services, it's the women's toilets upstairs that sprang a leak and have been dripping down onto our ceiling tiles for a while. Eventually it soaked through before it collapsed all over Ross's desk.' Norma looked from Max to Ross and rolled her eyes, a cheeky grin on her face.

'You can wipe that smug expression off your geggie, you cheeky mare. I note your bloody desk survived intact, whereas me, the bloody gaffer, gets deluged. It's a conspiracy, I tell you. Bloody women either not turning off taps properly or pishing too much, which bearing in mind how much tea you sup is more likely.'

'Ooh, that's harsh, inspector, and possibly a little misogynistic?' said Norma, fighting to keep the smile from her face.

Ross picked up his dog-eared A4 diary that was smeared in soggy dust. 'Ah, bawbags, it's all over my diary. This office is a bloody shite-tip. I'm off to see that fud in building services and he's getting telt that I want a deep bloody clean in here fucking pronto,' he blasted before storming out of the office, his jaw set firm and his face brick red.

'Morning, Norma,' said Max, stepping around the sodden ceiling tiles, sitting at his desk and opening his laptop after flicking a shard of plasterboard from the lid.

'Morning, Max. I got your message about the Munros and I've sent a few enquiries off. I'm also putting some bits and bobs together on the five deaths. Your pal is correct. The rate of death has gone up exponentially, and without any obvious explanation, but no one seems to have noticed. I'm pulling in all the reports of the incidents, and looking for commonalities. How was your leave, by the way?' she said, sipping from a large mug that had WORLD'S BEST MUM emblazoned on it.

'Nice. Just one night on the Black Isle to see my Auntie Elspeth, probably the last chance before the bairn arrives.'

'How's Katie?'

'Huge and grouchy.'

'Poor Katie. Want a tea? I'm making another.' She stood and brushed some biscuit crumbs from her immaculate business suit.

'Are you actually chain-drinking tea?'

'Thirsty work. You want one, then?'

'Jings, what the bejesus has happened in here?' said DC Janie Calder as she came into the office, a large rucksack over her shoulder. Her face was lined and pale, and her eyes were heavy with fatigue.

'Leak from the ladies' upstairs, only Ross's desk seems to have copped it, which is pretty funny,' said Max. 'Tea?'

'Aye, gasping. I bet he's fuming.'

'Aye, a bit. How was the course?'

'Hellish. No bloody sleep, and the instructors were top-end undercover operators, and every one of them was a mental case. They all sounded like they'd been in *The Sweeney*, but they knew their stuff. It's a good course.'

'It's a good addition to your portfolio for your accelerated promotion, being undercover trained.'

'Is it? I never bloody know, as I'm so behind on my portfolio, because you buggers make it that I'm always doing the job, so I never get a chance to *tell* everyone just how well I am actually doing the job.'

Max chuckled. 'You ready for your first deployment then? What you gonna be? Contract killer? Bouncer? Bodyguard? Or gangster's moll?' he said, grinning.

'Do I look like a gangster's moll?'

'Hardly. See the message I sent?' said Max, rapidly changing the subject.

'Aye. Doesn't look right. Anything obvious?' said Janie, sipping at her tea.

'Norma is just sorting the data, and we're getting some of the fatal accident reports. My pal seems to think that the attending cops were just ticking boxes, but you know what occurred to me the more I thought about this last night?' Max leant back in his chair and scratched his chin.

Janie shook her head. 'I don't like it when you think deeply about stuff. It always means lots of work, and often extreme violence.'

'Well, when you think about it, it's the perfect way to kill someone with almost zero risk of getting caught. If there are no witnesses, a quick shove and it's all done, right?'

'Aye. If it's a motiveless attack, no witnesses, no CCTV, phones won't help, and there's unlikely to be any forensics.'

'I have something, and I don't think you'll like it,' said Norma, her face serious.

'Go on?' said Max.

Norma cleared her throat. 'All the women had put on Facebook posts ahead of climbing, and all had only partially secured profiles, meaning anyone could look at them. Four out of the five were on Munro-bagging groups, as well.'

'Hold up, are you saying . . .' began Max.

Norma's face was grim. 'Aye, I am. I think someone is stalking Facebook groups, and picking off lone climbers.'

7

'**WHAT?**' **SAID MAX,** mouth agape in shock.

'It means any members of that Facebook group could see their posts. Most of them had even been in conversations with group members about the hills before they climbed them, so there would have been plenty of time for someone with ill intent to intercept them. Look, I've screen-grabbed their posts and photos, here.' She tapped at her screen, and Max and Janie went around to look at the photos. There was a long silence as the three of them stared at the images. All women whose lives were lost in an instant, needlessly and senselessly.

'Shite. This isn't good, and if the investigations have been cursory, this could be a big banana skin for the Chief when he's trying everything to shake off all the corruption issues we keep exposing. I think Ross is going to need to flag this sooner rather than later.'

'What am I going to need to flag, and why me? I'm carrying this bastard team, and you lot would sink without my tactful negotiating strategies and incisive leadership,' said Ross, stomping back into the office, his face like thunder as he flopped down heavily in his chair, grimacing. The chair creaked arthritically.

'The Munro shover,' said Janie.

'When did you creep in? I know you're now a top-end sneaky-beaky bastard, but don't go all surreptitious and covert on me in my own shitty, decrepit cesspit of an office. I heard you did well, by the way. Well done.'

'I'm fine thanks, boss. Course was great, and I came second from top.'

'I didn't ask that, but well done, I suppose. I'm proud of you. Did the Met cover all your stuff in their "I've Met the Met" stickers?'

'There were a few, but we were mostly too busy.'

'Any updates?' said Ross.

'You tell him, Norma,' said Max.

Ross's face fell as Norma explained the Facebook links, and he rubbed at his craggy face with his hands.

'Okay, I get it, and I don't like it. It sounds sinister, to say the least. If I was going to top Mrs Fraser, I'd take her up a deserted Munro and shove her off. You'd never get convicted for it, that's for sure.'

'You've clearly given this some thought, Ross-Boss. Need we be worried?' said Norma, peering around her monitors.

'Nah. She's a trying woman at times, but I think I'll stick with her. So Max, give us the full low-down.' Ross rubbed his hand through his swept-back hair, leaving a trail of dusty plaster debris on the thin thatch.

Max explained the meeting with Shay, and Norma filled in the gaps with the information she'd managed to extrapolate from the systems she had access to.

Ross stood and silently stared at the gallery of images of the women on Norma's screen, his heavy features serious. 'What do we think?'

Max just shrugged and nodded towards the pictures again.

'Do we think we're talking about a lack of investigation by cops, or SFIU and Crown Office?' Ross's eyes didn't leave Norma's screen.

'Impossible to tell without all the data, reports and findings. We need access to it all, so maybe if the Chief authorises a "thematic review"?' Max waggled his fingers to indicate quotation marks.

'Ah bollocks, not another "thematic review".' Ross waggled

his own fingers and scowled. 'They always end up in very bad news for all concerned.'

'Once we have all the material, we can make a proper call as to whether it's poor initial investigation by cops, or whether it's down to poor follow-up by SFIU.' Max raised his eyebrows. 'There's another possibility, of course.'

'I don't like that possibility, and I haven't even heard it yet,' said Ross.

'That someone charged with investigating, or managing, the death inquiries has something to hide.'

'See, fucking told you. I hate that possibility. If we've someone covering up evidence, or being wilfully negligent, then it's a shagging great brouhaha waiting to happen.'

'Of course, it could be something *else* as well,' said Max, standing up and stretching his shoulders.

'Whit?'

'It could be a bent cop shoving women off a cliff and covering it up.'

Ross groaned and rubbed at his eyes. 'Craigie, you're pushing me 'awa the line, man. I'll phone up Miles "Moneypenny" Wakefield and get us a slot with the Chief.'

'Is Miles the Chief's staff officer now?' said Max.

A grin spread across Ross's face. 'Aye, and it's funny as fuck. Since the Chief's last bag man is now locked up in Saughton jail, he's been looking for a new one. Miles wasn't happy to be moved from managing all the murder teams to being the Chief's secretary. I asked him if he sat on the Chief's knee when taking a letter.' Ross guffawed, wheezily.

'How did he react to that?' said Janie, a huge smile splitting her face.

'Told me to go fuck myself.' Ross picked up his phone and dialled, then said, 'Detective Chief Superintendent Wakefield, Ross here. Is the boss man in?'

Ross paused, grinning, as he listened.

'Can you slot us in for fifteen minutes as soon as, always assuming you're not currently giving him a foot rub, eh?' He pulled the handset away from his face, at the tinny blast coming from the receiver.

'Ach, I'm only messin', man. See you then. No sugar for me, and see if you can rustle up some of those wee tea cakes I know you keep in your drawer for special visitors. Oh, and Mrs Fraser's birthday is soon, can you sort some flowers for her?'

'I've suddenly realised what you and the Chief Constable have in common,' said Max, shaking his head.

'Whit?'

'Neither of you is getting promoted again. What time?'

'Eleven. Let's get the data worked up. Norma, can you come up with one of your gibberish Anacapa charts that mean fuck all to me, but everyone else seems to be impressed by?' said Ross, standing and picking up a dustpan and brush. He stared at the sludgy mess on his desk with a scowl.

'On it like a car bonnet, Ross-Boss. Although they're called i2 charts, and they bring clarity to confusion.' Norma glared at Ross through her spectacles.

'And another thing, we need more to properly link these deaths. If there's something linking these women, or anything we're missing, I need it before I meet the boss. If all we have is a few women who posted on Facebollocks over the course of a year, then it may be a stretch for him to authorise us to dig; it's not like we're short of work. Janie, can you get cracking and make some calls?' Ross rubbed his hands together and yawned.

Janie just stood there, transfixed by the images of the dead women on the screen, her eyes narrow; she hadn't seemed to hear Ross. Her eyes just flicked from image to image, her brow furrowed.

'Janie?' said Ross.

Janie looked up, her face a touch paler. 'There is something about them all,' she said, her voice tight.

'What?'

'I didn't notice at first, as four are wearing hats, but it's definitely there.'

'Jesus suffering fuck. What?' blurted Ross.

'They're all blonde.'

8

SUE BROWN FELT a surge of adrenaline as she heaved herself up with just her fingers into a tight crevice on a sheer rock face that stretched down almost ten metres. Her arms were screaming in pain as the lactic acid began to flood the muscles, and she leant back on the top rope that was attached to the climbing harness around her legs and hips. She adjusted her feet where they were slotted into the crevice in the rock, or 'schist', as her climbing partner had corrected her. She'd always been keen to try rock climbing, and had done some indoor bouldering at The Ledge in Inverness, but it hadn't been satisfying. It had felt like what it was – artificial and unrewarding – and she'd really wanted to experience climbing on real rock.

So, it had been a bonus when she met her latest date after a little back and forth on an internet dating app. Mikey seemed a nice man who was lean and fit-looking, with a grey-flecked beard, a ready smile and a shy disposition. They'd been for a couple of coffee dates in Inverness, and when he'd told her he was an experienced climber she was delighted, and moreover, desperate to have a go. It may have seemed odd to some, but for someone like her, a third date climbing the twelve-metre crag at Huntly's Cave in the nearby Cairngorms was perfect. She didn't like posh restaurants, anyway.

'You okay there?' came the call from Mikey, his soft, slightly odd Scottish accent echoing off the sheer craggy cliffs.

'Aye, just taking a breather. My arms are sore,' she said, looking back at his smiling face. She used the back of her hand to wipe the film of sweat from her brow, and pushed a tendril of her blonde hair back under her cap.

'Take your time, and climb when you're ready,' came the same steady and calm voice. It was reassuring and comforting, and she felt her stomach soften.

They had met in Grantown-on-Spey earlier that morning and then she'd followed in her car as he had driven a couple of miles north on the Old Military Road where they'd parked in a layby. They had left the cars and crossed the wall and railway line, and were soon at the top of the deep crag, which he'd assured her was perfect for a beginner, being secure and solid, and just twelve metres in height. He had attached a rope to a karabiner that had been driven into the rock with a piton at the top of the crag, which he had thrown out over the edge. Within just a few minutes they were at the foot of the small cliff in a chilly tree-lined ravine.

She'd changed into the brand-new climbing shoes that she'd bought for the date, and tucked her approach trainers into her rucksack, which she ditched at the foot of the cliff next to Mikey's.

He had strapped her into the harness and shown her how to tie the figure-of-eight knot that was secured onto the karabiner at her waist. Mikey had attached the other end of the rope to the belay device on his own harness. He'd grinned with charm as he pulled the slack on the rope, and she felt the tension bite, the harness tightening against her hips.

She had attacked the blocky, dry rock with enthusiasm, finding the hand- and footholds easy to locate and feeling the ever-present and reassuring tension on the top rope that Mikey was feeding through the belay device as she ascended, his soft words of advice easily heard against the echoey crag.

It was exhilarating, so much more so than the fake rock faces at the indoor climbing wall, and she had felt all the stresses that had been plaguing her over the last six months begin to evaporate:

the ending of a relationship, the loss of a job and unwell parents in Glasgow. She was just a hundred per cent focused on getting up this sheer rock face. It felt primeval, and that with every foot she ascended, she lost a little more of the tension that had been ever present in her muscles and mind. She felt free.

So, she was feeling proud that she'd only needed to rest now, after a ten-metre climb, as she shook out each of her hands in turn and leant back, allowing the tension on the rope to support her weight as she gathered her strength for the final three metres. She thrust her hands back into two nice-sized handholds and heaved again, her biceps straining as she pulled herself up back onto the rock, feeling the rope at her waist slacken.

She paused for breath, lifting her left foot up to a fissure in the rock, just a couple of feet away, but it missed, and slipped on a damp patch. All her weight was now just supported by four digits of each hand, until she managed to return her flailing foot into the deep crease in the rock. Her heart leapt into her mouth and began to pound, as the breath escaped her. Where the hell was the tension in the rope? She was just there on the rock, unsupported. 'Mikey?' she called out, trying to keep the panic from her voice.

There was nothing. A deep, impenetrable silence gripped the gorge. 'Mikey?' she called again, more urgency in her voice, and the blood started to rush and whoosh in her ears.

She firmed her grip in the handholds and looked over her shoulder.

Mikey was nowhere to be seen, and the rope from her harness just snaked down the cliff limply, swaying slightly. Sue gasped, unable to process what she was seeing. *Where was he?*

'Mikey?' she said, trying to keep the panic from her voice. Surely, he'd just nipped off for a wee, or something, but the rational part of her brain realised that it was unlikely.

Her blood turned to ice and she began to hyperventilate, as horror crept in. She firmed her grip on the handholds of the rock and pulled herself into the cliff face. She was stuck there, unable to go up or down. 'Mikey?' she now screamed, the high-pitched wail reverberating off the sheer walls of the gorge.

Then, a shadow fell across her face. She looked up, and there was Mikey, standing at the top of the gorge, staring at her from just two metres away. His face had changed. It had gone from shy smiles and gentle humour to coldness, flat and unfathomable. His eyes seemed to have sunk back in their sockets, and had darkened and lost even the slightest trace of emotion. He reached forward, fiddled with the karabiner that was buried into the rock, and the rope fell away, tugging at her harness as it hit the ground, ten metres below her.

'Mikey?' she whispered, her entire body quivering like a bowstring, tense and knotted, her breaths urgent and shallow as she felt the blood drain from her fingers. Despite the chill of the dark, shadowed and tree-lined gorge, she felt sweat break out on her back.

'Mikey, please?' she pleaded, her voice hoarse.

Mikey acted as if she had not even spoken, and held his phone out in front of him, pointing it at her without changing his expression. She buried her face into the rock, opened her mouth and let forth a scream that was nothing more than a stifled croak, as her abject terror had constricted her voice box, rendering it useless.

When she lifted her face from the rock, Mikey was gone. She looked up at the edge of the rock face, just a few feet up above her, and stretched out a desperate hand, slick with sweat. She found a small crevice and dug her fingers deep inside it. She suddenly felt a burst of hope in her chest; with one big pull, she could be up and out of this hellish situation, her feet on the firm ground just above her head. She tensed her muscles, and gritted her teeth, her earlier terror now being replaced with utter determination. She was getting off this godforsaken rock, or she was going to die trying.

Looking to her left she saw a protruding shard of rock. A perfect point for her foot. With a roar, she removed her left foot from the safe ledge and wedged it against the shard and heaved, pushing hard while pulling with her hand. With a monumental effort, she pulled herself up, her free hand reaching up and finding a narrow fissure in the surface. One more big pull, and she'd be out. 'Come on!' she yelled, as she threw her hand up to a root jutting out from one of the trees in the canopy above her.

Suddenly, there was a forceful tug at her waist, and the previously slack rope became taut against her harness. A terrible pain raged in her fingers of the hand that was holding the thick root, as her grip began to fail. She glanced down, and there was Mikey, at the foot of the rock face, rope in one hand, his phone extended towards her in the other. Another sharp and violent tug, and she was falling, back first through the cold Highland air, almost in slow motion, the ground rushing up to meet her.

The impact, when it eventually arrived, was catastrophic, an immense and all-consuming crash as her back hit the rocky ground. The devastation of sudden, terrible forces shattered her, completely and totally, as her head struck the earth.

But there was no pain.

The last thing she saw was Mikey, phone pointing towards her, his crooked teeth bared in a mirthless smile, his eyes blank and dark.

9

MIKEY LOOKED ON as she gasped her final breath, the crumpled form quivering just slightly and then relaxing, her eyes filling with a confusion that led to nothing. He held the phone in place, zooming in on her face for a moment, before closing the camera app down and looking at the thumbnail image. He quickly reviewed the footage, a smile playing around his thin lips. The close-up terror on her face at the top of the cliff, then the plummeting body hitting the rocky ground like a sandbag, then the *coup de grâce*: focusing on her face as the life ebbed from her fragile body. His eyes took in the blonde hair that now cascaded from under the cap and was spread across her shoulder, stark against the Gore-Tex.

The best bit. The transition. The unknowable process of life leaving a body. The transformation of a living, breathing, laughing and loving person becoming what she now was. An empty corporeal vessel. Nothing. Just meat and organs. A harsh chuckle escaped his lips.

He'd liked to have filmed some more, but he was aware that it was getting late, and that he couldn't rule out another walker or climber arriving. He checked that flight mode was still engaged on his phone. He always did this, being the careful man that he was. It meant that his phone was not talking to any cell masts and wouldn't put him at that location, even though he was intending to ditch this phone as soon as was appropriate. He would never be caught, because he knew how to not be caught. 'Leave no trace' was his motto.

He snapped on a pair of blue nitrile gloves that he had pulled out of his pocket, and he went to the broken and bloody body, removing her climbing harness and untying the rope, which he methodically coiled up. He tucked the harness away in his rucksack and placed the rope on top. He then went into the pocket of the individual's soft-shell jacket and pulled out her phone, a new-looking Samsung. The screen was cracked and splintered, but it was intact and seemed to be working. He pressed the home key, and when the lock screen appeared he lifted the woman's limp hand. He tried the index finger and the screen vibrated. *Try again*. He pressed her flaccid thumb against the reader, and the phone unlocked. He quickly swiped through the screen until he found the icon for the dating app that he had used to make contact with Susan, or Sue, or whatever her dull and insignificant name was. He pressed and held the icon until it began to flash, and a small menu appeared below. He pressed the 'uninstall' icon and the app disappeared. All their chats had been via the app, and as the photo he'd used had been an irrelevant image of someone wearing sunglasses and a beanie pulled low, he was confident that there was nothing for the cops there, either. His dating profile had been set up with fake information, so he was untraceable, even if they did forensically download the phone, which he doubted they would.

He placed the phone on the stony ground next to the corpse and stamped on it twice with his heavy boot, splintering the screen and cracking the housing. The cops would find it, but it was now questionable as to whether they would be able to extract any data from it, even if they tried to. It was more of a risk to remove the phone from the scene, and even if they managed to get into it, or its cloud backup, there was nothing there to identify him. He'd been very, very careful. They would assume that it had been damaged in the fall, which suited him just fine.

He left her rucksack where it was, propped against the wall of the cliff, with her walking shoes inside. Leaving her climbing shoes on her feet would tell a story. A stupid woman who had been to the indoor climbing wall a few times and who had recklessly decided to go bouldering on real cliff faces and had ventured too high before falling and tragically dying. No witnesses, no case.

'Mikey' shouldered his rucksack and took the coil of rope and slung it over his shoulder, and headed off out of the gorge, whistling tunelessly.

10

DETECTIVE CHIEF SUPERINTENDENT Miles Wakefield looked up from his desk, his face registering a mix of disdain and disapproval, as Ross barged through the door, an inane grin on his wide face.

'Good morning, Miss Moneypenny, I'd toss my hat on the stand, but you dinnae have a stand, and there's no hat big enough for my heid, in any case,' said Ross, affecting a Sean Connery accent as he and Max approached Miles.

Wakefield didn't look the slightest bit amused by the scruffy-suited Ross. 'Just how long am I going to have to put up with all the secretary jokes, Ross?'

'Ach, not for long. Has he begun to sexually harass you yet?'

Miles just shook his head, ruefully.

'Heard the one about the secretary who changed the boss's password for him?' Ross was almost hopping from one foot to the other with glee.

'Obviously not,' said Miles.

'Secretary changed it to "dick" but computer said, "Not long enough."' Ross burst out laughing.

'If I say you can go in, will you shut up telling stupid bloody jokes?' said Wakefield, the weariness etched on his face.

'Aye, if you make the coffees, Miss Moneypenny.'

'You can bloody whistle for coffees,' said Wakefield, turning to his computer screen, scowling.

The oak door to the Chief's office swung open, and the tall, lean Chief Constable Chris Macdonald appeared. 'This sounds suspiciously like an outbreak of morale out here; what's going wrong?' he said, a smile playing around his lips.

'DI Fraser thinking he's a comedian, sir,' said Wakefield with a slight shake of his head.

'Come in, Ross, I don't like the sound of the one-liner you sent me. Coffee?'

'Aye, that'd be grand, a flat white for me. Max?' Ross looked at Max with a grin.

'Espresso would be nice,' said Max.

'Miles, do the honours, will you?' said Macdonald, turning and disappearing inside the office.

'Don't forget the biccies, Miss Moneypenny,' said Ross, winking at Wakefield, who flipped the bird in return, without looking, as he scratched with his pen at a notepad, his face set firm in a heavy scowl.

'So, Ross. I've read the very brief summary that Norma sent, and I have to say I don't like it at all. However, correct me if I'm wrong, but we don't have any actual evidence, yet.' Macdonald raised his eyebrows.

'No evidence, just unpleasant coincidences. If it wasn't for Max's helicopter pilot pal, we wouldn't even have that.'

'So, is this a bit of a leap? And I'm not using that word advisedly. Is it just that a number of lone walkers have died on the hill?'

'Aye, but the numbers are concerning, as is the point that they posted on social media about it ahead of time. I always said that social media was shite and dangerous, so it looks like I've been proved right. I just want us to be able to investigate it, boss.'

'I have to say, the most concerning thing is the hair colour. All blondes?'

Ross nodded.

The Chief opened his mouth to respond, and then shut it again, trying out all the pieces of the puzzle to see which fit and which didn't. His eyes narrowed.

Ross shifted in his seat before he spoke. 'Look, we've nothing serious on now, and even if the goal is some "organisational learning", I don't see the harm. If we have an issue with fatality investigation, then I'd call that a serious reputational risk if we don't get ahead of it.'

They all turned as the door clicked, and a sour-faced Miles entered the room with a tray of steaming mugs.

'Ah, Miss Moneypenny, we've been expecting you,' said Ross.

Miles merely grimaced and deposited the tray on the desk, before heading straight back out again.

'You're a bad man, DI Fraser. I'll have to put up with his mood all day now. I agree with you, however. I'll put the feelers out with the Crown Office, and the Fatalities Investigation Unit, and tell them that we want to do a thematic review, to identify any risks to business, or some such nonsense like that. I don't want to step on the toes of the new staff at the Crown Office, after we jailed their boss recently, but this is very much their bag, so I'll need to be diplomatic.' Macdonald was referring to the corruption case that Max and the team had recently worked on.

'I can see how you rose to the rank you now hold, boss. You're awesome at all this management bullshit.' Ross sipped his coffee and nodded approvingly. 'You should also keep Miles on as your bag man. Good coffee.'

Macdonald smiled. 'I'll speak to James McDougal at SFIU and tell him what we're looking to do. Maybe a "dip sample" of past fatal accident investigations?'

'Aye, sounds good. I'll have Norma send over the suspect cases to make sure they're in the ones we want to dip sample.'

There was a buzzing noise on the coffee table next to Max. He picked up his phone and glanced at it.

'Max, can you sort out your social life another fucking time? We're in the Chief's bloody office,' said Ross, scowling.

Max continued to stare at the screen.

'Is it Katie?' said the Chief.

'No. It's Shay. There's been another fall.'

11

THE JOURNEY FROM Tulliallan to Huntly's Cave took just over two hours, with Janie driving at her customary high speed while Max navigated and occasionally ducked down when the speedo nudged a hundred miles per hour, and the hidden sirens wailed.

Max had called Shay immediately after receiving the text in the Chief's office, and he had passed over the details. A lone woman in her thirties at the foot of Huntly's Cave in the Cairngorms. A local walker had called it in and the search-and-rescue helicopter was called out, but she was dead on arrival. No obvious cause. Local cops were on-scene now.

The Chief had despatched them immediately. 'I want you up there. We need a second pair of eyes on this, right now. I'll call the area commander and tell them you're coming. Thematic reviews on death investigation for a study that's been ordered, okay?' he had said, gravely.

Janie was a first-class driver but a terrible passenger, which was why Max rarely drove the big Volvo pool car that they shared. That, plus her obsession for a clean and tidy vehicle meant that he was happy for his partner to take the burden.

'You are a very good driver, Janie, but you do shite me right up sometimes. That last overtake of the big lorry was a little risky.'

'Loads of room, stop being so bloody frit. How close now?' she said, as she steered the big car through the narrow road that they had followed out of Grantown-on-Spey, a large town in the

Cairngorms National Park. They continued on through the town until they returned to the lush and rich countryside.

'Not far, another mile up the road, and there should be a layby. I suspect there will be cop cars parked up as well,' said Max, glancing at the sat-nav screen.

Max's suspicion proved to be correct. As they rounded the next bend there was a phalanx of police vehicles tucked into a layby, together with a Mountain Rescue Land Rover, and a Crime Scene Investigators liveried van. At the end of the layby there was a small Toyota hatchback. Max stared at the small car, which had a sticker in the rear window of the Loch Ness monster.

Max pointed to the car. 'Can you get Norma to check that car out?'

Janie squinted through the windscreen and tapped away at her phone. 'I'll bet you're right, that'll be her car.'

There was a buzz as the response came back, almost immediately. 'Registered to Susan Brown, at an address in Inverness.'

Max nodded. 'The cop looks happy, right?'

A middle-aged, hi-vis-clad cop was leaning against the van, his cap perched on the back of his head. He waved Janie and Max on, as if directing traffic. They pulled up alongside and Max lowered the window, proffering his warrant card to the constable. He had a rather bovine face, with heavy-lidded eyes and a chin that spoke of a less-than-accurate shave. He held a cigarette in his hand, which he dropped on the ground, and radiated a sense of deflated boredom.

'DS Craigie and DC Calder. Who's in charge of the scene?' said Max, smiling widely.

The cop stared at the warrant card and sighed. 'Where are ye frae?' he said in a thick Glasgow accent.

'Policing Standards Reassurance from Tulliallan. We're doing a thematic review on fatality investigations.'

He snorted derisively. 'Inspector Campbell, he'll be scunnered youse are here. He disnae like people at his scenes like, and he's hung-over tae fuck, as he got steaming last night at the Chief Inspector's leaving do. He hardly ever drinks, so he's pure suffering. Looking fair peely-wally, he is,' he said, his words delivered rapidly, as he cracked a smile at the prospect of his boss's misfortune.

'Is that Inspector Gordon Campbell?' said Max, furrowing his brow, casting his mind back to the curmudgeonly duty inspector that he'd encountered on one occasion.

'Aye, "Cordon Gordon". You know him?'

'I've heard of him, but that was in Edinburgh.'

Max and Janie had previously encountered 'Cordon Gordon'. He was a rather officious duty inspector with a fastidious attitude to crime-scene cordons.

'Aye, he's been transferred and he's no happy aboot it. Hence, he gets verra particular, like. I'd mind tae have plenty reasons to be here, aye? I'll radio aheid noo, but yiz'll need to convince him why yiz're here, like. Pull over tae the side, and tuck well in.' He pointed over to a parking spot at the side of the road behind the van.

Janie nodded, manoeuvred the Volvo and parked it up. 'He seems a happy-chappy.'

'Aye, but then being put in charge of the vehicles by a hung-over Cordon Gordon is hardly a plum job, is it?'

'It was why I was so keen to get out of uniform. No one liked me, so the sergeant and inspector always pinged me for scene guards. Bastards.' Janie's face hardened.

'No one liked you?' Max looked at his partner, trying to hide a grin.

'Aye, they all thought I was a wee bit weird, like.'

Max shrugged. 'Fair point.'

'Piss off.'

'A little disrespectful, constable,' said Max, opening the door, his rucksack in his hand.

'Okay, piss off, sergeant. Now, shall we get going? I'm hungry.'

'You're always hungry.' Max slammed the door, and they headed back to the uniformed cop.

'Know where you're going?' he asked.

'No, fancy enlightening us?' said Max.

'Through the gap in the wall and then cross the Dava Way old railway line, then a few hundred yards along to the top of the crag, you'll see everyone doon the bottom. It's no far, ye cannae miss it, mind.' He checked his watch and made a note on a formatted pad.

'You've a scene log, for the cars?'

'Aye, that's Cordon Gordon for ye. He wants a log before ye get tae the scene, as well as at the scene. Man's a rocket, like, and he'll be giving you pelters for being here.'

'What's your name, pal?' said Max.

'Danny McSorley.' He smiled for the first time; clearly Danny wasn't used to anyone paying him attention, which was probably why he was currently minding the vehicles.

'Been in Highland long?'

'Just over a year, came up from Strathclyde. They'll nae get me awa' from here, noo. I'm a climber, and I love the hills, you get me, so this is bloody heaven for me.'

'You live close by?' said Max.

'Aye, I've lived in Grantown ever since joining Northern Constabulary a while back, before the disaster of the amalgamation into Police Scotland. Doesnae matter how much of a weapon Cordon Gordon is, I'm staying, it took me long enough to get back up here.'

'Well, nice to meet you, Danny. And my condolences on Cordon Gordon – Edinburgh's gain is your loss.' Max extended his hand, which Danny shook with a firm, dry hand, his face softening a touch.

'Mind how ye go, track's rough.' He nodded, pulled his phone from his pocket and began tapping at the screen.

Max and Janie walked through, and then after a few more steps a deserted-looking track appeared that stretched away into the distance. They were soon heading into a dank and dark wooded area, where they came to a green wooden sign that read HUNTLY'S CAVE CRAG – 150 M on one side and FORRES – 20 MILES on the other side.

They followed the sign and onto a rooted and dried earth track that headed down into the tall pine trees. The path was twisty and rutted, and studded with protruding granite rocks, before it opened out into a wider grassy area. As they moved on, the landscape changed, and slate-grey boulders sloped away into apparent nothingness. An information sign was staked into the dried earth. HUNTLY'S CAVE, it read, with a block of text giving some historical context.

'I remember something about this from history at school. Huntly was a supporter of Bonnie Prince Charlie, and hid on a rock, or something like that,' said Max.

'I think you'll find that it was Charles the First, not the Young Pretender. You obviously weren't listening in lessons,' said Janie, who had a degree in history.

'Well, that's as may be, but it's almost the same.'

Janie shook her head. 'It's nothing like the same. Charles the First died in 1649, the Young Pretender wasn't born until 1720.'

'Whatever.' Max shrugged as he walked towards the edge of the precipice and peeped over, keeping his feet firm on the immovable granite slabs that led to the cliff.

'Is it high?' said Janie, not moving much further forward.

'Aye. Not as high as Dunnet Head, but enough to ruin your day if you fall off the top. Come and have a look?' He turned, smiling, but knowing that Janie was not a fan of heights.

'Nah, I'm good.' Janie remained rooted to the spot.

Max noticed the tree growing out of the edge of the cliff,

seemingly defying gravity. He looked down and saw the sea of hi-vis jackets that were partially obscured by the boughs and foliage of the surrounding trees.

'How far down is it?' said Janie from afar.

'Ten metres, minimum. Probably more. Come on, let's get down there.'

'How do we do that?'

'Pathway over there – it's steep and rooty by the looks of it, so we'll need to be careful. I can see why they need the Mountain Rescue Team to pull the body out. Not one for amateurs. Let's go.' Max set off and began to descend the narrow, twisty track, thankful for the recent spell of dry weather, as the path would have been treacherous had it been muddy.

The temperature was significantly cooler at the bottom of the crag, the trees and sheer cliffside casting an inky shade in the clearing. Blue-and-white police tape was stretched around the foot of the crag, inside which was what looked like a pile of red clothing in a heap. A body. A forensic-suited CSI officer was snapping away with a professional camera.

There was a small clutch of cops at the perimeter of the cordon, and about six men and women all standing around an empty stretcher. Their yellow-and-black soft-shell jackets were all emblazoned with CAIRNGORM MOUNTAIN RESCUE.

Max noticed a peak-capped inspector glaring at them, his moustache quivering with indignation as he briefed his team who were standing by the cordon.

Max turned to one of the mountain rescue team, a slight, middle-aged man. 'Any ideas what happened, pal?'

'A walker called it in.' He pointed to an ashen-faced woman sitting on a rock at the edge of the clearing, with a small spaniel, talking to a uniformed cop. 'She was up here with her dog, who dashed away to the body at the foot of the cliff. She called it in, and the local cops shouted for us. It's gonna be a tricky job getting her up the steep track to the road, hence us being here.' He slapped his hand against the aluminium stretcher.

'Have you seen her?' said Max.

The man shook his head. 'Cordon was up when we got here, and that uniformed inspector is being a bit of a fanny. A bit of a sense of his own importance, I'd say, but don't look now, he's coming over.' He nodded behind Max.

Max turned to see the inspector marching towards them, adjusting his glasses as he picked his way through the rocky ground. He was a slightly overweight, middle-aged man, who was dressed in full uniform.

He began his diatribe before he'd even reached them, his bushy moustache bristling as he spoke. 'Now look here. This isn't a spectator sport. Who are you, may I ask?' He stopped, hands on hips, his eyes as grey as the rocks that surrounded them.

Max produced his warrant card and proffered it towards the inspector. 'DS Craigie and DC Calder from Policing Standards Reassurance at Tulliallan.'

Inspector Campbell's brow furrowed and his eyes hardened. 'And? I've not requested any assistance, and I think you'll find that as duty officer, I'm responsible for this scene.' He jutted a finger at Max accusatorially.

'We've been asked by our management to come and review the processes. We're carrying out a thematic review on unexplained death investigations, sir. I assure you it's all in order,' said Max, a smile touching his face.

'Well, I've heard nothing of this, and I think I will be the one to decide on these matters, not some silly quango from Tulliallan. May I remind you that a woman is dead?'

'Sir, rest assured that we are authorised to be here, if you'd like to check—' he began, but Inspector Campbell was having none of it.

'Sergeant, that is enough,' he interrupted. 'I am trying to

ascertain if there are any suspicious circumstances at this tragic event, and I will not have my investigation stymied by the likes of you.' He glared at Max. Suddenly, there was a tone from the front pocket of his hi-vis body armour. He looked down and pulled out his phone. 'Inspector Campbell.'

His face froze, and he stared at Max and Janie, his eyes wide.

'Well, yes, sir. They've just arrived, and—' He paused as he listened to the caller. 'But, sir—' He turned his back and walked a few steps until he was out of earshot.

'Sounds like a call's gone in,' said Max, smiling at Janie.

'Aye, I gave Ross the heads-up on the way down, once the cop by the cars told us it was Cordon Gordon. I knew he'd be a dick about us being here,' Janie said, sniggering.

'You're learning fast, constable.' Max nodded, impressed at his partner's foresight.

'You've taught me well, sergeant. Ross was delighted to be able to stick the boot in; you know how he likes pissing off senior officers.'

'Aye, almost like a sport to him,' Max said, trying to suppress a smile, as the inspector turned to stare at them.

Inspector Campbell's face was a picture, his voice now full of oily acquiescence. 'Of course, sir. As you wish.' He disconnected the call, and returned the phone to his pocket, placing a firm gaze on Max, but the fight had clearly evaporated from him. 'That was the divisional commander for Highlands and Islands. It seems that I'm to afford you every courtesy. In fact, Chief Superintendent Carmichael was most insistent, a direct order from the Deputy Chief Constable, it seems.' He flicked his eyes between Max and Janie, looking puzzled.

'Thank you, sir,' said Max.

'What do you need?'

'Access to the scene, if possible. Once the CSIs have finished, but before the deceased gets moved. I'd like to assess the fall site, and rock face. Also, any of her belongings that are available, and whether she had a phone with her. Of course, I'll need to see decision logs, and scene planning strategy evidence. All looking to improve best practice moving forward.' Max smiled, his delivery polite.

Inspector Campbell sighed and shook his head a little before replying, 'Well, it seems I have no choice, but you'll have to wait until the CSIs have finished.' He rubbed at an apparent itch on his cheek.

'Any early observations?' asked Janie.

'It seems she was attempting some kind of unsupported climbing and fell; crazy behaviour. She's wearing climbing shoes, and her rucksack is leant against the cliff face with her walking boots tucked at the top. I've not looked beyond that.'

'Any idea who she is?' said Max.

'Not yet. I was leaving searching the body for ID until the CSI had finished. Other than making sure she couldn't be helped, the first officers on scene just withdrew, secured the scene and called it in. Paramedics were here fast enough, but apart from declaring life extinct they couldn't do anything. No witnesses that we know of.' He sighed again and shook his head.

Max looked at Janie. 'I suspect she could be called Susan Brown. There's a Toyota in the layby registered in that name.'

'Could be a dog walker?' said the inspector, wincing slightly, clearly kicking himself that he had failed to check the car out.

Max just smiled and shrugged. 'Where will she go once we're finished?'

'MRT are here to stretcher her out to the road, and then the undertakers will take her to the mortuary at Raigmore, ready for a PM, whenever that will be.'

'Special?' said Max, referring to a special post-mortem, normally used for unexplained or suspicious deaths.

'I suspect so, but it depends on what the Fiscal says. I've already let him know, and he wanted a full response as we've done with CSI. The on-call DI at HQ in Inverness will be responsible for ensuring that her circumstances are investigated, in case there's anything in her personal life that points to this being something other than a tragic accident.'

'Is an SIO from the MIT coming to the scene?' said Janie.

'It seems not. The DCI at HQ in Inverness is happy for me to handle the scene, and his team will pick up the follow-up enquiries. I think they're very busy with a murder.' He shrugged.

'Any pathologist attendance?'

Inspector Campbell just shook his head.

'Really?' said Max.

'I know, DS Craigie. I'd like a pathologist and CID to come, but it doesn't seem that it is a priority. I guess as detectives, your presence is actually rather welcome, if Inverness can't spare anyone.' A smile touched his previously implacable face, as he no doubt realised that having two qualified detectives present would be useful for his report.

'Happy to help, sir. We'll just hang around to check out the scene, and then we can do everything else remotely once we get access to the reports, and the HOLMES account.'

'HOLMES?' said the inspector, framing the word as a question.

'Aye, Home Office Large Major Enquiry System,' said Max, furrowing his brow.

'I know what HOLMES is, sergeant, but I can tell you this much. This incident won't make it onto HOLMES. I suspect that beyond a cursory review by an SIO from Inverness this will be handled locally, and not on a linked system. We don't have the resources to staff an incident room for every death on hills and cliffs. We'd have no detectives for murder inquiries.'

Max opened his mouth to retort, but then closed it again, aware of why they were here. He looked over at the scene, and the white-suited crime scene investigator heading towards the scene tape. 'Looks like CSI is done,' he said, pointing to the tent behind Inspector Campbell.

They went to the tape, where the lead CSI was ducking under it, lugging a holdall and a rugged-looking camera case. He pulled down his hood and mask, exhaling with relief.

'DS Craigie, this is John Grant, he's the crime scene manager. John, DS Craigie is from Tulliallan, and is here at the behest of the senior leadership team. We've been instructed to offer any assistance,' said Campbell, jutting his thumb towards Max.

'Glad to know you, Max,' said John, who was in his thirties and heavily built with a goatee beard, and a mane of hair that he was smoothing back into shape after the hood had messed it up.

'Anything to report?' said Max.

'Deceleration trauma looks the most obvious. Huge head injury to the back of the skull, so it looks like she landed on her back. It'll need to wait for the PM, but I can't see anything to point to foul play, but then, if someone had just shoved her, I wouldn't find it, would I?' He shrugged.

'Any clues on ID?'

'I've not searched the body. Feel free to crack on yourselves, now that I've preserved the hands for examination and photographed the scene and body. There's a phone next to her that must have fallen from her pocket. It's almost been reduced to its component parts as far as I can see, so I doubt we'll get anything from that. Not much more for me to do, really. I can't see any major evidence loss by just getting her out of here and to Raigmore.'

'Can we take a look?' said Max, feeling the familiar sense of dread begin to bite at the prospect of being up close with a dead body.

'Yes, as long as you suit up and book in with the scene guard. There's a stock of suits, masks and overshoes in the scene bag with the guard. I can't overstate how important scene preservation is, sergeant,' said Campbell, stroking his moustache.

'Okay for us to search for ID?'

'I guess so, it'll make my incident report a little more defendable, if you do it. Right, I need to check on all the troops and get the undertakers organised to remove her, once the MRT have stretchered her to the road, so if you'll excuse me.' He nodded and then strode off, full of bluster and self-importance once more.

Max took a deep breath and closed his eyes, mentally preparing for what came next.

'Want me to do this, Max?' said Janie, her voice soft.

Max opened his eyes, and shook his head, ignoring the prickling sensation and beads of sweat that were breaking out down his spine. 'No, we can both do it. I need to see it up close with my own eyes. There must be something there – we just need to be perceptive enough to recognise what it is. Come on, let's get suited up.'

Within a couple of minutes, they had each donned a Tyvek forensic suit, nitrile gloves and rubber overshoes, and were ducking under the scene tape. They approached the form that lay at the foot of the cliff ten metres away. Max felt the blood begin to rush between his ears in time with his rapidly accelerating heartbeat. He breathed steadily and evenly, holding each breath in for a count of four, as his counsellor had taught him a few years ago. It was all he'd really taken from the sessions, but he found it calming and cathartic.

'All good?' said Janie.

'Aye. Looks like she fell straight down from the thick protruding root up there, right?' Max pointed up at a tree root that was sticking out from the top of the rock face.

'If she got that far.' Janie did a full 360-degree spin, taking in the entirety of the scene, her eyes flicking from side to side.

Max took another deep breath before looking down on the crumpled figure on the ground. She was on her back, her legs extended in front of her, rubberised climbing shoes on her feet with Velcro straps holding them in place. Her legs looked unbroken, and straight. Her arms were by her sides, and one of her fingers was stained with dried, congealed blood. She had long blonde hair that was obscuring her face, and a puddle of black, glutinous blood had spread underneath her head, which was at a sharp angle. Max guessed that her neck was almost certainly broken. 'I'm betting she did. There's a karabiner in the rock just below that root.'

Max took a deep breath, and without looking at her face, moved in closer to the woman's bloody finger, peering through the clear plastic bag that had been placed over her hand and secured with tape. The nail had been ripped clean out. He looked back up the cliff, directly above them, his eyes focusing on the thick root and the karabiner that sparkled as a shaft of sunlight pierced the leafy canopy. Max stared at the palms of her hands, which were red raw and spotted with blood that was even visible through the crinkled plastic.

'I bet she was holding onto that root up there, by the top of the cliff. Look at her finger, and her palms are red, and almost look friction burnt. This isn't right.'

Janie looked up towards the top of the cliff. 'I see the karabiner, but where's the rope?'

'The karabiner may have been there a while – this is a regular climbing spot – but you're right. Where's the rope? She's got climbing shoes on, which look brand new. This is wrong, Janie. It's all wrong, you don't boulder up that high – no climber would without a rope – and why is she on her own? People don't climb like this alone, it's just not done.' Max shook his head, trying to repress the anxiety that was gnawing in his gut.

'I can see that it feels wrong, but can we *prove* that it's wrong? Without a witness, what do we have?'

'Aye, I guess, but it's the absence of evidence that concerns me.'

'You always say absence of evidence isn't evidence of absence.'

'And it's true. There'll be something, we're just not looking properly.'

Max looked to the victim's side, and saw a smashed Samsung smartphone in a leather case that had seemingly fallen from the pocket of her jacket. The case was open, and the phone screen was battered to bits. 'Seen the phone?'

Janie nodded. 'It's seen better days.'

Max reached for the phone and saw the flash of something in the flap of the case. It was a bank card. Max carefully slid out the card, which looked new. It was in the name Susan Brown. Behind it was another sliver of plastic, which Max tugged at and slid out of the case. It was a driving licence that bore the face of an attractive, blonde-haired woman. The name read Susan Ann Brown, with an address in Inverness printed on the card. The date of birth revealed that she was thirty-eight. Max sighed; thirty-eight years old, and dead on the floor of a shady crag, all vestiges of life extinguished, and for what?

He looked up from the licence into the face of the corpse, his heart pounding in his chest. Breathing hard, he gently brushed the golden hair away from her face. It was as pale as alabaster, with the lips pulled away from her crooked teeth, which seemed to snarl in a bloody grimace. Her eyes were open wide, reflective of the terror that she must have experienced as she plunged onto the unforgiving rock. A solitary line of blackening, drying blood was stark as it had carved its gruesome trail from her nostril to her lips where it had congealed. All traces of colour had been drained away when her heart had stopped. Max sighed, a deep sorrow washing over him as he handed the driving licence over to Janie.

'Get the card to the inspector and get the cops to go to the address. There's a death message to deliver. We also need to see what Barney can do with this phone.'

'But it's knackered, Max.'

'I know, but if she was here with someone else, there'd maybe be evidence of that on the phone – either texts or social media.'

'But it's totally busted up.'

'You know Barney. He'll find a way, either by the components, or maybe the phone's backup.'

'I can't see how.'

Max looked again. The screen was totally decimated, and some of the components had spilled from inside. Shards of glass littered the earth around where it lay. Max frowned. All wrong.

'We need him to try. It's way *too* knackered, Janie. It's in bloody bits; if it was in her pocket and she fell on her back, which she clearly did, how did it get battered like that?' Max felt the whooshing blood in his ears intensify.

'What are you saying, Max?'

'I think someone smashed her phone after she fell.'

12

MAX AND JANIE were sitting in the incident room at Inverness Police HQ building, being studiously ignored by all the other officers who were beavering away on what was apparently a new, and potentially hot, Cat A murder. The on-call SIO, who had identified himself as DCI Struan O'Neill, had been friendly enough and had got mugs of tea for them, but he seemed frustrated and harassed.

'I've an urgent progress meeting. As soon as that's done, I'll come and speak, I promise. No more than twenty minutes,' he'd said, his ruddy cheeks flushed.

The twenty minutes had stretched to an hour before he appeared from the meeting room and joined them at the spare desk that they were sat by.

'I'm so sorry, guys. The divisional commander stressed that I was to cooperate with you, some review team, aye?' he said, running a hand through his thinning russet hair.

'That's right, boss. Policing Standards Review from Tulliallan. Wanted to talk about the fatal accident inquiry at Huntly's Cave,' said Max.

'Aye, it's come across my desk. Hold up, I think I have the summary here. I thought Gordon Campbell was handling it?' he said, sorting through a sheaf of papers, before extracting a single sheet and placing it down on the desk, then reaching for a pair of spectacles from his shirt pocket.

'A little worried about it, boss,' said Max.

'As I understand, a lone woman bouldering at Huntly's cave

fell. Climbing shoes, but no rope?' He studied the sheet of paper, his forehead creased in concentration.

'That's the one. Did anyone mention the phone?'

'No, I heard nothing. All I've heard is that there are no witnesses, no CCTV, no suggestion of an angry ex, or similar. Fiscal's been informed and has ordered a special PM. I was planning to review again after that. What are you basing your suspicion on?' He looked up from the paper at Max, his face a picture of confusion.

'The phone. It had fallen from her pocket but seemed to have been smashed to bits. I'm worried that someone may be covering their tracks if they've had prior contact with the victim,' said Max.

'Says here that the phone is battered beyond recovery, and it's believed that it was damaged in the fall. She fell from over ten metres, I heard?'

'It would seem so,' said Max.

'Well, we wouldn't be able to use our kit to download it, and even if we did, I have eighteen phones from our current Cat A murder ahead in the queue for examination. Look, I don't mean to be rude, but unless something comes from the PM, I don't see what we can do.'

'Well, do you mind if we have a wee poke about?' said Max.

'Be my guest. Next of kin has been informed, with no obvious leads. The poor woman was single but shared a flat with a friend in town, who has been informed. Apparently, she'd got into bouldering at the new climbing centre in town and wanted to try out a real rock face. Fiscal is waiting for the PM before deciding what to do next, so any poking around you do, please make sure you've a good record of it, as I'm going to have to do a review at some point – although God knows when I'll get the chance. Now, I don't want to be rude, but I really must get on. I've a meeting with the Superintendent in a minute, and he's fucking raging at the community response after the stabbing.' He stood, as if to go.

'One thing, boss. The phone, mind if we try and get it

downloaded? We have access to a few extra resources . . .' Max left the sentence hanging.

'Knock yerself out, pal. Be glad of the assistance. Just keep us in the loop of anything you find, eh?' He nodded, and almost jogged off towards an impatient-looking uniformed superintendent at the edge of the open-plan office.

'Jesus, they're totally willing to just write this off,' said Janie.

'Aye, I know, and I don't want to make too much of a fuss. This is either bloody awful laziness, incompetence or possibly something else,' said Max, swigging his tea and screwing up his face.

Janie narrowed her eyes as she looked at Max. 'Then why not make a fuss, or escalate?'

'In case it's something else. We're better off staying under the radar and skulking about in the shadows for a bit, while we see what we can find. If this is more than incompetence, we need to not spook them before we've had a chance to bottom it all out. Have you seen Barney recently?' Max was referring to Barney Illingworth, a retired ex-MI5 technical surveillance expert who assisted the team with their covert tactics. He was a laidback Yorkshireman, who mostly lived in a campervan, but was the most skilled and dedicated operative that Max had ever worked with.

'He's about. He's been avoiding everyone as he's enjoying the grace-and-favour flat that he's been squatting in which the Chief seems to have forgotten he gave him the keys to. What are you thinking?'

'That phone. No way would a standard XRY or Cellebrite machine be able to download it, and if they send it to a lab it'll take ages. If we get it to Barney, he may be able to crack it quicker.'

'Good call, shall we grab it and dash, then?' said Janie, standing up, and dusting biscuit crumbs from her jeans.

Max looked at his watch. 'Aye, but it's still early. Let's go and see the flatmate.'

13

Edinburgh, 1985

HAMISH WOKE WITH *a yelp, his body lathered in a thick, mucky sweat as he lay in his bed in the high-ceilinged bedroom at the house in Stockbridge, his breath escaping him in rasps.*

The dream had been as usual. A total blank. Nothing. No memory of the horror that was responsible for tearing him from his sleep like this.

His teeth were chattering in the cold room, and his heart sank as he felt the familiar warmth against his pyjama bottoms. He reached under the covers and immediately smelt the acrid stench of his urine-soaked sheets. It felt like all the blood was rushing to his face, and terror gripped his insides, ice-cold and fearsome.

There would be consequences.

There were always consequences.

He looked at the LED display on his bedside clock-radio, a gift from the always kind, but almost always absent Uncle James. It was 2 a.m. He cursed under his breath, 'No, no, no, please, no,' his voice trembling along with his hands, as he reached over and flicked the bedside light on. A weak yellow light illuminated the room.

He felt the tears begin to prick his eyes, the panic catching in his throat, as he pulled back the covers and stepped out of the bed, the biting cold attacking his legs as the thin fabric of his pyjamas clung to his skin. He crept across the creaky floorboards, his heart in his mouth as he reached the dark mahogany chest of drawers. Holding his breath, he gently slid a drawer open and pulled out a clean pair of pyjamas. They were neatly folded, put there, no doubt, by the kind and smiley housekeeper who worked there four days a week. No way did Auntie Eunice do housework – she considered it beneath her.

Hamish was pulling his clean pyjama bottoms up when he heard the door open. The chill gripped even tighter, and he quaked uncontrollably as the acidic voice pierced the dead silence of the night.

'You repulsive little fucking pissy-wretch,' said Auntie Eunice, her alcohol-slurred, cut-glass English accent delivering the ominous words with even more menace.

'Auntie Eunice, I'm sorry . . .' began Hamish, his voice thick and tight with the terror that was gripping his insides, as if his blood had turned to ice.

His aunt's face was twisted in an ugly rage, her teeth bared in a snarl, her lipstick smudged. The stench of cigarettes and gin filled his nostrils, as she strode across the room, a cane in her hand, which she whipped with terrible force right across his shoulder. He fell to the floor, into the foetal position, experience telling him that this was the only way to minimise the beating. He lay there as the cane cut the air, the swoosh of the bamboo in his ears, time after time, lashing against his exposed buttocks and back.

But twelve-year-old Hamish didn't cry out.

He never cried in pain.

It only made things worse.

14

SUSAN BROWN'S FLAT was a compact space above a convenience store on the east side of Inverness. Her flatmate, who had introduced herself as Stroma Leckie, was tearful, and dabbed at her eyes with a tissue as she sat on the threadbare sofa in the small living room.

'It's just such a shock. She was a lovely girl, I cannae believe that she's just gone.' Stroma's jaw quivered and the tears spilled over onto her cheek.

'Do you know much about her life, Stroma?' said Janie.

'She worked at an estate agent on Castle Street. It's such a shame, she'd just been promoted, as well,' she said, picking at a thread on the arm of her sweater and sniffing.

'Friends and family?' said Janie, scribbling into her notebook.

'Mum and dad and a sister in Glasgow. She'd moved up here with her ex, who buggered off overseas with offshore work, which was why they split. He was no good for her anyhow, so he wasn't so much of a loss, being as he was so far up his own backside. She was getting back out into the world, though. She'd had a few dates in town, in fact she seemed quite keen on the latest one.'

'You know anything about him?' said Max.

'No, sorry. Some kind of outdoorsy type, although she hadn't said much. I think they'd only met once or twice. She loves—' she paused and sighed before continuing and correcting herself, '*loved* the outdoor thing, whereas I don't like it so much when the pavement runs out. She mentioned something about bagging Munros, or climbing, but I didn't take much notice. She had been going to the new climbing place in town for a wee while, and was really getting into it; she even bought the weird shoes. She wanted me to go along, but I'm way too scared of heights.' She sighed again, deeply, and shook her head, before blowing her nose with the tissue.

'How did she meet the new boyfriend?' said Janie.

'Internet, I suspect. Never fancied it myself, too many bloody weirdos out there, I said. I met my boyfriend the normal method. Why are you asking all this? Do you think that it wasn't an accident?' she said, suddenly fixing Janie with a firm stare.

'We're just looking for background, Stroma. The Procurator Fiscal will want some answers, so we need to ask the questions. Did Sue have a computer or tablet?' said Janie, with a reassuring smile.

'No, just her phone and a work computer that never came home. She refused to bring her work home with her, which was why it'd taken way too long for her promotion. She was glued to her phone, though, always on social media, or the dating sites.'

'Any idea which ones?' said Janie.

'Not sure, but I think it was one of the popular ones. She was always moaning that it was all the same local creeps hassling her on there. She was a bonny wee thing, as well.'

'Does she have a diary?' said Max.

'I think so – it may be in her room?'

'Mind if we take a look?' asked Max.

Stroma's eyes widened a little. 'Is that really necessary? Shouldn't it be her family that does this?'

'We're wondering whether she was alone when she fell, so maybe there are some clues in her room. We'd really like to find who she was dating, just to rule them out, you understand,' said Max, smiling as he stood.

Stroma shrugged. 'Help yourselves, second door on the left.' She pointed towards the hall.

Max nodded, and headed into the dark and dingy hall, Janie and Stroma in tow. He stopped at a chipped wooden door, which swung open on creaky hinges. The room was a small double, with an unmade bed in the centre. It was shabby and untidy, with a dressing table at one end and a dilapidated wardrobe at the other. There was a photo tacked to the woodchip-covered wall of Sue with an older couple, all smiling broadly at the camera.

Max pointed at the photograph. 'Sue's folks?'

'Aye. They'll be devastated, and they're such sweet people. Is someone telling them?' She dabbed at her eyes again.

'Aye, it's been done,' said Max, softly.

Janie picked up a pink A5 notebook from the dresser and held it up. 'Is this her diary?'

Stroma looked up; there were fresh tears on her face. 'It must be.'

Janie began to leaf through the journal, before handing it to Max. 'Look at today.'

The date was marked with several crudely drawn stars, and a single word in looping, child-like writing was encircled by a heart.

SilverFox

Max said nothing, just reached into his pocket, pulled out his phone and dialled.

'Now then, what's going down?' the broad Yorkshire accent of Barney boomed in his ear.

'You busy?' said Max.

'Only in that I'm driving, and I can multitask, lad,' he replied, cheerily.

'Can you get to Inverness? Something has come up.'

'On me way, mate. Janie sent me a message saying I'd mebbe be needed, and as I'm reet bored in't flat I thought I'd spark up the tech-mobile and head your way. With you in an hour; where'd you want me? Local nick?' he said, and Max could hear the smile in his voice.

'No, not the police station, too many eyes and ears. We need somewhere that we can work in peace and quiet. I'll send you a pin drop. See you there in an hour.'

15

'THIS IS TYPICAL, shippers. I don't see you for bloody years, and then you can't stay away,' said Shay, his mouth split with a wide grin.

'I paid attention to what you said, pal. This is Janie, and this is Barney. Janie's my partner in crime, and Barney, despite his grandfatherly appearance, is our technical expert.'

'Glad to meet you both.' Shay shook hands with them and added, 'Now, you've got full use of our standby room, it's dead quiet in there at the moment. Not that I mind in the slightest, but is there a particular reason you don't want to do this at the local cop shop?'

'Walls have ears, and I'd prefer to keep a low profile,' Max replied.

'That bad?'

'Maybe. Can't be sure, but we're not happy about the fall. A few questions, and we're hoping the lassie's phone may have some answers.'

'Well, crack on then. There's a decent coffee machine, and one of the lads is a coffee snob, so there's only the best quality stuff there. Also heaps of biscuits, so help yourselves. I'll have to leave you to it, as I've a management Zoom meeting, but pop up and see me in the ops room when you've a minute.' He nodded, grinned and bounced off.

'Well, he's morale on a stick, eh?' said Janie, as they climbed the stairs.

Max grinned. 'Nickname used to be Tigger at school.'

Within a few minutes they were sitting in the crew room, which had the look and feel of a school staffroom, apart from the good coffee and widescreen TV.

'Reet, show us this phone then,' said Barney, sitting down on an armchair and opening his heavy-looking holdall.

Max handed over a sealed evidence bag containing the broken Samsung phone, which Barney turned over in his hands with professional interest.

'Someone did a bloody number on it, that's for sure, but as long as the main chip is undamaged, I may be able to retrieve summat. Can I open the bag?'

Max nodded, as he accepted a steaming cup of fragrant coffee from Janie. 'Go for it. It's not like the cops in Inverness are that arsed.'

Barney reached down into his bag and pulled out a pair of scissors and a scratched metal box the size of a pencil case. He snapped the lid open, revealing the contents: a set of micro screwdrivers and other miniaturised tools.

He put on a pair of nitrile gloves and then slit the evidence bag open with the scissors, before removing the cracked phone and laying it carefully on the low table in front of the armchair. He paused to take a proffered coffee cup from Janie.

Inhaling the aroma, he sighed. 'Your mate didn't exaggerate, that's a cracking-smelling coffee, lass.' He took an exploratory sip and nodded appreciatively.

'I thought you were a tea drinker,' said Janie.

'I am. Yorkshire bags, of course, and they have shite-looking PG Tips, so I went for coffee.' He took another sip before setting the cup down on the table.

Barney reached into his shirt pocket and pulled out a pair of plastic-framed spectacles with a missing arm and balanced them on his nose. He picked up the phone and turned it over in his hands, hissing in disapproval. 'Been brayed at least twice and look – there's a scuff here on the screen by the charging port. Hold up.' He reached into his bag again and brought out a small magnifying glass. He hunched closer to the screen, squinting through the glass and rubbing the tip of a tiny screwdriver against the scuff. He examined the end of the tool with interest. 'I'd say that's a rubber scuff, as if someone's hit it with the sole of a shoe or summat. This weren't caused by a rock, and it didn't happen in her pocket, that's for sure.'

'What, so are you suggesting that it was stamped on?' said Max.

'I suspect it would be hard to prove, but yeah. I reckon it's a possibility. Lockheed's theory of exchange or whatever you buggers always talk about with forensics, and all that bollocks.'

'Lockheed is an aerospace company, Barney. I suspect you mean Dr Edmond Locard's 1920 exchange principle, as in, when two objects come in contact, each one would leave with something from the other,' said Janie.

'God, you're a nerd, typical of you to not only know the theory, but the year he came up with it,' said Max with a chuckle.

Janie retorted by flicking two fingers in his direction.

'Shit, will that get the MIT team interested?' said Janie, returning Max's smile.

'I can't see it. Clever all-round chap that Barney is, he's not a forensic expert in trace evidence, and he's not even openly on the books. No, we need something else. Can you power the phone up?'

Barney shook his head. 'I don't want to boot it up, in case that fries it. I've another idea.' He went to his tin box and pulled out a small sliver of metal. He pushed it into the side of the phone and extracted the SIM card. He then pulled out his battered laptop from inside the bag and attached the phone to the computer. He stared at the screen, the light reflecting in his wonky spectacles before he began to tap at the keyboard. You could almost hear the cogs turn, as he quietly muttered to himself. He looked up, peered over his spectacles and gave his learnt opinion. 'It's fooked, mate.'

'What, totally "fooked"?' said Max.

'Well, I can't get in the normal way, so all the connections must be cream-crackered.' Barney lifted his cup and drank deeply.

'What, so it's hopeless?' said Janie.

'I didn't say that. I'll just have to be a bit more creative, that's all, mate. Don't fret, Uncle Barney is on the case.'

'That's what I feared,' Janie muttered.

'First thing is to check out the SIM card, you never know what's on that, and then I'll see if I can dig out the chip and get into that. May take a while.' Barney began to whistle tunelessly as he pulled out his micro screwdrivers and a large magnifier on a stand.

'Stop bloody watchin' me work, makes me bloody nervous, and I won't get it done any quicker. Bugger off and go and look at helicopters or summat. And get me another brew, I'm gasping.'

*

'See what I mean, shippers?' said Shay, as he tapped the iPad screen in his well-appointed office.

'I do. No obvious reason for any of them to fall.'

Shay had shown video clips that had been shot by the search-and-rescue helicopters of each of the rescues.

'So, what can you do about it?' said Shay.

'We're in the process of reviewing what was done with the fatal accident inquiries, but it's slow going. The worst we have so far is that the inquiries into the deaths were sketchy, to say the least.'

Shay narrowed his eyes. 'What, as in suspiciously sketchy?'

'Hard to say, until we drill down into the data, which won't help us moving forward. We need a lead on what may happen in the future.'

'What d'you mean?'

Max fixed Shay with a hard stare. 'If this is what I suspect it is, whoever it is won't stop. If they've killed multiple times, they'll continue, so we need to stop them before they do.'

'How?' Shay's eyes were wide with surprise.

'It's why Barney is doing what he's doing. If Sue Brown was shoved off that cliff at Huntly's Cave by someone she knew, or had been in contact with, there'll be a lead in that knackered phone.'

Janie appeared in the doorway. 'Barney has just got excited; I think he's maybe found something.'

'Excited?' said Max, feeling his heartbeat quicken.

'Well, he said, "Well, I'll go t' foot of our stairs" and raised his eyebrows.'

'Blimey, that is excitement, for Barney. Let's go.'

'Best of luck, shippers,' said Shay.

Max and Janie almost jogged down the stairs and back into the crew room, where Barney was sitting in the armchair, contentedly chewing on a slice of toast. The phone was in pieces on the table in front of him, next to his open laptop.

'You've cracked the phone?' said Max.

'This is lovely toast, mate. Decent bread, I'd expected shite sliced white, but they've a lovely loaf from a bakery.'

'Barney, will you stop dicking about. Have you cracked the phone?' said Max, his face darkening.

'Oh, no. Thing's proper cream-crackered. Told you that already.'

Max's forehead furrowed. 'So why do you look so bloody happy?'

'No point looking like a miserable bugger, is there?' Barney shrugged.

'Barney?' said Max, feeling the tension in his shoulders increase.

Barney sighed, a big smile stretching across his face. 'Well, I was able to breach the password protection with a brute force algorithm I got from a pal, and then I reckoned that she may have used the same password for other applications, so I hacked her email, which meant I could get around two-factor authorisations.'

'But you said the phone is buggered?'

'It is. Totally and utterly fooked. The floating gate MOS memory is gone, and the application processor is fried.' He flicked at the components on the table dismissively. 'More than one way to skin a cat, though. Because I cracked her password, I was able to access her phone account, which meant I've access to her last cloud backup, from early this morning. The whole thing is backed up safely on my computer. Emails, apps, GPS, Google searches, the lot, all in spreadsheets, documents and photo files. Want to see them?'

'Jesus, Barney. This would have taken weeks conventionally. I hope you've not breached protocols,' Max said.

'Well, as I dunno what the protocols are, I've no idea.'

'Get the spreadsheets to Norma, straight away. Can you search the whole thing for a keyword?'

'Easy as owt, what do you need?' said Barney, composing himself over the keyboard, looking up over his glasses.

'Search for "silver fox", and permutations of the same.'

'Ooo, nice idea, sarge,' muttered Janie, nodding appreciatively.

Barney tapped at the keyboard, his face a mask of intense concentration, whistling softly under his breath. 'Got it. Three results. One in a dating app cache, and a couple in WhatsApp messages.'

'Dating app?'

'Yeah, hold up, I'll bring it up.' Barney tapped again, before turning the screen around. 'Here you go.'

There was a photograph on the screen of what appeared to be a man dressed in climbing gear, suspended on the side of a cliff, attached by a rope on a harness around his waist. He wore tight trousers and a snug T-shirt. He looked lean and fit, and he was facing the camera, a thumb aloft. A baseball cap was pulled low on his head, and his eyes were obscured by mirrored sports sunglasses. The photo had been taken at a distance, so his features were blurred and fuzzy.

'Could this be our man she was climbing with?' said Max.

'It definitely is.' Barney pressed the arrow on the keyboard and the screen shifted to a page of messages from a screenshot of a chat function.

Suey B: I'm so excited for tomorrow!
SilverFox: Me too. Huntly's is a great spot, you'll love it!
Suey B: Promise me I won't fall to my death.
SilverFox: You'll be grand. If you can boulder, you can climb. See you at the layby on the A939, Old Military Road, at 8?
Suey B: So excited x

Max said nothing, he just stared at the screen as he dialled on his phone.

Ross's voice crackled in Max's ear. 'Where the fuck have you been, you workshy nugget, daundering around the Highlands giving it Charlie big spuds, while Norma and me are at the coalface, eh?'

'We've got a lead, Ross. We need to move before this scumbag kills someone else.'

16

MIKEY SECURED THE cam deep into the fissure on the rock face and activated the spring. He tugged against it, satisfied that it would easily take his weight. He fastened the karabiner that was attached to the short length of rope that was secured to his harness, and leant back, shaking his fingers out. He reached behind into his chalk bag and dusted. It was hot and sultry, and the midges were swarming his sweaty face and neck, but he didn't swat at them. All his years living in the Highlands had taught him that it was a fruitless exercise, but he was relieved that he had liberally slathered himself with Smidge before he'd started his climb.

Mikey loved solo climbs more than anything, and he loved traditional climbing. 'Leave no trace' was his watchword. Just him and the rock, with just some cams and safety ropes, to prevent certain death. The sensation of being alone was exhilarating, and almost primeval. And he was totally alone today, on a fairly simple rock face in the Cairngorms that was not a regular haunt of the sport climbers. He liked it this way. It was peaceful.

And it was why he was useful. No one knew the Munros and rock faces of the Highlands like he did.

His phone buzzed in the pouch that was secured on his waist. He'd normally have ignored it, but things were getting hot, and he was in demand, and that meant that there was money available. He adjusted his feet against the rock face and jammed another cam into the fissure, securing it to his harness with another safety rope.

Happy that he had a backup anchor, he reached for his phone. It was a direct message from the forum. He opened it up and smiled when he saw who it was from.

Destroyer_666: How long until the next event?

He wiped his sweaty and chalk-stained hand against his stretchy climbing trousers, and typed, Soon. Stay tuned.

Destroyer_666: Excellent. Sooner the better. The last one was beautiful, the look on the stupid whore's face when she went over the edge, but we need more close-ups. Everyone's going nuts.

Mikey chuckled and tapped out a reply: I've a beauty coming up, including a real close-up. Tell the others to expect it very soon, but the price will have gone up.

Destroyer_666: 😊 can't wait.

Mikey grinned as he tucked his phone back into the pouch. He steadied himself, reached up onto the face, digging a hand into the deep crevice, and heaved himself back against the hard granite. He released the cams and began to climb again. Totally unattached and free climbing – the sense of familiar elation coursed through him as his lean and sinewy body ascended.

He felt a surge of energy in his chest as he pulled himself up that sheer, unrelenting cliff face. He was indefatigable and irrepressible, but now he had a purpose. He climbed on, fast and skilfully as he needed to get to the top of the face quickly. He had work to do.

17

'NOW THEN, WHO wants tea? Oh, and I've a pan of stovies on, anyone hungry?' said Auntie Elspeth, who was standing in the doorway of her small living room, her lined face wearing a beaming smile. Max, Janie, Ross, Norma and Barney all looked up from the various seats that they were perched upon.

'Oh aye, I'm that bloody hungry I could eat a scabby donkey,' said Barney, an unlit roll-up wobbling in his mouth as he spoke.

'My lip-reading is pretty decent, so I think I got the gist of that,' Elspeth said, her eyes sparkling with mischief. She loved to host and had agreed immediately when Max had asked if they could camp out at her cottage in the seaside village of Avoch on the Black Isle. They hadn't wanted to go to the police station, as their presence always caused a stir, and the nature of the subject matter meant they needed to be away from public spaces. Elspeth was also a superb cook, and they were all hungry.

'I'd put it a little more delicately than that, Elspeth, but I think I can safely say that we'd all love a bowl,' said Norma.

'Aye, not half, and can I apologise for the senile old fud over there. Taking him anywhere is like taking your overly opinionated and crude old grandpa out to a nice restaurant,' said Ross, jabbing a finger in Barney's direction.

'Ach don't fret, Ross. I'm not offended, and if I was, I'd tell old Barney to get tae fuck.' Elspeth smiled and disappeared out of the room and into the kitchen as the others all chuckled.

Barney shrugged in a 'who me?' fashion, but instead of

retorting, he stood and plucked his roll-up from his lips. 'Gonna have a quick puff on this outside before we get into it. I've not 'ad a fag for ages,' he said.

'Lying old bugger, I could almost see blue smoke billowing out of your van windows, but go on then.' Ross nodded. 'You've done your bit, and I hate to say it, I'm impressed. No way would forensic services have extracted that data, and then retrieved her last fog backup, and certainly not within the next month.'

'Cloud,' said Barney, heading to the door.

'What?' Ross's face reddened.

'Cloud backup. Not fog, you daft lummox. Now if you don't mind, I'm gonna smoke me tab, and watch the sunset. It was looking grand out there when we arrived, and I could do with the fresh air.' A grin formed across his lips.

'Aye, well. Chances of any air being fresh near you are very slim, you crusty old bastard, just a smell of pish and Rich Tea biscuits,' Ross almost bellowed at Barney's retreating back.

Janie stifled a laugh behind her hand.

'You can mind your manners, you bolshy mare. Cloud? Fog? How the fuck am I supposed to interpret all this tech bollocks? Right, what do we know?'

'I know that I don't need you referring to me as a "bolshy mare",' said Janie, her grin slipping.

Ross opened his mouth to offer a retort, but then snapped it shut, and his eyes softened a touch. There was a silence that permeated the room for a brief moment.

When Ross next spoke, it was in a far softer tone. 'Aye, maybe. Sorry, Mrs F would tear me a new one, if I said things like that to her,' he said, his eyes casting down.

Janie smiled warmly. 'Nae bother, Ross.'

'Max?' Ross looked across, his face colouring.

Max cleared his throat and updated the rest of the team with all the progress since visiting the scene and recovering the phone from Huntly's Cave.

'So, the locals aren't even interested, by the sounds of it?'

'Plates are very full. Local CID are on a Cat A murder,' said Max.

'Aye, as may be. Question is for us, with our counter-corruption ninja hats on, and looking at this in the round, is whether it's deliberate, careless or something much worse.'

Norma cleared her throat. 'I've been cross-checking all the cases that your helicopter pal flagged up, and I'd be very concerned. There are a few striking features that link them. One, they were all novice climbers; two, they were all blonde women of a similar age, thirty to forty; three, they'd all just come out of relationships; and four, they all posted about their activity on Facebook before they climbed the Munros.' She paused and looked up from her laptop screen.

'Go on?' said Ross, his voice low.

'It's very striking that beyond brief enquiries at the scenes, and speaking to helicopter crews, or land-based mountain rescue teams, no one seems to have done much more, and the Fiscal's service seems to have been very easily satisfied. SFIU have apparently done thorough reviews, but on no occasion did they order a full police inquiry on any of them. Just the post-mortem, a quick chat with the bereaved family, and that was kind of it.'

'Statements taken?' said Ross.

'A couple, but very brief, and hardly a deep delve into the backgrounds to exclude angry exes, and things like that. Not one of the victims had their phones interrogated.' Norma removed her glasses and polished the lenses, before resettling them on her nose while a silence filled the room.

'How about the fatal accident inquiries at the Sheriff Courts?'

Norma shrugged. 'I've read the reports, all seemed light touch, but not all have come to court – wheels turn slow and that.'

'So, we now have potentially six unexplained deaths of women, in just over a year if we include A' Chralaig and Huntly's Cave. And we now have a strong suspicion of third-party involvement with what we found on Sue Brown's phone,' said Max, drumming his fingers on the wooden arms of his chair.

'How do we prove that third-party involvement, though?' said Janie. 'What do we actually have? We know that she was with "SilverFox" on the day she died, and I suspect that the phone was deliberately smashed, but we have no clue who the bugger is. The photo isn't much help, and could never be used to identify anyone, could it?'

'Anything else on "SilverFox"?' said Max.

'Not really, well, not yet. I've been swamped with all the other stuff.'

'It's not a great picture, which is why the bastard probably used it,' said Max.

A thick silence enveloped the room, only broken when Barney came back in, whistling softly, followed by the acrid aroma of tobacco smoke.

'Jesus, you polluting old bugger, you stink. What's Max's lovely auntie gonna think of you contaminating her wee cottage, eh?'

'Well, as she cadged a roll-up from me, not much, I guess. We had a nice natter while we had a puff; scoff's nearly ready and it smells grand. So, what's occurring?' Barney said, as he fell back into the squashy armchair he'd been occupying.

'Well, if you weren't nicotine addicted, you'd know. Basically, it looks like cops and/or SFIU aren't doing their jobs properly, either wilfully or lazily, and we can't identify who the SilverTwat is.'

'Oh, you'll not ID him from that photo.' Barney yawned and rubbed his face.

'What makes you so sure?' said Max, frowning.

'Stock image. I thought it looked a bit suspect for a dating-site profile picture, so I reverse-image searched it. It's a stock image from a climbing website.'

'Hold up a fucking minute, why haven't you mentioned this before?' said Ross, his face darkening.

'Only just found out meself. Before Auntie E came out, I was farting around on me phone, and it just occurred to me.'

'So, it's a dead end, then?' Ross sighed.

'I didn't say that, did I?'

'What are you on about, you old bampot?'

'Well, I widened the search parameters, and I found it on a social media site. That photo is a member of a couple of climbing forums, and it's a profile picture on a Facebook page for a bloke called Mikey SilverFox. Hardly anything on the profile, and I reckon it's just been set up very recently, but he's a member of a group called Munro-Bagging Newbies or some shite like that. I bloody hate social media, but this is a cheeky lead, right?' Barney grinned, clearly very pleased with himself.

'I'd never thought I'd see the day that a nicotine-addicted pensioner would get the upper hand on you whippersnappers in social media research. Well done, Barney, we have something to work with.' Ross nodded approvingly, and somehow grudgingly at the same time.

'You're welcome. Means I can justify the flat.'

'Don't get bloody used to it, you old goat. Right, suggestions? You youngsters need to up your bloody game.'

'I've a suggestion,' said Norma. 'IP searches with Facebook, backed up with phone data and attached email searches. It'd need a load of help from the intelligence bureau and comms intel unit, but we may get a phone number, or we may get attached data. We also may get something from the dating website.' Norma was animated, her cheeks reddening with enthusiasm.

'Okay, make a start with that, Norma; how about research with all the other potential victims. FaceAche?' began Ross.

'Big problem here, Ross, is that it's just me. This is the analytical work of several researchers. Social media companies are notoriously slow, and often just ignore data requests, particularly as most are located in the USA. By the time I got any sense back from them, he could have struck again. I can do the work, but I need more staff.'

'Right. I'll see what I can do, I'll call Miles and see if we can get backup for you.'

'I've an alternative, or at least a parallel suggestion,' interrupted Max.

All heads turned to him. 'Go on,' said Ross.

'Look, we can go after the historic stuff, in fact we should. Like Norma says, it's the work of several analysts, so let's get that underway, but this isn't the priority, is it?'

'Well, what is, then?' said Ross.

'Protecting his next victim, and that's where my suggestion lies. We need to take him out of the game before he gets a chance to do the next one, and this is our only real advantage.'

Ross shook his head, his jowls wobbling, slightly. 'Max, you're gonna have to bloody spell it out for me.'

'Right, now we do have an advantage. He doesn't know we're onto him. We don't know who he is, we don't know where he is, or what he looks like, but we know *how* he may do this, so I've an idea.' Max folded his arms and sat back in his chair, a wry grin appearing.

'Stop pissing about, just tell us.'

'Let's dangle a carrot and bring him to us.' Max's smile widened.

'What are you blethering about?' said Ross.

'We have a newly trained undercover officer ready to go.' Max nodded towards Janie.

'What?' said Janie, her eyes swivelling to Max.

'Simple. We know some of the Facebook groups he's potentially stalked. Let's give it a shot. I reckon we could get a profile quickly set up, have Janie appear to be a lonely woman out of a damaging relationship, and see who bites?' said Max.

A silence descended on the room, and you could almost hear the cogs turning.

'But I'm not blonde,' said Janie.

'Wig?' said Ross, trying to keep the smile off his face.

'No wig, wigs always look terrible unless done by a serious professional, and we don't have time for that. We just need an innocuous photo, probably in a hat, that shows that Janie's not hideously ugly,' said Max.

'What if he doesn't bite because she's not obviously blonde?' said Ross.

'Adds weight to the theory. Janie can just wear a cap, make it ambiguous, and keep her profile very brief. Worth a try, surely,' said Max.

'Irrespective of whether Janie is totally hacket or not, I'm not sure about this, boys and girls. How do you feel about it, Janie?' said Ross, turning to look at her.

Janie's face was pale, and her eyes flat, and she paused before answering, the slightest of tremors in her voice. 'I'm up for it; if the objective is just to bring him out into the open, I may not even need to engage with him,' she said, nervously pushing her hair back from her face.

'Excellent work, let's make it happen, then.'

'I could get a pal to sort out a Facebook profile reet quick. He's done all sorts of shit like this in his time, and he'd do it for us for a favour,' said Barney.

'Who's that then?' said Ross.

'Mate of mine, ex MI5, now a private IT consultant. He's helped us before, and he'd sort it way quicker than we could using his AI-enabled programs that he spends his life trying to counter for big companies,' said Barney.

'Do we need it, can't I just set up a new one?' said Janie, the colour returning to her cheeks.

'You could, but it would look brand new,' said Barney. 'My

mate Clive could make it look older, and more genuine, and he does something with AI and photos that I don't really understand, but the profiles he's set up in the past look years old.'

Max opened his mouth to speak but then froze as his phone buzzed, and he saw the message from Katie. *Call me ASAP, something's happening x*

Max's stomach tightened, and he felt the blood drain from his face.

'Max?' said Ross.

Max held his hand up. 'I need to make a call now. It's Katie.' Without waiting for an answer, he jumped to his feet and headed out of the room, through the kitchen, and into the back garden, where Elspeth was pottering with a watering can, her eyebrows rising as Max strode past her, his phone to his ear.

'Max, I think something is happening,' said Katie, her voice thick, and fearful.

'Are you okay, babe?'

'I keep getting contractions. They started light, but now they're much stronger.'

'Have you made the call?' said Max, his mind roiling with conflicting emotions, fear, excitement, worry. Was this it? Was life about to change, forever?

'Yes. Midwife says to just keep an eye on timings and if they get much closer, I should come in.'

'Have your waters gone?'

'No, not yet. How far away are you?' she said, and Max could hear the fear in her voice.

'I'm at Elspeth's, but I'm leaving now, okay?' Max looked at his watch and saw that it was almost 7 p.m.

'Please, Max. I'm scared.' She began to weep, and Max felt as if his stomach was being ripped from his abdomen.

'It'll be fine, babe; any problems you've John and Lynne next door. I'm on my way.'

'Please hurry.'

'Leaving right now, I love you.'

'You too.'

Max jogged back into the house. Elspeth stood looking at him, hands on hips as he passed her.

'I need to go home, now. It's Katie, sounds like things are happening,' said Max, breathing hard.

Ross stood up, his face impassive. 'Right, go now. Janie, you take him, he's a pish driver and will take forever. Go now, and don't spare the horses, I'll write off the speeding tickets.'

'But the case—' began Max.

'Fuck the fucking case. Your missus needs you. It may surprise you to learn that you aren't God's gift to criminal investigations. Norma and I can manage fine without you, ya fanny. We even have Old Father Time here to chip in with the tech stuff, so get going now. Of all the things to miss in your life, the birth of your first or, in fact, *any* ankle-biter isn't one of them, so piss right off, right this second,' he said, grinning, and clapping him on the shoulder.

Janie leapt to her feet, car keys in her hand. 'Let's roll, Daddy.'

Max nodded. 'Thanks, guys, and Janie?'

'Aye?'

'Never, ever call me Daddy again.'

18

KATIE LOOKED TIRED and scared when Janie dropped Max outside the cottage in Culross, her face pale and her hands clutching her stomach. Notably Nutmeg didn't move from Katie's side, she just looked at Max and wagged her tail nervously.

'I'm so glad you're here,' she said as Max bent down to kiss her cheek.

'How are you feeling?'

'Contractions every six minutes, and they're pretty intense. Midwife is now advising us to go in for a check-up,' she said, as Max stroked her damp cheek.

'Do you think this is it?'

'I don't know, Max. The contractions haven't changed timing-wise, and they're no stronger, but they're horrible. I'm worried.' Fresh tears spilled from her eyes and ran down her cheeks. Max picked up a tissue from the coffee table and wiped them away.

'Is your go-bag still packed and ready?' said Max.

'Yes, in the bedroom.'

'Then we're going, right now.'

*

'False labour, pet,' said the smiling and bustling midwife who had introduced herself as Catherine. She had a soft Highland accent and a kind face with twinkling blue eyes, and she radiated comforting efficiency.

Max had driven a groaning Katie at breakneck speed to the maternity unit at Kirkcaldy just over half an hour away. They had been ushered into a treatment room and very soon Katie was being examined by Catherine, whilst Max sat by Katie's head, stroking her damp brow.

'False? But the contractions are still really gripping, like someone has a bloody vice inside me,' said Katie, a look of disappointment replacing the fearful one.

'Worse than when they started, or less?'

'Possibly a little less.'

'It's fairly common, and it's a very easy mistake to make, particularly when you have strong and regular contractions, like you have had. However, yours have been six to seven minutes apart for several hours, and your cervix isn't dilated whatsoever. Unfortunately for you guys, that wee toot isn't quite ready to come out yet.'

'Does it mean things are imminent?' said Max.

'Maybe, maybe not. We're very much in the action zone, timing-wise, but there's certainly no suggestion that it's going to happen in the immediate future. You're still only thirty-eight weeks, so plenty of time yet. Go home and get lots of rest. Do you have a TENS machine?' said Catherine.

Katie shook her head.

'I'll send you away with one, they can really help with the discomfort, but if I was a betting woman, which I'm not, I'd say that these contractions will dissipate in the next few hours. I'm confident you're not ready yet; baby's head isn't fully engaged.' She smiled with encouragement, but Max could sense that she was already thinking about the next patient.

'So, we're good to go home?' said Max.

'Aye, get home, and get some rest while you can. Once junior turns up, sleep will be a precious commodity.'

'And should I stay home from work?' Max asked.

'Do you want to?' Catherine's blue eyes bored into Max's. She had clearly fielded this question many times from fathers-to-be.

'What I want doesn't matter, but parental leave doesn't begin until he or she puts in an appearance,' said Max.

'Well then, go to work. Average first labour is twelve to twenty hours, so you'll have time to get home.'

Max just nodded, not looking at Katie, fully aware that she'd be glaring at him, right now.

'Look, folks. We do this all day, every day, and ninety-nine per cent of births are totally routine, and at your stage, most go to term or beyond. We're ready when you're ready, but you're not there quite yet. So go home, and get some rest, and I am very confident you'll feel much better tomorrow.'

'You're sure?' said Katie, a look of anti-climax on her face.

'I can never be totally sure, because this is nature we're dealing with, and nature takes its own sweet course. If I were you guys, I'd enjoy the time you have as just the two of you. There'll be three of you soon enough.'

19

CATHERINE WAS RIGHT.

They'd got home just after midnight, to the delight of Nutmeg who, as was now customary, attached herself to Katie like a limpet, resting her shaggy, blonde head on her bump, as Max made the tea.

'It's definitely easing, I think the paracetamol has helped a little, and the contractions aren't so severe.'

Max said nothing as he sat. He just kissed his wife gently on the forehead.

'Are you angry with me?' said Katie, taking Max's hand.

'What?' said Max incredulously.

'Dragging you away from your job. I know how much your work means.'

'Katie, nothing is more important than you. The others are handling it all. I can join them when you're feeling better, so don't for one second think that.' Max stroked her forehead, and she lay back into the soft fabric of the sofa, her eyes closing.

'But . . .' she began, but then she stopped.

'But what?' said Max.

Katie shook her head. 'It's fine.' Her jaw was tight.

'Katie, seriously, what is it?' Max's stomach clenched. He knew that she was holding back.

'I'm worried, Max.'

'But you heard the nurse, things are gonna be fi—'

Katie's eyes flashed, and she interrupted. 'Not that. Not the birth, I'm worried about you, Max. About us. All of us. Me, the baby and you. And your job. The bloody job. I know how much it means to you, how much you put into it, and how much you care, I just . . .' She stopped, mid-sentence, and her eyes filled with tears.

'Katie . . .' began Max, but Katie jumped in again.

'I'm scared that I'm going to be doing this on my own.'

Max felt the blood rush to his head.

'Katie, listen to me. I love you, and I know already I love whoever is in there.' He rested his hand on her stomach. 'I want to do this together, of course I do, but I also have to pay the bills, and the job pays the bills. I'll still do the job, but you and the wee fella will always be number one.' He leant forward and planted a kiss on her forehead, wondering how much of what he was saying was completely true. Could he put the job second? Would he walk away from it?

Could he remain a police officer, and be a good dad? His mind reeled with the enormity of it.

'Is the job progressing?' she said, sleepily.

'Aye, it's fine. I'll head back up tomorrow, but I'll take the bike. I could be back here in a wee moment if things start to happen. You heard Catherine. Average is almost twenty hours. Inverness is only a couple away.'

Katie's eyes were closed, and her breathing was soft and steady, her chest rising and falling. She was fast asleep already. Max stood up, gently disentangling her hand from his and laying her head down onto a cushion. Nutmeg tucked herself into the crook of Katie's arm and sighed. Max took a fluffy throw from the other chair and laid it over her.

He crept down into the hall and flicked through his phone, checking the WhatsApp group. There was just one message from Ross that was timed just a few minutes ago. *Best of luck, dickhead. Let us know when you know.*

Max dialled, and Ross answered immediately, surprisingly without any type of abusive prelude. 'Any news, pal?' he said, his voice full of anticipation. Despite his bluff, crass and sometimes oafish exterior, Ross was actually a dedicated father and husband, with a long-suffering wife and two daughters, all of whom he doted on.

'Aye, false alarm. False labour, with loads of painful contractions, but she's all well. Midwife reckons we're not ready yet.'

'You did the right thing, pal. She needed you there. Is she okay now?'

'Yeah, contractions are easing, and less painful, and she's sleeping. What's happening there?'

'Plenty, but it's all in hand, so you don't need to rush up here.'

'What's happening, though?'

'Max, does it matter? Why not stay down at home for a couple of days, eh? We've got it covered.' Ross was clearly hiding something.

'Ross, I'm not daft, and I'll find out one way or the other.'

'Okay, Barney's geek pal created a very convincing FaceAche profile for Janie. Not that I'd know, because social media is for vacuous wankers, but between them all they've created a profile, and she's joined a number of groups, including one called Munro-Bagging Newbies. Look at the link I'm sending you.'

Max switched the call to speaker phone and waited for the inevitable bluff and bluster as Ross wrestled with the unfamiliar social media.

There were beeps, tones, sighs and oaths down the line. 'Fucking stupid bastarding shite, why do grown-ups use this crap, hold up – here it is.'

There was a ping as the link arrived. Max clicked on it, and a Facebook page opened. The photo of Janie was from a distance, and she was dressed in a blue windcheater, dark walking trousers, and had a baseball cap on her head, along with mirrored sports sunglasses. A quick scan down the feed showed a few other photos, none particularly close up, but all could have easily passed for Janie. It was clear that Barney's contact had been busy.

'This is impressive. It looks like a profile that's been around a long time, but has suddenly come into more regular usage after a change in life circumstances,' said Max.

'Aye, that's the point, after a relationship split, and the photos are enough to know she's no' a minger, but not too much that she'll be recognisable forever. See the other photos, and the timeline? Barney's mate did something with photos, and it looks like there's some kind of history. Apparently, lots of it is AI-generated from a couple of photos of Janie.'

'Has it worked?'

'It seems so. Jane Henderson, recently having escaped a troubled relationship, has a date tomorrow afternoon with our friend Mikey-Fox to go and bag Cairngorm.'

'Mikey-Fox? So, he is changing profile names.

'Aye, and he's used another stock image that could be anyone, but he's said she'll recognise him because of his red baseball cap, which makes a change from a carnation in the lapel. It's him, Max. It's definitely our man. Game on.'

20

THE DREAM WAS bad.

It was worse than it had been in a long time, tearing Max from sleep with a sudden gasp, as he sat bolt upright in bed, breathing heavily and lathered in sweat.

He'd been right there. Afghanistan, with his patrol of soldiers in the scorched run-up to the patrol base. He could almost smell the dried-up sand, the coppery tang of the blood that was flowing from Dippy and staining the desert floor in Helmand province. He squeezed his eyes shut, trying to drive the images out of his brain, but it was so difficult. The light in his friend's eyes fading, and then going as the flicker of life left his ruined body. Ruined by an IED set by the Taliban.

Max choked back the tears that were threatening to overwhelm him. *Not now*, he thought, gritting his teeth. Katie didn't need to see this.

He lay back on the damp sheets with a sigh, his breathing returning to normal as Nutmeg shifted across to his side of the bed from her new favoured position, tucked into Katie's back. She whined softly and nuzzled at Max's cheek with her icy cold nose. 'Shh.' Max tickled her silky ear, and she settled down again.

He had been free of the dream for some time now, but the experience at Huntly's Cave had brought it back in lurid, Technicolor vividity. He looked across at the digital clock, and sighed again when he saw that it was only just 5 a.m., and the dawn light was seeping through the crack in the curtains. He knew that he would not sleep again now, so he knew what he'd have to do. Silently he pulled back the covers and eased out of bed, thankful that all his running gear was in the cupboard in the long hall outside the bedroom. Nutmeg's ears pricked up, hopefully, and Max nodded. She almost dived off the bed, her tail thrashing wildly. She knew what always happened after these early morning wake-ups, and devoted to Katie though she was, nothing would stop her wanting to go on an early run.

Within a couple of minutes, Max was dressed in shorts, T-shirt and trainers, and silently left the house. He jammed his earbuds in and selected a mix of harsh guitar music by Mogwai. He broke into a run, Nutmeg trotting effortlessly alongside him as they ran in the milky morning light, heading down the track into the wide-open vista of the Culross morning. As Max ran harder, the pain that bit in his legs and heaving chest became therapeutic, and the memories of Dippy, Afghanistan, Sue Brown and all the others began to assume their normal positions. Passengers with him, rather than drivers driving him.

He felt a little better. Not all better, but a bit better.

*

'You okay?' said Max, as a bleary-eyed Katie shuffled into the kitchen, a cotton dressing gown over her shoulders, a confused look on her face.

'I didn't hear you get up?' she said, yawning expansively.

'I couldn't sleep, so I went for a run. Nutmeg was delighted.' He kissed her on the cheek and stroked her hair. 'How're you feeling?'

'Better than yesterday. God, that coffee stinks,' she said, wrinkling her nose. Katie was still very resentful that her previous love of coffee had been corrupted by pregnancy and she very much enjoyed blaming her husband for this.

'Tea?' said Max, with an apologetic grin.

'Yes, you bugger. Mint tea. Did you have the dream?' She eyed him balefully.

'No,' said Max, a little too quickly.

'I can smell burning,' she said.

'Pardon?'

'It's because your bloody pants are on fire, you fibber. You only wake early when you have the dream. Did something happen at work?' She accepted the steaming cup from Max.

'Another death. This one in the Cairngorms, a climber apparently fell to her death. We went to the scene.'

'Surely that's not your remit?'

'Toast?' said Max, changing the subject.

'Yes, please, and that's not answering the question I asked.'

'It's not our remit, but there's been a few too many deaths in the Highlands of women either on Munros, or in this case, apparently climbing. We've a couple of leads, and we're linking them. Let's talk about something else,' said Max, popping four slices of bread into the toaster.

'Okay, what are you planning today?'

'Depends on how you're feeling?'

'Like a great big heffalump, with swollen ankles, sore hips, and I'm always too bloody hot, but no contractions.'

'So, back to normal?'

'Well, this normal, yes. Are you wanting to go to work?'

'What do you think?' said Max, carefully.

'I don't want you eating into your paternity leave before junior makes an appearance, that's for sure. I think you should go to work, as long as you promise to take three weeks off once this wee thing arrives, and not look at your work phone once during that time.' Katie sat at the table and placed her cup down, before folding her arms and eyeing Max. He knew that look.

'A hundred per cent. I want to get to know junior as much as

94

you do. Once he or she pitches up, I'm on leave. Anyway, there's no way Ross would let me go back. Despite all the bluster, he's a right softy, particularly when it comes to weans.'

'I hope you're being careful, and not doing anything dangerous?' she said, chewing, the crumbs on her lips.

'It's just routine stuff, babe. Thematic reviews of unexplained deaths, and stuff like that,' Max said, biting into his own toast.

'Total bullshit, but go on, get going. Let me know when you get there, and don't do anything daft. This little person needs their dad when he or she shows up.' Katie's hand went to her swollen belly.

'I promise.' Max stood up and kissed her on the top of her head.

Within a few minutes, he was dressed in his bike gear and on his big KTM Adventure motorcycle. He took off, heading north towards whatever came next. His guts churned with a mix of fear and excitement.

And for the first time ever, it wasn't work that was stirring these emotions.

21

MAX PARKED HIS KTM in between the Volvo and Barney's campervan in the car park of the Cairngorm ski centre, the large winter sports venue at the top of the Cairngorm Mountain range. He pulled off his helmet and stashed it in the bike's top box along with his armoured textile jacket and leather gloves, leaving him dressed in jeans, a hoodie and walking boots. He pulled a windproof soft-shell jacket out of the box and slipped it on. Max had spent plenty of time on Munros and he knew that even with the current perfect weather, it was still Scotland.

He pulled his phone out of his pocket and refreshed the screen. No messages or calls from Katie. He breathed out, but it didn't release all the tension in his gut. The fact that he was at least three hours away from her was disconcerting to say the least, and not for the first time, he wondered whether his job and his family life would ever coexist. Could he do anything else? He squeezed his eyes closed, snapped them open again and quickly composed a message.

Just arrived, all ok, babe? x

The reply came back almost immediately. *I'm fine, and settled. Lynne is here, and is making a big pan of soup. X*

Max sighed and felt some calm return. Once again, the weather was spectacular, with the sun beating down from a vividly blue, cloudless sky, with a moderately stiff breeze taking the edge off the warmth. He took in the magnificent view that stretched out away from the grand Cairngorm Munro behind the centre, and down to the sparkling, iridescent Loch Morlich a thousand metres below.

In winter it would have been bustling with skiers and snowboarders, and the car park would have been rammed. But today being midweek, it was almost empty, the ski lifts hanging limp and swaying in the breeze above the scarred and scraped nursery slope. Rather than the hordes of winter sports aficionados there were just a few ramblers, and some disappointed sightseers who had come to ride the funicular railway only to find that it had been closed for repairs.

Max went in via the shop and into the small café, and ignoring the CLOSED sign pinned to the door, he shoved it open to find Ross, Barney and Janie all sitting with a small clutch of people dressed in the now-familiar Cairngorm Mountain Rescue soft-shell jackets.

'You took your time, you skiving fanny,' quipped Ross, as Max sat down to puzzled looks from the Mountain Rescue Team members. Ross was dressed in ill-fitting combat trousers and an ancient Barbour jacket that was shiny and greasy. His leather walking boots appeared to be, if anything, older than the Barbour.

'Forgive Ross, guys. We like to refer to him as "irascible",' said Janie, with a smile. She was dressed for the mountain, in grey walking trousers, boots, and a new and expensive-looking blue Gore-Tex jacket.

'Aye, well, if I knew what that meant, I'd possibly be offended, but I don't, so fuck you. Anyway, now that you've seen fit to join us, can I introduce Inspector Tom Jeffries, who is the Mountain Rescue coordinator for Highland, and Sergeant Ed Smith, his deputy.' Ross pointed at a lean and fit-looking middle-aged man, with salt-and-pepper cropped hair and a wide smile. Sitting next to him was a short and stocky man, with a shock of wiry brown hair and a pale face with a dark beard. Tom stood and offered a hand, which Max accepted, while Ed just smiled and nodded.

'MRT coordinator? Plum job, that?' said Max.

'Aye, it's the main reason I transferred up north. Part time, unfortunately. Ed and I work in the custody block at Inverness when we're not doing this, much as we'd like to do it full time,' said Tom.

'We asked Tom and his team to come up to offer some local assistance with getting bodies on the hill to deter any nastiness. Unfortunately, the local MIT don't seem too interested and think we're fishing, which is possibly true. Fortunately, Miles Moneypenny is a pal of Tom's, and he put the word in, so we've backup.' Ross nodded in satisfaction, clearly pleased with himself.

Max nodded at the rest of the team members.

'Let's go over there. You two coming?' said Ross, looking at Tom and Ed.

Tom nodded. Ross, Barney, Max and Janie, and Tom and Ed all gathered around a table away from all the others.

'No other cops?' said Max.

Ross shook his head. 'Too risky, and they'd be a bloody liability, anyway. This is just an opportunity to get a look at SilverFox, or whatever his stupid name is, and identify a vehicle, as there's no way up here without a car.'

Max's face registered disapproval.

Ross's brow furrowed. 'Don't give me that bloody look, we've done all the risk assessments, and we have a plan A and a plan B. First and best is that he turns up as arranged, and is identifiable. Janie's arranged to meet Silver-bollocks at eleven by the funicular entrance. He's told her he'll be wearing a red baseball cap, and black jacket, as his picture is so generic. We'll have the place plotted up by then with backup teams, and cameras running. As soon as we think we have him in situ, Janie will send him a message saying that she's running a wee bit late, and all being well he will look at his phone at exactly the right time, and we'll have him on camera. If we're confident it's him, Janie can send another message a few minutes later, and suggest that he goes into the café to wait for her. We'll have people in the café, and we can cover it all well. Him reacting to her messages will be our confirmation that we have the right man.'

'And then what?' said Max.

'If he follows the script, Janie will wait half an hour and then send another message, saying her car has broken down, and postponing. Key is, we'll have him on film, and we'll move to phase two.'

Max sighed. 'I though the plan was for Janie to go undercover, and engage?'

'If we have to, we will. We have to be clear we have the right man, and if we can only do this by engaging, then that's what'll happen. We need to be flexible. She's wearing a covert body camera, but that's not ideal for a few reasons. One, I know Janie is a bit of a hard case with all the origami-shite you two weirdos dick about with, and she's packing her CS spray, but we don't want to expose her to unnecessary risk. Two, there's hardly enough of us to contain this if they go up the hill. Barney has his wee helicopter, but it's not ideal if Janie needs backup.'

'Are we missing an opportunity to go a little further?' said Max.

Ross shook his head again. 'All we want to do is get a good look at him, and get some snaps, and hopefully a vehicle. This will let Old Father Time here do his sneaky bastard trick of lumping up his motor with a GPS tracker, and maybe getting inside if we can, and bugging the bastard up. Chief authorised all tactics yesterday, so we're good to go. We get him and the car, we get a home address, and we're moving.' Ross folded his arms.

'Fair enough, I suppose. What are we going to use the guys for?' Max nodded at the Mountain Rescue Team.

Tom cleared his throat. 'I'll get my boys up towards the summit at various points, and on the MRT radios, plus Ed will be ready on the quad if he's needed as backup, like. We'll let SilverFox arrive and then once he's identified we can make ourselves obvious – last thing we want is Janie in danger.'

'Janie's also frit with heights, so stay close.' Ross sniggered.

'Thanks,' said Janie, shaking her head, her face a little paler than normal.

'Are we all ready, then?' said Ross.

'Camera tested and all good, Janie?'

'Aye, Barney has it fed to his iPad,' said Janie.

There were nods all around the table.

'Let's get the boys out, some up at the top, some down here, and dot around all the popular walking routes, okay?' said Ross.

There were more nods.

'Okay, let's do it.'

They all rejoined the rest of the group, and Ross stood in front, managing to catch every eye in the room. 'Right, guys, this is a funny one for you, I appreciate, but it's a vital job today. This here is Janie, and she's one of ours who we're trying to use as bait to lure a nasty bastard out, and you're our eyes and ears on the hill. So, get a good look at her, and anything dodgy-looking, get on the radio. We're all tuned in.' He pointed a stubby finger at Janie. 'You can't miss her, in her blue pac-a-mac.'

Janie's eyes flashed with irritation. 'Pac-a-mac? Ross, this is a Rab Gore-Tex. Top of the range, and cost me two hundred quid.'

'Well, don't bother expensing for it. It looks like the cagoule I had as a wean that folded in on itself into a pocket and had a wee stretchy belt. Does yours do that?' Ross's face was impassive, but his eyes glinted, mischievously.

Janie sighed. 'No, Ross, mine doesn't fold into a pocket. Now can we get on with this?'

'Aye, ready to move in five,' said Ross, standing up to show the meeting was over. Everyone stood, and began to drift away to collect kit, and prepare. Max beckoned Janie closer.

Max looked at Janie, her face a little paler than normal. 'You okay?'

'Aye, why shouldn't I be?'

'First deployment? I know Ross is being all casual, like, but this bastard hasn't read the script, mate.'

'Meaning?'

'The one thing to remember on any deployment is that the plan never survives contact with the enemy. You ready for that?' Max's face was deadly serious.

Janie rubbed her hand through her hair, nervously. 'Aye, I reckon so, but I'm shiting a brick, here.'

'You'll be grand. Just be flexible, and remember what they taught you.'

'I'm more nervous about the heights.'

'Don't be. The heights are fine. It's a bastard shoving you off that isn't. If you go up the hill with him, keep your wits about you, and don't get into any situation you can't control, okay?'

Janie's jaw firmed, and she nodded determinedly. 'I'll not let you down.'

22

JANIE WAS SITTING at the far edge of the car park on a wall with a VW Camper for cover giving her a clear view of the funicular entrance. She was close enough to see if Silverfox arrived, but not close enough to be spotted. There were a few more walkers about, heading down from the summit of Cairngorm, all happy and rosy-cheeked after the effort of climbing the steep Munro. She looked at her watch and saw that it had just turned eleven. She was still here, pretending to be Jane Henderson, a recently single woman seeking a climbing partner.

Her covert earpiece crackled in her ear. 'Eyes on people, we're now live, and waiting for SilverFox to join us on the plot, all units acknowledge,' said Ross.

Janie clicked the tone button on the transceiver that was in her trouser pocket twice, acknowledging the message. She listened as Max and Barney also replied, followed by the Highland lilt of Tom. 'That's all my people up the hill. I'll communicate with them direct on MRT handheld sets.'

Janie swallowed down the knot lodged in her throat. Even if the objective was simple – to draw SilverFox into the open where he could be observed and followed – this was not what she'd anticipated as her first assignment, but it was both exciting, and nerve-shredding.

She felt a buzz in her pocket. She pulled out her phone and saw that there was a direct message on the Facebook app. It was from MikeyFox.

Are you here? Couldn't see you in the car park.

Janie frowned, as she typed a reply. *I'm here, by entrance to funicular.*

Janie waited, seeing the dots pulsating as he typed his reply. *I got timings wrong. Sorry. I thought you'd stood me up, so I walked up the hill a ways. I'm at the mid-station on the terrace benches. Only a fifteen-minute walk straight up the track. Meet me up there? I've a flask and a picnic? View's amazing. We can head for the summit from here? Sorry, I'm an idiot* ☺

Janie's stomach tensed, reflexively. She reached for the transmitter button in her pocket and spoke, her lips barely moving. 'He's just messaged. He's saying he cocked up the timings and is at the mid-station picnic terrace. He wants me to go up.'

There was a pause before Ross spoke. 'I don't like this, Janie. Tom, how far up is the mid-station?'

'Not far. Fifteen minutes only; one of my guys is up there, I'll ask him what's happening,' said Tom, his voice calm and soothing.

'Received. What's this bastard up to?' said Ross, his voice tight.

Tom's voice crackled in Janie's ear again. 'Jack has eyes on the terrace from a distance. There are a few people there that he can see from his position two hundred metres away. I think it's probably safe; he's not gonna try anything with witnesses up there.'

'Any match for the description of our man?'

There was a pause.

'Jack says it's hard to say from his position, but it's such a vague description. There are a couple of males sat on their own. No red cap, though, and he can't see if any of them were using a phone.'

'Bastard's changed the plan. Janie, what do you think? Are you willing to walk up?'

Janie pressed the button. 'Yeah, I'm good. If there are others about, then it's safe if I have to engage with him. I'll reply saying I'm on my way up.'

Another pause. 'Okay, proceed, but if he's on his own when you get up there, walk on by. We'll get some others to close in on the mid-station. Take your time, and don't engage on your own unless there are others sat close by. Clear?'

Janie felt her synapses begin to fire with the excitement of her first engagement with a live target. No more role-plays with bolshy, experienced undercover officers, but a face-to-face with a real target. She almost leapt to her feet, pressing the transmitter as she did. 'All received. I'm on my way, heading up now.'

'Received. Now no buggering about getting brave. Remember the objective, Janie, we just need to be a hundred per cent clear that our man is there so we can get a face and a photograph. Barney, are you ready?'

Barney's voice sparked up on the net, as relaxed as ever. 'I got you, I'm launching the eye in the sky now, and I'll see you in't van.'

'Received, Barney. Make sure it's not audible,' said Ross, no longer the foul-mouthed, sarcastic buffoon, but a focused and capable operational leader.

'It won't be. Camera's that good on this one I can fly proper high.'

'All received. Janie is live and en route to mid-station; eyes on, people, and ready to intervene if required. We're live, radio silence unless urgent.'

Her phone buzzed again. Another message. *?*

Janie tapped out a reply. *On my way.*

The reply was almost instantaneous. *See you up here, you'll see me on a bench.*

Cool. See you soon x

Janie slid her sunglasses on her face and set off on the steep incline that headed up the Munro, feeling the comforting outline of her PAVA incapacitating spray in her pocket.

The game was on.

23

IT DIDN'T TAKE long before Mikey saw her. He watched the blue jacket stark against the deep green and granite grey of the landscape, making her easy to spot, as she picked her way along the tricky, rock-strewn path. She moved easily and with some grace, and he could tell that she was fit and active. A smile played across his lips as he watched her progress with ease. So many of the others had been lazy and unfit. He chuckled as he thought about the stupid, inferior hags who decided that just because their pathetic relationships had gone south, they could 'rediscover' themselves by playing around in the wild open spaces of the Scottish Munros.

They'd all regretted it, he thought with a snigger as he felt his excitement begin to bubble, working hard to not let a chuckle escape his mouth. He tucked tighter behind the conveniently placed rock, but the bitch seemed unaware and was just walking quickly and confidently towards her destination.

He briefly wondered if he should let her go a little farther before he struck, for the fun of the stalk as much as anything. He crouched down behind the rock as she strode past, all her attention paid to the sheer, unforgiving drop that sloped away at an alarming rate onto jagged and deadly rocks hundreds of feet below.

He moved, silently and skilfully, to keep up with her. He chuckled, knowing that he knew the terrain better than anyone. It would be at least another fifteen minutes before she arrived at her destination.

She'll be mine before she gets there, he thought.

24

JANIE STRODE EASILY and smoothly, almost without any discernible effort, as she ascended the hill towards the mid-station. Being fit was important to Janie. She and Max often trained together, either at the gym at Tulliallan, or occasionally at Max's home gym. She'd trained in multiple sports all her life, and she still practised jiu-jitsu and mixed martial arts as often as her duties allowed. Her physical abilities had got her out of trouble on more than one occasion during her police career, and it gave her confidence knowing that as a comparatively diminutive woman, she would often be underestimated. Janie liked to be underestimated; it gave her an edge, particularly in the patriarchal and occasionally misogynistic organisation that the police could be.

She picked up her pace as she rounded a bend in the track, which she imagined during the ski season would be a pure white, combed and primped piste, whereas now it was just a rocky and stony track with a steep, almost sheer drop to her right. She looked behind her and saw no one, and the curve of the path meant that she could see no one in front of her.

She was all alone. She firmed her jaw, gritted her teeth and powered up the harsh incline, heading towards the mid-station.

*

Ross and Barney were sitting next to each other in the back of the campervan, huddled around the iPad, which was attached to a small remote that Barney was using to control the drone buzzing high enough above them to be inaudible from the ground.

'Where is she, then?' said Ross.

'Hold up.' Barney zoomed out, focusing the lens on the funicular railway entrance, and then following the track up until he halted on a tiny figure dressed in a blue jacket.

'That's her shite cagoule. Zoom in.'

The footage was remarkably clear as the frame tightened in on Janie, who was striding confidently up the steep incline towards the mid-station building ahead.

'Bugger me, this is a good bit of kit, Barney. I'm always surprised that an old fart like you knows how to use this kind of tech. I'm way younger, and I can't even wire a bastarding plug.' Ross nodded in admiration.

'No one wires a plug anymore. All stuff comes with a plug attached.'

'Good job Mrs F always deals with crap like that anyway. Any sign of anyone else near Janie?'

Barney zoomed out. Janie was closing in fast on the building, which Ross estimated was another three to four hundred metres away from her location. 'No bugger anywhere near. Shall I go and look at who's on the terrace?' said Barney.

'Aye, go for it, but make sure you can't be heard.'

'I'm at three hundred metres, and in this wind no bugger will hear owt.' Barney flipped the controller and zoomed out, before refocusing on the large wooden terrace in front of a long, low chalet-style building that was just to the left of the top of a ski lift. He flicked on the controller again, and zoomed in.

There were three picnic tables with occupants: a young couple, with the contents of a picnic spread out in front of them; a woman sitting by herself looking at her phone, a large bottle of water in front of her; and a lone man who was just sitting, gazing out over the view.

'Zoom in on that chap,' said Ross, tapping at the iPad screen.

Gently and steadily, Barney adjusted the controls and zoomed in tight on the man's face. He was middle-aged, tanned, and was wearing a blue baseball cap that obscured the top half of his face. He was dressed in a long-sleeved top, and there was a rucksack on the table.

'Could that be him? I don't trust the bastard about his red cap. Come on, look up, you bastard,' muttered Ross, but the man's head remained down, as he seemed to be fiddling with his phone.

'Possible,' said Barney, looking up from the screen at Ross.

Ross blew his cheeks out. 'Has to be. How much more battery time do you have?'

'Not that much. I'll be able to stay on until Janie reaches him if she gets a wriggle on.'

'Hopefully Max is close.' Ross reached for his radio and raised it to his lips. 'Max, are you nearby?'

'Yep, just out of sight of the terrace, but I can move up once Janie's in position for close protection,' said Max, the sound of wind buffeting his message.

'We're gonna have to bug out in ten minutes because of battery on this stupid wee helicopter, so before we do, you move up and take a seat on the terrace. There are two tables free. You receive?'

There was a short pause before Max replied, 'Received.'

'Right, come on, Janie. We need you here, now. Where is she, Barney?'

'She's just out of sight, rounding the bend. Want me to get back to her?'

Ross felt his face flush, as it always did at times like this. 'No. That has to be him on that bench now; she's just on that track. Leave the drone where it is. Janie'll be fine.'

25

MIKEY SAW HER again, exactly where he knew she'd be, approaching the pinch point where the track tapered. His knowledge of the hill had meant he could anticipate exactly where she'd emerge, and he knew the alternative route. He had her exactly where he wanted her now, which unfortunately for her, was the narrowest point of the track.

He felt the familiar grip of excitement begin to bite as he crouched behind a large lump of granite, feeling, as he always did, more alive than at any other time in his life. That almost visceral surge of power.

Life and death, he thought. Women like her had never paid him even the slightest attention. Always the same curl of the lips, the scowl in the eyes as they looked at him and then dismissed him as unworthy. *They'd fucking learn*, he mused, as he gritted his teeth in preparation for the inevitable.

The scrunch of her boots became audible as she strode along the track towards his hiding place. He steadied himself, tensing his tight, wiry muscles, ready for the strike, like a predator watching and preparing to kill.

He pulled a phone from his pocket, activated the video camera and looped the strap around his wrist. The prey looked like a capable sort of woman, but he always erred on the side of caution, and the last thing he wanted was the phone disappearing over the edge of the almost sheer ridgeline.

He felt rather than saw her pass the rock and eased himself

into action, noiselessly emerging from behind his hiding place and onto the track immediately behind her blue-clad form. She had stopped, rooted to the spot, admiring the admittedly staggeringly beautiful view. She reached into her pocket, pulled out her phone and began to take photographs, oblivious to the world around her. Typical of people like her, he thought, all so quick to pull out the ever-present phones to record what they saw, never relying on their memories.

Silently, he moved into the final kill position. Maybe she sensed him, possibly a disturbance in the light, but she turned, her attractive face open-mouthed in shock, her eyes wide with confusion.

He did not hesitate. He rushed forward and shoved her as hard as he could towards the lip of the precipice.

She did not stand a chance. She flew forward, her boots catching on a shard of granite buried into the track, and she was catapulted over the edge, her arms cartwheeling as she tried to regain the balance that had deserted her with the explosive force delivered.

And then she was gone, tumbling, head over heels, before she hit a sharp and jagged rock with a sickening crack.

26

JANIE HEADED AROUND the sharp bend in the track and emerged, heart rate slightly elevated as she reached the mid-station.

'All good?' she murmured into her mic.

'Aye, all clear, and just the one lone male at the table on the deck. Move up,' said Ross.

Max's voice crackled in her ear. 'There's no one else close by, just the few on the terrace, clear to move up.'

Her belly tightening with nerves, Janie walked around to the long, low mid-station building, and ascended the wooden steps that led to the deck where there were three tables occupied. The couple looked up from their picnic, and there was the suggestion of smiles from them, but only fleetingly, before they continued their conversation. Janie pulled out her phone and tapped in a message to Facebook.

I'm here, where RU?

She stared at the screen, but the tick remained grey, with no suggestion that the message had been read. She looked over at the lone male, who was sitting at one of the tables staring at his phone and yawning, but he didn't raise his head.

Janie sat at one of the empty tables and typed again.

?

The lone man didn't flinch, he just continued typing on his phone. There were footsteps behind Janie, and the man looked up. His face lit up in recognition. Janie turned and saw an attractive woman appear and almost run over to the man, whereupon he leapt to his feet, and they embraced like star-crossed lovers.

Then there was an urgent voice in her ear. It was Tom, the Mountain Rescue coordinator. 'All units, urgent message, reports of a female walker fallen on Coire an t-Sneachda, a mile away from the ski centre. All MRT teams are meeting at ski centre for deployments, and the search-and-rescue helicopter is on its way from Inverness right now.'

Janie pulled out her phone and dialled.

'Janie?' said Ross.

'What the hell's going on? He's definitely not up here, and he's not answering messages.'

'I don't know, but there's been an MRT shout on the other side of the hill, a few miles away at the Coire. A lone female walker has fallen, and is seriously injured, and Mikey-bollocks isn't fucking here. He was never here, Janie, the bastard knew we were coming. One of the MRT is coming to grab you in their Land Rover, and will also pick up Max. I want you both to the scene as soon as possible before any other cops get there. If there's shit there to find, I want us to find it first.'

Janie scrubbed at her short hair with her spare hand. 'You know what this means, don't you?' she said, her voice tight and low, aware of the nearby people.

'Aye, you're damn right I do. There's a leak. Someone leaked what we were doing and yet Mikey whatever his name is still came. This evil bastard is playing games. Worse than that, he's fucking taunting us.'

27

MAX AND JANIE arrived at the nearby Coire an t-Sneachda having cadged a lift in the MRT Land Rover as far as they could, and then jogging the rest of the way. The pounding note of a helicopter engine became louder as they rounded the final bend in the track, before they stopped dead, breathing heavily, astounded at the sight that met them.

The Coire was a massive glacial corrie, which stretched around them in a huge arc, almost like a cauldron, sloping away almost vertically five hundred feet, and a mile across. It was staggeringly beautiful, with the grey granite stark against the ice-blue sky, but it wasn't the sight of the corrie that astonished Max and Janie.

A hulking red-and-white AgustaWestland AW189 helicopter was above them, the deafening engine noise and violent downwash from the rotors kicking up grit, dust and the thin peaty soil. An orange flight-suited winchman was being raised up to the hovering behemoth, a stretcher attached with the casualty strapped tightly in. Max shielded his eyes and watched as the stretcher was expertly manoeuvred into the side door of the helicopter. The door slid shut after a wave from the winchman, and the helicopter note changed, as it turned and moved off at speed, engines roaring.

Within a minute, a deep, cloying silence had replaced the ear-splitting engine noise, and Max and Janie jogged across to the two red-jacketed MRT members who were staring at the departing helicopter, hands limp by their sides, a rope at their feet that disappeared over the edge of the Coire. Max looked over the steep edge and saw what appeared to be litter but was clearly the detritus of the casualty being treated by the winch paramedic. There were bandage wrappers and bloodstained pads all clustered around a bulbous, jagged piece of granite. Another man that Max didn't recognise was standing with the team members. He was bearded, wearing large mirrored sunglasses, dressed in a grey windproof and a peaked cap pulled low. He was deathly pale and trembling.

The nearest MRT man turned to look at Max, his face white. 'That was horrible.'

'I bet, what's your name, pal?'

'Chas,' he said, his voice a little wobbly.

'Dead?' said Max.

Chas shook his head just slightly. 'Paramedic on the helicopter came down, but it was a bugger getting him to her safely. We rigged up the lines, and we abseiled down and he managed to stabilise her enough to get her out, although he was banging on about her terrible blood pressure, a really horrible head wound, as well as broken bones. It was hard getting her on the stretcher.' He shook his head and blew out his alabaster-pale cheeks.

Max clapped him on the shoulder. 'Good work, Chas. Who called it in?'

'This gentleman did.' He pointed at a grey-jacketed walker. 'Max, this is Rory Jones, a walker up from Inverness. Rory, this is Max, and he's a police officer. Can you tell him what you found?'

Rory nodded briskly, his hamster-like cheeks wobbling a touch. 'I've just done the Cairngorm route, so was on the return via the Coire, and I saw her as I rounded the bend, and she was just down there, still as a statue like, so I called 999,' he said in a soft Scottish accent that had a trace of something else in it.

'Did you go down to her?' said Max.

He shook his head. 'Not without ropes, I just called you guys. Too steep for me.'

'Did you see anyone else?' said Janie.

He shook his head. 'There was a guy who walked past me, heading up the hill towards Cairngorm about ten minutes before I saw her, but other than that the hill is so quiet. I just hope she pulls through.'

'Can you describe him?' said Max, his antennae beginning to quiver.

Rory furrowed his brow. 'I didn't take that much notice, but he was maybe a bit younger than me, stocky, and he was all in black, I think. Oh, and he had walking poles. He looked like a proper climber, I'd say.'

'Did he say anything?' said Max.

'No, just nodded, head down. Like I say, I didn't take much notice.'

'And you say he was heading up the hill?'

Rory nodded. 'I suspect taking the reverse route up to the summit, nowhere else for him to go.'

'Did you see anyone else?'

'There was a young couple in matching neon jackets who were about three hundred metres ahead of me. They just headed on down the path towards the ski centre so they can't have noticed her, although she must have been there. I wouldn't have seen her, but I'd stopped for some water, and put my pack down on the path, so when I leant over to go into it, I saw her. They'd disappeared around the bend by then.' He shook his head and wiped his eyes, which were damp with tears.

Max reached across and put a hand on the man's shoulder, seeing his own reflection in the sunglasses. 'You've done great, Rory. If you hadn't called it in, she'd have definitely died. She has a chance, now. Does anyone have any idea who she is?' Max asked, looking at Chas and his colleague. They both shook their heads.

'She was never conscious, and I didn't look for any ID. Should I have?' said Rory.

'No, not at all. Can you describe her?'

'From what I could see from up here, she looked quite slim, blonde hair, average sized. She was wearing a blue jacket, black trousers.'

Max and Janie exchanged a glance, eyes widening.

'Blonde?' said Max, turning to Rory.

'Aye.' Rory narrowed his eyes.

'You should be proud, pal. She now has a chance,' Max looked at Janie. 'We need to search between the edge and where she was found. I take it that's not your cup of tea?'

Janie's normally pale face lost a little more colour. 'I can't say it's a dream. How about I take Rory back to the car and get a witness statement?' she said, hopefully.

'Good idea, I'll search the scene.'

'Fine. Rory, is your car at the ski centre car park?' said Janie, turning to look at the walker. He just nodded.

'Great, then Janie will go with you back there, and get a witness statement from you. Is that okay?' said Max.

'Sure, I'll do whatever you need. I hope she'll be okay. The hills are so dangerous, even in this beautiful weather.'

'I hope so too. Thanks for everything.' Max nodded.

'Let's go, Rory,' said Janie, touching the walker's arm gently. They set off down the path back towards the ski centre.

Max got his phone out of his pocket and dialled as he watched Janie and Rory navigating the rocky track, Janie almost having to jog to keep up with Rory's long, loping strides, indicative of an experienced mountaineer. He smiled to himself, thinking that the city girl that Janie was would not be enjoying this one bit.

'What's happening?' said Ross, without preamble.

'She's off to hospital now on the search-and-rescue helicopter; Janie's bringing the bloke who found her back for a statement.'

'Okay, I'm with Barney. You need anything from him?'

'Yeah, I want a full drone search of the side of the hill where we are, and where she ended up, and beyond. With that snazzy

4k camera on it, he may spot something I can't as it's a bastard steep hill. I also want him to look for a lone walker heading up to the summit. All in black with walking poles, he passed the witness on the path, and I don't like the sound of him. If he's up there we need to get hold of him, even if it's just as a witness. The hill is quiet, so he shouldn't be hard to spot.'

'He's just changing the battery and then he'll get it up. How long ago did he pass him?' said Ross.

'Well, it'd be shortly before the nine-nine-nine call, and it's a good few hours to the summit, so he should be able to find him if he goes high.'

'He's on it; anything else from us?'

'I think that we need a cop we can trust at the hospital. She's not dead, and if our man shoved her, we can't be sure that he won't want to go and finish the job,' Max said.

'Fine, I'll make a call. Barney says if you send him a pin drop, he'll send the drone over, and control it from here. He'll patch you into the footage, as he's too bloody lazy to walk there. Typical, using his peg-leg to get out of doing any fucking work.' Ross's voice was typically sardonic, but Max could detect the unease. This was as serious as it got.

The murderer, whoever he was, knew that he was being led into a baited trap, but he was confident enough not to stay away. He wanted more.

He even went ahead with the sham, safe in the knowledge that Janie was bait, and then he taunted them by engaging with her by text. He was playing with them, and they had fallen for it. The classic narcissist's playbook. He clearly felt omnipotent. He wanted to show the police that whatever they did, he was one step ahead.

And whoever he was, he knew exactly where the cops were, and what they were doing.

He clearly thought that he was the puppet master.

He was laughing at them.

28

MAX WATCHED THE pin-sharp footage on his phone screen, shielding it from the sun with his hand. The drone hovered thirty metres over the almost sheer drop on the edge of the corrie, sweeping slowly from left to right as it traversed the area in front of them. It zoomed in tight on the detritus from the first aid that had been delivered to the casualty, stark and vivid against the granite, before zooming out again.

'Is the footage clear?' said Barney over the radio.

'Clear as a bell – I'm surprised we have such a good signal.'

'Enough height, and proximity to the ski centre has it sorted. We're lucky.'

As the drone shifted position, something glinted thirty metres below where Max stood. 'Barney, stop there, did you see that?' said Max into his radio.

The drone stopped stock still, the camera zooming in tight on a spot. 'Summat glinted a way down the rock face below you. Aye, I got it. Hold up.' The image zoomed in further until it stopped, the 4k image clear and steady.

A mobile phone, fundamentally intact despite the cracked screen, a foreign object against the dusty rocks and rubble just behind a small patch of scrubby-looking grass.

'Got it? I reckon thirty metres down from where she was. Think you can reach it?' said Barney.

Max looked at Jack, who pointed at the ropes at their feet,

secured around a boulder, the other end of the rope snaking down over the edge of the corrie.

'Yeah, I can get it. You have enough battery to check for the walker?'

'Yeah, I've about half an hour left. All in black, cap and walking poles, right?'

'Yeah, that's it,' said Max.

'I'll go high and scan, and I can active track anything I spot. The zoom on this baby is beltin'.' The drone's motor suddenly increased in pitch, and it shot upwards, almost immediately disappearing.

'Think we can get me safely down the face – about thirty metres – to that patch of grass?' said Max, looking across at Chas.

'Be safer if we get someone up here with a harness and a belay,' said Chas.

Max's face was firm. 'We don't have time for that, we need to get that phone urgently. There could be some decent evidence on it. Can we do it?'

'Aye, no bother. We'll just secure you in with a bowline around the waist and we can just ease you down there. It's steep, but it's not sheer. I can do it, if you prefer? You've not climbed for a while,' said Chas, raising his eyebrows.

'No, I'm good, ideally better if a cop retrieves it to save you having to do statements. I did a fair bit of climbing as a youngster,' said Max, with a grin. To demonstrate this, Max picked up the end of the 10mm rope, and quickly and efficiently looped it around his waist and secured it with a snug knot.

'You know how to tie a bowline, so I feel a bit more relaxed,' said Chas.

'Never forget, do you?'

The earpiece crackled in Max's ear. 'I've swept over the route from height. No trace of any lone male walker in black. I'm pulling the drone back in, battery's getting low,' said Barney.

'Yeah, that's received, Barney,' said Max, his finger on the earpiece.

'By the way, you've got some numpty of an inspector on his way to see you. Got a bit mardy wi' Ross, he did. He may have the hump, but Ross is putting a call in now to smooth the waters.'

'Wasn't Inspector Campbell, was it?' said Max.

'No clue, but he was a bit of wazzock, and I reckon he'll be grassing on Ross for his choice language.' Barney chuckled, the voice distorted in Max's ear.

'Do you have kit to download it with you?' said Max.

'All in me van, bring it down when you're ready.'

Max hung up, shaking his head with wry amusement at Ross's typical dealings with authority. It could be amusing, but it could also be counter-productive, and now he was going to have to deal with the fallout once whoever the inspector was arrived. He cleared his thoughts, ready for the task at hand.

'Anyway, are we ready, Chas?'

Chas nodded and picked up the coil of rope. He nodded to his colleague who took up position just behind him, both firmly gripping the rope.

'Nice and easy now,' said Max, leaning back and easing himself over the lip of the corrie.

It was pretty straightforward, using the tension on the rope, being steadily lowered by Jack and his colleague, and it only took a couple of minutes before Max arrived at the spot that Barney's drone had picked out on the almost sheer cliff. Max traversed across to the patch of scrappy grass, and there it was, the sunlight reflecting off the cracked glass of the otherwise undamaged smartphone. He pulled a pair of nitrile gloves from his pocket, and letting all his weight be taken by the rope, he quickly snapped them into place and steadied himself on the rope, once more. He took a deep breath, leant down, and picked up the phone.

Reaching into his pocket, he pulled out a small evidence bag, slipped the handset in and tucked it in his pocket. He pulled three times on the rope. 'Coming up,' he shouted, his voice bouncing all around the sides of the corrie.

He felt an immediate pull on the rope, and began to walk straight back up the cliff, almost dancing in between the rocks and boulders, and within a few minutes he was at the top, his shoulders burning with the effort.

'All good?' said Jack, as Max appeared over the edge of the corrie.

'Aye, all good,' he said, puffing with the effort, cuffing away a bead of sweat from his brow.

'Should we be sealing this place off?' said Jack.

Max shook his head. 'No need, it'd take someone very determined to interfere with the scene, and I have what we needed. I need to get this to Barney,' he said, untying the rope from around his waist and letting it drop to the ground.

'Looks like we have company,' said Jack, nodding over Max's shoulder.

Max turned to see a couple of uniformed police officers striding towards them, and he groaned inwardly at the sight of 'Cordon Gordon' marching over to them, with PC Danny McSorley in tow a few steps behind, a holdall on his shoulder and a pre-formatted scene log in his hand. Gordon's demeanour was one of bristling resentment.

'Now this seems to be becoming a habit, DS Craigie. What the bloody hell is happening here, and why do I have to hear about a serious accident on my patch from the Coastguard?' he said, almost stamping to a halt immediately in front of Max.

'Good morning, sir. Did you encounter my DI in the car park?' said Max.

'If we mean the incredibly rude and scruffy man in a campervan, then yes. Is he actually an inspector?'

'He is,' said Max, trying to keep a smile from breaking out on his face.

'Well, I was none too impressed. As duty inspector for this region, I bear the responsibility for major crime, and/or accident scenes, and it would do him well to remember that.'

'Did you tell him that?' said Max.

'Yes, and he told me to, and I quote, "Get tae fuck".' He paused, his moustache bristling as he pursed his lips.

PC McSorley said, his voice uncertain, 'I think he actually said, "Get tae fuck, ya wankspangle", sir.'

'Not helping, Danny,' said Inspector Campbell.

Max had to bite the insides of his cheeks to stop the grin appearing.

'It's not funny, sergeant.'

'Apologies, sir. Look, we happened to be here on another covert matter, working with the MRT when the shout came in, so we responded. My colleague DC Calder is recording a witness statement from the walker who found the casualty, and I'll make sure that you get sight of that. Has an SIO been appointed?'

'DCI O'Neill is aware, and monitoring from Inverness. Again, he'll be waiting for my scene report. Can you brief me on what you know?' he said, contrition replacing the earlier indignation.

Max summarised what the witness had said earlier.

'I see . . . so no actual information on how she came to be down there?'

'Unfortunately not.'

'Any name?'

'Not yet.'

'Any reports on her condition?'

'Looks very bad. Seemingly a significant head injury, and some fairly obvious fractures to her limbs. Unconscious.'

'I've despatched an officer to go to Raigmore now. He's going to recover her clothing for forensic examination. Any other information? How about the walker I heard about on the radio, the one all in black that the witness mentioned?' The inspector removed his hat and wiped his damp brow with a handkerchief. He sighed, and massaged his temple. 'How the hell am I going to secure this scene and search it? It's almost vertical.' He removed his cap again, and scratched at his greying hair.

'If it helps, we used a drone to scan the scene. I have the injured woman's phone here,' said Max, holding up the smartphone with a gloved hand.

Inspector Campbell raised his eyebrows. 'How did you manage that?'

'Chas here lowered me down. We need to check what's on that phone, sir. It's the only lead we have. For one, it may give us her identity.'

'I agree, but it's my responsibility. PC McSorley has some evidence bags; give it to him and I'll arrange forensic examination.' He held out his hand.

'With respect, sir. That's a bad idea. I have an expert right here who can examine it immediately, as in within thirty minutes. If there are any leads, we need to strike fast. If she was pushed, it's possible that the victim and the killer arranged to meet up there, and there could be a trace of that plan on this phone.' Max held the handset aloft.

'That's as may be, sergeant, but this is my responsibility and the phone needs to be downloaded in accordance with established protocols, and with the rules on criminal productions.' The inspector raised his sweaty hand to his glasses and pushed them back up his nose.

There was a long pause as Max and Inspector Campbell stared at each other.

The impasse was only broken when the inspector's phone rang. He kept his gaze on Max as he answered. 'Inspector Campbell,' he said. 'Ah, DCI O'Neill, I'm on-scene now.' He turned and walked away, his voice lowering.

Max looked at PC McSorley, who responded with a huge grin, clearly enjoying this a great deal.

Inspector Campbell returned, his face red and flushed, and once again he removed his cap and pocketed his phone. A rueful smile crossed his face. 'DCI O'Neill's compliments, DS Craigie. We would be very grateful for any assistance you can offer us.'

29

Chat – FTF

Tor Browser

Wyatt-Lawman: I'm hearing all sorts of chatter. Was it Mikey or Doss?

Bagger: Mikey, he won't let Doss do another one, as he thinks the filming on A' Chralaig was crap. This one's in the Cairngorms, but she's not dead. Helicopter to Raigmore, although I'm hearing that she's unlikely to survive. I think we're okay, but he's getting too reckless. They put an undercover cop up on the hill, who had been speaking to him on Facebook. I tipped him the wink that he was being set up, but rather than lying low and not turning up he shoved someone else off the Coire. He's a mad bastard. The cop they used as bait wasn't even a blonde, and you know how he feels about blondes. He's taunting them, and it's gonna go wrong.

Wyatt-Lawman: Shit, this is way too much, and he's out of fucking control. He's let his hatred of women overtake common sense. This soon after he pulled that woman from Huntly's Cave is just reckless in the extreme. Do they have any leads?

Bagger: No, they can't have, but this is too close. We've survived this long, and now he decides that he's untouchable.

Wyatt-Lawman: What's making him go crazy like this?

Bagger: The psycho was fine until he lost his job. He was happy just to share our 'questionable' material, but since he was sacked, he's gone nuts. He's blaming blonde women for all his troubles. Mind you, the videos are making us a fortune.

Wyatt-Lawman: That's true. Have you warned Doss not to do anything stupid? He's fucking in awe of Mikey, and he may decide to go rogue.

Bagger: I'll make sure he knows.

Wyatt-Lawman: If he keeps on at this pace, we'll all go down, and that cannot happen. Talk to Mikey, and talk to Doss.

Bagger: I will.

30

MAX AND BARNEY were sitting in the campervan as the kettle began to sing on the gas hob. Max looked out of the window and watched with interest at the body language on display: Ross was apparently having a 'heart-to-heart' with Cordon Gordon. Ross seemed mildly amused at the brick-red face of the hapless inspector, who was jabbing a finger in his direction, his expression contorted in anger or frustration, whereas Ross wore a seraphic smile.

'Happen Ross is enjoyin' his self.' Barney chuckled as he plugged the iPhone into the familiar worn and chipped metal box on the Formica-topped table next to his laptop. A few taps on his computer, and he slotted an SD card into the box. He sighed and folded his arms as he looked at the whirring icon that indicated that the phone was downloading.

'I know, he looks particularly smug. Cordon Gordon is working himself up into a real lather. It's unusual to see, as Ross would normally just throw a load of four-letter words at him and storm off. That's what power does to a man. Tea?' said Max, as took the kettle off the hob.

'Teabags in't tin.' Barney nodded at a scratched Yorkshire Tea caddy.

'I've no idea how he made his current rank,' said Max, grinning to himself as he dropped two bags into two stained mugs, and poured on boiling water.

'I reckon he had summat on someone. It could only be chuffin'

blackmail. A man that swears that amount must be a reet old—'
Barney stopped mid-sentence and stared open-mouthed at his
computer. There was total silence in the van, only disturbed by
the sounds of a mug being stirred.

'Reet old what?' said Max.

'Barney, what's going on?' said Max.

Slowly, Barney raised his head and looked at Max, his eyes
wide. He swivelled the laptop around. The screen was filled with
a shot of blue sky, only punctuated by a few clouds.

'What am I looking at?' said Max, handing the tea to Barney.

Wordlessly, Barney snaked his hand around the side of the
laptop and tapped on the trackpad. The image jerked, and the
video restarted. It was a clip of the view from the top of the corrie
where Max had been just a short while ago. The video panned
around as if the owner of the phone had been using the handset
to admire the view.

'Just how beautiful is this, Mum? Looks like you can see
everything in the world from up here,' crackled a voice in the
background, distorted by the soft wind.

'Barney . . .' began Max, but his mouth snapped shut as the
image violently jerked upwards, and spun at what seemed at
lightning pace before a dark figure filled the screen, just for a
flash. The footage then went crazy, as the victim tumbled down
the side of the hill, and Max could almost imagine the frail body
smashing into the unyielding granite.

'Replay it and get ready to pause.' Max didn't take his eyes
off the screen, as Barney swivelled the laptop back around and
tapped at the keys. He turned the screen to face Max again, the
footage halted.

The screen was three-quarters filled with a face, the lips pulled
back in a snarl that showed stained and uneven teeth. Max took
in the cap, the grey windproof, and lined face and fat cheeks,
and he felt that familiar sensation grip his stomach. In the large

mirrored sunglasses was the reflection of the terrified woman, her mouth open in a scream. A mix of excitement, fear, anxiety and something else held Max like a vice.

Anger.

Anger at himself for missing what the image on the screen was now proving. Anger at himself for missing what had been right in front of him on the edge of that corrie.

The man staring at him from the screen was Rory Jones.

31

Tor Browser

Bagger: Have you heard?

Doss: Aye, on the Coire?

Bagger: Yes. Keep your eyes and ears open. Mikey has lost the plot, this is way too close.

Doss: Mikey is the man. He's untouchable.

Bagger: It's that attitude which is going to get us caught. Do nothing, no more until we know where this goes. Mikey is playing with fire.

Doss: Mikey is too clever to get caught, and he's teaching me well.

Bagger: He's good but he's being reckless. Your worship of him is blinding you. No more until we authorise it, understand? We've been so careful, let's not fuck it up now.

Doss: Fine

32

'**WHERE IS THE** bastard now?' said Ross, his expression not changing. Max delivered the news as they stood outside Barney's van, Inspector Campbell eyeing them, lips pursed, and stroking his moustache.

'He left about an hour ago straight after I'd taken his statement,' said Janie.

'Did you get a car for him?' said Max.

'Yeah, he was in a dark Golf. I made a note of the registration plate here.' Janie dug into her pocket and pulled out her notebook, flicking through the pages. 'I'll call Norma and get her working on it. I also have his phone number, so I'll do the same with that.' Janie stepped to the side and dialled.

'Shit, we had the fucker. We had him in our grasp,' said Max.

'Hold up, didn't he dial 999?'

'That's what I was told. Janie, get Norma on that as well. Okay, this is way more important than the historic cases. All efforts now into finding Rory Jones?' Max said to Janie, who nodded, the phone pressed to her ear.

'Why would he do that?' said Ross.

'He mentioned a couple of walkers in high-vis jackets. Maybe he was worried he'd been seen down the hill so thought that calling it in was the safest option.'

'Seems reckless to me, the necky bastard. Janie, anything?' Ross looked at Janie.

'The car is registered to a woman in Glasgow, no markers, no trace, no intel. Almost certainly cloned. Intel on the registered keeper throws up nothing. I bet the bastard had false plates on,' said Janie.

'You sure you wrote the plate down, right?' said Ross.

'Hundred per cent. Norma has confirmed that the number he gave to me is the same that called nine-nine-nine; she's running all the checks on it right now and is assuming she has authority to expedite?' Janie looked at Ross.

'Yes, soon as possible, and get Miss Moneypenny on the case for authorising cell site and data requests. I want to find him pronto.'

'Automatic number plate recognition?' said Max.

'Aye, ANPR as well, even if it is a shite plate, we'll still get activations,' said Ross to Janie, who nodded and moved away as she spoke to Norma.

'Options?' said Max.

'As I see it, we have two choices. We go noisy, announce it on all the radio channels, and let it be known we want him nicked on sight—' Ross paused.

'Or?' said Max.

'Well, we know he's the pusher, but he doesn't know we know. He almost certainly won't know that we have him on film shoving that poor wee lass. Can we keep this quiet?'

'I think we can. There's no suggestion he's an immediate threat, and we have some leads. We scour the data, work the phone, work the ANPR, and we find him without this going on general release. He may feel totally safe, right now. Let's keep it that way.'

'Aye, there's also hardly any bloody cops up here, so if he keeps his head down, we'll never spot the bastard. Shit, shit, fucking shit,' Ross blasted, his face redder than normal.

Janie rejoined them, scribbling in her notebook. 'All data requests are going in, and Norma is arranging for a uniform unit to visit the registered keeper's address. If the car's on the drive, then that will prove we're dealing with a cloner.'

'Nice thinking, but the bastard has an hour on us. How far could he have got?'

'If he wants to head south, he's twenty minutes from the A9, but with all the average speed cameras on that road, he'd be unwise. Simple fact is that he could be anywhere. We need something else.' Max nodded as Chas entered the café and walked over.

'Max, can I have a word?' he said, nervously, his lips twitching a little.

'Of course.'

'Something has just occurred to me. I saw the man who found the poor lassie in the café upstairs earlier on, before we all got started. When we went to the shout on the Coire, I thought he was familiar, but then I realised something. He said that he'd done the Cairngorm route, so up to the top of the hill, and then down through the Coire an t-Sneachda.' His pronunciation of the corrie was flawless.

'And?'

'Well, I'm pretty fit, and I know the routes like the back of my hand, like, but no way could I do it that fast, so I don't buy that he could have done that route in that timeframe. No chance.'

'Have you told anyone else about this?' said Max.

A shadow passed across Chas's face, and he looked a little pensive. 'Well, I told Ed, and he told me to come and tell you. It looks suspicious, is all I'm saying. Why would he lie like that?' Chas shook his head.

Max looked at the MRT man, acutely aware of the need to keep this tight. 'Okay, thanks, Chas. We'll look into it, but keep it all to yourself, maybe; it's all a bit sensitive?'

'Of course, but they have CCTV in the café, so you may get some footage of him.'

'Good call, we'll get on that now. Thanks, mate.'

'He was in the queue in front of me, and he bought a coffee and a cake. He then just sat down, and seemed to be looking at his phone. I also thought it a bit odd that he kept his sunglasses on inside.'

'Nice one, Chas,' Max said.

Chas nodded. 'Are we free to go?'

'We'll need a statement from you at some point, but it can wait. We'll speak later, yeah?'

Chas nodded and left.

'Right, let's get going, people. Pull in whatever favours you need to get this data in urgently. Let's all make ourselves useful, and regroup in thirty minutes, okay?' Ross looked at them each in turn, his jaw firm and eyes hard.

'What are you gonna do?' said Max.

'I'm calling the Chief. If we're staying quiet about a killer on the loose, I'd better get some top cover.'

33

MIKEY – OR RORY Jones (depending on who was asking) – pulled over at the side of the road into a deserted layby on the A86 that ran alongside Loch Laggan, the main route from the Cairngorms through to Fort William.

Checking both directions, he saw that the coast was totally clear. He went to the front of the car and pulled out a slim screwdriver to lever off the number plate, which had been affixed earlier that day with sticky pads. He repeated the action on the rear, before he opened the boot and pulled out the car's original plates. Within a few moments, both plates were affixed to the front and back of the car. Checking that the coast was still clear, he carried the other plates to the lochside, and tossed them as far as he could, watching them splash into the almost black water. He chuckled to himself as he got back into the car, and slammed the door shut. He pulled out his phone and replayed the footage that he'd recorded just a couple of hours ago. He felt the familiar stirring of nerves as he watched, hoping to God that it was satisfactory. The others didn't expect Hollywood standard, but they needed good images. Particularly of the faces of the unfortunates.

It had been a close call, but he wasn't sure at all that the couple in the dayglo jackets hadn't seen him. If they'd phoned the cops, and someone came, it would be hard to explain why he hadn't if they'd caught up with him, so he'd called it in. It was a risk, and he was glad of the disguise, but he hadn't been able to resist taunting the stupid fucking cops like that. While they were looking for him on the top of Cairngorm, he was doing his thing on the Coire. He almost guffawed at the headless-chicken approach of the cops and the MRT idiots, although he was a little surprised that the woman wasn't dead. He was sure that the crack he'd heard when she hit the rock with her stupid blonde head would have been sufficient. However, it seemed that paramedic winchman had managed to keep her alive, somehow. Inconvenient, but not catastrophic.

He needn't have worried about the video clip. It was a good one. He stared, transfixed, and slowed the footage down, taking in every frame as the blonde bitch turned, her face riddled with shock and terror as she fell, a tangle of splintering limbs as she collided with the unforgiving granite.

His mouth gaped open as he watched, her jerky and hesitant descent down the corrie, before he reached her. It had been a big risk to scale the cliff for the close-up shots, but for someone like him, with his climbing skills, it had been worth it. The images were startling, and would be way more lucrative. Her blonde hair darkening with the flowing scarlet blood, her face like bread dough and her terror-filled eyes looking at him with a mixture of despair and hopelessness. He paused the footage, and drank in the image. They were going to go crazy for this one, and he knew then that it had been worth the risk. The cops were far too stupid to catch him, and he cackled out loud at how easily he had played them.

It was beautiful.

He quickly accessed the dark web using the Tor browser that was hidden in the dark recesses of his phone, and uploaded the footage. He knew that he wasn't supposed to do this, and the others would go mental if they found out, but this was too good not to share.

It only took a couple of minutes, and there it was, all ready and available to view to the select few. It didn't take long before the reactions began.

Destroyer_666: beautiful, did you see the look on the bitch's face?

BitchesDie_hard: Maaate. That's a doozy.

Waffen_Sturm: Der Kopf der blonden Hure platzte wie eine Wassermelone.

A message pinged up from the secure chat. It was from Doss. *That was stunning, mate. You're a genius, but Bagger is panicking.*

Mikey tapped out a reply. *Ignore him, he's a pussy.*

He was reaching for the ignition when his Motorola buzzed again. Another message on the app. He closed the Tor browser and opened the message. He sniggered when he saw that almost inevitably it was Bagger.

Bagger: What have you done?

He smiled and typed. *This is a good one, you're gonna love it, man.*

Bagger: She's not dead. You idiot. She's gone to Raigmore, but she's not dead. I hope you didn't leave any trace?

Mikey smiled again; Bagger was such a flapper. *Of course I didn't*

Bagger: Have you ditched your SIM for the phone you made the call with?

'Of course, I have. I'm not stupid,' he muttered out loud as his fingers tapped at his phone.

Bagger: Where are you?

He typed out a response. *Going home.*

Bagger: You can't go home. You have to sort this situation. What if she wakes up. And there were cops up there, you knew that, right?

Mikey cackled. *Of course I knew. You told me. Stupid undercover cops who know nothing and they'll never trace me. The one I met was an idiot. She took my witness statement like a dumb plod.*

Bagger: What if she recognises you?

I doubt I'll ever see her again, but even if she did, she would never recognise me. No one ever does.

Bagger: Get it sorted. Get it sorted now.

Mikey looked at his phone and was surprised to feel a touch of nerves nipping at him. He wasn't scared of the cops; they'd never get close to him. Wrong number plate, wrong phone number, and he never stayed long in any one place. It was how he had stayed ahead of the police for so long. He flipped down the sun visor and blinked in the bright sunshine, his lined and tanned face, hidden by the mirrored sunglasses, which he now removed, stared back at him through the mirror. He tugged at his beard, which was long and scratchy. He sighed at his chubby hamster cheeks, before opening his mouth and reaching inside, pulling out two wads of densely packed cotton wool. His features morphed into the lean and lined face he was used to seeing in the mirror. It had been uncomfortable, but worth it. Now anyone describing him would only remember the beard, chubby cheeks and sunglasses. People only noticed the obvious and were often oblivious to the subtleties.

He reached into the glove box, pulled out a beard trimmer and stepped out of the car, checking both ways again, before wandering down to the lochside. He switched on the trimmer and it began to buzz like a demented wasp. He squatted down on his haunches by the loch, and ran the clippers over his lush beard and within a few minutes it was gone, leaving just a tight stubble behind. He scooped the hair up from the dusty and rocky ground and tossed it into the loch, where it dissipated.

Returning to the car, he rubbed at his itchy face and pulled his cap off his head, scrubbing at his thin, greying hair. He needed to go back to his lodgings, shower and get rid of his clothing. It was also probably time for a change of car. Not difficult, all fairly routine, and easy to do. He'd done it many times before.

Once that was all done, he'd take care of the Raigmore situation, if still necessary.

He smiled as he got back into the car, tuning the radio to Smooth FM, and began singing along to the ballad that was being played, as he headed off, the window open, and the fragrant Highland air wafting in through the window.

He chuckled, thinking about what fools he'd made the police look. Mikey hated cops, he hated them all, and taunting them was almost as much fun as it had been pushing the woman off the hill.

Almost.

But not quite.

A good day's work.

34

MAX AND JANIE were looking at the flickering screen in the upper-level café in the main ski centre. It was reasonable quality, and it didn't take too long before they had found their man. He was easy to spot with the mirrored sunglasses obscuring half his face, but the peak of his cap seemed to almost constantly be in the way of them getting a decent look.

'He'd be hard to pick out in a line-up, bloody shades make him look like a wee beastie,' said Janie, as she watched the man approach the counter and speak to the server, who was currently standing next to them. She was a young woman with dark hair piled on the top of her head, and a large smile across her glowing face. Her name badge announced that she was called Marian.

The café was quiet, with just a couple of people sitting at tables drinking coffees and eating sandwiches. A young mother was seated feeding a hefty baby with a bottle. Max's eyes were drawn to them, and his thoughts immediately turned to his wife and unborn child over a hundred miles away. He scratched at his shaved scalp, before Marian's voice dragged him back to the task at hand.

'I did think he was a bit odd, like. Sunnies inside and all that, but he was polite enough. He bought a latte and a cake,' said Marian, in a local accent.

'Any chance his cup hasn't been washed up, yet?' said Janie.

Marian shook her head. 'Dishwasher's been on several times since then, sorry.'

They continued to watch the security footage of him accepting his coffee with a smile and then paying with a card of some type. He then turned and went to sit over by the large picture window that framed the staggeringly beautiful view across the landscape.

'Can we get anything on the card if we can isolate the transaction on the till?' asked Max.

'I think so. I can see the exact time, and the cost would have been six pounds twenty for the coffee and a cake. Coffee and walnut, I think it was.' Marian smiled as she squinted at the screen.

'That'd be really helpful,' said Max.

'Tell you what, I'll make you some coffee, and I'll try and work it out. Take a seat while I do it, it may take me a few minutes,' she said, nodding at a nearby table.

Marian was true to her word, and it only took a few minutes before she was depositing two coffees on the table, along with a scrap of paper. 'It was actually easy; we've not been so busy, and I could isolate it by time and amount. He paid with a debit card, number's there. Will that help you?' she said.

'Very much so, thank you,' said Max. Janie picked up the piece of paper and quickly photographed it, then sat tapping on the phone.

Janie sipped at her coffee, then said, 'Sent it to Norma. Ross has pre-emptively got the authorities ready for it, so we should get recent transactions, quickly, and we're getting an account-monitoring order urgently authorised for future transactions.'

The doors to the café crashed open, and Ross and Barney wandered in, Ross already scowling.

'Where's my coffee, you selfish buggers?' he said, as he sat down with a grimace.

'You look sore, Ross,' said Max, raising his mug and sniffing appreciatively.

'Aye, fucking gout's making an appearance again. Bastard thing.'

'Ouch, sorry about that,' said Max.

'Too much port and red wine, Ross. Didn't Henry the Eighth have gout?' said Barney.

'Well, you'd know, bearing in mind you're old enough that you were probably putting bugs on Anne Boleyn's bedchamber to see if she was behaving, eh? Anyway, port and wine, my arse. I barely bloody drink.'

'Marian, can we have two more coffees, please? It seems that my boss urgently needs caffeine,' said Max to the waitress.

'Damn fucking right, I do. I'm bloody knackered. Right, any progress?'

'Yeah, Marian here has identified the bank card our man used to buy his coffee and cake and Janie has sent the details to Norma. All authorities are in place, I hear?'

'Cake?' Ross's face suddenly lit up, ignoring Max's question.

'Yes, cake. Want some?' said Janie.

'Obviously, coffee and cake.'

'I'll sort it,' said Janie, standing up and going to the till.

'Ross, eyes on the prize. Authorities?' said Max.

'Yep, with my customary efficiency, I got Miles Moneypenny to get the Chief to do forward-facing authorities for communications data, bank transactions and the like. Everyone is on tenterhooks ready to get us whatever we need. Still being kept on the downlow, for obvious reasons.'

'How about the victim at the hospital?' Max asked.

'I've had words with DCI Struan O'Neill at Inverness. I know him of old, and I trust him as much as anyone in this bloody force. He's arranged for a guard there, but he's not releasing any details more widely than that. He's content that we carry on doing what we're doing, probably because he got told to be happy about it by those above. We don't have long to get to the bottom of it, but the Chief is authorising that we keep going. It's not like we're losing much – we have enough to charge the evil motherfucker, as soon as we get hold of him. That video is bloody dynamite. We just need the break.'

There was a pause in conversation as they all looked at one another; as always, the weight of expectation bearing down on the small team.

Janie reappeared with two cups in one hand, and a plate containing several cakes. She deposited them down on the table, a little coffee spilling onto the wooden surface. Ross's hand shot out rapidly and grabbed a piece of carrot cake. 'Yes, ya fuckin' dancer,' he said, sinking his teeth into the cream-topped dessert. Predictably, a lump of the frosting detached itself from the top of the cake and, in what seemed like slow motion, fell, landing on Ross's shirt front.

'Ah shite, ya fucking walloper,' he spat, rubbing at the stain, only succeeding in smearing the topping across his shirt.

Barney sniggered. 'Christ, man. You really are summat. We can't take you anywhere, can we?'

Ross opened his mouth to retort, but paused, as Janie's phone began to buzz on the table.

'It's Norma,' said Janie, picking up the phone.

'Put her on speaker,' said Max.

'Norma, it's Janie and you're on speaker. Everyone's here.'

'I have news. Ross-Boss, I don't know what fires you lit under people's arses, but things are happening double quick. The bank card was issued just three days ago by Instabank, which is one of those accounts that's app based, with no branch. Much like we had on the Davie and Frankie Hardie case a while back. It's in the name of Rory Jones who resides at an address in Fort William.'

'Anything to confirm that?' said Ross.

'Well, no, but I am as confident as I can be that it's a gash account set up somehow by whoever is behind this.'

'How so?' said Ross.

'Rory Jones died three months ago, aged eighty-eight.'

'What else?'

'Not a great deal of transactions on it, and there's currently five hundred quid in there. But the card was used at the O2 phone shop in the Eastgate Shopping Centre in Inverness yesterday just before 6 p.m.'

'What's the number?' said Max.

'I don't know, yet. All we have is a transaction number, and amount of a hundred and forty-eight quid.'

'Any other transactions?' said Max.

'He bought fuel at Morrisons supermarket in Inverness yesterday, and maybe something inside the main store, but that's it.'

'Burner account, burner phone and a burner car. He's a careful bastard,' said Ross, shaking his head, almost in admiration.

'Norma, how about the number that he gave me when I took his witness statement?' said Janie.

'Burner. No longer active.'

Janie looked suddenly embarrassed, and shrugged, almost apologetically. 'How about the name and address he gave me. Any trace on Rory Jones?'

'All bullshit. The address in Fort William exists, but that's all.'

'And a burner address. Fuck, this bastard is very good. Right, priority is getting that phone number nailed down. Max, you and Janie get to Inverness, urgently, and find out the number. I'm betting he's gone and bought himself a new phone, and a burner SIM. We get those, and we have something to work with.'

'What are you two gonna do?' said Max, standing.

'Grandpa can drive me back to Tulliallan. I need to be there, as I've a feeling my negotiating and other interpersonal skills will be required there very soon. You two stay up here for now, in case something comes up from the phones and bank data. We've no idea where this bastard is, so it pays to split resources, yeah?'

'I'll need to call Katie, but sure.'

Ross paused, and looked at Max. 'I should have thought of that. You can go south, if you like, and I can stay. Mrs Fraser will understand, even if she'll no doubt give me massive pelters.'

Max shook his head. 'I'm good. I've my bike still here, which I'll park at Inverness nick, so I can make a quick getaway if needed. I'd rather stay, Ross.' Even as he was saying the words, he was wondering if they were true. Guilt flared in his mind about Katie at home alone, but then the sight of the corpse at the foot of Huntly's Cave flared more brightly. He needed to catch this bastard.

'You sure? What will the missus think about that?'

'She'll be fine. It's best I stay, in case we get a sudden lead, and Janie and I are best placed to deal – you're not exactly nimble on your feet with gout beginning to grumble,' Max said, grinning, although he was certain that it wasn't convincing. His mind was whirling with conflicting emotions.

'You can piss off. Do me a favour and go and speak to the DCI at Inverness while you're there and keep him updated. Okay, troops, the Chief has our backs on this, but the clock is ticking.'

35

NORMA WAS SITTING in the office, squinting at the screen, as Ross and Barney walked back into the shabby space.

'Ah, Jesus suffering fuck, has not a bastard been in to fix the ceiling?' Ross blurted out, throwing his bag on the floor.

'Oh, aye. They came in and fixed it, but then it bust down again,' said Norma, her eyes twinkling.

'And you can awa' and bile your heid, you cheeky mare.' Ross scowled, flicking lumps of plaster off his desk.

'Ross, if you call me a "mare" again, I'm taking my bloody laptop and working from home,' Norma said, sharply. Her eyes were hard, and the usual perma-grin was gone.

Ross closed his eyes, and sighed. 'Sorry, I'm trying, but occasionally it slips out.'

'Forgiven,' said Norma, her grin instantly returning.

'Looks a reet state in here, Ross. What's the management doing about it?' said Barney, as he flopped into the sagging, ancient-looking armchair in the corner of the room.

'You may well bloody ask. That fud in building services has taken a dislike to me ever since I called him a useless fanny the other day. Any update, Norma?'

'Aye. Max and Janie went to the shop, and have all the details about our man buying a phone. New number, address given, and bank details, most of which we know.'

'But we have the phone number, excellent. Data?'

'I'm expecting it any second now. The nice man at the single point of contact promised to help. I think he's due a bottle,' said Norma.

'Nothing else on any of the banking intel?'

'Only what we know already. No new activations, no card uses, zilch.'

'ANPR?'

'One activation on the A9 at Kingussie, but nothing else.'

'Heading south, then?' Ross clicked his tongue as he opened his laptop with a scowl.

'I've a direct link into the mannie that looks after ANPR, and he's promised a live update if there are any further activations. There are definitely cameras at Perth, and then more the farther south you go.' Norma stood and stretched her back with a sigh.

'Yet nothing?'

Norma shook her head, as she sat back down, heavily.

'Shite, is this bastard a ghost?' said Ross.

'Tea?' said Barney.

'First sensible thing you've bloody said all day.'

Barney stood up and wandered over to the small fridge, on top of which was a battered tray with a stained kettle and half a dozen cups on it. 'Bloody 'ell, the cups are chuffing minging again.'

'Stop moaning, you old fud, it's not like you're doing anything else, and yet I bet you're still charging us three hundred quid a day and living in your stolen flat,' Ross barked, his face red.

Barney opened his mouth to retort, but was silenced by Norma, who was suddenly animated.

'Shush, you two. I have the phone data,' she said, sitting upright in her chair and adjusting her spectacles, squinting as she looked at her screen.

Ross stood with a stifled oath and walked around her desk so that he could see the document she'd just opened.

'Okay, without your usual tech babble bullshite, just tell me where the murderous fuck-head is.'

'Last activation on the phone was just ten minutes ago – it hit a cell mast at postcode IV2 3UJ. I'm just plotting on a map, now.' Norma tapped on her keyboard, her face set in concentration.

The map zoomed in, before it steadied.

'IV postcode, that's bloody Inverness,' said Ross, his face growing even more red, as he rubbed his hands through his thinning hair.

Norma turned to look at him, her eyes wide with alarm. 'It's hitting a cell mast on top of Raigmore Hospital.'

A silence descended in the office that was thick with tension. Ross said nothing, just strode back to his desk, picked his phone up and dialled.

'Get to Raigmore Hospital, now.'

36

MIKEY WALKED THROUGH the large revolving door at Raigmore Hospital, striding confidently towards the reception desk, adjusting the small rucksack over his shoulder as he did. He put on his most charming smile for the receptionist, who was sitting with a phone clamped to her ear, as she nodded to acknowledge him.

He rested his palms on the countertop, a sense of utter calm in his chest. It was a skill he had learnt over the years climbing many of the world's most challenging hills and rock faces, that he no longer feared anything. He knew that he wouldn't be caught, because he was too smart, and because he would never let himself be caught.

Above all, he didn't fear death. He'd had so many close shaves in his life that in his mind he was already dead. He had died many times and it was meaningless. How could one fear nothingness? He knew there was no afterlife, so how could that be something to be feared? Death was release from reality.

'Sorry, can I help you?' said the smiling receptionist, whose name badge said Mary. She was young, blonde and attractive, and her smile, while ostensibly warm, was fake as she surveyed him with disdain. All women looked at him like that.

They'd all learn one day, the tight bitches. Despite the mounting sense of rage, Mikey showed his teeth in a wide grin that he was sure did not reach his eyes. He reached into his pocket and pulled out a small leather wallet, which he flipped open displaying the silver crown above a thistle at the top and the motto 'Semper Vigilo' just above the bold letters POLICE SCOTLAND. 'I'm DC Michael Anderson, here about the lady who was helicoptered in from a fall in the Cairngorms.'

37

Edinburgh, 1986

HAMISH INSERTED THE key into the door of the house in Stockbridge and pushed his way in, dumping his kit on the floor. His fingers ached and his triceps were straining, but he was feeling good after the session at the climbing wall. His instructor had really been impressed, and he'd progressed another level. He'd soon be ready to get out on the real rocks.

He hung up his jacket on the hook and listened. The house was silent and peaceful, almost as if it was asleep. Things had been much nicer as Uncle James had been home for almost two weeks, and it had been at his insistence that they'd gone to the climbing centre. Hamish had instantly fallen in love with it. The sensation of pulling himself up the wall, the belay securing him in, was just inspiring, and he knew he'd found his thing. All the boys at school had a 'thing', be it football, rugby or basketball, but none of the team games were for Hamish. Climbing was an individual skill. Using your strength and ability to ascend a sheer cliff – even if it was composed of an artificial rock, it was still a serious challenge, and one that required all of his concentration and effort. It was almost primeval. The desire to climb. To conquer. A battle of wits against gravity. He knew that he'd found his place.

Added to this was the fact that his aunt had been away at her sister's for almost a week. So he was feeling more positive than he had in years, and he hadn't even wet the bed for a few weeks.

It felt like he was turning a corner, and that he might find a way to be happy.

He went to the drawing room, where Uncle James normally read for an hour in the late afternoon, but it was empty and the silence was only punctuated by the rhythmic ticking of the large, imposing grandfather clock.

'Uncle James?' he called out as he went to the kitchen, which was just as empty as the drawing room.

He bounded up the stairs, two at a time, towards his bedroom. 'Uncle James?' he called out as he pushed his door open.

'Uncle . . .' The words caught in his throat, and he stopped as still as a guardsman called to a halt. His heart suddenly began to thump in his chest, and his face flushed.

Auntie Eunice was there in the centre of the room, her blonde hair piled high on her head, wisps of it across her face and a sneer on her flushed face as she held up one of the girly magazines that he had hidden under his bed. A copy of Mayfair that he'd bought off a pal at school.

'Auntie . . .'

'Don't you fucking "auntie" me, you little perverted shit. Bringing pornography into my house? How fucking dare you,' she said, her words slurred, and a line of drool on her chin. Her mascara was smudged like coal dust on her damp cheeks. She looked like a witch.

'But—' began Hamish.

'Don't you fucking "but" me, you little wretch. James has left me because of you. You little bastard. You've ruined my life.'

Hamish said nothing; he just turned on his heel and walked out of the room.

Auntie Eunice was not to be denied her moment, however. She streaked out of the room behind him, grabbing the collar of his shirt and pulling him backwards, slapping him hard as she turned him to face her. It hurt. It hurt a great deal, but Hamish said nothing, and he didn't react. He just stood and looked at her, his eyes cold, and a calm descending on him. Something changed. He did not know how, or what, but at that moment, a little piece of Hamish was lost. Or maybe, something new had arrived.

And then . . . Self-awareness. He knew what had changed.

He was no longer scared. He was stronger now, and was almost as tall as his aunt, and the fear that had dominated the last four years left him, as if he was discarding a rather too-tight sweater. He looked at her, straight into her eyes with defiance, his eyes blazing.

Her sneer turned into a scowl, which then morphed into naked, unmitigated rage, as she pulled back her palm and struck him with a heavy backhand that was studded with rings.

Hamish smiled at her, turned and walked away towards the staircase. 'Fuck you, I'm going out,' he said, without turning around.

Hamish had taken the ten steps to the staircase when she reached him. She grabbed a handful of his thick, wavy hair and pulled.

'Don't you bloody walk away from me, you little shit.' She spun him around to face her, her smudged red lips pulling away from her teeth, wafts of fetid, stale alcohol and cigarette-laced breath assailing his nostrils. The scowl turned to a grimace. 'No wonder your mother killed herself. Who would want to put up with a little bed-wetter like you.' She laughed, a gurgling, phlegmy sound, and pushed past Hamish towards the stairs, her fluffy mule slippers clicking on the tiled landing.

Hamish felt no rage and no anger as he shoved his aunt hard, in the centre of her back, the explosive force propelling her down in a tangle of limbs as she cartwheeled down the staircase, coming to rest at the first bend in the sweeping edifice. Her neck at a rakish angle, blood flowing from a nasty gash on her temple. Her eyes were wide open, her mouth sagging as blood flowed from her broken teeth.

Hamish stood there, mouth agape at the sight of his dead aunt, his insides as cold as an Edinburgh winter's day. He felt as if his whole body had been struck by lightning, such was the energy that was coursing through his veins.

He smiled.

He then began to laugh.

38

PC JIM LENNOX yawned as he sat on a hard chair outside room seven in the intensive care ward, and looked at his watch; he groaned when he saw that he still had several hours to go before he would be relieved.

The intensive care unit was a hive of activity, with lots of scrubs-clad doctors and nurses bustling around, and the whole atmosphere was one of busy efficiency. They were all friendly enough to him as he sat there, and one nice nurse had provided him with a tea a while back, but that was basically it. It was one nurse per patient, so they were all full on.

The poor, as yet unidentified, lassie in the bed was in a terrible state, hooked up to every machine, her head swathed in bandages and her eyes taped shut. She was in an induced coma, he had been told by her smiley nurse, Sian, with kind eyes and flame-red hair.

He knew nothing about the patient, and the risk assessment by the sergeant had amounted to 'someone above me has said that someone may want to finish her off, nae idea why, so eyes about you Jim-boy, and dinnae nod off'.

The tapping of shoes in the corridor made him look up from his musings, and he saw a suited middle-aged man, with a rucksack on his shoulder and a serious look on his face, walking towards him. As he got closer, he reached into his pocket and pulled out a warrant card, which he proffered with a half-smile.

'I'm DC Anderson from the Major Investigation Team, pal. Down to seize the victim's clothing and take hand swabs.'

Jim looked at the warrant card, and then up to the newcomer. 'Don't recognise you, pal. Where are you from?'

'They're pulling a new team in from all over. I'm based at Gartcosh. For some reason it's got busy in the Highlands, eh?' He grinned.

Jim raised his eyebrows. 'Aye, that's for sure. The CID are all running about like crazies on another murder. Is this an attempted murder case, now?'

DC Anderson sighed. 'Seems to be heading that way, although no bugger is telling us why. All very hush hush. Can I go in?'

'Hold up, there's a nurse in there all the time, so we'd better ask.' Jim stood and pushed the door open a crack. Sian was over the patient's bed and fiddling with one of the multitude of lines that were going into her.

'Sian, I've a colleague here from the Major Investigation Team, wants to take her clothes, and do some hand swabs, is that okay?'

Sian looked up, a puzzled look on her face. 'Is this a serious crime, like?' she said.

'Seems like it,' said Jim.

'Well, her clothes are in the bag there.' She pointed to a clear hospital bag, which was dumped in a corner.

'Hi, I'm DC Anderson, am I okay to take them, for forensics, like?' The newcomer smiled, warmly.

'I guess so; what was it about hand swabs?' she said, looking perplexed.

'Just some dry swabs of her palms, you know, just routine,' he said, reaching into his bag and pulling out a small, sealed plastic bag that contained what looked like a number of oversized Q-tips.

Sian shrugged. 'Aye, that's okay, I have to stay in the room, though.'

'Fine by me,' said DC Anderson, entering, and pulling out a large, clear plastic evidence bag with a numbered self-seal strip at the top.

Jim felt his phone vibrate in his pocket. He pulled it out and looked at the screen; it was his wife. He glanced up at DC Anderson who was snapping on a pair of blue nitrile gloves and shaking the large evidence bag open ready to transfer the clothing into it. 'I'd best stay on watch outside the room,' said Jim, backing out and taking up his position on his chair once more as the door swung shut.

'Hey, sweetheart,' he said, answering the phone.

'Jimmy, that bloody school . . . they've suspended Logan, caught him vaping in the toilets,' she blasted down the phone, her voice shot through with anger.

He sighed, wearily. 'What?'

His wife sounded angry – very angry about what their eldest had apparently done. He listened as she ranted and raved about the injustice of it all, not really taking it in.

A couple of minutes later, the door opened, and DC Anderson emerged, clutching a bulging evidence bag, as well as the rucksack over his shoulder.

Jim held his hand over the phone. 'All done?'

'Aye, easy as, pal, I'd best get these back to the incident room, DCI is barking for them. Take care, and don't get too bored. I'm sure the lassie in there will make you another cuppa soon, eh?' he said, before walking off towards the exit.

'Not you, love. Carry on, what did Logan say?' he said, returning to the stream of vitriol that his wife was letting fly.

He sat there listening for a few more moments before a muffled thump came from the room. His wife asked a barbed question. He turned and looked at the door. What was that? He listened, trying to filter out the sounds of the bustling ward. He shook his head, his wife's severe tone dragging him back.

'No carry on, pet,' he said, turning back to his phone, only just listening as she droned on.

Then a metallic crack. A sharp noise, as if something had fallen. 'I'll call you back, love,' he said, rising to his feet.

Then a strangled, hoarse scream, from the room. His heart lurched and he rocketed to his feet, shoving the door inwards.

Sian was struggling on the floor, trying to get to her feet, her face brick red, her eyes wide and full of alarm. 'Help!' she screamed, her voice rasping and throaty, a line of sputum dripping from her mouth and onto the floor.

Jim's stomach turned to water, as he rushed up to Sian and knelt at her side. 'What the hell's happened?' he said, but he knew. In his heart he knew that he'd screwed up massively.

'It was him, he tried to kill her. Get him, get after him, now.'

39

MAX AND JANIE burst through the hospital doors and into reception, listening to the chatter on the radio, and the anxious commentary from the cop. '*4073, urgent assistance required at Raigmore ICU. Attempt on the life of patient, suspect has fled purporting to be a cop with warrant card. Male, about forty, six feet, in a suit, short grey hair and glasses, suit and tie. On his way from ICU into main hospital, I'm giving chase.*'

'He'll be heading down here, no doubt,' said Max, as he scanned the reception area.

'*I think he took the stairs up; I'm giving chase,*' came the out-of-breath message, echoey and frantic.

'Up? Why would he head up?' said Max. 'Chasing officer, we're holding the bottom of the lift shaft and stairs. You confident about him going up?' he said into his radio handset.

There was no reply, just dead airspace.

'Staircase and lifts are down here,' said Janie, jogging off along the corridor, ignoring the people stopping and staring at them.

Within a minute they were standing outside the lifts, in a large vestibule with the fire escape door to the left leading to the staircase.

'What do we do, Max? Stay here and hold this position? He's got to come out at some point, and it has to be this way,' said Janie.

'Unless he decides to go to ground for a while, or ditch out of a window?'

'I bet they're restricted opening.' Janie opened the doors, went into the staircase and stopped. 'All quiet here, how many floors?'

'Eight, I think. If he goes to ground, it'll be a bloody nightmare.'

There was a ping, and the lift light lit up, the doors beginning to slowly open revealing a capacious lift, packed with a mix of patients, staff and what seemed to be visitors. They watched the group file out, but none were wearing suits, as described by the officer. Max looked towards the staircase again, which was quiet and empty.

He watched with interest as the group from the lift began to head off towards them. An elderly man in a wheelchair being pushed by a male nurse dressed in scrubs seemed agitated. Max noticed that next to them was a grey-haired man in casual clothes, who was looking from side to side, his movements jittery, until he stopped, and recognition flashed across his face as a young woman ran from behind them and embraced him.

Max sighed, his eyes drawn to the nurse in scrubs, as he was struggling with the wheelchair. He was middle-aged and smiling kindly at the patient in the wheelchair, releasing the brake and beginning to move off towards their position. Max sighed. Not in the lift, so probably on the staircase as first thought.

He turned to Janie. 'I think we need to stay here until we get reinforce—'

'What?' said Janie, a puzzled look on her face.

Max didn't reply. He stared at the nurse just ten yards in front of them who was still struggling with the brake on the wheelchair, trying to release the mechanism with his shoe. Max zeroed in on the shoe, trying to work out what was wrong with the picture.

'Max, reinforce what?' said Janie, raising her voice a touch.

The shoe.

A plain black Oxford lace-up. Not gutties, not Crocs, not sandals, as you'd normally expect, but a formal shoe.

He looked up at the nurse, who stared straight back at him, his eyes hard and flat. He moved off, towards them, and towards the exit, his stride long and loping. Max knew it then. He'd seen that walk before, as the man approached, just five yards away, now.

'Stop! Police!' he bellowed, rushing towards the man, who responded by violently shoving the elderly patient in the wheelchair hard towards Max, before turning and sprinting away back towards the lifts. He shoved the door to the staircase vestibule open and bound up the stairs, revealing that he had a small rucksack on his back. The wheelchair smashed into Max's shins, and the pain jolted him into action. With a roar, Max sidestepped around the wheelchair and gave chase, Janie hot on his heels.

Max was fitter than average, but the speed with which the man bounded up the stairs, three at a time, was astonishing, and he began to open a gap on Max and Janie. Max didn't slow. He heard Janie shouting into her radio for assistance as they ascended the stairs, Max puffing and blowing as he did, flight after flight, his lungs bursting, but their quarry was always keeping the distance even between them.

As they hit what felt like the fifteenth floor, but must have been no more than the seventh, the smacking of feet on concrete stopped, and there was silence from above.

Max slowed as he rounded the corner, and saw the door at the top of the stairs swing shut. He went forward, breathing heavily, his heart pounding and legs screaming in pain, and put his hand on the door handle. He nodded at Janie, who was just a few steps behind him. 'Ready?'

'Aye, knackered, but let's do this,' she said, the sweat beading on her forehead.

Max flung the door open. The corridor was long and narrow and led to a stout-looking door marked AUTHORISED ACCESS ONLY. WORKING AT HEIGHT REGULATIONS APPLY. The man stood there, facing them, panting heavily, but in control. He was breathing deeply, but his eyes were hard, dark, and full of menace.

'Let me see your hands,' said Max, approaching with caution to where the man stood.

'You've no idea, you poor saps. Look at you, I'm older than both of you, and you could barely keep up with me, especially you, you bitch. Such a stuck-up cow, you barely noticed me on the hill. Well, you're noticing me now, eh?' he said, looking at Janie and sneering. He spat on the floor, his voice harsh and ragged, his eyes fixed on her.

'Hands, now!' said Max, just as the door behind them swung open, and a uniformed cop appeared in the corridor, a yellow Taser in his hands and a bodycam attached to his hi-vis ballistic vest.

'Nice timing, pal,' said Max.

'Who're you?' said the cop, between breaths.

'DS Craigie and DS Calder. What's your name?'

'Jim Lennox. He attacked a member of staff in ICU, and he may have killed the patient, injected her with something. He had a warrant card and said he was DC Anderson from the MIT, the bastard. Who the fuck are you, and what did you do to that poor lassie?' he snarled, through clenched teeth.

A chuckling noise came from him, a throaty, phlegm laden noise. 'It is a genuine warrant card, you stupid bastards. You've got nothing, and you know nothing at all,' he continued to guffaw.

'Hands on head, dickhead, or you're getting fried,' yelled PC Lennox as he advanced, Taser outstretched in his hands, as the laser dot quivered on the attacker's chest.

He showed no fear as he looked down at the dancing red dot; he just began to laugh, his wide eyes shining with excitement.

'What did you inject her with, you bastard?' said PC Lennox.

He just grinned, his face shining, almost triumphantly. 'You've no idea what you're dealing with. No idea at all. This doesn't end with me; this is so much bigger than you can ever imagine.' He let out another laugh, just as the metal door behind him opened inwards, shoving him forwards. A shocked-looking workman in hi-vis jacket and hard hat appeared in the doorway.

'What the hell—' he began, but the man in scrubs was lightning quick, pushing the workman out of the way and exploding through the open door with a roar, out onto the roof and heading towards the balustrade. Max, Janie and PC Lennox immediately sprang into action, PC Lennox almost shoving Max out of the way to get through the door.

'Anderson' didn't hesitate as he ran towards the roof's edge, determination evident with every loping bound, his scrubs flapping as he closed in on the edge. He was going to leap to his death, Max was totally certain of that fact. 'No, stop!' yelled Max.

Then there was a pop to Max's side and 'Anderson' stopped dead, as if he'd been shot. His back arched and he let out a strangled cry as he hit the concrete of the hospital roof like a felled oak, his face connecting with the surface with a sickening crack. Two small darts were protruding from the green scrubs with fine wires attached to the yellow Taser in the outstretched hands of PC Lennox, who was bellowing, 'TASER, TASER, TASER!'

Breathing hard, his jaw firm with aggression, his arms ramrod straight, PC Lennox released the trigger, and the target relaxed, groaning faintly, a bubbling noise coming from his face.

'Anderson' rose to his knees, blood dripping from his smashed face. He stiffened again as the Taser crackled, and let out another bloodcurdling cry. He fell back onto the concrete, quivering, the familiar strangled cry coming from his damaged mouth.

'Stay still, you bastard, or I'll fucking fry you again,' spat PC Lennox.

Max looked at the cop, whose face was white as a sheet, and put his hand on his shoulder. 'Jim, steady, pal, eh.'

PC Lennox said nothing, just continued to stare at the man who was still moaning on the deck.

'Jim?'

PC Lennox looked at Max briefly and nodded. 'Aye, I'm okay.'

'I'm gonna take your cuffs off your belt, and secure him, okay? It's all good, we have him, yeah?'

Max reached to the cop's belt kit, snapped the rigid cuffs from their holster and advanced to the assailant, kneeling at his side. All the fight had gone from him, as he lay face down on the concrete, blood oozing from his shattered nose.

'Right, I'm gonna cuff you. If you resist even slightly, a very pissed-off PC Lennox will turn you into a human lightning rod, do you understand?' said Max.

He said nothing, just buried his face into the concrete.

With practised ease, Max applied the cuffs behind the detainee's back, and then released the fastenings of the small rucksack and pulled it away, tossing it to Janie, who caught it effortlessly. She snapped on a pair of nitrile gloves and unzipped the bag. She peered in, and slid her hand inside, pulling out a leather wallet. 'Well, well, well. Detective Constable Anderson, if indeed that is your name.' She let the wallet fall open, revealing the crest of a Police Scotland warrant card.

The man in scrubs said nothing, just spat bloody mucus out onto the concrete.

'Also have a VW key and a locked Motorola in here, and what looks like an insulin pen.'

'Call it in on your radio, Jim,' said Max, reaching for his phone and dialling.

'Why is it that every time we do a thematic review, it always ends in carnage, Craigie? Tell me you have him?' Ross said by way of opening gambit.

'We have him. Is Norma there?'

'Aye, currently making her way through a box of Tunnock's

that the bugger won't share. Anyway, what the fuck is going on? Last time I checked, I'm supposed to be in charge and you're supposed to tell me shit.'

Max brought Ross up to date.

'So, the bastard was going to chuck himself off a fucking hospital?'

'Aye, and if the uniformed cop hadn't zapped him, he'd have been a Jackson Pollock on the concrete eight storeys below.'

'Jackson who?'

'Never mind, suffice to say, he wouldn't have survived the jump, and the paperwork would have been interminable,' said Max.

'Nice job, I hate paperwork as you well know. What do you need from us?'

'Janie is sending a picture of a warrant card that our man has on him. We need it checked urgently. Also is Barney there?'

'No, he was bored and was getting on my tits so I told him to head north to support you two.'

'Support us with what?'

'With bloody anything apart from getting on my tits here. He left an hour ago.'

'Good decision, we'll have work for him.'

'He shouldn't be long; you know what he's like when he's bored, so he'll be raring to go. Is it all over, then? Got him bang to rights in the act of trying to finish off that poor lassie from the Coire?'

'I don't think so, Ross. I think we may just be getting started.'

40

IT WAS CLOSE to an hour before PC Lennox slammed the cage door in the prisoner transport van, leaving the suspect scowling at them, his nose flat as a pancake, and at least two teeth shattered. He did not look like a broken man, however, and he stared at them with utter hatred blazing in his deep eyes as the main door shut with a bang.

'Good work, Jim.' Max clapped him on the shoulder.

'What do you mean good work? My sergeant is going to be bloody scunnered with me, and I'm already persona non grata on the team. I let the bugger into the ward with a snide warrant card.' He massaged his temples, and his face was deathly pale.

'No, you didn't.' With a gloved hand, Janie held up the warrant card that had been found in the rucksack.

'What?'

'Aye. Genuine. I've had our analyst and researcher check it out.'

'What, already?'

'We don't hang about on Policing Standards Reassurance. DC Michael Anderson was a serving cop in Glasgow until a year ago, and the mannie in the van is definitely him.' Janie held out her smartphone showing an image of a fresh-faced uniformed cop. He was younger, but there was no doubt. It was the same man.

'Shit, that's him; so he was a cop? Bloody hell, no wonder he managed to blag his way past me.'

'Indeed. He resigned under a very significant cloud after some kind of inappropriate conduct allegations were made. Tried it on with a victim of a serious sexual assault, you know, creepy text messages asking her out and that, and even a dick pic. Her mum cliped on him when she found the messages on her phone. Chucked his cards in before he could get disciplined, and the powers that be decided not to pursue criminal charges, which is somewhat odd.'

PC Lennox shook his head. 'Shite, what a scumbag.'

'Even worse, and I accept that I'm no criminologist, but his background is very concerning. His real name is Hamish Michael Anderson, mother died when he was nine, and he was mostly brought up by an abusive aunt who died after she "fell"' – Janie mimed the inverted commas with her fingers – 'down the stairs at their posh house in Stockbridge when wee Hamish was just thirteen.'

A voice sounded out from behind them. It was a uniformed female inspector, who had just arrived. She had kind eyes and an easy smile. 'You okay, Jim?'

'Aye, how is the victim, boss?' His eyes were full of fear and sadness.

'She was lucky. He didn't succeed, and she's going to be fine. Nurse was smart enough to get the line out of the patient and a new one in before the poison hit her. Insulin apparently, he left the syringe in there. It was one of those single-use things that diabetics use, so they knew what it was. She's still very poorly, but not because of anything that happened back there.'

PC Lennox opened his mouth to speak, but his voice cracked and his eyes welled with tears. 'I thought I'd failed, boss. I thought she was gonna die,' he said, the colour draining from his face.

'You caught him, Jim. You made it right, so don't beat yourself up over it, eh?' she said, her voice gentle.

'Is the nurse okay?' he said, with a catch in his throat.

'She's fine. You know what these Highland wifies are like, Jim. Tough as old boots.'

'Listen to the guvnor, Jim. You did well,' said Max.

'Go and get yourself in the car, and I'll run you back to Burnett Road. MIT team are taking over, and they'll need your statement, but he's your collar, you get to book him in, yeah?' she said, gently.

PC Lennox nodded, and cuffing the tears from his face, he walked off.

'I'm Inspector Rafferty, thanks for helping Jim out. He's a decent cop, just lacks confidence. I'm not sure many would have denied a man who looks like a cop with a genuine warrant card access to a victim in those circumstances.'

'I agree, he did well. Has this been reported up?' said Max.

The inspector nodded. 'DCI O'Neill has assumed responsibility, and he has a reception committee waiting at Burnett Road for strip-searches and retrieval of property. Is that his rucksack?' She pointed at the bag in Janie's hand.

'Aye. We think he's a car nearby, leastways he has a VW key in it, and a phone, and we have our tech expert coming up. My boss, DI Fraser, is liaising with DCI O'Neill now.'

'Is that DI Ross "Fuck-You" Fraser?" said Inspector Rafferty, with a half-grin.

'The very same. You've met him, then?' said Max, laughing.

'Let's say we've encountered each other. Bark way worse than bite. Best get the bag and the car back to Burnett Road when you've found it.'

'Of course. Can we get our guy to download the sat-nav?'

'No argument from me, but maybe square up with the DCI, eh? I know what you CID lot are like. I'd better get Jim back; I'll leave you two to sort the details out, but the MIT will want your statements, okay?'

'Nae bother, boss,' said Max.

Inspector Rafferty nodded and then almost trotted off to her marked car.

'Our inestimable leader never fails to make an impression, does he?' said Janie.

'Indeed. Any ideas on locating this car?' Max held up the VW keys in gloved hands.

'Old-fashioned way?'

'Is there any other?'

'Nah, come on. It's a big car park, so it may take a while.'

*

In fact, it took only about ten minutes walking up the rows of cars, pressing the unlock button on the fob before the lights flashed on a plain-looking, almost brand-new black VW Golf.

'Same car as up on Cairngorm, but he's changed the plates. In fact, look . . .' Janie squatted down and pointed to two dark smudges on each side of the plate. 'Used sticky pads to put false plates on. I'll get Norma to check these ones out.' She tapped on her phone for a second. 'Do we get a low-loader in and take it back to a pound somewhere?' said Janie, eyeing Max.

'What do you think, Ms Accelerated Promotion?'

'I think you're referring to accelerated high potential who hasn't moved anywhere or got any chance of promotion for three years?'

'Aye. Only because you don't want to stop working with me,' Max snorted.

'What, the man who makes it so I'm never at home with my girlfriend?'

'The very same. Barney should be here soon, so maybe let's let him have a wee lookie first?' Max raised his eyebrows, questioningly.

'So, you're saying that we shouldn't use established protocol?' said Janie.

'I'm saying that time is of the essence, and I don't think we really understand what we're dealing with, yet.'

Janie looked at Max, quizzically, but said nothing.

'I think there may be others.'

'What?' Janie looked astonished.

'How did he know what we were doing on the hill? How did he know that you were bait? Because I'm bloody certain he did. He has world-class arrogance, but he knew, Janie. He knew all about it.'

Janie rubbed her face. 'Shit.'

'Remember what he said, before he ran off in his suicidal quest: "This doesn't end with me."'

'Could be bullshit. He was full of it. He has an ego the size of this bloody hospital.' She pointed to the big building.

'The way he was staring at you when he said the things he did. Everything he's done, the risks he took to try to kill the lassie in that hospital. It was pretty clear to me, especially since learning why he was hoofed out of the force.'

Janie narrowed her eyes. 'Go on?'

'I think he has a big problem with women. In fact, I think he hates women, that's for sure, but I think we have a bigger and more immediate issue.'

'Oh Jesus. No. Not again.'

'Aye. I think he had a bent copper feeding him live intelligence. And they're still out there. This is nowhere near over.'

41

Chat – FTF

Tor Browser

Wyatt-Lawman: I'm hearing all sorts of alarming things? Tell me they're not true?

Bagger: Unfortunately, yes. He's in custody at Burnett Road now, being booked in. It's all been locked down tight, and he's being held incommunicado.

Wyatt-Lawman: He can't talk.

Bagger: He won't talk. The guy is a total maniac, but he won't talk. He's a true believer.

Wyatt-Lawman: You better be right.

Bagger: I am right.

Wyatt-Lawman: On the upside, have you looked at the forum?

Bagger: No, that's your area of expertise, why?

Wyatt-Lawman: The one at Huntly's Cave is going viral. Worldwide. He must have uploaded it from his phone. Serious amounts of views, and it's making a fortune. I just hope he keeps his mouth shut, or we won't get to spend it.

Bagger: He'll never talk, I guarantee it.

Wyatt-Lawman: You'd better be right. Do we think that Doss will take over the front-line duties now that Mikey's out of the game?

Bagger: What, you want to keep on going?

Wyatt-Lawman: After a break, yes. Doss managed very nicely on A' Chralaig, didn't he. That clip made good money, despite the fact that Mikey thought it was crap. People will pay for anything.

Bagger: Doss would jump off a cliff himself if Mikey told him to. He was the true disciple, kind of pathetic, really.

Wyatt-Lawman: Then we're good to go. Just need some time, and maybe a change of method, but I see no reason why we need to stop forever.

Bagger: Christ, you lot are crazy. I want this to stop.

Wyatt-Lawman: You have no choice. We're all in this together, remember? Mutually assured destruction. Nuclear option.

Bagger: Aye. I have to go, it's all happening.

42

MAX AND JANIE sat in their Volvo, which they'd repositioned by Anderson's VW while they waited for Barney to arrive. They both just sat, not talking, sharing yawns after the punishing hours, as the Highland summer sun began to dip below the horizon.

'We should really get this lifted, and back to Burnett Road, you know,' said Janie.

'Aye, I know, but I want Barney to look at the sat-nav before it's moved, in case lifting it somehow cocks it up. We can't track using plates, and we can't be sure what plates he's been using. GPS will confirm exactly where the car's been. Looks to me like the car's been bloody valeted, so leads may be at a premium. He's a proper careful bugger, which is to be expected given his former employment.'

'I guess. I'm knackered, and want to go home for a bit, and it's making me grumpy.' Janie stretched, arching her back against the leather seat, and yawned.

'I know. Katie wasn't too happy when I called her saying I was unlikely to be home tonight.'

Max's phone buzzed on the dash. It was Norma. She sounded as bright and cheery as normal.

'Right, I've done a deep dive on the VW, intel-wise. Want the info?' she said.

'Sure, don't you ever go home?' said Max.

'I am home. Hubby's put kids to bed, and I'm on the systems remotely, want to hear?'

'Go on.'

'Well, VW was purchased three months ago, in Falkirk. A private sale after it was advertised on Auto Trader. It's still shown registered to the old keeper. Anderson paid ten grand for it, which he transferred from a different app-based account that was set up a week previously, and is now inactive with just twelve quid in it. Same address in Fort William as the account that purchased the phone in Inverness. I'm still waiting for the full financial profile on that address.'

'Anything else on the address?'

'A bit more. It's listed as empty, as it's currently going through probate; the old guy died intestate. No next of kin, and obviously no will, but there's something else. The address is listed on Airbnb, dead cheap.'

'That seems a bit odd?' Max rubbed at an itch on his cheek.

'Maybe needs a visit. The phone number for the host is registered to the next-door neighbour.'

'Okay, we'll check it out. He must have been getting his head down somewhere, and who knows what we'll find. As the Motorola is clearly a burner phone, I'm betting he has another handset out there. That could yield all sorts.'

'Indeed. By the way, I've checked out the number he bought in Inverness, and after he left you lot, it was used a couple of times. One hit a mast close to Loch Laggan, and it then hit another in Fort William, so it all ties in.'

'We'd best get there, once we're finished here,' said Max, thinking of Katie.

'Aye, well. Best of luck – anything else you want me to do?' said Norma, brightly.

'No, you get on with your life, and leave us poor buggers at the coalface,' said Max, mid-yawn.

'Will do, byeee!' She rang off.

Max and Janie just looked at each other with flat, tired eyes.

'Shall we get the car searched? Barney will be here imminently,' said Janie.

Max nodded, and wearily got out of the car.

They donned full forensic kit while they thoroughly searched the car, but all they recovered was a single Yale key, a packet of mints and three brand-new SIM cards still in their blister packs. The familiar cap and sunglasses were tucked deep in the glove box. The car was immaculate, and had clearly recently been completely wiped down, as the plastics gleamed and there wasn't a trace of dust or debris on the carpets, or the fabric seats.

Janie slammed the door, a clear evidence bag in her hand containing the items they'd retrieved. 'Nothing to write home about, although the hat and glasses are useful to the MIT team for matching with the footage the poor victim caught when she was shoved.'

'Slam-dunk case on him. Heads up, here's the ageing ex-spy,' said Max, pointing as he pulled off his face mask.

There was a scrunch of tyres on tarmac as Barney's van pulled up alongside the VW.

'Now then,' said Barney, limping slightly as he eased himself out of the van, the metal of his prosthetic leg flashing in the fast-departing sun.

'Good trip?' said Janie.

'Pleasant. Views coming up the A9 are always lovely. What do you need?' he said, stretching his back, with a grimace on his craggy face.

'Firstly, anything technical you can do with this car? It has sat-nav, so wondering if you could do anything with that? You managed it on the drugs case a while back.'

'I can 'ave a look. Owt else?' he said, as he plucked his worn leather tobacco pouch from his pocket and deftly began to roll a cigarette.

'This Motorola,' said Janie, holding up the handset in her gloved hand.

'Easy as owt. Let me get that running first and then I'll look at the car.' He applied a flame from a battered old Zippo to his skinny roll-up and inhaled with visible pleasure.

'Great, can we crack on? It's getting late and I think we need to get to Fort William tonight. If we can locate an address, who knows what we'll find,' said Max.

'On it like a car bonnet, lad. Give us the phone, then.'

'Gloves first?' said Janie, tossing a pair of nitriles over to Barney, who caught them with ease, the roll-up wobbling between his lips. He took a final long drag, before he dropped the half-smoked cigarette on the ground, and stepped on it.

'Let's get cracking, then,' he said, snapping the gloves into place and taking the phone from Janie. He opened the sliding door on the van and flicked a switch, which bathed the interior in a weak yellow light. He stepped into the van, and reached for the now-familiar scratched metal box and plugged the snaking lead into the handset.

Max's phone buzzed again; it was a message from Katie. *I guess you're not coming home tonight, then?* ☹

'I'm just gonna make a quick call,' said Max, unzipping his forensic suit and stepping away from the van.

'The fact that you've called me immediately definitely means that you're not coming home, doesn't it?' said Katie, her voice sounded hoarse, and there was a tremor to it.

Max felt his heart sink at the tone in his wife's voice. She sounded sad. 'I think not; we've had a very tough day, babe.' He massaged his temple with his free hand, but he didn't elaborate. The last thing she needed to hear now was about attempted suicides, or death in the Munros.

Katie sighed, deeply. 'I'm sad, Max. I'm sad and sore, and I'm feeling a bit lonely. I miss you,' she said, her voice cracking.

Max felt his stomach lurch, as if someone had punched him from inside. 'I'm so sorry, babe. We've work to do before I can get back, but I'll be home tomorrow, as soon as I can get everything up here sorted.'

Katie said nothing, but Max could hear her begin to weep, softly, and felt a lump rising in his own throat.

'Katie . . .' he began, but she got there first.

'I'm sorry, Max. I'm so sorry to put this on you, I know how important your work is to you, and I know you're doing important stuff, so it's unfair of me to land this on you, but I'm really missing you, and I really want you here.'

'I know, and I'm sorry. You don't deserve this, but I will get back tomorrow. It's a big case, and I just can't leave the others."

'They're all big cases, Max. All of them. They're all big, important and bloody urgent. I sometimes wish . . .' She paused, and Max could hear her weeping. He screwed his eyes shut, and massaged his temple with his free hand.

'Katie, I—' he began, but she jumped in, again.

'I'm sorry, Max. I don't want to make your life hard, and I know what you do means so much, but I sometimes want my husband here. Particularly now, when we're about to become a family. Look, I'm gonna go, I'll feel better after some sleep.'

Max had no idea how to react, or what to say, so he just apologised again. The words tasted bitter and sour, and he felt pathetic and weak.

'I know. I know you're sorry, and I know you'd come home if you could. Look, I'll be fine; John and Lynne are checking in on me.'

Max paused, and closed his eyes. 'I'll be home tomorrow, I promise.'

'I know, I'm probably just overtired. I'm going to bed. Love you.' The familiar three tones on the phone indicated that she had gone. Max's head reeled with guilt and his face began to flush, just as he realised that he wasn't alone. Janie was standing next to him, a concerned look on her face.

'You okay, pal?' she said, softly.

'Katie's sad—' He stopped, feeling the need to compose himself.

'Do you need to go?'

Max shook his head.

'It must be tough for her.'

Max nodded, but said nothing, unsure if he could keep a steady voice.

'You know we can do this without you, right? I mean, you're good, but nobody's indispensable,' she said, softly.

Max took a deep breath, as the images of the dead victims swirled in his mind. 'I need to stay. I need to see this fucking job through, Janie. It's too important.'

'They're all important, Max. Always are. If you need to go, go. You're gonna be a dad soon, and you want to be there for Katie.'

'I'm all good,' he said, his voice firming, and thoughts clearing.

Janie looked at him, long and hard. 'Sure?' She reached out and touched his shoulder, gently. Just a fleeting brush, but it carried all the concern that her face showed for her friend.

Max nodded, and forced a half-smile.

'Barney has something on the phone,' she said.

'What, he's broken in already?'

'Aye. "Shite cheap Motorola" was his considered opinion. Apparently, the internal GPS on maps is interesting. Come on, he's very pleased with himself.' Janie walked off to the campervan, where Barney was looking at a computer screen.

'What's the score?' said Max as he joined Janie at the campervan door.

'He's not the sharpest tool in the box. It's a burner, but it's still linked to an email account, which I suspect he uses for all his burners; that's summat Norma can look into.'

'Okay, go on?'

'Right, when he bought it in't shop in Inverness, he put in the new SIM, and then logged in using the email address. An anonymous Gmail one. When he did that, it would install the apps he's used in the past, if he hadn't deleted them. So, Google, Spotify and similar, but he had also installed a secure messaging app, Wickr.'

'Any messages on it?' said Max.

'We don't know. He has auto delete on, set for ten minutes. So once the message has been sent, it's there for just ten, then it's gone forever. No way can it ever be recovered. Special Forces even use it as it's so effective. But it shows what he's been up to.'

'Damn, so it's no use to us, then?' said Max.

'I didn't say that. This phone is bloody dynamite, mate. He thinks he's clever, but he isn't. He's left his GPS enabled, so we know everywhere he's been since he switched this phone on, all in lurid colour on Google Maps. I think we know where he's been staying in Fort William. You just have to know where to look. And there's something else.'

'What?'

'There's one video on the download. He deleted it, but not properly, so I was able to recover it. He's clearly not that savvy on computer forensics, the wazzock.'

'Is it bad?' said Max, feeling his skin prickle.

Barney shook his head, a tiny movement that barely registered, but the meaning was clear. It was evident in the set of his eyes, the firmness of his jaw. Barney was tough as teak and had seen it all, but there was a shadow over his face. He sighed. 'Nay, lad. It's worse than bad. It's bloody horrible, but it'll bury him.'

'Show me,' said Max, his throat constricted as if there was a golf ball trapped in it.

He watched, Janie by his side, as Barney played the footage. It was not the greatest quality, but Max knew that he'd never forget the jerky, grainy piece of digital video. He knew that it would be etched on his mind forever, and that it would be at the top of the long list of things he had seen that he would never wipe from his memory.

As the rock was smashed down on the helpless blonde woman's temple, Max knew that nothing would ever be the same again. All thoughts of Katie, and the baby suddenly left his mind, and a sudden determination gripped him like a vice.

Whenever he next got the opportunity to sleep again, the nightmares would surely tear him awake without mercy.

43

HAMISH MICHAEL ANDERSON stared straight into the eyes of the attractive blonde custody officer who had introduced herself as Sergeant Cotton. She avoided his gaze as she went through the booking-in procedure in a perfunctory and efficient manner. An older, hard-faced and bearded sergeant sat next to her and stared at him with eyes that seemed to blaze with anger. The cop who'd arrested him, PC Lennox, stood to one side of Anderson, wordless after he'd delivered the verbal account to the custody officer. Another cop, more morose-looking, stood behind them both as security, silent but glaring at Anderson.

Anderson's face was a mess, and his broken nose was covered with a gauze bandage that was spotted with blood. Dark circles were already forming below his eyes. His nose throbbed wickedly, despite the analgesics that the surly custody nurse had handed him.

Anderson answered the questions monosyllabically, never once removing his gaze from Sergeant Cotton, his face impassive.

'Do you want a solicitor, Mr Anderson?' the sergeant said, her dove-grey eyes looking straight at him. He held her gaze unblinkingly, feeling the familiar cold grip on his stomach. The bitch would never entertain him if he tried to speak to her in a bar, but now she feared him. Now she respected him, even if she visibly loathed him. He could smell her fear like a cheap, sickly perfume. Fear was tangible, and fear was intoxicating.

A smile played on his lips, and he moved his tongue across their dry, chapped surface. He chuckled, a harsh sound that came from the back of his throat.

'That's enough of that. Answer the custody officer's bloody question,' said the other sergeant, his eyes hard.

The female sergeant looked to her colleague, her face registering disapproval. 'It's okay, Ed, I've got this,' she said, as she turned back to face him. 'Mr Anderson, a solicitor?'

'Yes,' he said, in little more than a whisper. She almost flinched at his words, her eyes widening. It was remarkable how much hate he conveyed in that one word: so much loathing and frustration at a life spent in the margins.

'Y-e-e-s,' he repeated, drawing the vowel sound out further than necessary.

He'd spent his life being invisible, especially to women. It used to bother him, make him angry that he was constantly rejected by the stuck-up bitches, beginning with his slut of an aunt.

Well, they were noticing him now. His smiled widened, and he chuckled, amazed that he felt no fear. Not a trace.

They were all terrified of him.

'That's enough of that, man,' said the cop who'd arrested him. The stupid dumb bastard had barely looked at his old warrant card when he'd flashed it in the hospital.

Anderson turned to stare at the white-faced PC Lennox, who had a suggestion of a tremble in his bottom lip. He stared at the other cop, his expression flat and unemotional. Anderson looked beyond them to see half a dozen others, all in plainclothes, watching the proceedings, all probably members of the MIT team that were going to be dealing with him. There was a sense of anticipation in the stuffy air of the custody suite. He turned his eyes to PC Lennox again and held his stare for a full beat before the custody officer cleared her throat and spoke again.

'Mr Anderson, do you have a preferred solicitor, or should we call the duty?'

He turned his head slowly to face her, and paused before replying, 'Duty is fine,' his voice quiet but firm.

'Right. Go with PC Lennox and PC McSorley, here.' She pointed to both of the uniformed cops. 'I'm authorising a strip-search for any concealed items, and your clothing is going to be seized for forensic examination. Do you understand?' She looked directly at him, her pale face impassive.

He nodded.

'I'm also authorising that hand swabs and nail clippings are taken. Understand?' she said, her confidence rising and her jawline firming.

'My solicitor?' he said.

'I'll call the service right now. As soon as they arrive, you can have a consultation before you're bedded down for the night. You'll not be interviewed tonight as inquiries are still ongoing, but I imagine your solicitor will want to talk to you tonight owing to the gravity of the offence.'

He said nothing. Just continued to stare, holding her gaze without feeling a flicker of discomfort.

The air of triumph was there amongst the cops, the smug bastards thinking that it was all over. That they'd caught their man. He chuckled, ignoring the hard looks coming his way from the idiots in the custody office.

It was not even close to being over.

44

BARNEY TAPPED AT his keyboard after he'd inserted the SD card into the side of his battered computer. A few clicks and a map suddenly filled the screen. He snorted with mild amusement before looking up at Max and Janie.

'That were real easy. Simple plug into the car's GPS unit within the sat-nav circuit board and download, and it was easy to import and overlay into a map. It's all here, bugger's been all over – look.' He jabbed a stubby, calloused finger at the screen.

Max peered over Barney's shoulder at the map of Scotland, which showed a series of lines and blue blobs.

'Shit, that's a lot of moves and stops. Can we filter by times to coincide with when he purchased the car?' said Max.

'Probably, but it'd need software I don't have on this laptop, and it'd need Norma to filter it to really nail down the evidence that the inquiry team are going to need to back up their case.'

'Shame.'

'It's not all bad, I can see today's activities easy enough, although getting the timestamps will probably need a bit more sorting. From what I can see, he left Fort William early this morning, went to Cairngorm ski centre. I can then see that he went back to Fort William before heading here. What I can't tell at the moment are the times. I'm sure it'll be in the data, but it'll just need some time to extract.'

'This is brilliant evidence, Barney. Totally corroborates all the evidence we have and now it tracks him to all the crime scenes, and then takes him back to his base. And I'd assumed that the Fort William place was a burner address. How accurate will it be?' said Janie.

Barney scratched at his chin. 'I'd say to within three metres.'

'Does it put the car at a specific address in Fort William?'

'Well, it looks to me like it's parked up on the drive at the address it's registered to.'

'What, the Airbnb that the neighbour is clearly subletting?' said Max.

'It's certainly been there. I can't see for how long, although I'm not sure his phone is putting him there. I'll need to do a bit of digging to see if I can narrow that down.' Barney looked up, his face bathed in the light from the laptop.

'Are you in a rush to be anywhere?' said Max.

Barney waved his finger around inside the campervan. 'I'm always home, me. What do you need?'

'Me and Janie will head to Fort William and check out the address. He may just hole the car up there, so we need to be sure. We simply have to identify where he's been putting his head down, as there must be evidence there. Anderson had a key in his pocket, so worth a try, eh? If you can stay here and wait for the low-loader to come and remove the car?'

'Fine by me, lad. I'll pop the kettle on, it's a grand evening, and I can sort out the phone data. Always happy when I'm on the clock and the Chief Constable is picking up the tab.' He gave his easy, slow smile. Nothing fazed Barney, whether it was sitting about in a car park, or being in a covert listening post inches away from international criminals. He'd just smile and say, 'Fine by me, lad.'

45

IT WAS AS dark as it ever gets in the far northwest of Scotland in midsummer, as Max and Janie arrived at Fort William, the large Highland town in the shadow of Ben Nevis. The Munro was like a massive, amorphous dark blob that loomed imposingly over the town, like a black guardian angel.

They drove through the deathly silent streets until the sat-nav told them that they were at the address where everything suggested that Michael Anderson was living. A modest, 1970s semi-detached house on a small estate on the outskirts of Fort William, it was bathed in the sharp, pale moonlight.

'That's it,' said Janie, as she drew the Volvo to a stop.

'The one on the left?'

Janie looked at Max. 'Aye, one on the right is the one renting it out, probably a bit sleekit, like.'

'I'd call it enterprising,' Max said, 'while the probate wheels of justice creak on by. Shall we?'

Janie stifled a yawn. 'Aye, why not.'

They got out of the car and eased the doors closed, keen not to make any noise. They walked up the cracked and weed-knotted path where they were met by a half-glazed door with faded, peeling paint that may have been red, but had been turned silver in the moonlight.

'Seen the key box?' whispered Janie, tapping at the small enclosure that had been fixed to the architrave. Janie flipped at the numbers, but the box was locked tight.

'Try the key.' Max nodded towards the lock.

Janie just shrugged, and tried the key. It didn't fit. 'So, what's this key for, then?'

Max moved from the door to the window and peered in, the curtains being wide open. The room, which could have once been a living room only had minimal furniture, looked uncared for, and was dank and looked depressing.

Janie bent down and peered through the letterbox. 'Looks very empty to me.' She leant forward again, and sniffed loudly. 'Smells empty, as well.'

'Makes a change that it doesn't smell of death. That's what we normally encounter when we do this kind of thing.'

Max stepped back along the cracked path a few steps, and looked up at the first-floor windows, which were not shielded by curtains or blinds.

'Something not right about this place. Advertised on Airbnb, but no curtains, hardly any furniture and no signs of life. It doesn't add up.'

'What's going on?' A sudden, tentative voice made them both spin around. A middle-aged woman wearing a dressing gown and slippers was standing on the path, her hands clasped in front of her, almost as if in prayer.

Max pulled out his warrant card and held it up. 'Police. Who are you?'

'I'm Mrs McCoist. I stay next door. Is there a problem?' she said, concerned.

'Who's living here, Mrs McCoist?' said Janie.

'Nobody. It's going through probate after old Rory died a while back.' The words almost seemed to catch in her throat, and the nerves were palpable.

'So, tell us about the Airbnb, then?' said Max, gently.

'I've no idea what you're talking about,' she said, clasping her hands even tighter.

'Mrs McCoist, we know it's been listed online, and we know it was listed from a number at your address. Now, we couldn't care less about that, we just need to know who has been renting it from you, and we need to get in.'

She visibly relaxed and sighed. 'I've no idea who it is. A mannie did rent it, and has continued to for a few weeks now, but I've never seen him.'

'What, never?' said Max.

'Well, I've heard the door go a couple of times, and noises from within, but only very infrequently. I also saw him walking down the path to his car, but he was just a shape. I never spoke to him once.'

'How was he paying you?' said Janie.

'Via the website, I was a bit reluctant to rent to him, as it was a brand-new account, and he had no reviews, but it's not like this is a prime place for an Airbnb, so beggars cannae be choosers, eh? Look, am I in trouble? The place was empty, there are no relatives, so it made sense while it was just empty to make a little bit of coin out of it, eh? Only fifty a night. Surely, I'm no in trouble for that?' she said, her voice trembling.

'Mrs McCoist, I don't care about it at all. Now, do you have a key?' said Max, his voice not harsh.

'It's in the key box. I used to look in on old Rory daily so he had the key box put on so he wouldn't have to get up to let me in. He was a lovely wee auld chap, but so lonely.'

'Aye, I can imagine. Number?'

'What, my phone number?'

Max sighed, the exhaustion biting hard as he raised a finger towards the door. 'Key box?'

'Oh, yes, of course, that makes more sense. It's four-three-two-one.' A small, thin smile stretched across her sallow cheeks.

Janie reached up to the container and swivelled the tumblers around until the digits were aligned. After she flicked down the catch, the box dropped open and a key fell into her hand.

'Are you sure I'm no in trouble?' said Mrs McCoist, in little more than a whisper, genuine fear touching her eyes, which were coal black in the half-light.

'No, well, not with us, just maybe don't tell the tax man, and maybe don't mention it to the local council. Now, you go back to bed, we're just going to take a wee look inside,' said Max, smiling.

She nodded, turned, and padded down the concrete path and headed back home.

Janie slotted the key into the door, and twisted and pushed. The door opened with a sharp creak. 'Shall we?' said Janie.

They stepped into the uncarpeted hall, where there was a small pile of post on the floor. Janie quickly snapped on a pair of nitrile gloves, and stooped to pick it up and leafed through it.

'Anything?' said Max.

'Mostly pish, but there's what I'm pretty sure will be a bank card in this one, recent date on postmark, and addressed to Rory Jones. I'd say it's ex-DC Anderson's newest snidey bank account ready for his next job.'

'We'll take that away with us. Let's check the rest of the place. You fancy upstairs?'

'What if there's an axe-wielding homicidal maniac up there, ready to remove my nappa from my shoulders, eh, sarge?' Janie began to ascend the creaky staircase.

'I'll mourn your death, constable.' Max headed into the rest of the ground floor of the house, walking to the sparsely furnished kitchen. It had basic utensils, appliances and a chipped Formica-topped table with a single chair. Max opened the fridge, and found that it was empty apart from a putrid-looking plastic bottle of milk. The date showed that it was weeks old.

He moved through to the lounge, which just had a worn sofa and an old, bulky TV in the corner. Other than that, it was empty.

'Upstairs is stark as everywhere else. Just one room made up with a single bed with linen that I reckon is older than the house.

No one has slept in it, that's for sure,' said Janie as she entered the kitchen.

'No bugger's stayed in here for weeks, and certainly not "Rory Jones".' He mimed quotation marks with his fingers.

'So why bother with it then, and where is he actually staying?' said Janie.

'Gives him some legitimacy, I guess. Registers his phone, bank accounts and car here, and allows him to get mail safely. He's not stayed here, that's for certain.'

'So where's he been? Sat-nav and phone put him in Fort William.'

'I'm willing to bet that Yorkshire's answer to James Bond's Q will have an answer.' Max pulled out his phone and dialled.

'Ayup, you found 'im?' said Barney.

'No.'

'Not surprised, he's not been kipping there. I'm just getting me head around the car's data, but I suspect he's about five minutes from where you are now. The GPS on this car is actually pretty accurate from what I can see and has plotted his movements beautifully since he bought it a few weeks ago. Most nights it's been parked up on a drive of a nearby address. I'll text it to you, but it needs checking out. Something on the coordinates doesn't look quite right.'

'Nice one, Barney, we'll get straight on it.' Max hung up.

'What do you know?' said Janie.

'A new address, nearby, although Barney says there's something odd about the coordinates.'

Janie nodded. 'We'll find it.'

'Aye, we have to find it. The bastard has been laying his head down somewhere near here, and we can't go back without identifying where. He's a serial killer, and we all know of a nasty habit they can have?'

'I'm not sure I do,' said Janie.

'Serial killers like to keep trophies from their victims.'

46

HAMISH MICHAEL ANDERSON was sitting on the plastic-coated mattress in his cell, trying to clear his mind and focus on what to do next. He knew it was all over for him, personally, even though his previous arrogance had led him to believe he never would be caught. He didn't care. In fact, it was almost a relief. He'd accepted that he was a dead man many years ago.

He hated women. He didn't care about being judged, either in this life, or the next. His mind reeled as the vision of his Auntie Eunice swam into his mind. Her cruel smile, her beehive blonde mop, her foul breath, and worse, how she made him feel. Lower than a snake's belly. Well, he fucking showed her, and he showed all of them.

The small opening rattled, and a face appeared at the cell wicket. It was Malachy, the taciturn blue-uniformed custody support officer, who had treated him with barely disguised loathing ever since he'd arrived in this stinking cell block.

'You not sleeping?' he said.

'Could you, if circumstances were reversed?' said Anderson.

'Probably not, but then I never threw innocent women off cliffs. Custody sergeant wants to know if you want food.' The support officer's eyes were hard.

'What's on offer?'

'Microwave curry, or microwave spag-bol.'

Anderson snorted with derision. 'Tempting. I've a distant memory of the curry not being too vile.'

Rather than answering, the support officer just grunted and slid the metal wicket shut with a sharp rattle.

Anderson sighed as he looked at the graffiti scratched into the thickly painted walls, wondering if this was going to be it forever. Staring at impregnable walls and plated-glass windows. His bruised and battered face throbbed relentlessly. He brushed the tender skin with his fingers; it felt almost hot enough to fry an egg on. He cursed the bastard cop who had Tasered him, his hand going to the sore spots on his arse that still stung. He wished he'd gone out exactly like he'd always imagined he would. In a blaze of glory, his job done, the bastard cops beaten.

The rattle of the cell wicket awoke him from his reverie, and a cardboard food box was thrust through. He accepted the box, and the Styrofoam cup that followed. 'It'll be bloody roasting, so take care. *Bon* fucking *appetit*,' said Malachy, before he slammed the small hatch shut again.

Anderson sat down on the mattress, placing the cup on the floor. He opened the box, to find the familiar plastic and clingfilm of a microwave curry meal for one. He sniffed, and his memory surged of handing out similar meals to prisoners when he'd been a jailer in other custody suites years ago. He picked up the plastic spoon and dug into the neon orange gunge. It wasn't actually that bad, and despite the situation he was in, he found that he was actually hungry. He chewed at a gristly lump of what could have been chicken, but could just as easily have been lamb, such was the pungent flavour of the sauce. It was fairly meagre, and within two minutes he'd scraped the plastic tray clean. He tossed the box onto the floor of the cell.

Then something caught his eye.

The plastic tray had fallen from the cardboard box and had been upended. Something had been taped to the bottom. He reached down, his skin prickling with excitement.

A note. A small scrap of paper had been taped to the bottom of the tray. Carefully he picked off the note, the tape still attached, and looked at the small, neat handwriting.

A smile stretched across his face. He rolled the paper up between his fingers, raised his hands to his mouth and popped the note in, swallowing the scratchy, tape-covered scrap, washing it down with the unpleasant cup of tea, or possibly coffee.

He chuckled as he felt the note slide down his throat.

47

'IS THIS IT?' said Janie as she pulled the Volvo to the side of the road in front of a double-fronted detached property. It was a smart, new-looking building that was half-clad in timber, with a long drive that led up to a double garage. There was a brand-new Mercedes saloon parked, dark and inert on the drive.

Max looked at the pinned location on the map on his phone; the red dot was planted square at the end of the drive. 'Aye, looks like it. Barney said that he's sure that the phone has been right here, and that the car GPS put it right on this drive, so it has to be.'

'It's late. Reckon we knock, or just try the key?'

'Something about this doesn't feel right. Norma emailed me all the details she can find on the place. Owned by a Mr and Mrs Harrison, and that car is the only one registered here. Nothing on them; they were victims of a fraud a while back, Mr Harrison is an offshore worker. I say we knock first.'

'Norma is almost as job-pished as you, Craigie. She's still up?' Janie stifled a yawn with the back of her hand.

'Aye, I told her to hit the sack. Come on.' Max opened the car door and stepped out into the balmy evening, pulling the key that they'd found in Anderson's bag out of his pocket as they walked up the long drive. The door was sleek pale wood with a long brushed-aluminium handle, and a solid and modern lock. Max looked at the key. 'This definitely isn't for this door any more than it was for the last place.' He turned the plain Yale over in his fingers.

There was a kid's scooter in the open porch, which Janie pointed at. 'Kids in here. Softly, softly, yeah?'

'What you trying to say? I'm not Ross,' said Max, smiling as he jabbed at the doorbell. Soft chimes were audible from within the house.

There was nothing, just total silence, and deep darkness from within the property.

Max reached forward and pressed again; the chimes repeated like distant, soft church bells.

A light came on in an upstairs window, muted by curtains, which were then pulled back, and a face appeared, heavy and lined, as it looked down towards them in confusion. Max held his warrant card up towards the first-floor window, the metal badge shining in the moonlight. The curtain fell back into position, but within thirty seconds there was a rattle and a few muted clicks from the front door, which opened on silent hinges. A puzzled middle-aged man in a T-shirt and shorts appeared, his face full of sleep and irritation.

'Help you?' he said, in a soft Highland accent.

'Mr Harrison?' said Max.

'Aye.'

'DS Craigie, and DC Calder, sorry to wake you. Does a Michael Anderson stay here?'

His brow furrowed. 'No, just me and my wife and kids. What's this about?' he said, without hostility.

'How about Rory Jones?' said Max.

Mr Harrison's brow furrowed again. 'Name's not familiar.'

'Owns a VW Golf?'

Realisation dawned on the man's pale face. 'We've an Airbnb guest in the hut in the garden who has a Golf, I did'nae mind his name, though. Look, what's this about?' he said, a touch of irritation becoming evident in his voice.

'We've a man in custody for a serious offence and we think he's been staying here. Does this look like it could be the key to the hut?' Max held out the Yale.

Mr Harrison looked at the key. 'It's a Yale, so it could be.'

'Can you describe him?'

'Barely spoken to the fella. Middle-aged, scruffy beard, shoogly teeth, as I recall. He kept his self to his self, but now you come to mention it, he did say his name was Rory. I think he liked bagging Munros, like. I mind seeing him with ropes, and always dressed in hill gear.'

Max nodded at Janie. 'That's the man. Mr Harrison, we need to get into the hut, he's been arrested for something serious. Will you grant us permission?'

'Aye, of course. You want me to come?' he said.

'Not unless you want to.'

'I'm good. If you go to the side of the house, the gate's open and the hut's at the far end of the garden. Let me know if the key does'nae work.'

*

The hut was a little more than Max was expecting. It was a pristine one-bedroom chalet-style building, constructed from larch, with bifold doors and modern furnishings. It comprised a single living space, with a corner sofa in front of a TV and a small kitchenette. It was immaculately clean and tidy, with no personal possessions anywhere to be seen.

'Nice place,' said Janie, as she snapped a pair of nitrile gloves into place.

'Better than your tenement, eh?'

'I wouldn't go that far. I have a serious hi-fi.'

'And your saxophone, which I don't believe you can play,' said Max, grinning.

'I can, I'll just never play it in front of you. Now, can we get on? I'd like to get back to said flat, one day.'

Janie opened the small, but sleek fridge, which turned out to be moderately well-stocked with ready meals and a few bottles of beer. 'Looks like this is where he was actually staying, not just the mail-drop place before.'

'Aye, even more evidence here. Look . . .' Max had opened a drawer on a coffee table in which was a wallet that contained several banks cards, a sheaf of banknotes and a driving licence in the name Rory Jones. 'And lookie here, more work for Barney.' Max held up an iPhone in his gloved hand.

Janie looked around and pushed open a door, which led to a compact bathroom. There was only a bag of toiletries on the vanity unit.

Max pushed open the remaining door, which led to a bedroom with a neatly made double bed in the centre and a compact cupboard to the side. The cupboard had a number of garments hung up on the rail, and clean underwear on a shelf at the bottom. Everything was well ordered. 'A methodical man, is DC Anderson,' said Max, as he began to rifle through the clothing, systematically checking each piece.

'Must be something else here. No way does a serial killer live like this; there'll be more,' said Janie, appearing at the doorway. She opened the bedside cabinet drawer and saw that it was totally empty, and then stood back, scanning the room critically. She looked at the foot of the bed and noticed some light scratches in the laminate flooring by the lower edge.

'We need to lift the bed,' she said, her voice hard, and her eyes determined.

'I reckon you're right. Nothing in the cupboard. We must be missing something.'

Max gripped the end of the bed, and lifted. It was surprisingly light. Janie ducked down and peered underneath. 'Bingo,' she said, triumphantly, reaching below the bed and pulling out a scratched and worn-looking briefcase.

It was a square and boxy thing, with a three-digit tumbler combination lock on each clasp.

'I had a briefcase similar when I was at school, older than the hills, that,' said Janie.

Max chuckled. 'A briefcase?'

'Aye, what of it?' said Janie, looking perplexed.

'Not seen *The Inbetweeners*?'

'Oh, ha, ha. No, I wasn't known as Briefcase Wanker, sergeant. We need to get into it.'

'We could just bust it open?'

'Bad idea. What if he's rigged it for that, or we damage something inside?'

'Barney would be into it in seconds,' said Max.

'Hold up.' Janie held the opening switch and pulled it to the left with her thumb until it would go no further. Keeping pressure on the button she began to swivel through the digits one at a time, starting with the inner wheel, her face rapt with concentration.

'Janie, three digits means that there's a thousand potentials, we really don't have time for this,' said Max.

'Shh. I'm concentrating.' Janie continued to swivel through the digits, advancing the middle tumbler as she went. She continued this for about two minutes, before the lock pinged open, the combination locked in at 219. Janie grinned, and dialled in 219 on the other clasp and snapped it open.

Max stared at her, open-mouthed. 'Sorry, how?'

'My house mistress at school used to keep the exam answer sheets in a case just like this. We figured it out quite easily. If you pull the catch over as far as it will go, keep it tight and then just scroll through each of the tumblers quickly, you'll eventually get to it. Takes a maximum of six minutes.'

'No wonder you got good grades, I'm impressed. Let's see what we're dealing with, then.'

Janie carefully lifted the lid just an inch, pulled out a penlight torch and shone it in the gap. 'All looks okay. No weird booby traps or anything.' She flipped it open wide. An old and scratched laptop was inside, along with a 4G dongle and a charger. The letters FTF were scratched into the surface of the lid of the laptop.

'FTF?' said Max.

Janie just shrugged and pulled out the laptop, resting it on the bed along with the charger and dongle. She flipped through the lid compartments and pulled out a plastic wallet, which contained four syringes, each with a capped needle. There were also eight small glass vials each marked, ACTRAPID-100 INTERNATIONAL UNITS/ML INSULIN HUMAN.

'Note that one syringe is missing. That's significant, aye?' said Max.

Janie nodded. 'Maybe he's diabetic?'

'No idea, but we should let custody know, in case he's not bothered to tell them.'

Janie rummaged in the bag a little more, pulling out a leather pouch, about the size of a pencil case. She looked up at Max, who just nodded. She unzipped the bag and peered inside.

'Oh, Jesus suffering fuck.'

'What?' said Max, looking at his partner's face, which was growing pale.

'You were correct, Max. The bastard *has* taken trophies.' Janie upended the pouch, and emptied the contents onto the duvet top.

A driving licence in the name Leanne Wilson.

A silver locket, smeared in blood.

A hair grip.

A smashed pair of sunglasses.

A lip balm.

A slim gold watch, spotted with dark blood, the bezel cracked and smashed.

A bloodied and cracked tooth.

Max exhaled softly and picked his phone from his pocket.

'Max?' said Ross, his voice thick with sleep.

'Anderson is now a confirmed serial killer. We've found all his trophies. Get him locked down, Ross. Get him watched twenty-four/seven. This boy has nothing to lose.'

'What do you mean?'

'Given a chance, I reckon he'd top himself.'

48

ANDERSON WAS ONLY half-listening as his solicitor, who'd introduced himself as Jacob something or other, droned on across the desk from him. The consultation room was a half-glazed space that wasn't covered by CCTV, and there was no recording equipment in there, since it was where legally privileged information was shared. It felt like a goldfish bowl, not helped by the miserable jailer, Malachy, staring at them from outside the room where he'd been ordered to stand guard.

'Mr Anderson, did you hear what I said?' Jacob looked at him with tired eyes from behind thick-lensed spectacles, his heavy cheeks wobbling as he spoke.

'Aye, interview in the morning, and you'll come back. Fine.'

'Just remember, Mr Anderson. Say nothing, talk to no one, and do absolutely nothing until I'm back here. I cannot overstress that point enough. Say one thing off the record, and you can be sure that it will make its way very much *onto* the record. Am I clear?' He stared directly at Anderson, his face serious.

'Crystal. Nae bother.' Anderson reached for his Styrofoam cup and took a sip from it, as Jacob raised his finger to Malachy, indicating that the consultation was over.

Malachy propelled himself away from the wall that he'd been leaning on, and opened the door, just at the exact moment that Anderson sent the cup across the desk, its contents spilling over the papers that had been spread all over the Formica-topped table.

'Oh, bloody hell,' said Jacob, grabbing at the papers and brushing at the water that had splashed all over his grey slacks.

'Ach, you clumsy fud,' said Malachy, before disappearing into the medical room next door.

Anderson reached under the desk, feeling with his hand into the far corner. It was there, smooth and sleek, and attached to the table's underside with tape. He pulled it off and palmed it, just as Malachy came back into the room with a fistful of paper towels, which he handed to the solicitor.

'I'll see you in the morning, Mr Anderson,' said the seriously pissed-off Jacob.

'Aye, sorry and all that,' he said, trying to keep the grin off his face.

'Come on, then. Time for you to get your head down, boy,' said Malachy, ushering Anderson out of the room, and back into the custody suite.

'Sergeant Smith, that's Mr Anderson all finished with his solicitor. He'll be back in the morning for an interview,' said Malachy, as he led Anderson to the space in front of his desk.

The inspector looked up. 'Ah, Mr Anderson. Good timing, I'm Inspector Tom Jeffries, duty inspector. I'm required to review your detention after a certain time to make sure that you're being kept in accordance with all the rules. I'm authorising further detention now, so that you can be interviewed tomorrow, understand?'

Anderson shrugged and yawned deeply.

Inspector Jeffries nodded, and tapped at the computer keyboard. 'I'll update your solicitor of this, okay?' He picked up the ringing phone on the desk and listened to whoever was talking, and then his eyes opened wide as he glared at Anderson. Anderson knew then that whoever it was, was calling about him. There was something in the inspector's glare. He knew that things were progressing. He had no time to waste.

'Aye, whatever,' said Anderson, already walking off back to

his cell, jamming his hands in his tracksuit pockets as he trudged down the corridor, his gutties squeaking on the polished floor, Malachy and Smith close behind.

'Get your head down, pal. You've a busy day tomorrow,' said Sergeant Smith.

'You want the lights down?' said Malachy, as he ushered him into his cell.

'Aye, may as well try and get some kip,' said Anderson, falling onto the hard, unrelenting bed, and pulling the blanket over him.

Malachy just sneered at him and shook his head.

The door slamming reverberated, almost shaking his fillings loose, and the lights went down; not totally out, but much dimmer. He knew then and there that he needed to act now, or he may not get another chance. He pulled the item he'd taken from the consultation room from his sleeve, keeping his hands under the coarse blanket. He knew what he'd have to do. But not yet.

He'd know when.

The bastards would regret crossing him.

49

JANIE PROPELLED THE Volvo fast and skilfully out of Fort William heading back towards Inverness, ninety minutes away, as Max updated Ross on the phone.

'Fucking hell, so how many souvenirs has the bastard taken?' said Ross, his voice harsh and mechanical as it came from the car's speakers.

'Hard to say entirely. There may be more than one per victim, but if it was one each, then seven,' said Max.

'Seven? Shite.'

'Aye, exactly.'

'Are you heading to Inverness? The MIT are gonna have to take this on now, and they'll need to beef their team up. I've already alerted Miles Wakefield, and he is getting resources scrambled. At least we know we have our man now, and as an ex-cop he'd have been able to get the low-down. We can take our time trying to uncover who his source was, but I think we've done our side of the business, Max. Brilliant work, both of you. And you know how I feel about praise.'

'Aye, maybe,' said Max, unable to put his finger on the cause of his reticence.

Ross's tone took on a caustic edge. 'What's that miserable bastard voice for?'

'Something's still not right, Ross.'

'I'm sure, but we've been full-on with this, and we need some rest. I also should point out that your lovely wife is the size of a bastard hoose and is probably missing you for some strange fucking reason.'

'I know, I know, but something is still wrong,' Max said, rubbing at his eyes, which felt gritty and tight. His thoughts shifted to Katie at home, probably in bed with Nutmeg next to her, probably worrying about the baby. His insides boiled with guilt. He should be with her. Ross's harsh voice brought him back into the present.

'Look, we need to sit down, go through what we've got and dot t's and cross i's, or some shite like that, but it's the wee small hours, and we all need a break. Get to Inverness, hand over the productions from the briefcase, and get a hotel. Then get back here tomorrow and we can reassess, okay?'

'Aye,' said Max, the fatigue beginning to bite hard.

'What's Grandpa doing?' said Ross.

'Meeting us at Burnett Road. I want him to take a look at the computer before anyone else does. If they send it off, Christ knows how long it'll take, and they have plenty to interview and charge him with. The video on the phone from the victim on the Coire is bang to rights, but there's something about this whole situation that still feels unfinished.'

'Aye, maybe, but you guys have blown the whole fucking thing open. Get back, get all the productions into the MIT and then get home. For once, I think we have time on our side.'

Max wondered if this was true as his thoughts shifted away from the investigation towards his wife, a hundred miles away.

50

THEY MET BARNEY at Burnett Road nick car park where they handed the laptop and iPhone over for him to quickly assess before they contemplated their next move. It took just one minute for Barney to give his considered verdict.

'I don't like the look of this beggar. It's a piece of junk old thing, but from what I can see it's encrypted to buggery. Leave it with me, but it may take a while. If I rush it, it could wipe, and I suspect that'd not be great.'

As they walked into the CID office Max immediately recognised DC Doreen Urquhart sitting behind a desk next to a huge crate that was full of clear plastic evidence bags. DC Urquhart was a criminal productions specialist and was exacting in her standards, but she was not fast, and would never be hurried. 'Seen it's our old pal Doreen on productions again. I'm glad we gave Barney the head-start with the computer and phone. Once she gets hold of it, we'll never see the bastard again,' whispered Max as he nodded at the harassed-looking DC, who was noting bag numbers and recording them into a ledger.

'Good decision, sarge. It's why you get paid the big bucks, but we'd best hand over the trophies and stuff; they'll need them for interviews tomorrow.'

PC Lennox was seated behind a nearby desk, scribbling into his notebook frantically, his body armour discarded and his black wicking top shabby.

'You okay, Jim?' said Max, as he sat in the empty chair opposite.

He almost flinched as he looked up from his notebook. 'I've had better days, man.'

'Get him all booked in okay?' said Janie.

'Yeah, but there's something really skin-crawling about the bastard. He creeped out everyone in the custody block, even Sergeant Smith and Inspector Jeffries, who are both old campaigners. I never thought I'd see them weirded out,' said Lennox.

'Did Sergeant Smith book him in?'

'No, Sergeant Cotton did, and he was really fucking weird to her as well. I'd say he does'nae like women. Ed told him to shut the fuck up, eventually.' He sighed and scrubbed at his face with his hands.

A noise from the corner of the office made them all look up to see a tired-looking DCI O'Neill striding over, yawning widely as he did. His tie was pulled low, and his shirt was crumpled.

'Anything on the search of Anderson's place?' he said without preamble, stifling another yawn.

'Aye, although he was using a pseudonym of Rory Jones. Place in Fort William,' said Max.

'Much found?'

'Aye. A phone and a computer that our tech expert is taking a preliminary look at now, if that's okay with you?'

'Aye, be my guest. In fact, that's a big help. We're going to restrict ourselves to basing the immediate case on the phone you found, and witness statements from the MRT people who got there after Anderson called it in. That'll be enough for the Fiscal to authorise the charge and get him to court quickly and remanded to prison. We can sweep the rest up once he's safely away, as it's going to be long and painstaking. I don't want him here longer than necessary,' said O'Neill, firmly. This was common practice in serious cases. Prove the obvious and immediate first in order to secure a charge that could be dealt with during the legal time limits.

'Nae bother,' said Max.

'Anything else found?' said O'Neill.

'Aye, trophies. Plenty of trophies – it doesn't look good, boss. I suspect that they'll lead to other victims we don't know about yet. There's a driving licence, a hair grip, some jewellery, some of which is bloodstained. We have a serial killer on our hands, here.'

O'Neill sighed, and almost fell into the vacant chair nearby. 'This is gonna be huge, folks. Like, really huge. I've had the DCC onto me already, wanting updates before we've even got moving. I've asked for a load more staff, which hopefully I'll be getting tomorrow.'

'Does it change what you do?' said Janie.

O'Neill shook his head. 'The priority remains the same. Get enough evidence to charge and remand on today's case. The rest can start once he's safely banged up. Anything else?'

'Just some insulin and syringes. Is he diabetic?'

O'Neill frowned. 'Not that anyone has told me, but I'll check. Good work today, guys. I'll be sure to extend my thanks into the right quarters, but apart from the tech assistance, I think we can let you go. We have our man, so we'll take it from here.'

He stood, nodded and left.

Max and Janie just looked at each other. They'd been working together for some time now, and they could almost read each other's thoughts.

'I know that look, Craigie,' said Janie.

Max just shrugged.

'So, what's next?' she said, returning his weary smile.

'Let's go and see how Barney is getting on with the laptop, check out the CCTV situation with Ross and then let's head south, and pick this up tomorrow afternoon. Unless you want a free hotel?'

'No way, it's early hours already, and I want to wake up in my own bed. How about your bike?' Janie said, wearily getting to her feet.

'It'll be fine at Inverness; I'm pretty convinced we'll be back up here sooner rather than later.'

'Shall we get weaving then, sergeant?'

'Janie?'

'Aye?'

'Call me sergeant again, and I'll drive home.'

'Now that's a fate worse than death, and with your grandpa-driving, it'll take all bloody night to get home. Let's go.'

51

SURPRISINGLY, IT WAS the London dream that ripped Max from sleep at close to ten the following morning. A flashback to that day a few years ago when he'd shot a bank robber who was about to let rip with a sawn-off shotgun. As always, it was the yawning chasm that was the double barrels swinging in a slow, deliberate arc wielded by the masked gunman outside the bank. His hands, clutching the Glock 19, seemed to be progressing with aching slowness through the treacly London air. The pistol bucking twice in his hands, the bullets smacking into the chest of the raider, his eyes widening in shock as he fell, already dead when he hit the floor.

Max sat up in bed, gasping, the breaths rattling from him, his sweat-soaked chest pounding, his mind feeling like a cog had worked loose.

'You okay, babe?' You're sweating and breathing heavily. A dream, or something you'd rather not share.' She grinned, as she sat on the bed with a grimace, and laid her hand on his chest, then pulling it away, her lips curling at the sweat.

'Aye, a wee dream.' Max sighed.

'Afghanistan?'

'London.'

'You okay now?'

'Aye, fine.' Max tried to smile, but he wasn't sure that it was reflected adequately on his face.

'You sure?'

Max nodded.

'Max, talk to me, please?'

'It's nothing, just a dream.' He leant across and pecked her on the cheek.

Red spots appeared on Katie's cheeks. 'Seriously, you can't keep doing this.'

'What?'

'Shutting me out. You've been having these dreams more regularly, Max. Why? Are you worried about the baby coming?' Her normally soothing voice was harder edged.

'Of course not. It's just been a trying couple of days, babe. I'll be fine, it's drawing to a close now.' Max wondered if this was even true, but he smiled at his wife, and kissed her again, hoping this would change the subject.

'I didn't even hear you come in. What time was it?' said Katie.

'Almost four. Janie dropped me off. How're you feeling?'

'Okay. Huge, and hips are sore, the little bugger keeps shifting around, and I'm not sure there's much room anymore.'

'Your bump has dropped,' said Max, looking down at Katie's swollen stomach, swathed in the thin cotton of her dressing gown.

'I look hideous.'

'You look beautiful.' Max reached for her hand.

'You're biased. I hope this sod comes soon. What's happening today?'

Max looked at the clock in on the bedside table. 'Janie's picking me up in half an hour.'

Katie's face fell, and she sighed, deeply. 'Why am I not bloody surprised?'

'Sorry, it's been a rough couple of days, and we've still lots to do. Nasty business – do you want to hear about it?' Max looked at his wife's face and wasn't surprised to see the sadness in her eyes.

Katie shook her head. 'No, I don't. In fact, no, I fucking don't in the slightest. I want my husband to faithfully promise me that he will be present for the birth of our first child.' She glared at him, her eyes damp.

Max felt his heart lurch in his chest, feeling a wave of overwhelming love for her. He squeezed her hand in his, and put his other hand on the bump.

'I promise. I'll be there. I love you, Katie.' He felt his face flushing.

Katie's cheeks reddened again, and her eyes hardened. 'As much as you love your bloody job?'

'What kind of question is that?' said Max.

'An obvious one. I've barely seen you, I've had a false labour, I'm sore, and I'm fucking lonely, and yet you still piss off to work?'

Max opened his mouth to retort, but then snapped it shut again. He lowered his eyes. 'Sorry. I promise. I just need to sort this job, and then I'm all yours.' Max's head was thumping, and shame filled him. An almost physical feeling of it overwhelming him. Tears pricked in his eyes.

Katie's demeanour instantly softened, and she raised her hand to his cheek and kissed him. 'Go on, sod off and get a shower, you stink, and Janie will be here any time. I'll make you a boiled egg. Lynne handed a dozen over the fence this morning.'

Max smiled, their eyes connected, and something passed between them. 'Just this job, babe, and then I'm done. On leave, I'll tell Ross, no arguments.'

Katie grinned. 'Now bugger off and go save the world.'

52

THE OFFICE WAS a hive of activity when Max and Janie walked in just before eleven. Ross had his phone clamped to his ear and was looking particularly dishevelled. His pale face was lined with fatigue, and his eyes were bloodshot and rheumy. His stubble was evidence of a poor, or absent, shave, and his off-white shirt was creased. He scowled as they walked into the office, and shook his head as he pointed at the handset. 'That's a load of fucking bollocks, Struan. It was my bloody people who uncovered this, and we are gonna keep poking around. It is most certainly not a fucking done deal, slam run or home bastard dunk,' he blasted into the handset, his face turning an even deeper shade of crimson than normal.

'Sounds interesting,' said Max, nodding at Barney and Norma who were sitting at her desk, conspiratorially muttering to each other and looking with intense concentration at Norma's bank of screens.

Ross clamped his hand over the phone and looked at Max. 'You've no bastard idea, Max. DCI fucking Struan O'Neill thinks this job is all done, the nugget. They're looking at all the trophies you two found, and comparing against the known victims, and hoping for the best as far as I can bloody see,' he almost growled, as he removed his hand from the phone and continued his diatribe. 'No, you fucking listen, Struan. My tech man has the computer and phone downloaded.' He jumped to his feet, wincing, and stormed out of the office, still barking into the handset.

Barney and Norma looked up and grinned at Ross's pugnacity. Next to them was a small package in a soft fabric wallet, with a cable snaking out of it and into Barney's worn old laptop.

'Going well, guys?' said Janie.

'Yes and no. iPhone you retrieved was easy enough to get into. Simple passcode protection, and he'd not been imaginative, shall we say. I've downloaded it, and it's ready to look at,' Barney said, not looking up from the screen of his laptop.

'That's good, right?' said Janie.

'Yes, I'm about to run it through some e-discovery software, and start comparing with Anderson's other phone, but the laptop is a different matter, so Barney says.' Norma tapped on her keyboard her eyes flicking between monitors, her face full of concentration.

'How so?' said Max.

Barney raised his head. His normal calm persona seemed to have been dented a touch; his eyes were full of frustration. 'It's a bit strange, as his phones have been slack as owt, but this computer has been professionally protected. Like, top end. Full disc encryption, serious password together with two-factor authorisation. I also suspect that it has remote wipe in place, hence I've put it in a Faraday pouch, so nothing can get in, or out.' He tapped the fabric wallet in between them.

'Can you crack the encryption?' said Max.

'Mebbe, but it's a risk. I know me way around cybersecurity, but I'm no hacker, and this bloody needs one. I'm worried if I use my normal steps and methods, that the whole thing will fry, along with whatever badness is on it.'

Max stroked at his chin, trying to push the fog of fatigue away. It didn't make sense. Anderson's phones had been easily accessed, and his car's GPS was active and unprotected. He'd been careful, but not to this level. There had to be something on that laptop, something that someone else had wanted to keep secret. So much so that they had installed professional-level protection on the old and battered laptop.

'Take all care then, Barney. If he's gone to that much trouble, then there must be something worth protecting on that shite-looking laptop. What do you suggest?'

'I could ask Clive.'

'Who the fucking fuck is Clive?' said Ross, as he stormed back into the office, his face wearing a scowl.

'Call with DCI O'Neill go well, Ross?' said Max.

Ross's brow bristled menacingly. 'Man's a total fucking wankspangle. Telling me that he wants the computer product for interview.'

'He wasn't bothered last night. In fact, he was positively delighted to have it taken off his hands,' said Janie.

'Seems that the Chief Super at Inverness is getting a bit busy, and some bullshit victims' group is giving him gip. He's worried that if they charge him with just the one murder there'll be negative press, or some bollocks like that. Since when did anyone give a shit what they think in the *Inverness Courier*, eh?'

'Tell him from me that he's talking shite. No one at a standard forensic computer lab would be able to crack this anytime within a week. Clive could, though – can you authorise?'

'Authorise what?' said Ross.

'A bit of brass for Clive, he's the best hacker in the business,' said Barney.

'Whit? Who's Clive?'

'Barney just said, Ross. He's a top-level computer expert. We need this, and we need to pay for it. It's make or break,' said Janie, her face showing irritation at Ross's bumptiousness.

'You can get tae fuck, you cheeky mare. Any biscuits?' Ross's frown shifted, and his eyes glinted, amusement hiding in plain sight in amongst the bluster.

'Biscuits?' said Janie, rocketing to her feet, her face hard.

'You're disregarding legitimate concerns of a women's victim's group, as if the fact that a serial killer has been targeting lone women is "bullshit," and then you ask for fucking biscuits. Who the hell do you think you are, Ross?' Max had never seen Janie so angry.

A confused expression replaced Ross's sarcastic scowl.

'Aye, it's a bit sexist, to say the least, Ross,' said Norma, although her even tone was not matched by the look on her normally bright face.

'What?' Ross's eyes narrowed, his voice suddenly unsure.

Norma removed her glasses and looked at Ross, her eyes a little firmer. 'Ross, you do realise what we're dealing with here? A brutal misogynist killing women for some hideous, perverted reason. You do remember you have two women working with you? Maybe have you considered how this is affecting us?' Her voice was matter-of-fact, but there was steel in the gentle delivery.

Ross opened his mouth, his eyes flashing in the customary fashion, ready to engage. Then his mouth snapped shut. There was a long pause in the room. He looked between Norma and Janie, clearly unsure whether this was a joke. He opened his mouth, but Norma interrupted.

'Let's not forget that Janie was actually in the eye of the storm here, Ross. She put herself in harm's way with this bastard, even if he was playing with us. Have you thought how that makes her feel? And while I'm at it, I'm having to read endless fucking reports on women being murdered, just for being women. Have you for even five minutes considered whether this is bothering us? The job is full of bloody sexists, and this case is just compounding it.' Norma sat back in her chair, steepled her fingers under her chin and fixed Ross with a firm stare.

The silence in the room was almost overpowering, as Ross's gaze once again flicked between Norma and Janie.

Eventually he spoke. 'I'm sorry,' he said, his normally hard scowl softening, and the corners of his eyes down-turning a little.

'About what?' said Janie.

'For not asking about how you two were taking it. Or making sure that you were okay about going undercover, or how you felt about digging into this hideous shiteshow, Norma. I know I'm a bit of a coarse bastard, and sometimes my mouth runs away with me, but you know I've always had your backs, eh?' he said, his craggy face looking a little downcast.

'Aye, well, it's all good, but it'd be nice to be asked, yeah?' said Norma.

'We know you have our backs, Ross. You're a good boss,' said Janie, smiling before turning back to her computer.

'Aye, I get it. I'll do better,' said Ross.

The office was again thrown into an uncomfortable silence.

Then there was a sudden snort of laughter from Barney. 'Shite, mate, they just handed you your arse on a plate there, didn't they?'

'You can fuck off, you daft old codger, ya bum's oot the windae,' retorted Ross, his voice back to its normal irascible tone.

The whole office descended into gales of laughter before Ross spoke again. 'So, what *is* actually happening with the computer?' he said, his previous calm returning.

'Clive,' said Barney, accepting a steaming mug from Janie.

'What the bollocking shite-balls are you wittering on about, Barney?'

'Clive's gonna tek a look, and he's willing to get straight on it. He's the best in the business, ex MI5, and the best hacker I've ever worked with,' said Barney, sipping at his mug, before pulling out his scratched leather tobacco pouch and plucking a Rizla from a pack.

'Who is Clive, you blithering idiot?' said Ross, falling back into his chair, and cramming the whole teacake into his mouth, shards of chocolate dropping onto his desk and shirt.

'Computer geek I used to work with in Box. He's a bit weird, but he's the best hacker and decrypter I know. I don't think that I can get into this computer without frying the contents.'

'Fuck's sake, leave it alone. Your pal can do it, then?'

'Clive will be able to, I'm sure.' Barney stood and began to make his way to the door.

'Where are you going, now?' said Ross, his voice full of exasperation.

'Going to smoke this, leaving you enough time to work your legendary negotiating skills and rustle up some wonga for Clive to decrypt this bloody computer. If they've gone to the trouble of using top-level encryption on a shite old Lenovo Windows thing, then there must be summat on it.'

'And then what?' said Ross, rubbing his face with his hands in frustration.

'Well, as long as you're successful I'll drive down to Clive in Halifax.'

'Halifax?'

'Aye, Halifax. Market town in West Yorkshire, I'll 'ave this and then I'll set off.' He picked up his laptop and pulled out the cable. 'I'm heading now, no time to waste, eh? Let us know when wedge has been approved.' Barney looked at Ross as if he was an errant and slightly dull child, removed the roll-up from behind his ear, popped it between his lips and left the office.

'Shite, I know the cussed old bugger is good at his job, but he pushes me 'awa the line, sometimes,' said Ross, although the smile he was trying to keep from his mouth was more than evident in his eyes.

'He's right, though, Ross. We have no idea where this job begins, or ends. I suspect that MIT want to put it all down to Anderson, but I don't get one thing.'

'What?'

'His motivation. I mean, why?'

'Why does any serial killer kill? Because they like it, eh?' said Ross.

'I know, and he's a classic serial killer, even down to taking and keeping trophies, but there's more to it. I don't believe he was working totally on his own. We can be certain that he was getting intel from someone inside the police, but there's also what he said to us on the roof. He said that it didn't stop with him. Was that hyperbole? Or is it, as I think it is, an indication that he's not the only woman-hating murderer out there? If he was filming the murders, who was he filming them for?'

Norma cleared her throat from behind her screens, and stood, her face draining of colour.

'Norma?' said Janie.

'You're right, I think, Max. I mean, about Anderson not working on his own.' Norma looked worried, her brow furrowed, and she was plucking at her earlobe.

'What is it?' said Ross, without his customary belligerence.

'I've just compared the sat-nav on the car with the GPS on the iPhone, and compared against the deaths that are of concern, and something isn't right.'

'Go on?' said Max.

Norma sat, and shuffled her mouse around her desk, as she stared at the monitor with the familiar intense concentration. 'I've looked at date and time parameters for the suspicious deaths, on the various hills that your pal Shay flagged up, and it puts Anderson's iPhone and his car nearby in each case, apart from . . .' She paused and clicked her mouse again.

'Apart from?' said Ross.

'The death that raised this case. The one a week ago on A' Chralaig where Leanne Wilson died . . .' She swallowed.

'Norma?' said Janie.

'As far as I can see. Anderson was in Fort William all day that day. His iPhone and car didn't move from the property you searched last night.'

'He may have left them there and used alternative means. In fact, that would actually be good tradecraft,' said Max.

'I don't think so. Firstly, he's used the car to get him to other venues at the times of murders, so why change his method for Leanne Wilson?'

'I'm suspecting that there's more?'

Norma nodded. 'The phone was used to surf the internet while connected to the wi-fi at the premises he was staying at, and he was using it to cast movies from Netflix to the TV in his room. Also, the car moved, but just locally to the supermarket where he bought fifteen quid's worth of groceries using ApplePay. He was definitely in Fort William when Leanne was killed.'

Ross audibly sucked air into his lungs, his craggy face losing a little of its colour. 'Does this mean what I think it means?' he said, his voice a mixture of anger and sadness.

Max sighed and scratched his fingernails lightly over his stubbly scalp. 'Aye, boss. It means that there was always more than one of them.'

53

Glasgow, 2005

'**LET US GO**,' *she said, her face red and tear-stained, and her eyes flashing with anger. Her accent was pure, unadulterated Glaswegian.*

Mikey laughed at the sight of the semi-naked girl. A cheap slapper they'd picked up earlier, after a very drunken evening of celebration.

'C'mon, babe, the others have had their fun, now it's my turn,' Mikey said, his head swimming with the effects of the alcohol he'd been imbibing for hours. The sounds of raucous laughing came from downstairs, as the others were still clearly getting in and amongst the booze that had filled the fridge.

'No. Nae more, I want tae go, noo. You lot are fucking sick.' She shook off Mikey's hand that had been gripping her tightly by the bicep, and shot to her feet, gathering her clothes from the floor of the scabby bedroom.

'Where're you going, babe?' Mikey guffawed, standing up from the bed, staggering slightly, and not bothering to cover up his nakedness, as she headed towards the door.

'Awa' from youse pure fucking perverts, that's fucking where.' She disappeared out of the door, and into the putrid little landing.

'Come on, Karen, don't be coy; we paid you, didn't we?' Mikey said, laughing as he followed her out of the bedroom. She spun around like she'd been shot.

'Paid me? Fucking paid me? Thirty fucking quid for a quickie, and then all youse fuckin' lot pitch up? Get tae fuck, I'm getting' the fuckin polis in, eh? See how ye like that, and I know youse lot are all coppers, see how youse like it in Saughton wi' all the villains, eh?' She turned to the stairs, her narrow back facing him as she dropped, her foot lowering to the first tread of the staircase.

Fury surged in Mikey's chest, and almost reflexively, he shoved. His hands rocketed forward, one either side of her spine. She flew into the void of the narrow staircase, the momentum of the shove spinning her head forward before it smashed into the thinly carpeted staircase. She tumbled down, head over foot, until she hit the bottom with a sickening crack. She lay there, motionless, her head at an impossible angle, her eyes open and empty.

She lay still. Utterly motionless, and silence gripped the grimy house.

Mikey giggled.

Then he laughed.

The door at the bottom of the staircase opened, and the others appeared, their faces white with shock.

'Mikey, what the hell have you done?' said the closest.

Mikey chuckled again. 'What have we done, boys? What have we done?'

54

BARNEY WALKED UP the block-paved path towards the uPVC door of the anonymous newbuild in a suburb of Halifax.

While Barney knew it was Halifax – he'd driven here after all, and had even seen the sign that proudly proclaimed, WELCOME TO HALIFAX, FOUNDED 1794 – he had to admit that he could have been anywhere, such was the ubiquitous nature of housing developments like this one.

Before he'd even got to the door, it was flung open and the dishevelled form of his old colleague, Clive, appeared at the door, smiling widely and showing crooked, off-colour teeth.

'Barney, it's great to see you, my old friend.' Clive stepped forward, arms aloft, a neon-coloured piece of plastic in his hand about the same size and shape as a highlighter pen.

Clive's stiff embrace was both surprising and uncomfortable, and suggested to Barney that his old colleague had had some input from someone, somewhere, that a hug may be a nice icebreaker to relax his usual awkward manner.

'Clive, good to see you, mate.' Barney stepped back from the man-hug, and clapped the computer analyst on the shoulder.

'How've you been, my old friend?' he said, bringing the neon plastic item to his mouth and sucking at it, noisily. A voluminous cloud of fruity-scented vapour erupted from the device and was exhaled by the still grinning Clive.

'Middlin' lad, nobbut middlin'. What the bleeding 'eck is that thing?' said Barney.

'It's my vape, Grandad. Watermelon flavour – it's delicious. Want to try?'

Barney screwed his face up. 'I'll stick to me Golden Virginia, thanks.'

Clive appraised his old mentor through thick-lensed spectacles, one of his eyes slightly off-centre. 'Come in, come in, it's been so long. Tea?' he said, stepping back from the door.

'Always tea, mate. You know that,' said Barney, as he stepped across the threshold and into the uncarpeted hallway.

'Excuse the mess, I've not long moved in,' said Clive, pointing at the brand-new chipboard floor and boxes that were stacked up underneath the staircase, next to a scruffy racing bike.

'How long?'

'Six months, I bought it off-plan once the money on the new job started kicking in. Private sector is the place to be; I'm earning loads now.'

'And still not unpacked, Clive? We spoke about this, eh?'

'Yes, but I've been busy, and time is just an inconvenience misappropriated by the corporeal bodies of the weak.'

'If you say so, lad. Still got the old racer?' Barney pointed at the bike.

'Obviously, why would I trade Dorothy in? Cars are the scourge of the world, Barney, you know that.'

'When did you leave London?' said Barney.

'Right after I left Box. It was all too much for me, was that London. Too many bloody Cockneys, too many cars, and too many bloody people, so I came home. I can work from here, and can work in me pants if needed.' He raised his vape to his lips and sucked, exhaling a cloud of vapour.

'Glad you aren't today, lad. Last thing I need to see is your spotty arse in your ripped Y-fronts.'

Clive exploded into paroxysms of hilarity way more than the quip deserved, but Barney smiled along with his old protégé.

'Barney, man. You slay me, it's because you retired from Box that I had to leave. They had me doing financial intelligence, I mean, what a waste of my formidable talents, eh?' he said, leading Barney into the next room that the builders had probably intended to be a lounge.

Barney pulled out his tobacco pouch. 'If you're exhaling that shit, which stinks like melted pear drops, mind if I spark up a rollie?'

'Be my guest. I'd never deprive you of your nicotine, mate. Roll me one, too?' He raised his eyebrows hopefully.

'Isn't the flavoured steam enough?'

'Can't beat the original and best, mate.' He exhaled the sweet and sickly vapour with a grin.

Barney nodded, and with his usual practised ease rolled two thin cigarettes, one he tucked between his lips, the other he handed to Clive, and offered a flame from the old Zippo.

'Pure bliss, mate,' said Clive, the smoke wisping from his nose.

The 'lounge' was nothing of the sort. A huge, expensive-looking computer table dominated the rear half of the room, and both front and back windows were shaded by plain shutters. The overhead lights had been extinguished, leaving an eerie gloom, as the only light came from the bank of monitors competing for desk space with empty cans of Tango and a large tub of Percy Pig sweets. Piled-up hard drives and servers were neatly stacked, lights blinking, under the desk.

Each monitor showed scrolling numbers, symbols and characters, all of which winked and blinked, giving the room a strange, hypnotic feel. Soft chill-out music seeped out of large speakers that sat in the corner of the room, stacked on top of each other. One of the monitors was split into a gallery display of surveillance cameras, which seemed to have every corner of the house covered, both inside and outside.

The room was uncomfortably warm, despite the three fans that lazily pushed the sultry air around the stuffy space.

'Bloody hell, lad, this place looks like the situation room in the bloody White House,' said Barney, as he surveyed the space.

'Great, isn't it? I've so much processing power that there's not much I can't achieve from this room. Right, make yourself comfortable, and I'll make tea.' Clive flicked on the overhead light, which bathed the space in a weak yellow glow.

'Where?'

'Sorry?'

'I mean, where shall I sit, lad? I remember you hate it when people use your chair, and there's no other furniture.' Barney knew from experience that to sit on Clive's chair was tantamount to heresy, and would be the only time that the genial-natured man would get angry.

Clive looked flustered for a moment. 'Hold on.' He disappeared out of the room, returning within thirty seconds with a small folding chair, which he put on the plain floorboards. 'There you go. Milk, no sugar, right?'

'Aye, whatever. Come on, lad, hurry up, time's a marching on.'

'Fine, fine, I'm on it. What do you need?'

'I need you to look at this.' Barney handed over the Faraday wallet containing Anderson's computer.

Clive accepted the package and opened the flap, sliding his hand in to pull it out.

'Whoa, careful. It's in a Faraday bag. I think it has a wipe program on it,' said Barney, his voice rising an octave.

'Barney, please, this is my environment, here. This whole room is a Faraday cage. Special instructions when the house was being built. Nothing in, and nothing out unless I choose.'

Barney's eyes widened, and he looked at the pristine plasterwork. 'Must have cost you a bob or two. I can't see it.'

'A fortune. But it's better to be safe than sorry.'

'Why not just line the room with foil. Few rolls of Bacofoil and you'd have been grand.'

'People might think I'm weird. Particularly if I have a lady in here,' said Clive.

'Has that happened much?'

'Not many times, if I'm honest.' Clive averted his gaze from Barney's, and he shifted in his seat.

'Well, if you do bring a filly in here, then maybe show her this room last, eh? Now, crack on then, no time to waste.'

Clive pulled the battered laptop out from the case and turned it over in his hands. 'This POS? You've brought this antique to me, Barney?'

'Aye, but I plugged it in to my set-up and didn't like what I saw. Plus, there's definitely encryption on discs, and I'm sure I saw the signature of auto-wipe in the boot sequence, so I stopped before I buggered it up.'

'Let me see, then.' Clive began to hum tunelessly as he opened the laptop and plugged in a cable that attached to one of the ports on a hard drive beneath the desk.

'Good decision, Barney. Definitely has an auto-wipe installed. Hold up, just freezing and disabling now.' He continued to hum, his eyes flicking from screen to screen, as the numbers and characters tumbled and scrolled.

'Okay, that's no problem, it's safe for now, so let's look at this encryption,' he said, swiping, clicking and scrolling using his mouse and his high-tech keyboard.

'What's it look like?' said Barney, trying his tea again. It was tepid and insipid.

'Hmmm. Well . . . just a minute. Oh, you bugger. Just a mo. Not bad. Bloody amateurs.' He grinned as he tapped a key with a flourish.

'Bad or good?' said Barney.

'Decent level of encryption, but I should be able to decrypt with one of the bespoke tools I created for Alfa-Guard 900x, which is what this system has running. I just need to get past the password, now, which is complex. Do you have an intelligence profile for the owner?'

'Aye. I can forward it, but not in your Faraday cage.'

'Okay, go into the garden and send to my webmail address, and I'll run the algorithm, but it'll take a while. He's using a multi-characteristic, alphanumeric password, but it is a manual entry, so it'll potentially have roots in familiarity. Forward it to me now, and I'll get cracking.'

'How long will it take?'

'Depends.'

'On?'

'The profile you send me. How detailed it is will determine how quickly the algo will work. I'll also use other methods alongside in case he's been sensible, and not used his dog's name, or summat daft like that.'

'The profile is pretty detailed; Norma is a brilliant analyst.'

'Then I estimate forty-five minutes. If lucky, that is.'

'If unlucky?'

'Then never.'

'So, we need to be lucky. I'll go and send it now.' Barney walked out of the room and into the front garden, drawing with pleasure on the cigarette between his lips.

He quickly located the email from Norma, which contained the profile on ex-DC Anderson and forwarded it to Clive. His phone buzzed in his hand, just as the email sent. It was Max.

'Ayup, lad, what gives?' said Barney.

'Barney, how are you getting on with the laptop?' said Max, his voice tight.

'Clive's on it like a car bonnet, mate. Why d'you ask?'

'Because things have just got urgent; this isn't a sweep-up job anymore. There's more of them out there.'

55

CLIVE SUCKED ON his vape, his eyes flickering between monitors as he inhaled the fruity vapour, the nicotine flooding his system and firing his synapses, as he scrolled, almost in sync as the characters and numbers rolled.

Barney had left him to it, returning to his van to ''ave forty winks, lad. Don't want to cramp your style', as he eloquently put it. This was fine by Clive, as he did not welcome distractions while he was trying to break a password, particularly one as strong as this.

It was a conundrum, this computer. He was confident that it had been using the dark web, as he'd seen evidence of a Tor browser in the datascript, but until he fully gained access to the hard drive, he wouldn't be able to properly tell. But it still rankled. A cheap, crappy Lenovo laptop, with minimal processing power and a basic Intel Core 19 processor, and yet protected by a sophisticated password, and decent encryption, as well as the auto-wipe program. It was protecting something, and it felt fifty per cent professional, and yet somehow, a little amateurish.

He'd programmed the personal information into the password algorithm, which he hoped would speed up the attack, and couldn't help but look at the intelligence report as the algorithm was running. The servers were all humming, and giving off significant warmth, as Clive had also set a rainbow table hacking tool running alongside the brute force attack using the algorithm to try to defeat the password.

The photo of ex-DC Anderson hadn't given much away, but Clive was self-aware enough to realise that he wasn't the best at understanding his fellow men. He looked pretty normal to Clive, despite the hard-looking eyes.

This had made the possession of a simple computer, protected by state-of-the-art cybersecurity, all the more perplexing. Just what, and why? Did he have unusual tastes in pornography? It wouldn't be the first time that Clive had uncovered evidence in cases like this, but it was normally hidden in the dingy recesses of the dark web.

There was a soft tone, and the scrolling stopped. PASSWORD CORRECT. Clive smiled, and nodded slowly. *Nice try, ex-detective Anderson, but no cigar*. He looked at the password displayed on the screen, simply a long series of numbers and letters, which meant nothing to Clive, but probably meant that the intelligence profile hadn't been of much help, and it was the rainbow table tool that had decrypted the password. He looked at the timer he had set. Twenty-eight minutes. Twenty-eight minutes to defeat a complex and sophisticated password was good going. Once again, a computer that Clive couldn't break into had yet to cross his workbench. The screen cleared on the computer, showing a standard Windows desktop with a background photograph of a mountain range.

Clive clicked into the workstream, and nodded appreciatively. It had been the rainbow table that had cracked the password, not the brute force. It seemed that this was becoming the norm.

He looked into the list of programs loaded on the laptop. There was no email, no apps, and no Word files. In fact, on first look there was nothing beyond a Tor Browser icon. A purple circle, half with concentric lines, half solid purple. The Onion Router.

The portal into the dark web.

The route to private internet browsing, protected by a three-layer proxy, just like layers of an onion. Private, secure and almost impossible to trace the users of.

The perfect haven for criminals.

But why would an ex-cop, and murderer of lone women, have a laptop computer that was free of any files, icons or apps and whose only purpose seemed to be accessing the Badlands of the dark web?

A cough behind Clive made him start and visibly jump in his seat, such had his level of immersion been in his task.

He turned to see Barney, a smile stretched across his face.

'You nearly gave me a heart attack, Barney. You should know by now to not sneak up on me when I'm working.'

'Sorry, lad. Success, I see. Under half an hour, and all. Brute force?'

'No, I was running brute force along with a rainbow table, which was sensible of me, as that was what cracked it.'

'I never understood rainbow tables, but then I'm a bug man, not a hacker.' Barney shrugged, clapping Clive on the shoulder in appreciation.

'Oh, Barney. Rainbow table is simple as anything, basically it works by doing a cryptanalysis quickly and effectively. Unlike brute force attack, which calculates the hash function of every string present with them, determining their hash value—'

Barney held up a callused hand to silence his old protégé. 'No need for that now, mate. I know my area of expertise, and hacking tools isn't it. What's on the computer?'

'Seemingly nothing.'

'What do you mean, nothing?' Barney's forehead creased.

'Well, on the face of it, zilch. As in, whoever managed this computer, tried to clear up after each usage, but he made a mistake, I suspect.'

'How so?'

'As you know, you never truly delete anything from a computer, unless you overwrite it. There are programs that can flood a hard drive with ones and zeros, but I don't think he's used one. It looks to me like he's been using it mainly to access the dark web, and maybe a few other bits, but normal usage.' Clive tapped at the Tor icon on the screen.

'Can we see the history of where he's been surfing?' said Barney.

'You don't surf the dark web, certainly not in the same way as you do via a Windows or Mac browser. You need a specific address. There's no dark web Google, well, not in the same way, anyhow. It doesn't retain search history, we'd need a specific address of where he's been to find it, and it's not stored on the computer.'

'So, we're screwed, then?'

'I didn't say that. This is a well-protected computer, but I don't think he created the protection. He's slack. There's some hidden photo and video editing software, but nothing's been saved on it. Give me one second.' He began to move his fingers along a remote keyboard, humming softly as he clicked, tapped and swiped.

'As I thought, there's a load of images and videos that have been deleted. Hold up, I'll just use a little bit of software to retrieve it.' He hummed again, tunelessly, as he worked.

'Boom. Done. Videos, stills, montages. A good few of them, as well. He thought he was so clever, but no way was he clever enough for Clive the conqueror.' He spun in his chair and punched the air, triumphantly.

'Have you secured them?' said Barney.

'Oh yes, saved onto my drive: the whole bloody computer.'

'Play the first one, then,' said Barney, his face and voice both sharp, as he stared at the raft of video icons on the screen.

Clive moved the arrow over the first of the icons, and clicked on it. The wheel spun, and he shifted the spinning icon onto one of the larger hi-def screens. The player filled the monitor, and three letters appeared in turn on the screen.

FTF

'FTF? That's what's scratched on the lid of the laptop. What's that mean?' said Barney.

The question was answered as each letter dropped and moved to the side, bouncing as it did and joined by another letter. A whistling noise came out of multiple speakers and ended with a 'splat' noise, as three words formed:

FAR TO FALL!

56

ANDERSON'S FACE WAS impassive as he sat across the table from the stony-eyed man who had introduced himself as DS McSween. The meaty-faced detective in the cheap suit stared at him, with barely concealed fury. Anderson tried but failed to suppress a grin from forming.

'What's so bloody funny? said McSween's colleague, a very attractive middle-aged female detective who had introduced herself as DC Urquhart.

Anderson said nothing; just moved his head so that he was staring straight into the deep-blue eyes of the detective, who was pointing at a laptop computer on the desk. She had played the video clip taken by the bitch he'd shoved off the Coire, just the previous day. It was pretty damning, and yet it had been mesmerising to watch. Her terror, reflected in his sunglasses, was strangely exciting to him. It was an angle he had never considered. He'd always enjoyed the images he'd recorded on his own phone, but to have it from the point of view of the victim was actually very satisfying.

In fact, as he felt a stirring in his trousers as he grew hard, he realised that it was a little more than just satisfying, it was a proper turn-on. The fear in her eyes, the perfect 'O' formed by her mouth just as she fell, disappearing from view, the footage tumbling and moving from blue sky to grey granite as the phone bumped down the steep cliff.

It was beautiful.

And it was his swansong.

His final performance, and it was a tragedy that there would be no encore. He sighed, and yet he felt no sorrow. He'd lived his life, and he would leave his legacy. His name would be mentioned alongside all the others. Peter Sutcliffe, Dennis Nilsen, Levi Bellfield and many more. He'd achieved what he intended.

Notoriety.

DC Urquhart's barked question pierced his reverie, and he looked up, his eyes boring into hers with almost burning ferocity. He knew what he looked like to her, as he'd practised this stare on many occasions in the bathroom mirror. She didn't avert her gaze, but he saw it in her eyes. A chink in her armour. He knew that she'd be thinking about this stare for a long time after the interview.

'I'm sorry. Can you repeat the question please, Detective *Constable* Doreen *Urquhart*?' he said, his voice low, drawing out her name way beyond what was required, enunciating every syllable for maximum effect. He had practised his voice, too, for just this moment, he had even recorded it on a few occasions so he knew how menacing he would sound. This was something to be savoured. An experience to linger over and enjoy. It was only the soft cough of the idiot solicitor, Jacob, or whatever his name was, that jerked Anderson away from the moment.

DC Urquhart's mask slipped, and her lip trembled, only just visibly, as she opened her mouth to repeat the question, her eyes full of barely concealed alarm. She took a full beat to compose herself, and asked the question.

'You've seen the video we've just played to you, clearly showing you pushing the victim from the edge of Coire an t-Sneachda. Do you have anything to say about it, Mr Anderson?' She sat back in the chair as she finished, her shoulders sagging a little.

Anderson leant forward, slowly moistened his lips with his tongue and breathed, 'No. Comment.'

57

BARNEY AND CLIVE stared at the video clip that was in lurid, hi-def colour on the large screen in front of them.

A long silence hung in the stuffy room, only punctuated by the whirring fans and clicks of the servers cooling.

The video was shocking. Barney had seen much in his life, in Northern Ireland, Iraq, Afghanistan, and various other deniable operations on behalf of HM Government, but he knew then and there that the footage he had seen of the woman being pulled off the face of a cliff by an unseen hand on a climbing rope would live with him forever.

When the footage zoomed in on her dying face, he felt an icy hand begin to grip his stomach. Barney wanted to turn away, but he couldn't move his head, as he watched the poor woman's dying breaths on the harsh rocky ground, the camera steady and tight on her desperate eyes, full of pain and terror.

'Holy shit, is this real?' whispered Clive, his voice shot through with dark horror.

Barney said nothing, he just stared at the screen as the footage went blank, just to be replaced with the now-familiar letters.

FTF.

'FTF? Far to fall? What are these sick bastards doing? Barney, there's bloody loads of these video clips in the deleted files on this computer. What's the bastard been doing with them? Creating them from phone-shot footage, clipping them up in standard video editor and deleting them?'

'No, I think that he's sharing them. He's taking the videos for others, and sharing them.'

'How? He's no email on here, no messaging, no social media and no internet browser beyond a Tor browser.'

'Then that's how he's sharing them. How can we find where he's been?'

'From this laptop, we can't. Tor automatically deletes search history, so we can't see where he's been on this, and as far as I can see he's historically been using a VPN.' Clive's fingers danced across the keyboard, like a concert pianist doing a Rachmaninov recital.

'I'm not that clued on Tor and the dark web. How would he locate whichever destination he intends to upload these videos to?' Barney stared at the scrolling numbers and characters on the screen that were almost hypnotic in the dim light of the room.

'We'd hope he had it stored somewhere – unless he committed it to memory – but a Tor page address isn't like a standard URL on a normal browser. It's mostly gibberish to the uneducated eye. Fifty-six numbers and characters followed by dot onion. Unlikely he'd remember it, and I can't find any trace of such a thing stored on the computer. As I said, it's practically empty.' Clive scratched at his wiry hair, a frown on his pale face.

Barney looked at the laptop, worn and scratched, but with no clue of any Tor address. He ran his hands over the casing, and onto the trackpad. Where would he store such a piece of information? Something was tickling his mind as he looked at the flickering screen of the laptop that was mirrored onto the much larger monitor above their heads. He clicked his tongue against the roof of his mouth as he often did when thinking. Then it hit him. It was obvious. He clicked on the Tor browser icon, which then filled the screen with a purple webpage that declared, EXPLORE. PRIVATELY. Barney moved the cursor into the web address box.

'What did you say his password was?'

'I didn't, but it was basically a long line of numbers and letters.'

'How many?' Barney turned to look at Clive.

Clive opened his mouth to answer, and then snapped it shut again. He tapped on the screen and copied a long line of numbers and letters. 'I've not counted, Barney, but that looks like it could be about fifty-six characters, wouldn't you agree?'

'I would. Try it.'

Clive's fingers flashed across the screen, entering 'http://' into the password box, and then copying and pasting the password into the address bar before finishing with '.onion'. He turned to look at Barney in enquiry.

'Go for it,' said Barney.

Clive pressed the return key. A webpage filled the screen. Just a plain blue webpage with three words in the centre.

Far. To. Fall.

A box underneath simply made one request.

Password.

'If he's used it twice, I bet he's slack enough to use it three times. Try it,' said Barney.

Clive pasted the fifty-six characters into the password box on the screen. 'Let's see just how lazy you are then,' he said, as he pressed return.

Login successful. Username MikeyMunroSkulker,
you have 459 reactions to videos.

58

THE SILENCE IN the fuggy, smoky room was unpleasant, and thick with tension, as Barney and Clive stared at the screen.

They didn't speak. They were both struck mute by what they had seen.

Twelve videos.

Just twelve thumbnails, each with a brief description underneath, the most recent simply read, 'Huntly's Cave, fall and close-up.' There was a button underneath which read, 'Pay to view' and a counter that seemed to indicate how many times the video had been watched.

'Am I reading this right, Barney? Have 1,475 people paid to watch that video?' said Clive, his voice tight as a bowstring.

'It looks like it.'

'How much has that made them, then?' said Barney.

Clive clicked on his keyboard, his eyes widening. He tapped at the screen again, before frowning and tapping some more. 'Almost fifty thousand.'

'What? Fifty grand?' said Barney.

Clive turned to Barney before he shook his head. 'Sorry, no. Not pounds, but SATS, or Satoshi to give the correct name.'

'What the hell is a Satoshi?'

'Bitcoin. Cryptocurrency. Named after Satoshi Nakamoto, the anonymous person who published the paper that kickstarted crypto, in 2008.'

'How much is fifty thousand SATS worth?'

Clive turned back to the screen and clicked again. 'On today's prices, about a tenner. Each view. One time only, no facility for customers to download.' Clive faced Barney, the shock still written in his face.

'What, so he's just made almost fifteen grand for that video that was made yesterday?'

'Looks that way. All in Bitcoin that will be zapped off to a wallet that is attached to the website.' Clive tapped at the keys, before nodding to himself. 'Yes, got it. He used a Bitcoin wallet, which I can't access from the website. Let me give it some thought.' Clive leant back in his chair and stretched.

Barney nodded. 'Can we watch all the videos? Not that I want to, but the investigation team will need to.'

Clive nodded. 'As we've logged in as Anderson, we have full access rights, and I can use some jiggery pokery to secure all of this as it now sits, so we don't lose any evidence. If I change the password from the actual Tor website, I can ensure that no one else will be able to log in and delete evidence. Should I do that?'

Barney considered this. It wasn't his call, but he was here now, and they needed to secure this evidence. He was confident that Ross would agree. He nodded. 'Do it.'

'Done. Do you want to see any more of the videos?'

'No, lad. We've done our job uncovering and securing the evidence; it's down to the cops to watch these bloody things, the poor beggars.'

*

After they'd finished, Barney turned to Clive, whose normal pale pallor was now white as virgin snow, and he trembled as he stared at the screen, his eyes wide.

'What the fuck is this about, Barney?' he said, in little more than a whisper.

'Looks like a snuff site. I've never seen anything like this, in all my bloody years . . .' Barney stopped, his mouth open, unable to form the words.

Barney clapped him on the shoulder, and stood. 'I need to make a call, and then we'll see.' Barney pulled his phone from his pocket, left the room and headed out into the garden. He dialled.

'About fucking time, Grandpa. I hope you've done whatever incomprehensible bullshit you set out to do,' said Ross, his voice seemingly forcing the typical sarcastic abuse.

'We've had a development. Clive cracked the computer and managed to access the dark web site that Anderson had control of. It's all there, Ross. All fucking there; he was running a fucking snuff site. There're twelve videos on there. I've not watched them all, but it looks like it's all women being killed.' Barney's voice had an atypical tremor to it.

Ross said softly, 'You okay, pal?'

'I'm fine, but we need to nail that fucker to the wall, Ross. I'm securing all the evidence now, but the MIT will need a team to dig deep into this, ready for the interviews and that.'

There was a pause and Ross cleared his throat.

'Ross?' said Barney.

'DCI O'Neill's just called with an update. Anderson has just been charged with murdering Susan Brown at Huntly's Cave and attempting to murder Shona Grant, who is the woman at Raigmore Hospital. He goes to Inverness Sheriff Court tomorrow morning. He's heading for jail on a seven-day laydown for the team to get into it properly.'

'But what about all this? Ross, there's shitloads of evidence on this computer, and it now involves many, many more people than just Anderson. Every bastard who watches or shares these videos is complicit – you should see the bloody comments,' Barney said, his delivery much faster than normal.

'Barney, mate. It's fine. Get all the evidence secured, get back to

Tulliallan, and we'll make a plan. We don't stop with Anderson, not a fucking bit of it. We'll charge him with bloody everything we can prove, but it's gonna take time; we have a bigger priority now. Getting whoever else is involved. All of them.'

Barney exhaled, feeling uncharacteristic tension in his temples.

'Right, I'm on my way back, and just say whatever you need from me to get every single bastard who's had involvement in this, even if it is just paying for one of these videos. These are the evillest bastards.' Barney felt his face flush with anger.

Ross's voice was clear, hard and determined, with no trace of his usual bumptiousness. 'We're bringing the whole lot of them down, Barney. Each and every fucking one of them.'

59

THE OFFICE WAS buzzing with activity when Barney returned, clutching the laptop under his arm. Norma looked up and smiled, her glasses askew, and her normally immaculate hair looking a little more dishevelled. Max and Janie were crowded around a laptop, both scribbling into notebooks.

'Ayup, team, what gives?' said Barney, cheerily.

'Pissing into the wind,' Ross replied, as he slammed his phone down on the desk.

'How so?'

'Struan O'Neill is still working on the theory that Anderson was working on his own, and at the moment they aren't looking for anyone else. He's such a twatopotamus,' he hissed, his lined face dark and heavy browed.

'Twatopotamus? Not heard that one before.'

'I've been saving it for an appropriate moment, and I've decided that this was it. Happy?'

'Very. Belting choice, lad.'

'Good work on the laptop, although I've had a look at the shit your mate Colin sent and it gave me fucking chills,' said Ross. 'Fucking thousands of people have paid to view those fucking hideous videos.'

'This won't be as easy, he's using Bitcoin, and *Clive* thinks that the Lenovo wasn't used to deal with that, so there must be another computer being used for the brass,' said Barney.

Janie looked up. 'And it's true. I'm liaising with the National

Crime Agency, and they're contacting the FBI; they'll get the best crypto nerds on it. Apparently, crypto isn't always as anonymous as people think, and the person I spoke to thought that by working the blockchain, they may be able to uncover where the money has come from, and where it went after they'd paid to watch the videos.'

'This is a little confusing. I'm out of my comfort zone with this,' said Barney.

'Fuck me, you are? Imagine how I felt when Norma started droning on about how many fucking Suzukis these freaks were paying to watch these videos.' Ross blew his cheeks out as he exhaled.

'Satoshi, Ross. Not Suzuki. Suzuki is a motorbike,' said Norma with a grin.

'Ach, piss off and get on with your bloody work.'

'I bloody hope that they can trace all the bastards, but they'll be feeling safe with the use of Bitcoin,' said Max.

'As always, we'll follow the money one way or another. Criminals always fuck up, and they always want the same thing whether the money is in pound notes, gold watches, or fucking Kawasakis, or whatever these bloody stupid things are called,' Ross said, belching quietly under his breath.

'What's that, then?' said Janie.

Ross's eyes were hard. 'They want to turn their Tamagotchis into nice things. No use to them when they're just numbers on a screen.'

'Good point, well made,' said Janie.

'Aye, we're already flagging up to Interpol, and our friends in England and Wales to get ready to start farming it out, and every single one of them that's identifiable is getting bloody nicked. Goes all over the place. America, France, Canada, Australia. By the way, don't ask about all the comments under each video.' Ross grimaced.

'Aye, it's not pleasant. Definitely incel vibes about it all. Rejoicing in women being bloody killed, about how the snobby bitches deserved it, etc.,' said Janie, with a curl on her lips.

'Thankfully, I've been deploying my usual – and may I say underappreciated – negotiation skills, and the Chief has directed that the cyber-crime team take over the mop-up of this, with the assistance of your old firm, Max.'

'What, the Met?' said Max.

'Aye, loads of purchases in London, I hear. Their cyber unit wants the easy wins of nabbing the bastards. Good for the stats at the year end when applying for funding, and that. You making tea, Barney?'

Barney said nothing, just shook his head resignedly and began making a whole tray full of hot drinks. 'If it's all getting farmed out, what's left for us to do?' he asked, as he handed a steaming mug to Ross.

'Plenty. Anderson is at Inverness Sheriff Court in the morning, and I want us there. One thing I've learnt in my time doing this type of work is it's always worthwhile turning up at court hearings and funerals. There's always an interested party at both. Always.'

'What do you want us to do?' said Barney.

'Work the data, dig deep on it. There's another one of these fucknuggets out there, and I want him found. Look into Anderson's background, his associates, where he worked, and overlay it with what we already have. If Anderson didn't shove that poor wee lassie from the top of that unpronounceable hill, some bastard did, and the answer is out there. He even videoed it, for fuck's sake.'

'Clive's offered to help with the data.'

'Who?' said Ross, his eyebrows bristling.

'Jesus. You've forgotten already?'

Ross broke into a wide smile. 'Nah, I'm fucking with you.

Clive the computer nerd. Aye, get him on it, we need all the help we can get.'

'What do you want me to do with the laptop? It's all downloaded and I don't need it anymore,' said Barney.

'Give it here, it needs to go back north, as Struan will want it for his productions.' Ross tapped his desk, and Barney laid the Faraday bag down.

'Right, folks. Time's moving on, and I promised Mrs Fraser that I'd get home at a reasonable time, and we have to be in Inverness Sheriff Court in the morning, so let's piss off.'

60

Tor Browser

Wyatt-Lawman: Mikey's at court tomorrow, I hear.

Bagger: Yes. Charged with one count of murder.

Wyatt-Lawman: He can't talk.

Bagger: He won't talk.

Wyatt-Lawman: You had better be correct.

Bagger: I am.

Wyatt-Lawman: Do they know about the others?

Bagger: Hard to tell. I'm not close to those at the centre of the investigation and there's a big cloak of secrecy around it all. I've an idea, though.

Wyatt-Lawman: ?

Bagger: Still planning, but it should confuse.

Wyatt-Lawman: Just be careful.

Bagger: I'm always careful, which is why I'm talking to you, and not sitting in a cell next to Mikey.

Wyatt-Lawman: Another thing. You said cops have Mikey's

laptop and phones. I'm deleting the website for now, just in case they manage to beat his encryption.

Bagger: Is that likely?

Wyatt-Lawman: No, but I don't want to take the risk, Mikey was an idiot with computers, and he may have got lazy. I'll set up secure comms by another means and let you know.

61

ROSS FELT A mildly pleasant sense of anticipation as he pulled his decrepit Ford Fiesta onto the drive of his house, which was a welcoming semi-detached 1930s building on a small, well-kept estate in Falkirk. He smiled when he saw that his wife's immaculate Nissan was tucked away under the carport.

His stomach began to rumble at the prospect of a decent meal at home with his wife, particularly as the kids were away. A nice bit of dinner, maybe a glass of wine, and then a movie sat on the sofa next to the woman he'd spent the last thirty-five years with. It was a good marriage, and he loved his wife dearly, but she did get frustrated with his dedication to his work. He couldn't help it. Ever since joining the police all those years ago, he'd been totally committed to locking up bad guys whenever he could. It was in his blood, and his desire to keep doing it had only strengthened since he started his current role with Max and the others.

He stepped out of the car and took in the fresh early evening air as he slammed the door shut and walked up to the front door.

It was locked fast. He frowned. This was unusual; his wife was always home before him, and her car was on the drive. Why had she locked the door? he wondered.

He slotted his key into the door and pushed it open, furrowing his brow in confusion.

The house was silent. Dead quiet, apart from the ticking of the hall clock.

'Honey, I'm home,' he called out, aping an American accent, as was his custom.

Silence.

A sudden creak made him start, just a touch. He turned to the lounge door, and Ted, their petite and svelte ginger tomcat, appeared in the doorway, stretching and yawning.

'Ya wee shite, I almost cacked my pants,' he said, stooping to tickle the cat's chin. Ted arched his back in delight and began to purr.

'Where's ya mammy, lad?' he whispered.

The cat turned and almost strutted into the lounge, with Ross just behind.

The house was quiet and inert, and the air was pleasantly warm and scented by the jasmine reed diffuser that his wife loved on the windowsill.

'Anyone home?' he called out as he passed through the comfortable lounge, noting his wife's spectacles on the coffee table. He frowned again.

'Hello?' he said, in the kitchen now, which was clean and sparkling.

There was a note on the kitchen island. Sharpie on a Post-it note, the chemical tang of the pen's ink indicative that it had recently been written. He looked down at his wife's smart cursive writing.

Gone out for dinner with Jennifer. Leftover mac & cheese in fridge. Don't wait up x

Ross sighed, disappointment flooding through him. Out with her annoying piss-head of a sister. So, no tasty meal in front of the telly with a glass of something chilled with his wife. He opened the fridge and looked inside.

The mac and cheese looked dry and unappetising, but his grumbling stomach made its presence felt once again. He pulled the glass dish out of the fridge, peeled off the clingfilm and jammed it into the microwave, jabbing his stubby finger at the buttons. He reached into the fridge and took out a tin of lager and popped the top, taking a long draught of the cold beer. He sighed, but then a smile formed on his lips, which quickly became a chuckle.

Fair enough, love, he thought. Why should she wait around for him all the time?

His phone buzzed in his pocket. He pulled it out and looked at the screen. It was Barney. 'What do you want, you senile old nugget?'

'Bloody charmin', and I'm phoning with interesting news.'

'Aye well, I'm starving, and I've a dried-up mac and cheese to eat, so hurry up.'

'Clive has just called. The website has suddenly gone down; deleted was how he described it.'

'What, we've lost everything?'

'No, he secured all the data on it as soon as he found it, but it's gone. Just before it went down, he captured an interesting exchange, between two characters in the chat function. I'll forward it to you now. Have a look – it's enlightening and makes something clear.'

Ross stared at the messages between 'Wyatt-Lawman' and 'Bagger' on the screenshot that Barney had forwarded to his WhatsApp, feeling the familiar rage begin to burn in his very core. He'd been a cop for many years, and the reason that he kept on doing it was for moments like this.

But these were worse than the normal bad guys. They were supposed to be on the side of the angels, but here they were dancing with the devil.

He forwarded the message to Max and Janie, and took another sip of his cold beer.

Tomorrow. Court. The bastard will be there.

62

'**WHAT THE FUCKING** fuck is this place?' blurted Ross from the rear of the Volvo as it pulled into the car park of the Inverness Sheriff Court, on the edge of the capital of the Highlands. The new building was vast and shone bright, blinding white against the pale blue of the morning sky. The early sun sparkled in the huge array of glass that made up the frontage of the imposing building.

'Impressive, isn't it? The old courthouse was bloody awful, cramped and falling to pieces,' said Max.

'It looks like a shagging great Bank HQ building. Look at the tasteful bastard sculpted gardens, and pleasant benches. I despair of the future. Courthouses should be horrible intimidating Victorian places that smell of death and pish. This looks like an airport terminal in Dubai, or some other shite hole. Just one with criminals hanging about all over the place.' Ross shook his head.

'I like it, it's modern and cutting-edge,' said Janie.

'Aye, that's because you're a millennial. Nae bloody taste of the old things.'

'Ross, I've a degree in history, but history evolves, and moves. It's not always linear.'

'Ah bollocks,' said Ross, shaking his head. His face was craggy and lined with fatigue.

'Aye well, that's as may be. Come on, court starts any minute, and we need to scope out who's there,' said Max, opening the car door.

The three of them passed through security having shown their warrant cards. The inside of the building was, if anything, more impressive than the outside. There were large, tasteful Scottish scenery prints on the walls, one of which was grandly titled *Caledonia Silva Rediviva*.

The exposed concrete walls, ducts and harsh overhead lighting, together with the glass atria in which shrubs grew, did give the place a very different feel to the average criminal court in the country. There was even a coffee bar.

Ross, predictably, was not impressed. 'Place looks like a giant fucking vodka bar in the West End of Glasgow. Should be full of fucking hipsters with shite beards and check shirts, not jakies and junkies waiting to hear how much they're about to get fined for smashing the boozer window last week.'

'Not impressed then, boss?' said Janie as they ascended the stairs towards court three, which seemed to be a hive of activity.

'No. Not one bit. If no bastard was hung by the neck until dead back in the day, then it's no' a proper court.'

'Looks like Struan O'Neill is here already. Look . . .' said Max, pointing at the throng of suited detectives and reporters all hanging around outside the court.

'Aye, every bugger will want a part of the ex-cop serial killer,' said Ross, as O'Neill turned to look at them. He approached with a nod.

'Morning, Ross. Couldn't stay away, eh?' he said, smiling.

'You know me, pal. Funerals and court appearances. We still have suspects outstanding.'

'Do we?' said O'Neill.

Ross just shrugged, clearly not keen to explain further. 'Who's the sheriff?' he said after a long pause.

'Sheriff Logan Muldoon,' said O'Neill.

'Will it be tried here?' said Ross.

'Shite, I doubt it. If there are more victims, which we all know

253

there will be, it'll be transferred to the High Court in Edinburgh, I suspect.'

An usher appeared from the court. 'All parties for case of Anderson,' she said, her voice carrying in the vast, open space.

There was a general increase in the buzz of conversation, and the crowd began to file into the courtroom.

Ross's distaste for modern judicial buildings wasn't improved when he entered the court. It was large and spacious, the walls lined in pale, slatted wood, and the juror benches were fronted by smoked glass. The place was airy and clean. The dock was situated slap-bang in the centre of the room, with a staircase that descended into the bowels of the building where the custody cells were housed, easily accessed from Burnett Road Police Station via a secure walkway.

There was a brief hubbub as people settled into seats, and gowned counsel took their spot in front of the dock and before the judges' bench.

The clerk of the court stood, and there was a sharp rap on the door.

'All stand,' said the clerk, and there were soft murmurings as the occupants of the courtroom got to their feet.

The Sheriff entered the room, resplendent in his wig and gown, his beard neatly trimmed and his rimless spectacles glinting in the harsh light. He bowed his head slightly and sat. The rest of the court followed suit.

'Yes, madam clerk,' he said in a rich baritone.

'First case, my lord, is that of the Crown versus Michael Anderson, who is in custody.'

Sheriff Muldoon inclined his head, his face reflective of the gravity of the situation. 'Yes, have the panel brought up.'

The clerk picked up a phone and whispered.

The court fell silent. Total, cloying and almost-visible anticipatory silence as the behind-the-scenes functions of the court swung into action, and the occupants of the room waited to see the serial killer for the first time.

Justice being seen to be done, in the full glare of the brightly lit new building.

You could almost hear the tension in the air, as it crackled like static electricity.

63

THE HOLDING CELL in the bowels of the court was tiny, and even more austere than the one in the police station.

'It's time,' said Malachy, peering through the Perspex wicket in the cell door, his eyes hard as he stared at Anderson.

'I just need a quick piss,' Anderson said, jumping to his feet and moving over to the small stainless-steel pan in the corner of the cell.

'Quick, you've a shitload of people waiting to see your ugly mug,' said Malachy without even a trace of humour, as he moved away from the door and snapped the metal hatch back up with a bone-jarring clank.

Anderson felt his pulse quicken. Now was the time. There would probably be no better opportunity than now.

It had to be now. It would almost be poetic, in front of all the ghouls together in the court upstairs, waiting to gain a look at him, the evil serial killer of women.

Well, fuck them. This was on his terms. He'd win. All the bitches in his life that had turned him down for being too bloody ugly, too blunt, not charming enough, would finally realise who they'd been dealing with.

They'd know, all right.

He reached into his baggy tracksuit bottoms and pulled out the object that he'd retrieved from under the table in the solicitor's room the previous day, and that he had kept hidden in his pants ever since. He'd use it to be remembered forever.

'Hurry up, Sheriff's waiting, Anderson,' came the harsh voice of the permanently angry Malachy.

'Aye, I'm ready,' said Anderson.

He felt a surge of triumph that was only dimmed by the beginnings of mild dizziness.

He'd won.

He always won.

There was a rattling of keys in the door. He smiled ruefully at the familiar sound, which he'd heard many, many times in the past, although from the other side. The door swung open, on well-oiled hinges, and two burly and scowling dock officers stood there, alongside the big jailer. He snorted in amusement. He was so important that it was going to take four of them to get him up the short flight of stairs and into the brand-new court building.

Pathetic bastards. What was he going to do? Fight them all?

'Right, come on then, sweetheart. You cannae keep his lordship Sheriff Muldoon waiting,' said Malachy, the sarcasm redolent in his voice.

Anderson shrugged, and stepped out of the cell, where the dock officers took one of his arms each, and they frog-marched him towards the staircase, just as his head began to spin, and he felt his face flush and burn up, as his excitement grew. The world was about to witness his greatness. *They'll never forget*, he thought as his mind began to swim.

He staggered slightly as he ascended the second flight, seeing the bright lights above him, and he could hear the slight hubbub of conversation as he emerged into the packed courtroom.

The Sheriff looked at him, his thin, craggy face impassive, but failing to mask the loathing in the deep-set eyes that surveyed him from behind the thick-lensed glasses.

Nausea began to grip his stomach, and he felt the prickle of sweat break out on his forehead, running down his face and stinging as it went into his eyes. The room started to spin wildly and he felt a sudden elation and euphoria as he staggered to one side, only remaining upright as the dock officer held onto his upper arm. He let his mouth sag open, feeling the wetness of drool run from his tongue, which felt like it had doubled in size.

'Mr Anderson . . .' The words from the Sheriff briefly pierced the maelstrom of his mind, and then there was nothing. Utter blackness descended and he fell into deep, impenetrable blackness, as chaos around him erupted.

64

THERE WAS AN almost collective change in the air quality as all occupants of the court sucked in a breath of surprise at the collapsing prisoner, only to be followed with immediate panic that was evident from the dock officers and escorting cops. Max, Ross and Janie watched in silence as dock officers and Malachy all went into first-aid mode behind the Scandi-chic pale wood of the dock. The three of them were standing at the back of the court, whereas DCI O'Neill had closed in to witness proceedings, his face flushing red.

Sheriff Muldoon barked orders. 'Clear the court now, and call an ambulance.' The clerk picked up his phone, hands shaking as he watched the unfolding drama, as people began to file out of the room, being snapped at by the usher, who was shooing them all towards the door.

Soon, it was just the three of them, along with DCI O'Neill, and a couple of his staff watching as Malachy began to perform CPR on the deathly pale figure of Anderson, who was now on his back being worked on. Anderson looked inert, and without any muscle tone, even though there was no way of telling whether he was alive or dead.

But Max knew.

He knew it was too late. The last time he'd seen someone in that condition they had died, and died on a kitchen floor by simply slipping away. He'd seen this all before.

'Insulin,' said Max, his voice low.

'What?' said Ross.

'He had insulin in his bag that we seized from his place in Fort William. This reminds me of that bloody case in Linlithgow last year.' Max's voice carried a trace of bitterness at the memory.

'How'd he get bloody hold of it, and has he been hiding it all along?' said Ross.

'Could it have been passed to him on his way from the custody block to the holding cell?' said Janie.

'I doubt it, it's wall-to-wall CCTV and he was escorted by the civilian dock officers, as well as the jailer. I can't see they'd all be in cahoots, and a handover would be too risky. It must have been in the custody block during his detention,' said Max.

Suddenly, the doors burst open, and two green-uniformed paramedics rushed in, rucksacks on their backs, and made their way to the dock. As they passed, Max spoke. 'I think we could be talking about an insulin overdose, guys. Just a feeling,' he said to the lead paramedic, who just nodded, as he hurried by.

'Surely he was strip-searched?' said Ross, not taking his eyes from the dock.

'He was,' said Janie.

'How'd you know that?' said Ross, turning to her, face quizzical.

'I checked the custody record online yesterday. Strip-search authorised by Sergeant Cotton as soon as he was booked in. Jim Lennox searched him. I'd say he was a fairly switched-on mannie,' said Janie.

'Good skills. I'm glad my influence is wearing off on you, my girl,' said Ross, without his customary mirth.

'This doesn't look good, does it? How long's it been since he collapsed?' said DCI O'Neill as he joined them.

'Fifteen minutes. Too long, if it's insulin, which I'm betting it is,' said Max.

'Insulin? What makes you say that?'

'We found some in the same bag he had his computer in. Quick way to kill someone. Or yourself, for that matter. I've seen it up close before. We need his cells locking down for a full forensic search, boss. Both in the court and in the police station. Two choices here: one, he had it secreted on him when he arrived, and it was missed by the strip-search.'

'And the other?' O'Neill's eyes were flinty as he turned to face Max.

'Someone in custody gave it to him. If the syringe isn't on him now, I bet it's in one of the cells. Mind if we search?' said Max.

O'Neill just sighed, and rubbed at his temples with his fingers, just as the two paramedics stood, one looking across at them and shaking his head. 'Aye, be my guest. I'm screwed if I know who else to trust right now. Go and lock both down, and get a flash search done before some bugger cleans them out. I'll get PolSA in later.'

'What are you going to do?' said Ross.

'This court is now a crime scene, as far as I'm concerned. I'm locking it down, getting a CSI team running, and then I'm calling the DCC, God help me.'

65

THE CELL IN the bowels of the court building was tiny, and about half the size of a standard police cell, which was to be expected considering what it was required for: temporary housing for defendants arriving from prison, or having been walked across from the police station a few metres away.

There was just a low sleeping platform, with the familiar thin, rubberised mattress on top of it. An empty Styrofoam cup was crushed on the floor, and despite the newness of the building, someone had still managed to scratch 'ACAB' on the wall.

'Jesus, this is a new fucking block, and it still stinks of jakies already. It's no' as fragrant as being up the top of a Munro, eh, Tom?' said Ross, as the crime-scene-taped cell door was unlocked for them by the unsmiling Inspector Tom Jeffries.

'Like I said, Ross. If I could do that job full time, I would, but the Chief Super is permanently scunnered with me, so I get lumbered with custody inspector duties. I'm well used to the stink of bloody jakies, although it's considered offensive to call them that now,' he said, bitterly.

'What, jakies?'

'Aye. These are vulnerable people, Ross, and we have a duty of care to them,' said Inspector Jeffries.

'Ach bollocks. Come on, let's get on with this. I'm betting you have some gloves, Janie?'

'A whole box here, Ross,' said Jeffries, pointing to a small shelving unit to the side of the door.

'Well, I'm no' doing it. No' putting my hand down cludgies is one of the reasons I became a DI.' He grinned and nodded at Max and Janie, who snapped nitrile gloves into place before entering the cell.

Janie headed over to the sleeping platform, and pulled the mattress off and onto the floor, poring over every inch of it, testing the seams, before moving to the pillow, which was made of a similar material.

Janie picked up the Styrofoam cup, and sniffed at it, before turning to Ross.

'Evidence bags are in my rucksack, Ross. Can you pass one? Best seize this in case he drank something,' she said, placing the cup back on the floor.

Ross muttered something about monkeys and organ-grinders, but went to Janie's rucksack that was just outside the cell door and pulled out a small self-seal evidence bag.

Max was standing by the stainless-steel toilet pan, and looked down at the water with distaste. Despite the cell being clean, there were yellowish spots of urine splashed around the rim of the toilet, and a big wadge of toilet paper in the bottom of the bowl.

Max sighed, and rolled up the sleeve of his sweatshirt. Gingerly, he dipped his hand into the water and eased the sodden lump of paper to one side.

A long and slender syringe lay at the bottom of the steel bowl, the light glinting off the needle, which was almost invisible against the stainless metal. Carefully, Max gripped the plunger end, between his thumb and forefinger and lifted it clear of the water.

'Bingo,' he said, looking at the syringe, which was identical to those that they'd seen in the bag that had contained the laptop.

Janie just nodded, holding something up in her gloved fingers. 'I suspect this is the cap off the syringe. I almost missed it on the sleeping platform.'

'So, it was insulin. The scummy bastard took the easy way out. Question is, how did he get it?' said Ross.

'It had to be in the police station; the walkway from there is full of CCTV with no blind spots,' said Max. He looked up at Ross, his face pale. 'We need to check Anderson's property, and we need to check the custody CCTV, urgently.'

Ross nodded, gravely. 'We bloody do, and we need to do it quietly and under the radar. Janie, if I make the relevant call, can you get hold of it, and start looking?'

Inspector Jeffries nodded. 'No need for that. I have the CCTV accessible from my login, I'll sign you in and you can review from a quiet office. We need to keep this on the downlow, but I'll have to inform the area commander.'

Ross exhaled, blowing his cheeks out as he did. 'No, don't even do that, Tom. I'll contact the Chief Constable, and he can go direct, without bothering staff officers so we can keep this as tight as a gnat's chuff. It has to be a cop there that gave Anderson that syringe.'

*

Doreen Urquhart was knee deep in evidence bags, a harassed look on her face.

Janie and Max were in the far corner of the office, staring at a screen. 'Go on, then,' she whispered.

Max cleared his throat, stood up and strode over to where Doreen was sitting.

'Hi Doreen, DCI O'Neill has told me we need to sign one of the production labels?' said Max, smiling at the scowling features of the productions officer.

'Can I ask why?' she said.

'Because we forgot to when we seized it earlier, and the boss wants all things dotted and crossed. Call him if you've any issues – he's said it's okay, and I don't need to open the bag.' Max smiled.

Doreen huffed. 'Have a productions number?'

'Aye, it's JRC/3. Should be a wallet containing syringes.'

Doreen went to her register and flicked through it. 'Aye, I have it here, it was seized by your colleague, but was handed to me by PC Lennox, who brought all the productions up from custody, and there were bloody loads of them. People seize any old shite, you know, and it's me that has to document it all. Pain in the bloody arse,' she grumbled, but went to a large black plastic crate and began to rifle through it, before coming up with a brown manila envelope. She upended the envelope and a small self-seal bag fell onto the desk.

'Help yersel', if you need to open it. I'll need a continuity statement, yeah?'

'I don't need to open it. I'll be back in a minute, Janie over there needs to sign it as well,' said Max.

'Aye, fine, but bring it straight back, no buggering off with it,' she said, turning back to her register.

Max studied the familiar wallet-pouch that they'd found in the premises in Fort William. He recognised Janie's signature on the label on the bag, along with her familiar writing of the description of the contents. 'Wallet/pouch containing four (4) capped syringes, and eight (8) vials marked Actrapid-100 international units/ml Insulin human.'

Through the bag, Max manipulated the wallet, managing to lift the top flap open to reveal the contents, but knowing what he was going to find.

There were only three syringes, and six vials in the wallet. Max exhaled, turning the bag over in his hands. At the bottom of the bag was a slit with clean edges that seemed to Max to have been made by a sharp implement. It was tiny, no more than half a centimetre, and it was barely noticeable. However, it was there, and it was big enough to manipulate a syringe out of the bag, along with two vials.

He sat next to Janie and deposited the bag on the table, and in a low voice, said, 'Have a look at the bag, but don't look at Doreen. There's a wee slit at the bottom, and one syringe and two vials have gone.'

Janie picked up the bag and studied it, her face impassive, as she handed it back. 'Bastards,' she whispered.

She was studying the screen on which the multiple camera angles of the custody suite were displayed.

'Anything?' said Max, nodding at the screen.

Janie shook her head. 'Not yet. Just watched him being booked in by PC Lennox. There was a full strip-search – of that there is no doubt – so unless he had it jammed where the sun don't shine, he didn't bring it in with him.'

'I think he'd have bust it up his jaxy when Lennox zapped him on the roof, anyway. I'm with you; somehow, some bastard passed that to him in his cell. Watch carefully and I'll return this to Doreen.'

'Aye, do I have a bloody choice?' said Janie.

'Not really, I also need to talk to Norma. I'll go out of here to make the call, walls having ears, and all that.' Max stood up and walked back to where Doreen was frantically searching through a heap of bags, a phone clamped to her ear, looking extremely agitated. Max just smiled and put the bag back on the table, before leaving the office and walking down the corridor.

He found an empty office a few doors down, got out his phone and dialled.

'About time, you bugger. I've been grafting down here, on my bloody lonesome, while you lot are swanning about in the Highlands. I've had to make my own tea.' Despite the remonstration, Norma's voice was as chirpy as always.

'No Barney?' said Max.

'No, he sloped off. I suspect to the betting shop, he was nose deep in the *Racing Post* for a while, not that there's much to do now that I have the computer downloaded, which is fucking awful, by the way. I'll need some bloody counselling after this.'

'Really?'

'It's the worst thing, Max. We'll all need a big debrief on this when the dust has settled, shite like this can leave its mark.'

'I'll speak to Ross. It's been a tough case.' Max couldn't help but think that was true in all ways, as he thought about Katie alone with Nutmeg at home.

'I've not watched most of the videos, but some of the comments and forum topics are skin-crawlingly bad. I'm not much up on incel culture, but I suspect the users of this Far to Fall site are all knee deep in it.' Her normally happy tone slipped a little.

'That bad?'

'Worse. So anti-women, all shite like "bitches deserved it", blah, blah.'

'Sorry, pal. I'll help when I get back, but we've a hot lead. Are you okay?'

'Aye. Worse for you lot; you're out there seeing this shite, so I'm not moaning.'

'Don't be afraid of taking a moment, eh?'

'Aye, I won't. It's all good, next tea round is on you, though,' she said; Max could detect a smile in her voice.

'I take it the news of Anderson's demise hasn't escaped you?'

'Ross told me. He's already got me looking for previous associates of Anderson working in Inverness or surrounding areas. I'm just waiting for access to his personal file that professional standards are dragging their feet about.'

'Aye well, someone here handed him the means to top himself, so we're scanning CCTV, and any leads you can uncover will be good.'

'On it like a car bonnet. Bring me something nice back from

Harry Gow's, yeah?' said Norma, referring to the popular Highland bakery that they'd both frequented as kids.

'Will do, ta.' Max hung up and looked at himself in the mirror that was on the wall in the office. His face was pale and lined, and he realised how little sleep he'd had since this case had kicked off.

His thoughts suddenly turned to Katie, and he was about to dial when his phone buzzed. It was a WhatsApp message from Janie, containing a video clip. It was of her computer screen, which had been maximised to show the inside of the cell in which Anderson was standing by the door taking something from the hatch. It looked like one of the cardboard boxes used to supply prisoner meals. The screen then flicked over to the cell passageway, which showed the custody support officer, Malachy, walking away from the cell. It then switched back to the inside of the cell, where the image zoomed in on Anderson. Max watched with an ever-growing mix of emotions. Shock turned to anger, which morphed into a steely determination, as he watched Anderson swallow whatever had been taped to the bottom of that ready meal.

He swallowed a note in the cell, came the message from Janie.

Max minimised the message, his mind on Malachy, the big, surly jailer, as he dialled.

'I was just about to eat, and you've disturbed me, you inconsiderate walloper,' said Ross.

'Ross, we need to meet now, and we need an urgent search warrant for Malachy the jailer's place.'

66

THE PROCURATOR FISCAL studied the triplicate sheets of papers, with a practised eye, reading the hastily put together document. His name badge identified him as Gerald McCaskill; he was a short, stout man with a neat salt-and-pepper goatee and thick-lensed glasses. He wore a rumpled pinstripe suit, the shoulders of which were flecked with dandruff.

'Very short notice, officer?' he said, his watery eyes firm.

'As a result of short-notice developments, and we need to urgently move,' said Janie.

The Fiscal eyed Janie as he studied the information provided in support of the search warrant.

'Okay, fine. I'll take you now to see Sheriff Muldoon, and we can only hope he's in a good mood.'

'Think he will be?' said Janie.

The Fiscal shrugged. 'Not every day you see a defendant die in the witness box, is it?' he said, standing up and slipping his jacket on.

'I guess, but it is genuinely urgent, and we are seeking a suspect in connection with the death,' said Janie.

'Have you no smarter clothes?' said the Fiscal, eyeing Janie's scuffed jeans and washed-out hoodie that was emblazoned with EDINBURGH MMA.

'Well, no. We're away from home for a few days, and this job has somewhat snowballed, sorry.'

'Ach, nae bother, he's a bit glaikit, but he'll want to hear what's happening. Come on, he's waiting in his chambers.' A smile suddenly softened his somewhat harsh exterior.

Janie followed McCaskill, as he crossed the shiny floor of the court corridors, and into court three, his worn shoes beating a tattoo on the hard surface. The clerk was seated behind a huge pile of papers.

'Am I good to go in and see his lordship, Maggie?' he said, cheerily.

The clerk smiled. 'Aye, he's waiting and expecting.'

Within a moment, they'd rounded the bench, and McCaskill was tapping on the pale door.

'Come?' came a voice from within.

McCaskill pushed the door open and nodded for Janie to join them.

Sheriff Muldoon was sitting behind his vast, wide desk, his eyes concentrated on a computer screen. He made as if not to notice the newcomers, instead continuing to tap away at the keyboard. Janie looked about the chambers, which were spartan, with no photographs or pictures on the walls; seemingly the only adornment was an old-fashioned coat stand, on which a set of robes hung. His wig was on the desk next to him.

'Yes?' he said, raising his eyes.

'Urgent search warrant application, my lord,' McCaskill said, handing over the sheaf of papers that Janie had only typed out forty minutes ago.

Muldoon took the papers and studied them, his grey moustache twitching as he read the contents. He raised a manicured finger and smoothed it over his eyebrows, before looking up again.

'This is very fast work, DC Calder?' he said, his eyes glinting from behind the spectacles.

'Yes, my lord. This is a fast-moving investigation, and the CCTV is clear that the suspect gave the meal, which seemed to include a note to the deceased, Michael Anderson,' Janie said, trying to quell the butterflies in her stomach.

'So, I see. Well, best of luck, it was quite a traumatic incident, having someone pass in my court. Please do keep me informed.' He uncapped a silver fountain pen, methodically signed all the warrant sheets, and handed them back, showing his stained teeth in a half-smile, before bowing his head back to his computer.

Janie gave a half-bow, as she accepted the search warrant, and she and McCaskill left the chambers, quietly.

'That was easy,' said Janie.

'Aye, he's free and easy with warrants – loves the cops, unlike most of his fellow sheriffs. Now, keep me informed of developments. The Procurator Fiscal service wants to keep a close watching brief on this case, being as serious and high profile as it is. Good luck.' He nodded and headed away.

Janie pulled out her phone and sent a text to Ross. *Success. Warrant signed and ready to rock and roll.*

Ross's reply was as expected. *What do you want, a medal?*

67

ROSS, MAX AND DCI O'Neill were all crowded around the computer screen in the glass-walled office. They watched the comings and goings of the busy office on CCTV but focused in on the activity of Malachy. Watching him enter the meal prep room and remain in there for a minute before exiting again, carrying the small cardboard box down to the cells and handing it over via the small wicket. Then a minute of Anderson eating, and then finding the note. The long, slow smile as he read, before he popped it in his mouth.

'Did you see that bloody smile?' said Max.

'Aye, it's like he's fucking delighted to see that he can top himself. What the hell are we dealing with here?' said Ross.

'Some type of weird bloody incel cult, from what Norma says. She's not enjoying interrogating the data from the computer, and that Far to Fall dark web bollocks,' said Max.

'Aye, I'll pick her up a pack of Tunnock's, that'll sort her out,' Ross said, without mirth.

'That'll deal with the PTSD of watching and reading from a load of women-hating bastards,' muttered Max, shaking his head, almost undetectably.

'When's the PM?' said Ross.

'Tomorrow morning at Raigmore,' said DCI O'Neill.

'Who's attending?'

'Just me and Doreen. I'm keeping it deliberately tight. What are you thinking?' O'Neill slumped in his chair and rubbed at his face.

'Malachy gave him the food, which had the note on, so he needs nicking, and we need to search his place thoroughly, agreed?' Ross looked at everyone in the room.

'He goes into the meal prep room, which isn't covered by CCTV, and then hands it over, so I think we have to, but there are different and more important questions,' said Max.

'Go on,' said O'Neill.

'How did he get hold of the syringe and manage to sneak it out of the bag without being spotted, and how did he get the syringe to Anderson? I've spoken to Lennox, and he is adamant that his strip-search was thorough; he even complained about having to see his hairy bollocks. I've seen nothing on the CCTV that suggests Malachy, nor indeed anyone else, in the custody suite handed over a syringe. I mean, they're not huge, but you'd need physical contact to get it to him.'

'So did anyone else have contact with him?' said Janie.

'Just his lawyer who had a twenty-minute consultation with him, but he was straight off the duty list, and had no contact with Anderson before he arrived. No way it was him, and in any case, we know the syringe came from the property you seized on the search,' said O'Neill.

'Where was the consultation?' said Max.

'The small room adjacent to the interview rooms. No CCTV there, owing to the whole client privilege bollocks, unfortunately.'

'I'll go and check it out, but I think we need to get Malachy in, now. Is he on duty?' said Max.

O'Neill shook his head. 'No, but he starts for late shift at three. Should we wait for him to get in?'

Ross looked at his watch. 'How about we surprise him at home? Means we can get the place searched, just in case shit gets leaky here when folk see us collaring him in the yard. Where's he stay?'

'I'll find out; you want some backup?'

'I think we're good, but we keep it close, yeah?' said Ross.

'Aye, I'll just need to let his sergeant know he'll be a wee bit late, or he'll be making phone calls, which may tip the wink a bit.'

'Fine, but leave it as late as you can, Struan, eh?'

O'Neill nodded.

'Right, folks, let's get saddled up. Struan, text me the address as soon as you have it. Let's go.'

68

Bagger: You need to move, now. They're onto you, and they'll soon be bringing you in.

Doss: What? How the fuck?

Bagger: I don't know, but I've just heard, you've no time at all, run, now. You know what you have to do.

Bagger: You there?

Doss: Yes, but fuck. Where do I go?

Bagger: I'm not interested. Just go now, or you'll be in custody, and you'll not get the opportunity that Mikey got. You'll never be left alone. Go now. You know what you have to do?

Doss: . . .

Bagger: You know, right? We all agreed, and Mikey has done the right thing. You have to do this.

Doss: . . .

Bagger: Doss?

Doss has left the chat.

69

THE VOLVO SWUNG around the corner into the street that O'Neill had told them Malachy lived on, a rundown road of pebble-dashed, post-war dwellings ten minutes from the police station.

'There's his car,' said Max, pointing to a dilapidated blue Vauxhall on the weed-encrusted gravel drive in front of a tired-looking bungalow.

'Are we going straight in?' said Janie.

Ross looked at his watch. 'He'll be leaving in a minute or two, if he's to make it for his clock-on time, and Struan is assured he's always punctual, even if he is a bit of a lazy curmudgeon.'

Janie pulled the car to the side of the road, fifty metres from the bungalow.

'Heads up, the door's opening, and he's out. Janie, move up and block the bugger in.' Ross pointed a stubby finger towards the house, where the door had swung open and Malachy had appeared, a bag slung over his shoulder. Janie engaged the Volvo in gear and set off, steadily towards the drive of the house.

Malachy showed no alarm, and didn't seem to be hurrying. He just made his way, keys in hand, towards the car, looking up at them only when they pulled up in front of his drive, blocking his Vauxhall in. His eyes flashed with annoyance, as he saw the Volvo draw to a halt. This expression slipped into one of confusion, followed by one of concern as he saw who was in the car.

Max didn't give him time to react. He was out and on the drive in a flash, and gripped hold of Malachy's arm.

'What the hell . . .?' he began, but he offered no resistance.

'Malachy, I'm DS Craigie, and this is DI Fraser and DC Calder. We're detaining you, okay?'

Malachy's mouth gaped open, and his eyes were full of genuine confusion. 'What's going on? I'm on my way to bloody work, man,' he said, which was borne out by the blue cotton trousers and blue polo shirt he was wearing.

'You know Anderson's dead, yeah?' said Ross, his voice hard and accusatory.

'Aye, of course, death in custody and all that, but it's nothing to do with me,' he said, his face draining of colour.

'We've seen the CCTV, Malachy,' said Janie.

'What about it? I was just doin' ma' job,' he said.

'We saw you deliver the meal just after he was booked in. We saw the note passed to him,' said Janie.

'What bloody note? I just gave him a microwave madras like he asked. It'll be all on the audio and that.'

'The note, Malachy. The note under the tray. We saw him take it off, read it and swallow it. You gave him the bloody note, man,' Ross said.

'I fucking didnae. I just gave him the box. I didn't even heat the bloody meal up, and I've certainly no bloody clue about any note,' he said, his voice hardening.

Max opened his mouth to counter, but then stopped. There was no CCTV in the meal prep room, and he had a memory of another figure walking into the small kitchen.

'Who did heat it up?' said Janie, realisation landing hard.

'It was that grumpy Weegie from Grantown who was up for the day, for some reason.'

'What, the grumpy bugger we met at Huntly's Cave – Danny something, or other?' said Max, heart pounding.

'Aye. That's the bugger, Danny McSorley; he moaned the whole bloody day about being away from the Cairngorms, he did, right enough,' said Malachy.

Max looked at Janie, and they then both looked at Ross. 'We need to find out where Danny McSorley is, right bloody now,' said Max.

Ross nodded and moved away, picking his phone out of his pocket.

'Seriously, guys. I'm to be at work soon, what's going on, eh?' said Malachy, looking at each of them in turn.

Ross returned, pale-faced.

'He's supposed to be on duty, but they can't raise him. He was at Grantown a couple of hours ago, but ditched his partner and disappeared. His radio has dropped off the net fifteen minutes ago; his patrol car is currently parked at the Cluanie Inn up by Glenmoriston.'

'The Cluanie Inn. Isn't that where Leanne Wilson stayed before she died on A' Chralaig?' said Janie.

'Aye, the very same. The bastard's gone back to the scene of the crime,' said Ross.

70

SecureMsg-FTF

Bagger: Are you away?

Doss: Aye. Im wellway

Bagger: They're searching for you.

Doss: theywont fand meman

Bagger: What are you on about, are you drunk?

Doss: bloootered. Bottle of goood whisky pal, on ma way to the hill. Where it all started for me. Miky showed the way, man.

Bagger: You know what you have to do. We all agreed. Mikey played his part, now you have to.

Doss: I know. Dinnae fret mann. I' fuck do/ wat.

71

ROSS, MAX AND Janie jumped out of the Volvo in the rear yard at Burnett Road, only to be met by DCI O'Neill and Inspector Jeffries who were waiting in the car park.

'Any news?' said Ross.

O'Neill just shook his head. 'I've got the Super to authorise an urgent ping on McSorley's phone. Looks like it's off now, but it last hit the cell mast closest to a pub where his car is parked, which makes sense. It's hardly populated; in fact, it's a quiet area.'

'How about his radio?' said Max.

'GPS puts it at the same location as his car. I'm guessing he's ditched the car with the airwave set inside. He'll know that we can ping his radio down to the metre,' said O'Neill.

'If I was a guessing man, he's away to hide in the hills. He knows the mountains as well as anyone, and let's face it, there's nowhere else around there,' said Jeffries.

'Aye, he told us he was a walker and climber,' said Max.

Sergeant Ed Smith appeared in the car park and jogged over, puffing slightly. 'I've called Jack from the MRT, and they're scrambling for whatever we need and are ready to guide, depending on where we think he's gone,' he said to Jeffries.

'Any clues as to where he might go, Tom?' said Max.

Jeffries screwed his face up. 'No real idea, but the weather's been so grand he could hide up there for ages, if he has food with him.'

'Are we sure he's planning to hide?' said Max.

Jeffries turned to face Max. 'Meaning?'

'Looks to me like they're part of some wild bloody incel cult. Maybe he's gone into the hills to top himself, like Anderson.'

'No fucking way,' said Ross. 'No more bastards escaping justice on their bloody terms by killing themselves; I don't like the bloody paperwork. We have to find him. Can we get the police helicopter up?'

'Already asked. It's broken,' said O'Neill.

'Shite. How far away is Barney?'

'Should be here any time. Why?' Janie asked.

'His wee helicopter thingy may be useful.'

'Battery life is a bit limiting, but may be handy once we get up there,' said Janie.

'Call him, and get him to divert to the Cluanie. We'll meet him there,' Ross barked.

Janie nodded, and pulled out her phone.

'How about the Coastguard?' said Max.

'What? He's gone into the bastard hills, not the sea, ya fud,' said Ross.

Max sighed. 'Ross, the Coastguard search-and-rescue helicopter, they do hills as well. In fact, they mainly do hills.'

'We'll need to put in a tasking request. I'm not sure they'd agree to this; it's probably not their remit to go and get suicidal coppers, they're not trained for it, and if McSorley has been doing what we think he's been doing then he's a danger to others. We need cops on the hill, not MRT,' said Jeffries.

'Let me make the call, at least,' said Max, reaching for his phone.

'Suit yerself,' said Jeffries, with a shrug.

Max pulled out his phone and dialled.

'Yo, shippers, what gives in copland?' came Shay's chirpy voice.

'Shay, I need a big favour,' said Max, moving away from the small group.

'Fire away,' said Shay.

Max explained the situation, unvarnished and unredacted.

Shay didn't hesitate, as Max had expected. 'Get yourselves here, shippers. I'll warm up the helo.'

72

DANNY MCSORLEY TOOK another deep swig of the cheap whisky, almost relishing the painful burn as the raw spirit carved a fiery path down his throat. He was drunk, now. Really drunk, and really scared. He knew what he had to do.

He unzipped his hi-vis police-issue body armour, spread it on the harsh, spiky granite rocks and sat down with a deep sigh, studying the bottle with a practised eye. Fucking Bell's. He didn't even have time to find a decent whisky, he thought as he took another swig.

He had nothing much to live for, being permanently single and always broke, but as he looked at the gaping chasm beneath him, he also knew that he didn't really want to toss himself off it into the oblivion of the sharp, unforgiving granite all those hundreds of feet below him.

The weather was still stunningly beautiful, and being in the Highlands in the height of summer meant that it wouldn't get dark for several hours yet. Maybe he'd stay for a while longer, enjoying the staggering view as he sat perched on the top of the ridgeline of A' Chralaig. The site of his first kill, and it seemed, his last.

He'd always loved the hills. It was why he'd moved from Strathclyde to Northern Constabulary with Bagger, after all the shite with the daft bitch. He loved the solitude, and he loved the raw, craggy peaks and the sense of achievement he felt from climbing to the roof of the country. Always on his own, just him, his kit and his wits keeping him safe. He'd done some mountain rescue, but hadn't really enjoyed it. For him climbing wasn't a team game.

He swigged again, the despair becoming deeper. He was expected to die to save the others.

Mikey had done it, but he'd always been a ruthless and mad bastard. He'd shown him the way on the hills, not just the climbing, but how to deal with the bitches. He knew how to cover his tracks, and how to select the best possible targets for the website.

McSorley chuckled without mirth, his mouth acidic and sour, as he remembered his first solo mission on this very spot. Mikey had done the research for him, poring over Facebook for the daft hags who were 'rediscovering themselves' by climbing Munros, and he'd identified the stupid tart. Leanne or something, her name was. She'd announced her intention to bag the hill for all to see on the social media site, with her big, beaming smile. It had made McSorley angry, as he knew that if he'd ever tried to talk to her, she'd act like he was something that she'd found on the bottom of her shoe, like all the others did. The look on her face was priceless as she'd tumbled down the sheer side of the ridge. The others had been ecstatic about the footage, which had made a bloody fortune. Not for him, mind. Bagger had been tight as fuck about that. It was gonna be him and Wyatt-Lawman who benefited from the money. Wyatt and Bagger were a couple of pathetic bastards, who would never have the courage to do the business on the Munros. They left it to him and Mikey. They liked the money enough; that was for sure. He knew one thing: with the nuclear bomb they all held against each other, they'd never grass. Grassing meant they all went down forever, and who'd want to be ex-police in jail?

Well, now Mikey was gone, and he was supposed to go the same way. He knew it would be easy, the slope was sheer, the height was vast and the granite unforgiving. Death would be instant.

But would the others do the same if necessary?

Would they fuck. He swigged again. He was one of the foot soldiers, the one expected to get the camera footage that the others would benefit from. Bagger just kept his distance and Wyatt sorted the money. Well, where was his fucking share?

His head swam, and he blinked away hot tears. It wasn't fair, while the remaining members would be there, sitting pretty, with the money rolling in from all the thousands of people sending their cash in, just for the privilege of seeing the videos.

He opened his mouth and let out a long, low, wolf-like howl.

He was going to die. But not yet. He was going to sit for a while longer, and maybe watch the sun set for the last time. Maybe the jump wouldn't look so bad in the dark.

He pulled out his phone, and went to the secure messaging app and looked at the last message from Bagger.

You need to do this now. They found the cop car with its GPS.

He sneered and took another swig from the bottle, which was nearly empty now. He narrowed his eyes to focus and composed his reply.

I'll see themcome, man. I'll dae it Bagger, nae frit. I ken this hill better than anyone. Why I klld the bitc here. Nae fuckr will get me

73

NORMA WAS ADDING to her chart on the largest of the screens, trying to make sense of the huge amount of data that Clive had dumped on her.

The dark web page was one thing, hideous as it was with the video clips of women falling, but the comments under each of the videos were, if anything, more disturbing.

> *@Incel4Life: Stupid bitch. Did you see the look on her face, not so pretty anymore.*
>
> *@womensuck: Fuck her, she'd have been a typical one. Wouldn't look at anyone that didn't have a full head of hair or a six pack. I love how her head caved in ☺*
>
> *@Bitches-die-in-pain: Oh maaan . . . this is just tooooo sweet! Love this site.*

Norma shuddered. Despite the jocular interaction with Ross about how she and Janie were feeling, it was unsettling to see and read what was on the website. She had a sudden urge to take a long, hot shower as soon as she got home.

Most of the videos had been uploaded by someone called @MikeyMunroSkulker but a couple had been uploaded by someone calling themselves @Bagger, who she assumed was the same individual on the message exchange that Clive had intercepted before the website had been deleted. He seemed to be carrying out some kind of admin function on the chat forum, talking about prices, details and hints to future videos that seemed to drive the forum users wild with excitement. Norma reached for her bottle of mineral water and took a deep draught from it, feeling a quiver of nausea. Her hands trembled just a little as she picked up her phone and dialled.

'Hello?' came a nasal, Yorkshire-accented voice.

'Clive?' she said.

'That's me. Is that Norma?'

'Yes, Clive, I'm wondering if you can help, as I'm drowning in data here, and trying to extract what's relevant. I've found two names that seem to be moderating the dark web page; one is obviously Bagger, who you identified before the website went down, talking to Wyatt-Lawman. The other is MikeyMunroSkulker, who we assume is Michael Anderson. Have you found anything?'

'Well, this is a coincidence, as I was going to call. I did a deep dive into the archive history of the webpage. It was tricky, but I used some AI-supported methodology and got a few fragments of the chat function that sat within the webpage but somehow in the background. It's complicated to explain, but I've found some communication history between Mikey whoever, Bagger and another couple of other names, Doss and Wyatt-Lawman. They don't all chat to each other, but Bagger seems to be consistent in all of the messages.'

'Any details?'

'Of the messages?' said Clive.

'Aye, the content of the messages.'

'Unfortunately not since the website went down. All the historic messages had an auto-delete function on them, and once they're gone, they're irretrievable, even by me. I was lucky with the one exchange that I saw almost live, and managed to screenshot before the website disappeared.'

'That's a shame, but the names and associations are useful for the chart. What else?'

'They've all been communicating, via the dark web, and on VPN-enabled connections, so there's no way of identifying where they are, or what device they sent the messages from, but I'd say that the individuals at the centre of this are Bagger, Wyatt-Lawman and Doss.'

'Okay, that's fine, I'll keep plotting and charting. Send me that exchange, yeah?'

'On its way,' said Clive, and then the phone beeped as he hung up.

Norma sighed and then minimised the screen. She needed to look at something else other than the contents of that hideous website, and the download of Anderson's laptop.

She turned to the summary of all the deaths of the women on the hills, which she'd just received, someone else having collated it all. They'd been so busy with all the hot taskings, and fast-time deployments, to catch Mikey that she'd not been able to get to them before now, beyond a cursory look. Some were still under investigation by the SFIU, but a number had been resolved without an inquiry. Only one had been the subject of a formal hearing at Inverness Sheriff Court. She opened the document and began to read. Her mind scanned over the names, dates and locations as they were entered into a table that she'd speedily put together. Then she stopped.

Of the deaths that Max's friend had flagged as being suspicious, only one had been referred for an inquiry, and on only two occasions had the Procurator Fiscal even ordered a police investigation.

She frowned; that didn't feel right. Why hadn't a full inquiry been ordered?

She clicked one that had been referred for an investigation and read the summary. There was no mention of the victim's use of social media ahead of her ascent up the hill. If Shay Hammond had discovered that, why hadn't the cops investigated?

She clicked on the case where an inquiry had been held just last year, the deceased being a lone walker female, called Fiona Howse from Coventry. The first page was a colour photograph of her. She was a young-looking, thirtysomething with an open smile, sparkling eyes and a short, bobbed blonde haircut. Norma stared for a full minute before turning to the next page. It was a technical legal document about the hearing at Inverness Sheriff Court, in front of Sheriff Muldoon and presented by the Procurator Fiscal, Gerald McCaskill.

Norma scanned the legal document and, once again, found no mention of social media use, but her eyes did lock onto the opening paragraph. One line caused a shiver down her spine.

Fiona had recently come out of a long relationship, and while the break-up was seemingly somewhat acrimonious, friends report that she was enjoying life as a newly single woman. She had only recently discovered Munro climbing, and while she was a comparative novice, I am not convinced that her inexperience was a contributory factor in her fall.

Once again, a newly single woman who met her end plunging off a Munro. She read on, despite the knot of anxiety sitting in her throat.

The cause of death was described as being . . .

due to a chest injury caused by, or as a consequence of a fall while climbing, damaging a lung, which resulted in the development of a pneumothorax and bleeding into the chest space, causing impaired respiration leading to hypoxia.

Norma sighed at the technical language used to describe the death of someone's mother, sister, daughter. It was just so sad.

She read on, stopping at the section marked 'Reasonable precautions'.

> There was no suggestion in the evidence that Ms Howse was not adequately equipped for the activity she undertook. There was no evidence to suggest that any other equipment would have made any difference. There was no evidence that she should have been using climbing ropes. I was not invited to speculate about that. On the face of it, she was adequately clad, had proper boots and was wearing a helmet.

The only observations and recommendations seemed to be about the Cairngorm Mountain Resorts reinforcing advice for lone walkers with regards equipment, route selection and ensuring that their timetables are widely circulated. There was no mention of her use of social media in announcing her intention to climb the hill on an unrestricted page. It all seemed to be a little slack.

Her phone buzzed on the table; it was a message from Janie.

Any updates?

Norma looked at the chart, and the legal report, and shook her head. It was too early, and she had no concrete conclusions. She composed a response. *Not yet, still data crunching, what you up to?*

About to get on a helicopter and fly up a bloody mountain after that McSorley bloke I told you about. He's hiding out up there somewhere.

Norma smiled as she typed, *How exciting, lucky you!*

I hate heights, so no. Gotta run, briefing time before we go.

Norma sighed. She loved her job, but sometimes she hated being stuck in an office.

There was a tone from her computer indicating that an email

had arrived. It was the report she'd requested on the circumstances of Michael Anderson's dismissal. She opened it, and began to read, sighing again as she did. Another closely typed and tedious official form.

She stopped reading, stood up and went to the kettle.

Probably her tenth of the day, but she needed the lift before she tackled the next task.

Such was the life of an analyst.

74

JANIE HELD HER breath as she strapped herself into the seat on the red-and-white helicopter alongside Inspector Jeffries, who just grinned and nodded at her. She settled the headset on her head and looked across at Max, who was sitting next to Sergeant Ed Smith. The two crew members that Shay had identified as Chas and Jimbo were both dressed in orange flight suits and helmets, busying themselves with the pre-flight routines. Shay and his co-pilot, a similarly chirpy guy who'd been identified as Macca, went through all their pre-flight checks with practised ease.

Despite her nerves, Janie was feeling confident about what came next. A report had come in from the mountain that a uniformed cop had been seen parking a car in the pub car park and had headed off up to the Munro. She leant forward in her seat and retied the long laces on her walking boots. Together with the Mountain Rescue waterproofs that she and Max had been given by Inspector Jeffries she didn't feel that they were too underdressed. She shifted uncomfortably in her discreet body armour and adjusted her handcuffs, gas and extendable baton that were attached to the utility belt around her middle. She looked out of the still wide-open sliding door at the blue sky. She couldn't remember such a period of almost perfect weather in Scotland, and despite the fears of climate change, at this particular moment, she was happy that the skies were clear. Climbing a mountain was one thing, doing it in foul weather was another.

Her headset crackled, and Shay's chirpy voice came over the intercom.

'Okay, people. We're all set to go, flight time about twenty-five minutes. We'll head straight there and see what we can see. Shouldn't be too hard to spot a uniformed cop on the hill, especially as it's one of the quieter ones. If it was Cairngorm, it'd be a bit more of a struggle.'

'Great, can't wait,' said Max into the intercom.

They'd had a short amount of time to plan before boarding the helicopter. Ross and DCI O'Neill were travelling down in the Volvo, and would meet Barney when he arrived. Max, Janie, Jeffries and Smith would all stay on the helicopter while Shay performed a sweep to see if they could spot McSorley.

'If we do spot him and you want to go down, we should be able to deal with that too. I can isolate the intercom, so you guys can hatch a more detailed plan before we put you down,' said Shay.

'Nice one. Can we do that now, Shay?' said Max.

'Over to you,' said Shay.

'Are we all here?' Max began.

'Tom here.'

'Ed's here.'

'Janie here.'

'Okay, assuming we spot him on the hill, what do we suggest?' said Max.

'Well, Ed and I are the experienced climbers, and we're both familiar with this hill. So if we need to split, I suggest it's in pairs – one of you guys with one of us. If we see him, Shay can drop one of us behind him, and then move the other pair ahead of him. If he's on the ridgeline, we'll have him in a classic pincer, yeah?' said Jeffries.

'Okay, agreed. Let's see if we can trace him first, but that sounds like a plan. We'll also have Barney and his drone very soon as backup.'

'Sounds good. Do we all have gas and batons? McSorley will, so we need to be ready,' said Jeffries.

'Yeah, we're all good,' said Max.

'We're in suck-it-and-see territory here, guys. We can't plan properly until we spot him. If we don't see him, we're going to have to go slow time, call in more cops and get the full MRT team in.'

Janie sighed. She just had a feeling that they needed to get hold of McSorley soon, or they'd have another suicide on their hands.

The helicopter's engine note shifted up a notch, and the crew became more animated and the checks increased. Chas, the winch operator, slid the door shut, and the helicopter lurched just a little as it ascended, and within a few moments, they were off, gathering height into the blue sky.

The intercom clicked in Janie's ear. 'Okay, that's us on the way, guys. Hold tight, be there soon.'

In fact, in only twenty minutes they were crossing the unrelenting rolling green and slate-greys of the mountain range, and then were above a snaking road with a building to the side.

'If you look at the screen that Bill is about to fold down, you'll see the cop car parked near the pub,' said Shay.

Janie turned in her seat and looked at the screen, seeing the pin-sharp image of the car park with the distinctive cop car below, the blue light on the top, and the vehicle-identifying digits on the roof.

'I'm gonna head towards the ridgeline, as that's where the witness reported seeing him heading. Hold tight for just a few minutes, keep an eye on the screen, and direct Bill to anything you want him to zoom in on, okay?'

The helicopter swooped in the sky towards the big grey and rocky expanse, the engine thunderous in Janie's ears, despite the headset. The operator zoomed the camera out wide, before tapping his finger on the screen and zooming in again. 'See that?'

he said, pointing at a bright-yellow pinprick just off the craggy pathway that bisected the grassy hill.

The camera's zoom function was impressive, and the item grew in the screen.

Janie saw what it was straight away.

It was a hi-vis police jacket.

Janie felt her stomach tighten and, flicking the switch on the intercom, said, 'That's his uniform jacket, and look to the side of it. That's his cap. He's divesting himself of his uniform.'

'We can't be sure where he's heading, though, can we?'

'It'll definitely be the ridge,' said Max, with utter confidence.

'How can you know that for sure? He could be going anywhere if he's topping himself,' said Ed, his brow furrowed.

'Because that's where he killed his first victim. He's revisiting the scene of the crime before he kills himself,' said Max.

75

NORMA SIPPED AT her eleventh cup of tea of the day, thankful that she'd now switched to decaff, as she turned the page on the report of the discipline hearing for Michael Anderson.

The case was completed just over a year ago, and it seemed to be something of a hush job. She'd seen a number of disciplinary reports in her time, and this one seemed somewhat of a light touch.

Then Norma saw it.

Involvement of PC 7456 McSorley

The complainant in this case suggested that DC Anderson was with PC McSorley during two of the interactions with her. His involvement was minimal, he had no contact with her on any occasion, but she is insistent that he commented, 'Nice tits, hen,' as the police car driven by Anderson moved off during their first encounter. I have challenged McSorley about this, and he is insistent that she must be mistaken, and that he did compliment her on her tattoos, and in fact said, 'Nice tatts, hen.'

PC McSorley.

Norma felt her heart begin to beat faster in her chest, and she swallowed.

McSorley and Anderson had worked together and had been

jointly involved in a complaint of impropriety with a female victim of crime.

She read on, getting to the recommendations of the report.

Recommendations

The evidence of the complainant makes it clear that Anderson pursued her with the intention of seeking an inappropriate relationship after dealing with her as a victim of domestic abuse. He was a man in a position of power over a vulnerable victim of crime, and he behaved in a manner likely to bring the service into disrepute.

However, in light of DC Anderson's resignation from Police Scotland at short notice, I am unable to progress this inquiry any further. Had he remained in post I would have concluded that there was a case to answer for gross misconduct, and if proven I am satisfied that Anderson would have been dismissed.

I do not believe that sufficient evidence exists to take further action against PC McSorley. However, I will issue him with written words of advice, which will remain on his personal file.

. . .

I have informed the complainant of my decision, and of the outcome of this investigation, and she seems satisfied and does not wish to progress any complaint against PC McSorley.

Respectfully submitted for your information.

Norma sighed. They'd missed the vital bit of information that linked McSorley with Anderson. This may have enabled the cops to intervene sooner. This would look very bad if the press got hold of it. She needed to speak to Ross.

'What? I'm in a car speeding thorough the Highlands, and I'm shite scared of the shite driver,' said Ross.

'I've some bad news.'

76

THE HELICOPTER SWOOPED over the ridge at what Shay had told them was a thousand metres. It almost resembled a knife blade, and followed the steep line until it widened slightly with huge, blocky granite slabs that led to the top of the ridge towards the summit of A' Chralaig.

Max was strapped in, looking at the screen of his phone. A text from Katie had made him jump. *Any ideas when you're coming home?*

Max tapped out a reply. *Not yet. Currently in a helicopter being flown by Shay!*

OMG, how exciting, why?
Doing a thing on a munro. All okay?
Fine. Jealous of the helicopter ☹. *Say hi to Shay for me, and be careful. X*

Max tapped out a reply. *Love you x*
The double ticks on the message remained grey. Clearly, she'd just put the phone down. Or was choosing not to answer.

Max sighed, wondering if she was as cheerful as the exchange seemed. His sudden morose mood was lifted when there was a shout over the headset from Bill.

'Something there, guys, at the cluster of granite rocks on the ridge. Shay, hold her steady while I zoom in,' he said. He worked the controls and the footage zoomed in tight on the peak of the ridgeline where there was a dark blob. The footage homed in on the top, the image clearing immediately. Janie was amazed at the quality of the camera. They must have been a mile away from the rocky outcrop but the image was pin-sharp as it zoomed in.

Then they saw him.

A black-clad figure flat out on top of a large slab of granite, his head resting on a neon-green protective vest.

Janie looked at the footage, and even from their height, she recognised him.

Without doubt, it was Danny McSorley.

'That's him, and I'm guessing he's pished. See the empty bottle to the side of him?' said Janie, looking over and nodding at Max, who shifted to get a view at the screen.

'Aye, that's him right enough. Shay, we need to get down, now,' said Max.

'That's no problem, guys, but I'll blow him off the side of the bloody ridge if I go down here. How about I drop two of you at the north of the ascent, and two at the south end? You'll have him sandwiched in then, and only an easy one-kilometre climb each?' said Shay, his demeanour calm and efficient, as one would expect who had flown multiple combat missions in hostile environments.

Janie looked across at Jeffries, who nodded, his jaw firm.

'Good idea,' he said. 'Drop us in first, and Janie and I will make the ascent, it's only a thirty-minute climb if you can drop us as close as you can, Shay.'

'No problem for me, it'll be a slightly longer ascent for you, Max, as opportunities for a drop are a little more limited on the north side of the buttress, but you'll still have him in the middle of you both. If you're quick, you'll be able to give him a nice wake-up call. Okay, hold tight, I'm descending over the ridgeline and out of his sight, not that I think the bugger's in any fit state. I could probably just winch you down, and you could surprise him,' Shay said, chuckling, as calm as ever.

'Perhaps not,' said Jeffries.

'Okay, well, south ridge it is. Get ready. Just a couple of minutes.' Shay worked the controls, and the helicopter tipped alarmingly and headed back the way they'd come.

Janie checked her kit, and breathed deeply, calming her nerves. Game on. She and Max looked at each other for a full beat, and then he nodded, his face hard.

'You ready for this, Janie?' said Jeffries.

'Aye, I don't like heights, and I don't like the countryside, so I'm grand.'

77

THE HELICOPTER BARELY kissed the soft, tussocky grass just at the bottom of the craggy path that led to the final ascent towards the ridge, when Janie and Jeffries both jumped out of the aircraft, and moved safely away, the downdraught buffeting them, and the engines roaring.

Janie turned to look, as the engine pitch changed, got louder, and the helicopter ascended again, Shay giving a thumbs-up as the huge Agusta roared upwards, gaining height quickly into the cobalt-blue sky.

Within a minute, it was silent again, with just a soft breeze that whispered around them, full of the scent of the grass.

Then they came.

The midges. Millions of them swarming across their exposed skin.

'Jesus, bloody midges are brutal,' said Janie, swatting about herself fruitlessly.

'Aye, wee bastards are unrelenting. Fortunately, your Uncle Tom here has some Smidge and a couple of nets. They're attracted to the CO_2 you're breathing out, so there'll be no respite.' He pulled his rucksack from his back, rifled inside it and tossed a small pouch to Janie. Unfurling it, she found a fine mesh net bag.

'Ya dancer,' she said, scrubbing her hands at her face before slipping the bag over her head and loosely tightening the drawstring.

'You'll want a squirt of Smidge for your hands, and maybe face, to take care of any wee stragglers that are under the net. When it's as still as this, they'll be brutal. If the wind's up at the top of the ridge, they'll no' be so bad,' Jeffries said, offering the bottle.

Janie squeezed a small amount out and spread it over her hands, before squirting a little more out, lifting the net and liberally applying it to her face, ears and neck. When done, she tossed the bottle back to Jeffries. She then pulled her waterproof hood up, and tightened the Velcro around her cuffs.

'All ready?' said Jeffries, a smile detectable behind the mesh of the net.

'Aye, as I'll ever be.'

'Then let's go. You have any phone signal?' he said.

Janie pulled out her phone and her heart lurched as she saw that her battery was also running very low. 'Hardly any, and my battery is awful low, anyhow.'

'No bother, it's always shite here; it'll get better as we climb. I've my radio, so I can keep in touch with Ed and we can make sure we get to Danny at the same time. It'll be a fairly stiff climb. Are you fit?'

'Aye, I do a bit,' said Janie, not mentioning the daily punishing exercise routines and twice-a-week MMA or jiu-jitsu sessions.

'Then let's go.' He turned and set off towards the stony and rocky path that went straight up towards the ridgeline.

Jeffries' pace was hard and unrelenting as they began to tackle the steep path, and soon Janie found her thighs burning as the lactic acid forced its way into her muscles, but she said nothing, just carried on, breathing hard as they trudged towards the top of the path.

As they hit the peak, the scenery fell away in front of them, leading towards the ridge, which looked sharp, dangerous and grey against the green of the grass. The wind had picked up and was now blowing in from the edge of the cliff, which was welcome, as it was cooling, but mostly, because it seemed to have chased the midges away.

'You okay?' said Jeffries, pulling up his face net.

'I'm good, particularly now those wee midgie bastards have sodded off,' said Janie, accepting his proffered water bottle and taking a long draught.

'Aye, they're unrelenting wee buggers, but they don't like the wind,' he said with a smile.

The path snaked away in front of them to a small clump of rocks where it seemed to narrow. Jeffries pulled out a pair of binoculars and raised them to his face. 'He's still there, flaked out on a flat rock. I reckon we're ten minutes walk away from him. I'll call up Ed and see where he is,' he said, tapping at his earpiece and reaching into his pocket, where presumably he had a button.

'Ed, you getting me?' he said, looking again through the binoculars and cocking his head.

'Aye, he's not far away. Let's get as close as we can; don't want the bastard to wake up and hurl himself off, eh?' he said, tucking the binoculars away, along with the water that Janie had handed back.

Jeffries reshouldered his rucksack and set off again, at the same merciless pace.

The path was narrow and rocky, and the sides sloped away alarmingly on each side. Janie felt the first pang of nerves as she realised just how high this ridgeline was. The scenery was absolutely staggering but she dared not look; rather, she watched each and every step she took, while resisting the urge to swat at the feeling of a million little beasties feasting on her skin behind the midge net.

She tried ignoring the discomfort and ever-increasing fear that gnawed at her insides, like a dull cramp. She forced the feelings down and just kept putting one foot in front of the other.

The path suddenly veered away from the ridge ahead and seemed almost impassable as it grew even more craggy. It cut into the grass and descended a few metres towards the small nest of rocks where they'd seen the flash of hi-vis that indicated where McSorley had been. Jeffries stopped and raised a palm, holding his fingers to his lips. He moved closer to Janie and whispered, 'Just on the other side of these rocks. He's on one of the flat ones, on his back. Let me edge forward to check, and I'll radio Ed.'

Janie nodded and knelt down, reaching for her phone and checking the signal. Even more worryingly, she noted that the battery icon was now in the dead zone. She closed her eyes and prayed that it would hold out just a little while longer.

Jeffries edged forward towards the rocks, his finger rising to his ear as he did, reaching for the radio button as he moved on soft footsteps. He reminded her of a cat stalking its prey as he used the natural features as cover. It was impressive to watch, she had to admit, and as uncomfortable as she was in this beautiful but dangerous environment, she was glad to be with Jeffries.

He crept up to the rocks and peered around the corner, before he turned and beckoned her to join him. Her heart in her mouth, and feeling it beating fast in her ears, she advanced to where Jeffries was. He nodded at her, and whispered, 'He's on his feet.'

'What do we do?' said Janie.

'Hold up.' Jeffries peered again around the rock at the edge of the path, which sloped away into a huge chasm to the side. Janie tried not to look at the drop, knowing that all her attention and efforts were going to be required to bring in the murderous cop. She steeled herself to spring into action.

Jeffries turned back and leant forward to whisper, 'He's just standing there, leaning against the rock, like. All dozy and pished as a fart. I think we can take him out ourselves. You ready?' His eyes were wide with excitement and anticipation.

Janie felt her stomach tighten, but she nodded.

'Okay, stand by, and on my mark.'

78

NORMA CONTINUED TO peruse the documents, after the slightly dismissive fashion that Ross had handled what she thought had been important information.

'That can well wait till later, woman,' he'd blasted before hanging up. So, she'd made another cup of tea, before looking at the report again to see if she could spot anything else.

She reread the last passage of it, something telling her that she was missing something.

> I do not believe that sufficient evidence exists to take further action against PC McSorley. However, I will issue him with written words of advice, which will remain on his personal file. He has expressed an interest to be redeployed to the north Highlands and Islands Division, and I am minded to recommend this. A fresh start with the reflective practice action plan will give PC McSorley the best chance to progress and, hopefully, flourish.

> I have informed the complainant of my decision, and of the outcome of this investigation, and she seems satisfied and does not wish to progress any complaint against PC McSorley.

She looked at the signature block of the author of the report, and she gasped, as she felt the colour drain from her face.

Inspector Jeffries. Tom Jeffries. The same man she'd spoken to when organising the MRT team. The same man she'd sent the briefing notes to.

The same man. The man who made the questionable decision not to prosecute Anderson, and not to sack McSorley. The man now on a manhunt high up on a Munro with her good friend.

Norma's hands shook as she dialled, and the phone clattered to the desk, before she picked it up again. 'Hi, it's Janie, I can't take your call right now. Leave a message.'

'Shit, shit, shit,' she said as she redialled, the number going to voicemail again.

'Fuck,' she hissed, her skin boiling, and she dialled again.

'Fuck's sake, woman, we're trying to catch a suicidal and murderous cop, what is it?' said Ross, his voice steel-edged.

'Is Inspector Jeffries with you?' Norma blurted out.

'No, he's up the top of a Munro with Janie. Why?'

'Call her now, call her right now, she's in danger.'

'What are you bloody talking about?'

'He's part of this, Ross. He was Anderson and McSorley's complaints inspector in Glasgow last year, and he's never mentioned it. He investigated the case that got Anderson in trouble and McSorley was complained about as well, and he never said a fucking thing, Ross.'

'*What?*'

'Jeffries is one of them, Ross. I think Jeffries is Bagger.'

79

JANIE HELD HER breath, as Jeffries counted down with his fingers – three, two, one – and then powered around the rock, and onto the narrow path, Janie just a metre behind. McSorley looked up, his face pale and his eyes widening in surprise as he was faced by the charging Inspector Jeffries, who grabbed him by both shoulders and slammed him against the rock.

McSorley barely jumped. He just stared at Jeffries with half-closed eyes, as he sagged on legs that appeared to be made of rubber. He was clearly seriously pissed.

'Danny, it's over, man,' Jeffries said, reaching down and unhitching the cop's utility belt, which fell to the dusty path, pulled down by the weight of the cuffs, extendable baton and gas.

'What the fuck . . .' began McSorley, but he seemed incapable of resisting as Jeffries just firmed his grip.

'Janie, call it in,' said Jeffries, looking at her, his eyes wide with excitement.

Janie pulled her phone from her pocket and looked at the screen. It was dark, inert and dead. Janie swore under her breath as she tried to reboot the handset.

Nothing.

'Janie, we need to call it in,' said Jeffries.

'My bloody battery has gone. Can you call it in on your radio?' she said.

'Aye, hold up. Now listen, Danny, it's over, yeah? I'm gonna release one hand, and then I'm calling this in, so don't piss about, okay?' he said, his voice as hard as steel.

McSorley looked broken. He nodded, drunkenly, and Janie could smell the stench of whisky from her position two metres away. 'I'll no' cause a stramash, Bagger, man,' he slurred.

Something flared in Janie's mind.

Then it arrived like an express train.

Bagger. She opened her mouth, and her hand began to move to her belt for her baton, when in an explosive and lightning-quick movement, Jeffries firmed his grip on McSorley's shirt and violently swung him towards the precipice, releasing him at the last second. He flew off the rocky edge disappearing from sight and into the abyss, a thousand feet down.

80

JANIE FELT LIKE she was moving through treacle as she went for her baton. Jeffries was faster. He raised his hand and a thin stream of liquid jetted out and splashed into Janie's face.

The pain was intense, immediate and overwhelming as the PAVA irritant spray bit into Janie's eyes, and she cried out with a mix of fear and fury as Jeffries rushed her and drove her backwards. They both fell to the rough ground, pain exploding in Janie's back as she collided with a sharp rock, just a few inches from the precipice that McSorley had just plummeted into.

'You stupid fucking bitch,' growled Jeffries as he pinned her to the ground, his hands around her neck. 'Could've left it, but you bastards had to interfere. Well, you can take a trip to the bottom of the cliff with poor old Danny.'

Janie let out a strangled cry, as the biting spray attacked her eyes and nasal passages, her eyes streaming with tears, and mucus flying from her nose. She opened her eyes and through the blur, she could make out the hate-filled face of Jeffries. He firmed his grip on her neck, his teeth bared in a snarl.

Janie's instincts kicked in and chased away the initial terror. She forced herself to open her eyes, despite the excruciating pain, as the synthetic capsicum solution bit harder. Fury overtook the initial fear, and she looked into his eyes, her vision blurred. But she knew. All her years of wrestling and jiu-jitsu told her instinctively that his body position was all wrong, and she could turn this to her advantage, despite the agony she was in.

She knew that Jeffries had made a mistake. A big mistake.

He'd underestimated her, like so many before him. This bastard, like so many police officers, thought she'd be a pushover. Well, he was about to learn a hard lesson.

She raised her hand and extended three fingers together, jabbing them hard into his eye. He howled in fury and pain but didn't release his grip on her neck. Her already compromised vision began to fail, as the interrupted supply of oxygen to her brain made an impact, and she knew she had to act now. She jabbed again, her finger finding the wet softness of his eye socket, and his grip on her neck loosened and shifted, allowing her to lower her chin, whereupon she sank her teeth into the web of his hand, hard enough to taste blood.

He screamed and released his grip, but then drew back his fist and struck, catching the top of her head. The pain was immense, and stars danced behind her eyes. She knew she had only one last chance against the much bigger man, so she released a wild elbow that smashed into his nose, driving his head upwards and to the side. He half fell away from her, his body slumping closer to the edge of the cliff. He released Janie's leg that had been pinned underneath him. She quickly whipped it around and over the inspector's shoulder. She dragged him towards her, catching him with her other leg and locking in around his neck, his arm trapped in between Janie's leg and upper body. He began to struggle, but it was no use. Janie let out a howl that was animalistic, with a mix of intense pain in her eyes and nose.

She'd practised this move many times in her MMA dojo. A classic jiu-jitsu triangle choke. A winning choke. If this was in a competition, Jeffries would be tapping out right now. But Jeffries wasn't tapping out, and she wasn't releasing him, either.

A finishing move, she knew it then and there. She applied the full pressure of the choke, her legs locked around his neck interrupting the supply of blood to his brain.

Jeffries went limp, and he sagged, his legs flopping into the void just to the side of them, and suddenly he was a dead weight. Janie scrabbled for purchase but the weight of Jeffries was pulling her with him closer to the edge of the cliff, and into oblivion. She knew then. She had no choice.

She would have to let him go, or she'd die with him.

81

JANIE LEANT BACK, trying one last time to pull the unconscious man back onto the path, letting out a yell as she did, before everything changed. A hand shot out from behind her, and grabbed hold of Jeffries' jacket collar, and heaved him back up onto the path. Max dragged Jeffries fully onto the path, and turned him onto his front. Ed suddenly appeared, and grabbed hold of Jeffries' trailing arm, and pulled him closer to the rock face.

'Good work, Janie,' said Ed, nodding at her.

'It's okay, release him, I have him,' said Max, as he snapped a handcuff on Jeffries' wrists, as the Inspector began to moan, softly, as he regained consciousness as the blood supply was reestablished to his brain.

'Aye,' said Janie, 'what took you so long?' She smiled, her eyes still stinging intensely, as she sat up.

'Sorry. Where's McSorley?' said Max.

'A thousand feet below us where Jeffries shoved him. Best call in the search-and-rescue helicopter; he may have survived, but I doubt it.' Janie almost collapsed and she sat against the rock, breathing heavily. Max secured Jeffries, and spun him around onto his front as he began to regain consciousness. He said nothing, just buried his face in the scrappy path, his eyes wide open.

'Already done, SAR are on their way,' said Ed, looking at Jeffries with utter disdain.

'Nice one, Ed.'

'I cannae believe that Tom has done this, I've worked with him for years,' said Ed, leaning against the rock.

'One thing I've learnt is that people often turn out to be not who you thought they were, Ed. Jeffries has just been added to that list. He's been part of these murders, and sharing the footage of them on the dark web. He's a bad man, and he's going to bloody jail,' said Max.

'Jeffries is Bagger. McSorley called him by that name, just before he shoved him over the edge,' said Janie.

'I know. Norma figured it out, and called Ross. Ross radioed it in to Ed and we ran up as fast as we could.' Max smiled.

The inspector groaned and shook his head, his eyes blinking blearily. Ed dragged him up into a seated position, his back against the rock. Jeffries just looked down at his boots, his face white as a sheet. Ed almost snarled, his eyes hard as he glared at his former boss. 'You bastard,' he said, face full of rage.

Jeffries said nothing. He just sat there, head bowed, quivering with fear.

Max grinned and clapped his colleague on the shoulder. 'You did good stuff, pal.'

'Aye, well, if I'd waited for you, I'd be deid, ya teuchter bastard,' she said, smiling despite the pain in her head, eyes and back.

'Well done, pal. Despite being a nugget of a Sassenach, you're no' so bad,' said Max, nodding and smiling at her, as he handed over his water bottle.

'Is it over?' said Janie, sitting up and wiping at her eyes, before sluicing them out with the water.

'Not yet. There's one left.'

'What?'

'Aye. Some bastard called Wyatt-Lawman. Clive has found all sorts on the computer. He's still out there, and we're bringing him in.'

'How are we doing that?' said Janie.

Instead of answering, Max knelt down next to Jeffries and began to sift through his pockets until he found his phone, a new-looking Samsung. He continued to search, delving into the pocket of the inspector's cargo pants, where he pulled out a cheap-looking Motorola. It may as well have had 'burner phone' inscribed on it. He woke the screen, which lit up. There were only two apps installed. The now-familiar Tor browser and a messenger app.

'Here we have a totally filthy phone, eh? Gonna give me the passcode, Jeffries?' said Max.

The inspector said nothing, just sat there, head bowed.

'Suit yourself,' said Max, before grabbing the man by the shoulder, dragging him away from the rock and dumping him on his front once more.

Jeffries balled his handcuffed fingers reflexively. Max grinned at Janie. 'Listen, Tom, here's the thing. I'm gonna get your fingerprint to open this phone whether you like it or not. Now, you've just been in a violent encounter with my hard-as-nails partner here, and during that struggle, it's possible you *may* have snapped some fingers, so my suggestion is, extend the finger you use on this phone, or I will make that possibility a bloody reality.'

'You can't do that,' he blurted out.

Ed stepped forward, knelt down and pushed his face close to Jeffries. 'Open your hands now, or I will fucking stamp on them, you corrupt shite,' he hissed through clenched teeth.

Jeffries turned even paler, and a solitary tear trickled down his cheek, but he extended his right index finger. Max pressed it to the unlock pad, and the phone lit up.

The messaging app showed that it had one message unread.

'What do you reckon?' Max said to Janie.

'We should get it done proper, like. Authorities and all that. But I suspect you have other ideas,' said Janie, her eyes still brick red.

'How long will that take, and will the message disappear before it does?' Max pulled his phone from his pocket and dialled.

'About bloody time, what the shitting fuck is going on?' said Ross, his voice harsh.

Max told him.

'Shite, I know I don't do praise, but that lassie is one for a square go, eh? What do you need?'

'Authority to pretend to be Jeffries on his phone, and contact the outstanding suspect. Also no one can know he's in custody.'

'I'll make the calls, but the Chief's already said he'll authorise whatever you need. Your pal in the helicopter is on his way to McSorley, who I assume is deid. They'll then bring you lot down with that scummy bastard, Jeffries. I'm making the call to get an ancillary custody centre opened up. I'll ask for Fort William; we certainly don't want him going to Inverness.'

'He needs to be on a suicide watch, and we need him incommunicado. No phone calls, no people informed, no solicitor. Nothing. We need the world to believe that Inspector Jeffries has not been arrested, and we are dealing with what appears to be a fatal accident in the hills.'

'Leave it with me, and I'll get back to you,' Ross said.

Janie nodded at Max. 'Do it.' They both walked a short way down the path out of earshot of Jeffries and Smith. There was the distant *whoomp*, *whoomp* of an approaching helicopter. 'Whatever you're doing, do it quick. Sounds like the airborne cavalry is approaching.'

Max clicked on the app, and a speech bubble opened.

There was one message on the phone.

Wyatt-Lawman: What the hell is happening?

Max looked at Janie and smiled. 'Are you thinking what I'm thinking?'

'I suspect so, let's make this happen.'

'Do we think that McSorley was Doss from the chats?'

Janie nodded. 'He has to be, nothing else makes sense.'

Max took a deep breath and tapped out a response. *Bagger: Doss is dead at the bottom of a Cairngorm hill.*

Wyatt-Lawman: How did he get there?

Max smiled. *Bagger: He went there to jump off, but lost his nerve. I gave him a helping hand* 😉

Wyatt-Lawman: Nice work, anything to tie it to you?

Max looked at Janie, who nodded. *Bagger: No, but they'll be careful. Waiting for backup now, and I suspect they'll treat it like a crime scene, so I'll need to lose this phone. We have a potential big problem. They have an expert working on Anderson's laptop and they're trying to break the encryption. Is it secure enough?*

'Ooo, I like that, you Machiavellian bugger,' said Janie.

'Who the hell is Machiavelli?' said Max.

'Really, you don't know?'

Max shrugged.

'Niccolo Machiavelli, commonly credited with being the father of modern political philosophy and political science. He served for years as a senior official in the Florentine—'

Max raised a hand. 'Boring nerd alert. I was just being sarcastic,' he said, with a grin.

'Piss off,' said Janie, looking at the inert phone screen.

Max chuckled.

'What's the bugger doing?' said Janie.

'He's thinking. Someone encrypted Anderson's laptop. I'm gambling that it's this mannie,' said Max, tapping on the screen.

The phone buzzed.

Wyatt-Lawman: That must not happen. It could lead them to the money. Can you get to it?

Bagger: Not immediately. They'll be treating this as a death in custody, and they'll be all over me as soon as they get up here. I can hear a helicopter approaching now.

Wyatt-Lawman: You must get it, by whatever means necessary. Where is it?

'He's shiting a brick, man. This is it. This is the opportunity.'

'I think so.'

Max furrowed his brow and tapped out a reply.

Bagger: Some forensic expert has it. I can probably find out.

Wyatt-Lawman: Just get it, and get it to me, urgently. There's vital information on it that I need to secure the money.

'The bastard's desperate, which means he'll be reckless. Let's push him.' Max typed out another message.

Bagger: They're gonna suspect me, man. PIRC will be all over me for a death in custody.

There was another long pause before the reply came through.

Wyatt-Lawman: Don't worry. It's just a fatal accident investigation on a Munro. Leave that to me.

Max looked at Janie, his mouth agape. 'What the hell does that mean? Who *is* this bastard? A senior cop? Again?'

'He must be. Who has the clout to frustrate such an inquiry?' said Janie, raising her voice, as the sound from the approaching helicopter became louder, and the big search-and-rescue AgustaWestland loomed level with them a hundred metres away. The door opened, and the winchman appeared. It dropped quickly, and out of sight below the precipice, the noise relenting a touch as it disappeared.

Max looked down and tapped out another message.

Bagger: Cavalry is almost here, so I need to wipe and lose this phone, urgently. How will I contact you?

There was long pause again. Max risked a peek over the edge of the cliff; the helicopter was there, the engines roaring, and the orange-clad winchman was dangling below, heading towards what looked like a broken shop dummy, several hundred metres down the almost sheer slope.

'What's happening?' said Janie, nodding behind Max.

'Take a peek?'

Janie shook her head, vigorously. 'No bloody way, I've had enough adventure for today.'

Max chuckled. 'The winch paramedic is going down, most likely for a body recovery.' The phone buzzed in Max's hand.

Wyatt-Lawman: I'll call your personal phone with one ring from a new burner. Get a new burner, and WhatsApp me a meeting place and instructions for handover. No contact. We can't be seen together. Exchange in Inverness. (Wyatt-Lawman has left the chat.)

Jeffries' Samsung buzzed in Max's hand, just one short ring, and a mobile number flashed up on the screen.

'He's bitten, and now all we need to do is reel him in,' said Max, a wide grin stretching across his face.

'When?' said Janie.

'Immediately. Every second counts, Janie. Whoever Wyatt-Lawman is, he's connected. We let the cavalry arrive, get Jeffries into custody. We finish this today.'

82

THERE WAS A reception committee waiting for them when the helicopter touched down at the bottom of A' Chralaig, and within no time at all the silent Jeffries was in the back of a police van.

The broken and bloodied body of McSorley was secure in a body bag strapped to a stretcher on the floor of the helicopter, with Sergeant Ed Smith sitting next to it. It had been agreed that he would accompany the body back to Raigmore to ensure full continuity and to hand over to the murder team officers who would be meeting him there.

'Good work, troops,' said Ross, nodding at Max and Janie as they stepped off the helicopter. As Janie got closer, Ross's eyes widened in alarm. 'Shite, you look like a fucking vampire that had a particularly rumbunctious night on the swally in a dive bar off Sauchiehall Street. What the bastarding hell happened to you?'

'Inspector Jeffries decided to introduce me to the fun of PAVA spray right in the puss,' said Janie.

'Need any medical attention?' he said.

Janie shook her head. 'No way. We've a golden opportunity here, and we need to strike now. Last thing I need is to dick about at a hospital.'

'Have you deployed your legendary diplomacy to get this locked down?' said Max.

'I have. Miles Moneypenny is doing a sterling job of making all the calls. Fort William custody is being specially opened and is taking Jeffries with a custody officer and jailer that Miles personally vouches for. Incommunicado is being authorised, and he'll only get an approved and vetted solicitor, but we all know that it's only a matter of time before it leaks.'

'Who's doing the interviews?' said Janie.

'Two of Struan's best detectives. He's worked with them forever, and they're good people, which leaves us to get on with tracking down the missing piece of this whole puzzle. Do you have a suggestion?' said Ross.

'I do. Did the laptop come north with us?'

'Aye, it's in the car in its Faraway bag.'

'Faraday bag,' corrected Max.

'Fuck's sake, whatever, Poindexter. Now, are you going to enlighten me? As I understand it from the messages you sent from the helicopter, whoever Wyatt Earp is, he wants the contents of the *Faraday* bag back. Who's gonna take it to him? You?'

Max shook his head. 'I don't think it can be a cop, unless we call up an undercover operator from outside Scotland, which we don't have the time for. This guy is clearly connected, and anyone we send, he may recognise, with disastrous consequences.'

Ross narrowed his eyes. 'Then who do you suggest, and when do we do it?'

'I've a slightly off-kilter suggestion.'

'I don't like your weird suggestions, Craigie.'

'Ach, it'll be grand, I'll explain in the car. Let's go.'

83

WYATT-LAWMAN LOOKED AT the burner that had just buzzed on the coffee table in his home, in one of the better Inverness suburbs. It was a WhatsApp from an unknown number. His heart lurched.

It's Bagger. I have it. Inverness crazy golf, 8 p.m. Bench closest to the kiosk. You'll need an Aldi blue carrier bag. Go in and sit down and wait. Someone I trust will exchange for an identical bag. Make it look natural, and follow his lead.

He looked at his watch, a sleek Tudor; it was almost seven thirty. He could feel his heart pounding in his ears as he looked at the message. He trusted Bagger – he'd known him for years – but this felt overly clandestine, although he accepted that they couldn't be seen together. But introducing someone new? He composed a message.

Who? This seems like madness.

The reply was instantaneous. *I don't think the cops believed me, and I wouldn't put it past them to put a team on me and follow me. I'll just go home. My associate has the item. This is the only option. Can you make it for 8?*

Wyatt-Lawman sighed, and rubbed at his temples. This made sense; they couldn't be seen together, and Inverness was a small place.

He tapped out a reply. *I'll be there. What does your man look like?* His thumb hesitated over the send button for a moment before he pressed it, his stomach churning.

The reply came back quickly. *Mid-forties, stocky, sunglasses. He's solid. I have to go. I'm ditching this phone now. No more contact. Ever. Just pay me what you owe.*

Wyatt-Lawman looked at the message, before he ejected the SIM from the phone and tossed it in the bin in the corner of the room.

He sighed and rubbed at his face, before he stood, picked up his keys and left.

84

MAX, JANIE AND Ross were all sitting in the Volvo in the parking bays opposite the skate park adjacent to the River Ness on the outskirts of Inverness, just a hundred metres from the entrance to the crazy golf.

It was a beautiful evening, and the air was pleasantly warm as it wafted through the open windows, accompanied by the familiar sweet, cloying smell of cannabis that was drifting over from a small clutch of teenagers who were sitting on benches by the concrete park.

'Fucking stoners, man. Look at them, eh?' said Ross, staring at the group of kids, all of whom had stunt scooters at their feet.

'All fairly typical stuff, Ross. Skateboarders are good, eh?' said Max, pointing at a kid, who could only have been about thirteen. He had a mop of blond hair and glasses and wore excessively baggy clothes, but he was skating with impressive skill, as he flew up a ramp, flipping the board in a gravity-defying manner, before reversing back down, with a flourish. All his fellow boarders tapped their boards on the concrete in appreciation.

'Are we all set, then?' said Janie, who had an iPad open on her lap displaying a wooden picnic bench that was in front of a small tea and coffee shack. An elderly lady with short grey hair was behind the counter handing ice creams out to a young couple, with a wide smile.

'Is that Gus's mum?' said Janie.

'Aye, that's the lovely Bet,' said Max.

'Who the fuck is Bet?' asked Ross.

'Gus Fraser's mum.'

'I'm still not comfortable using him. I mean, he's hardly squeaky clean, is he?' said Ross.

'Best I could do at short notice,' said Max.

Gus Fraser was an ex-cop who had bought the crazy golf course after leaving the police under a cloud a few years ago. He had heavily featured in an earlier operation they'd dealt with.

'Aye, I guess. Is the bastard coming?'

'Norma pinged his phone at a mast very close by. It went dead straight after we sent the messages, so who knows. Bloody hope so,' said Max.

'He'll come. He's greedy and desperate,' said Janie.

They sat there in silence for a few moments, just enjoying the momentary peace.

Max's phone buzzed in his pocket. It was Katie.

You okay?

Aye, fine. How're you? X

Missing you. When are you coming home?

Hopefully tomorrow. Any movement?

No. Just huge and uncomfortable. I had dinner with John and Lynne, they've been lovely. Promise me you'll come home tomorrow.

Max sighed, feeling like he'd been punched in the guts. *Bloody guilt*, he thought. Leaving his wife to deal with this on her own. *I promise I'll try, babe x x*

That's not a promise, but I understand x

There was a movement on the screen. 'Standby, standby, someone approaching, back to the camera,' said Janie, tapping Max on the arm.

gtg, speak l8er x x Max quickly typed, forcing the feelings of guilt and worry away.

'There we go, he's going to the counter. Come on, you bugger, turn around,' said Janie. Barney's van was parked up opposite the entrance to the gates to the golf course, a camera focused in on the bench in front of the kiosk. The man was dressed in suit trousers and a pale blue shirt. They still couldn't see his face as he conversed with Bet, who was chatting away, a big beaming smile on her face.

'Come on, Bet. Stop being so bloody sociable,' muttered Max.

'We need a face, Max. We need to see who this bastard is.' Janie's jaw was firm.

'Soon, pal. Very soon.'

85

WYATT-LAWMAN SAT DOWN at the bench, as instructed by Bagger, and snapped open his can of Coke, wishing it could be something much stronger. He felt a bead of sweat begin to trickle on his forehead as he took a swig of the thankfully cold liquid, and looked around him, pleased to see no other customers. He looked at his watch, seeing that it was just past eight, which seemed late for a crazy golf venue to be open. He slid the carrier bag under the table, which contained an A4 hardback notebook inside a zip-up laptop case.

His heart leapt as a man rounded the corner from the street, just as described by Bagger. Mid-forties, wearing shorts and sunglasses and with tidy brown hair. He was carrying a blue plastic carrier bag with the Aldi logo printed on it.

He almost bounded up to Wyatt-Lawman and sat down with a big sigh, wearing an even bigger smile.

'Hey, man, how's it going, eh?

'Who are you?' said Wyatt-Lawman.

'Our mutual acquaintance, Tom, sent me. I have no idea why, and I didn't ask, but he asked for a favour, and I agreed.'

'You have the item?'

'Aye. You have the money?'

He felt a sudden nip of fear and felt the colour drain from his face. 'M-money?' he stuttered.

The newcomer chuckled. 'Should see your face, man. No, you're grand, no money required, as I'm always good for a favour.

Fancy a pint?' he said, bobbing around from side to side, radiating warmth and enthusiasm.

'Er, no. I, er, need to be away from here, quickly. Can we do this?' Wyatt-Lawman felt his stomach boiling. This character was not what he was expecting, and he wanted to get away, immediately.

The courier smiled. 'Ach, you're no fun, man. It's a beautiful evening, but business is business, eh? Under the table, take my bag, and I'll take yours; you go first.' He smiled and nodded, before standing up and offering a hand.

Wyatt-Lawman stood and accepted the handshake, picking up the carrier bag as he did, noting the extra weight of what he was praying was a cheap Lenovo laptop. The same cheap Lenovo that he'd fitted with sophisticated encryption and auto-wipe software. The one that would lead him to the hidden password disguised within the system workings that would allow him to access the four hundred thousand pounds worth of Bitcoin in the secure wallet. He was ready. A grin spread across his face.

86

MAX WATCHED THE screen as Gus and their target shook hands. 'That's the signal. Barney, did you clock his car?' he said into his covert radio transmitter pinned to the inside of his polo shirt.

'I did. Blue BMW 3 series parked four cars to the left of the entrance in the bay. I've unlocked it, and the tracker is on and is working nicely. I even tucked a cheeky little listening device in there as well,' said Barney's voice, in its usual unhurried and casual delivery style.

'How did you do all that, in that amount of time?' Max grinned at Janie, who was shaking her head in admiration.

'Ask me about that later. We have Clive on standby in Halifax ready to do his thing.'

'You're a bloody star. Right, we have control; subject is turning and heading towards the exit. We should get a look at his face any time now,' said Max.

The figure on the screen headed straight towards the shot but was still a little small to identify. Suddenly, Janie sat up in her seat and her mouth gaped open. She pressed the covert radio button. 'Barney, can you zoom in on his geggie? We need this for evidence,' she said, her voice urgent.

'Geggie?' said Barney, a puzzled tone in his voice.

'Face, bloody zoom in on his face, you old fud,' blurted Janie with uncharacteristic irritation. On cue, the zoom function tightened in on the man walking towards the camera.

It blurred, as the auto-focus recalibrated, and then cleared.

'Well, you cheeky, dirty, amoral bastard,' said Janie.

'Who is it?' said Ross.

Janie snorted. 'Jesus, what's next for us? Bent, murderous cops, and now this.'

'What? Who the bastard is that?' said Ross, his eyes fixed on the screen but face quizzical.

'That is Gerald McCaskill, Procurator Fiscal for Inverness and the Highlands, and formerly of the Scottish Fatal Accident Investigation Unit. The man responsible for overseeing death investigations, including ones on Munros. The scumbag.'

Ross let out a short, sharp cackle. 'Well, what a turn-up. Right, let's get ready to do our job. I take it that Clarence is on standby to do the geekery?'

'If you mean Clive, then yes,' said Janie, as McCaskill turned and disappeared from sight.

'That's 'im into his car,' came Barney's voice from the campervan.

'We all ready?' said Max, switching from the camera view to the map application, a blue pulsing dot in the centre.

'Aye, I've just text Norma, and she's getting his address for us now, but we'll stay close in case he doesn't go home,' said Janie, pulling her seatbelt on and settling into the driver's seat.

'Coiled springs, motherfuckers. Let's do our thing, Barney. Phone Colin in Halifax and get him ready,' said Ross, his voice tight.

'On it, calling Clive now, and the BMW is on the move,' said Barney, his voice masked by static.

'Let's go.'

87

MCCASKILL PULLED UP in front of his home, a character property on a leafy road by the River Ness, which bisected the capital of the Highlands. He'd lived there alone for many years, having inherited it from his parents. He parked on the wide drive and got out of the car, slamming the door shut.

Within a few minutes he was in the big, echoey house and had poured a large whisky from a half-empty bottle of Singleton. He pulled out the laptop from the carrier bag and placed it on the kitchen table, noting the scratched letters 'FTF' on the top, which had been a bloody stupid idea by Mikey, probably done while drunk. He couldn't help but feel a surge of relief when he thought about the dead former cop. He was good at what he did, and was a ruthless bastard, but he was also dangerous to know. Now he and McSorley were gone, there was no one left to do the dirty work. Jeffries wasn't great at the hands-on stuff, so maybe this was it. The end. No more FTF. He sighed. It had been fun while it had lasted, but they'd probably pushed it as far as they could, anyway. Now he was away from the SFIU it would be harder to make the 'accidents' go away, and there would be far too much scrutiny that he could do nothing about. Again, he thanked the Lord that Anderson was gone, as he'd have never accepted that. All in all, it had worked out rather well. A chuckle escaped his lips.

He flipped open the top and entered the long string of characters into the login screen, thereby disabling the wipe program he'd installed a year ago. Mikey had been in charge of the laptop for some time, as he was the one filming and uploading the 'sequences', as McCaskill liked to call them.

McCaskill navigated into the system overview files and selected the file marked 'taskmanager-logfile.bin'. Once in, he highlighted the passage of what seemed to be gibberish and copied it. He smiled to himself, indulging in a bit of virtual high-fiving at his idea of hiding the login data deep within the operating systems. Unless you knew what you were looking for, you could use all the forensic tools in the world, and the numbers and characters would just look like junked files. It was why they'd needed him throughout this whole stupid enterprise. He was weak and didn't have the stomach for killing. He enjoyed the videos that Mikey and McSorley had shot, but he loved the money even more.

Quickly, he installed a Firefox browser and entered the web address for the Bitcoin wallet that he'd set up a year ago; the one that was full of lots of lovely crypto that he was about to move to a wholly new account, ready to be cashed into the bank account in the Caymans that he'd opened at the start of this business. He'd sort Jeffries with the fifty grand he'd promised, and the rest would be all his. Their little secret, each other's complicity ensuring that neither would ever spill the beans.

He pasted the long series of characters and numbers into the box, and began to go through the complex login process. The screen cleared, and the familiar egg-timer icon appeared in the middle of the screen as the bank went through the myriad security checks. He sat back and waited the usual thirty seconds, as he watched the screen, reached for his whisky and sipped at the smooth, peaty spirit.

Then he saw the cursor move.

It moved on its own, just as the egg timer turned into an arrow, and went to the logout button.

A dialogue box appeared on the screen. *Please log in.*

A flutter of nerves made him shudder, just a little. He clicked in the login box and pasted the numbers in again.

The screen wobbled. *Incorrect login sequence. Try again.*

He went back into the work file, copied the digits and characters once more, and pasted them in.

Incorrect login sequence. Try again.

He felt his face flush, and his insides turned to water. He tried again.

Incorrect login sequence. Try again.

'No, no, no, no. Fucking hell, no,' he hissed, trying once more.

Your account is locked. Please contact administrator for assistance. Your session has been discontinued.

He almost leapt out of his skin as he heard a creak behind him, spinning around to the source of the noise. He cried out in alarm, his hair standing on end, as he saw a man and a woman standing there, watching him with curiously amused expressions on their faces, and police warrant cards in their hands.

Recognition flared as he looked at the young woman in her hooded sweatshirt emblazoned with EDINBURGH MMA on the front. The cop from the court earlier who had come for the search warrant. He opened his mouth to remonstrate, but then he closed it again, and turned back towards the laptop. The screen went totally blank. Dead and inert as the night.

McCaskill just sat there, eyes wide and jaw sagging, as realisation crashed home like a runaway truck into a caravan. The moving mouse, the money. It had gone.

He knew it was all over. Tears brimmed in his eyes, and his jaw began to wobble as he started to weep, first softly then with deep, racking sobs. 'I've been so bloody stupid, but I didn't kill anyone. I want to tell you everything, but I've killed no one. I just looked the other way on the accident inquiries. Anderson blackmailed me; he was so dangerous, and I was so scared,' he babbled.

'Aye, whatever, pal. Is this the face of someone who gives a toss?' said a big, beefy man in an ill-fitting suit, who appeared next to the other two cops.

McCaskill rocketed to his feet and advanced towards them, his movements jittery and his voice wobbling, mewling. 'Seriously. I made a mistake, years ago, and then Mikey had me over a barrel. I'll tell you everything,' he said, almost plucking at the big man's sleeve.

The man closed in on McCaskill until they were almost nose to nose, his face like a slab of worn granite, and his eyes pure steel. 'Get this bastard out of my sight, before I do something I regret.'

88

THE CELL DOOR slammed shut in the block at Inverness, and Max looked at Janie. Something passed between them, and a smile spread across Janie's face.

A job well done.

Janie punched Max softly on the shoulder. 'Nice work, partner,' she said.

'Back atcha, pal.'

'Whatever self-congratulatory shite you two fucking weirdos are up to, make it stop or I'm gonna boak, eh?' Ross's voice was gruff and harsh, but there were the distinct beginnings of a smile forming in the corners of his mouth.

'What are we doing?' said Max, looking at his watch.

'If you mean are we processing the prisoners? Then the answer is no. Struan wants a joined-up interview strategy, and has a tier-five interview coordinator ready to devise a plan for both Jeffries and soppy-bollocks in the cell there. So, we just need to do statements, and we can get to the pub. I don't know about you freaks, but I could strangle a swally, and there's a no' shite pub close enough.'

'Sounds like Clive did a good job?' said Max.

'Who's Clive?' said Ross.

'Oh, shut up, ya nugget,' said Max.

Ross's hard face cracked and creased into a smile. 'Aye, Clive the hacker geek did a great job. Over four hundred grand's worth of Yamahas have been transferred away to a new coinbit purse.'

'You mean Bitcoin wallet?' said Janie.

'I know what I bloody mean. A slightly unusual legal situation, but I figured better in a facility controlled by us, rather than one that could have fucked it off all around the world in an instant. I'm impressed by Keith.'

Max just shook his head in exasperation.

'I think McCaskill is ready to bare his soul. How about Jeffries?'

'He's saying *nada*. They got him out for an urgent interview, and he didn't say a single word. Not one word, and he's now on suicide watch,' said Ross, stifling a big yawn.

'Inconvenient,' said Max.

'Not really. We've linked both of them to the laptop, and the laptop is incendiary. Clive taking control of the laptop remotely was a genius idea, which, of course I'm taking credit for. We also have you seeing Jeffries shove McSorley of a bloody cliff. I think we can leave it to Struan and his team. Now, who's for a beer?' said Ross.

Max said nothing. He just stared at his phone, which had buzzed in his pocket, feeling the blood drain from his face.

'Max? You look like you've seen a bastard ghost. What's up?'

Max held up his phone so Ross could see.

It was a message from Katie. *Are you there? The baby's coming.*

89

HAD MAX HAD a front number plate on the KTM, the speeding tickets would have been plentiful, but their absence, together with the spending cuts on roads policing, meant he didn't see a solitary police car, and Ross's promise to make any tickets go away had meant it wasn't a concern.

As he pulled up outside the cottage, he was disturbed to see that the house was in darkness. Taking out his phone he saw a message from Lynne.

Waters broke at 11. Gone to Queen Margaret's.

Max cursed under his breath, put his helmet back on and roared off again, his heart pounding and face burning.

Within fifteen minutes, he had parked outside the hospital and was jogging into the maternity ward where he was ushered into a private room by a smiling scrubs-clad midwife. She had a wide smile and a cheeky glint in her eyes.

'Och, darlin', I think you're in plenty trouble. Katie's been giving you pelters.'

'Shit,' muttered Max.

'Ach, nae bother, pet. Her pal has been doing a sterling job, but it's really action stations now. Leave all your horrible bike gear in the day room, wash your hands and get a set of scrubs on, man. When you're ready, come into room seven, okay?'

Max nodded. 'Aye, thanks.' His head was swirling, and his heart was pounding in his chest.

It must have been obvious to the midwife as she smiled and laid a hand on his arm. 'Don't fret, love. It'll be fine, but hurry up.'

Max quickly changed and washed his hands before he jogged in his too-big Crocs, and found himself in front of room seven. He could hear moaning and panting from within. He closed his eyes and pushed the door open.

'Ach, see. I told you he'd get here, eh?' said Lynne with a big smile.

Katie was on her back, legs up, sucking on an Entonox mouthpiece, her eyes shut tight. Her face was brick red and damp with sweat, but to Max she was more beautiful than ever.

'Katie.' He laid his hand on her shoulder.

Her eyes snapped open, and she tried to focus on him.

'You, you bloody bastard. This is all your fucking fault,' she said, although her eyes didn't reflect the anger in her words, instead the tears welled and spilled onto her cheeks.

'I'm so sorry, it was al—'

'Oh, shut up, you dickhead, and hold my hand,' she said between sobs.

'I tell you what, I'll leave you two to it,' said Lynne with a chuckle, and she padded off.

Max grabbed Katie's hand and she squeezed it tight, staring at him, a glint in her eyes. 'I fucking love you, you bastard.'

'I love you too, babe.' Max reached forward and stroked her damp brow, just as a contraction arrived. She gritted her teeth, and her face turned almost purple as she pushed, a strangled cry escaping from her.

'That's great, Katie. One big shove and we're done,' said the midwife.

Time seemed to stand still for Max, as he looked at his wife on the bed.

And then it happened.

'Whhooaa, that's a decent-sized one,' said the midwife, her voice full of delight.

Max felt like he was only barely in the room, as he looked to the midwife. She chuckled as she looked at him.

'Come on then, Dad. Step up?'

Max stood up and moved to the foot of the bed, head swimming, and he felt the breath leave him as if he'd been punched. It felt like a cog had worked loose in his brain as the midwife handed him a small bundle wrapped in a towel, and he looked down, his mouth gaping and his stomach churning. At that moment, Max knew that his life had changed forever.

Everything had changed.

The world had stopped.

He took the bundle, his heart pounding as he nestled the pink, soft weight from the midwife in his arms. The face squashed, red and yet achingly, heart-shatteringly beautiful. He tried to speak as he looked at the baby, but the words wouldn't come, they remained lodged in his throat.

'Come on, Craigie, I'd like to know, as well,' said Katie, who was looking at him with tired, but amused eyes.

'Over to you to deliver the news, Pops, but I can say that all is as it should be. It's a cracking healthy wee toot,' said the midwife.

Tears streamed down Max's face, as he stared into the eyes of his child and he tried to find the words.

'Hello, mate,' was all he could think of to say, as the tears he tried to blink away spilled down his cheeks.

'Craigie?' said Katie, her voice hardening.

'Katie, babe. Meet our daughter.' Max handed the pink, creased and now scratchily crying human being to his wife. When he saw the look on her face, wet with tears, he knew then at that moment that *their* life had changed forever.

He looked at Katie, and their daughter, and he knew.

He just knew.

Max pulled his work phone out of his pocket, raised it and

snapped a quick photo of Katie and their daughter. He composed a message into the team WhatsApp group and attached the photo.

A wee girl. Mum and baby doing well. I'll call in a few days, phone going off now.

Max powered down the phone and returned it to his pocket.

'You're not making work calls already, Craigie?' said Katie.

'No, babe. Quite the opposite.'

90

DS MCSWEEN RAISED his eyebrows at the solicitor next to Gerald McCaskill after he'd asked the question as to whether he wanted to explain his role. They were in the interview room at Burnett Road Police Station, a plain, functional space with scuffed walls and sultry, stuffy air, and at the conclusion of the interview introduction procedure.

'My name is Jacob Brown, solicitor from Brown, Joseph and Webb in Inverness. Before we begin, my client wishes to make a prepared statement. May I read it?' The lawyer looked directly at McSween, who was sitting next to DC Urquhart.

'Please do,' said McSween.

Brown nodded and lowered his head towards an A4 sheet of paper. 'I, Gerald McCaskill, wish to make this statement which I make of my own free will after consultation with my legal representative. I first met Michael Anderson and Tom Jeffries when both were officers serving in Glasgow and I was serving as a Fiscal Depute. I later became acquainted with Danny McSorley because of his association with Anderson. We all became friendly and socialised on a number of occasions over the course of a few years. During this time, we participated in something which I deeply regret, and had the potential to ruin my career. After this isolated incident I tried to break off our friendship. We then did not see each other for years during which I had moved from the Fiscals service in Glasgow and was working at the Scottish Fatalities Investigation Unit. During this time, I was approached by Anderson who asked me to overlook some inconsistencies, and investigative omissions following a fatal fall of a female on Ben Nevis. I refused, but then I was blackmailed and forced to agree, and did not recommend a further police investigation or Sheriff's fatal accident inquiry. I told them both that I wanted nothing more to do with them, and again, heard nothing for some time. However, they resurfaced last year, after Anderson left the police and blackmailed me into doing the same on several occasions. They threatened me, physically, and even worse, Anderson said he would harm my two children in Glasgow where they live with my ex-wife. I am ashamed of my actions, and as an officer of the court my behaviour has been reprehensible, but I firmly deny any involvement in any homicides. I will not answer any further questions.'

The solicitor looked up, nodded and handed the sheet of paper to DS McSween, who took it and studied it through a pair of wire-rimmed spectacles. He read it in silence before handing it to DC Urquhart without looking at her.

'Is that it?' McSween said, his voice laden with sarcasm, ignoring the snort of derision from his partner.

'That's all my client wants to say. He admits an inappropriate relationship with Anderson and Jeffries, and McSorley, and admits to being coerced into not doing his duties at the SFIU, which we acknowledge amount to an offence of defeating the ends of justice, but my client is not a murderer, DS McSween.'

'How about the laptop today, Mr McCaskill?' said McSween.

McCaskill wiped a shaking hand across his face. 'No comment.'

'Are you sure you want to stick with this?' McSween said, holding up the piece of paper between a thumb and forefinger.

'No comment.'

McSween looked up and stared for a full thirty seconds at McCaskill, who did not return his gaze. The silence in the room was thick and stale, and McSween sighed before he turned to DC Urquhart, who just shrugged.

'How about the laptop that you believed you were receiving from Jeffries?' said McSween.

'No comment.'

'Really? You were caught red-handed, man. We've a statement here from the computer expert who was remotely in charge of the laptop and witnessed – and recorded, I might add – you accessing a Bitcoin wallet and attempting to move a large amount of cryptocurrency. Anything to say about that?' said DC Urquhart.

The solicitor's head snapped up to look at the cop, his mouth open in shock, and his brow furrowed. 'I've not been informed of this evidence. Why not?' he said, his voice hard-edged.

McSween turned to face the lawyer, his eyes like grey pebbles. 'Because I chose not to. Does your client want to answer this reasonable question?'

McCaskill opened his mouth to respond, but the solicitor laid a hand on the man's shoulder. 'No. I want a private consultation with Mr McCaskill now, please.'

McSween continued to stare at the lawyer and a smile appeared on his face, although it didn't reach his eyes.

'Fine. Interview suspended, 9 a.m.'

91

JANIE AND ROSS were waiting in the custody suite when DS McSween and DC Urquhart reappeared, their arms full of files and bags of property. Sergeant Cotton was tapping away at her custody officer terminal, looking up as they all walked in.

'Blimey, that was quick,' said Ross.

'Aye, cagey bastard wants a break already. He didn't like it when I hit them up about your computer nerd pal,' said McSween.

'What's he said?' said Janie.

'Bullshit prepared statement.' McSween handed the sheet of paper to Janie, who took it and began to read, Ross looking over her shoulder, his face darkening as he read.

'What a lying shitebag. Blaming the others, two of whom are now dead, and then just saying he looked the other way?'

'Aye, about the size of it. I guess he thinks that his career is over, and he'll have to do a bit of time, but this is a total exercise in damage limitation,' said McSween.

'It's utter wank, is what it is,' said Ross.

'Hard to disprove. We found no other computers or phones at his home,' said Urquhart, her voice hard.

'What about Jeffries?' said Ross.

'Still not said a word. Seems like he's toeing the line of the FTF club. I suspect he'd top himself if he had the chance.'

'Wonder if he wants a cup of tea?' said Ross.

'Who, McCaskill?' said McSween.

'No, Jeffries. Must be thirsty, it's getting warm in here.' Ross turned to the custody officer. 'Shall I see if Jeffries wants a cuppa, or a water, sarge?'

Sergeant Cotton looked at Ross from her place behind the Plexiglass shield, and her brow creased. She sat back in her chair and swiped a strand of blonde hair from her eyeline. 'You know you can't ask him about his case, right?' she said, her voice laden with sarcasm.

'Goes without saying, but I can see you guys are busy. I could take him a tea, and let him know we'll need to interview him again.'

Sergeant Cotton appraised Ross with narrowed, suspicious eyes, but then grinned. 'Aye, why not. Glad of your help, sir,' she said, before turning back to her computer terminal.

Ross beckoned Janie towards the cell passageway with a nod. They set off down the long corridor, at the end of which sat a solitary cop outside a cell door that was ajar. A constant watch on a suicidal prisoner.

'You okay, pal?' said Ross to the cop.

'Aye, I'm good. Been here ages, though; know when I'm getting a break? I'm busting for a pish.'

'Off you go, son. We'll mind the prisoner,' said Ross. The guard leapt to his feet and hurried away down the corridor. Ross went to the cell and swung the door open.

Jeffries looked up at Ross, his face blank and expressionless, but morphing into surprise as he saw who was in the doorway.

'Ross?' he said, his face pale and lined.

'Tom. Need a drink?' he said.

'No, I'm good. What are you doing here?' he said.

'Just checking in on you; everyone thinks you're gonna top yourself, man,' said Ross, bluntly.

A hint of a smile crossed Jeffries' face. 'Those were supposed to be the rules, man. One of us goes, we all go.'

'What, even McCaskill?'

Jeffries eyes widened in surprise. 'You have Gerry?'

'Aye, he's mid-interview. Talkin' shite from what I can gather, referring to some kind of dodgy situation you buggers got into back in the day.'

'What, he's talking?' he said.

'Well, a wee bit. Prepared statement.'

The corners of Jeffries' mouth immediately began to twitch. 'I don't believe it. None of us would speak.'

'Well, you'll no doubt be interviewed again after he's finished, so you can see it then. I can't show you, you know that.'

Jeffries slumped on the sleeping platform and pulled up the sleeves on his grubby tracksuit top. 'Bastard,' he whispered.

'No matter. Won't change what happens to you. Best you sit tight. Your guard will be back in a moment, and they'll continue to listen to his bullshit about you and Anderson blackmailing him, or some other kind of pish. I mean, who wants to listen to the bollocks he's spouting about just looking the other way on the SFIU stuff? I'd better shut my big geggie, eh? Sure, I cannae get you a drink, or something to eat?'

'Are you bullshitting me, Ross?' Jeffries was suddenly animated, as if he'd been connected to a low-level electrical current.

'Why would I? You'll get all this served on you in the next interview. You can decide if it's bullshit or not, then.'

'Have they searched my house?' said Jeffries.

'I assume so. Why?' said Ross.

'Did they find it?'

'Find what?'

'You'd know if they had. You need to check again.'

'No one mentioned it; should they have?'

'Mutually assured destruction, man. If they'd found it, you'd know. Fucking bastard.'

'Mutually assured destruction?' said Ross, feeling his insides skip a beat.

Jeffries' face darkened. 'Operation McNulty. Mutually assured destruction, like the nuclear deterrent. Something you have that you hope you'll never have to use. We all have one. Now leave me alone.' He lay on his bed and covered his head with a blanket.

92

'OPERATION MCNULTY?' SAID DCI O'Neill.

'That's what he said, unsolicited, like,' said Ross, as he, Janie, DS McSween and DC Urquhart sat around the table in the conference room.

'Unsolicited?' said O'Neill, one eyebrow raised, questioningly.

'Aye, unsolicited. I just went to offer him a cuppa.'

O'Neill looked at Ross, his eyes narrow, before shaking his head, just a tiny amount. 'Right, I'll get on the phone and find out what it was – if it's legacy Strathclyde force it may take a bit of digging, as records got all buggered up when we amalgamated into Police Scotland, but I know who to call.'

'Ahead of you there,' interrupted Ross. 'My analyst Norma back at Tulliallan has the details already.'

'What?'

'Aye. Norma. She knows all the shortcuts, so don't be offended. Operation McNulty, an anti-prostitution inquiry in 2005 led by the vice team in Glasgow. Closed down a load of brothels and locked up a load of pimps. Everyone was terribly delighted, and in normal fashion a heap of people got commendations, right from the most junior officers to the Fiscal Depute who prosecuted the case. Judge was very complimentary.'

'So, what's the connection?'

'Want to know who got commendations from the judge?' said Ross, the subdued smile on his face telling its own story.

'Ross, stop pissing about,' said O'Neill.

'Aye, you guessed it. Anderson, McSorley and Jeffries all got commendations for dedicated police work in a challenging environment. Want to guess who the Fiscal Depute was? McCaskill, of course.'

'Jesus. They knew each other almost twenty years ago.'

'Seems so.'

'But why does Jeffries feel so compelled to mention it now?'

'Well, he may be a little offended that McCaskill broke the code of silence, I guess, and he specifically mentioned it in connection with the house search. He mentioned "mutually assured destruction", and compared it to the nuclear option.' Ross rubbed his hands through his thin, unkempt hair.

'What do you think he meant by that?'

'Well, I'm guessing that he means that they all hold something that would destroy them all. That's my reading of it, anyway.'

'What do you suggest, then?' said O'Neill.

'Let's search the houses again. All of them.'

93

JANIE UNLOCKED JEFFRIES' front door with the keys that they'd secured from his property record. It was a small, well-kept newbuild in Inshes in the east of the city.

The property was neat, tidy and furnished in a minimalist style, with no signs of any female influence in the décor. Pale wooden laminate, magnolia walls and some framed photographs of Munros and lochs.

'What are we looking for, then?' said Janie.

'Whatever. Something dodgy that links the bastards,' said Ross, loosening his tie. The house was hot and stuffy with a faint smell of an acrid reed diffuser.

'Well, let's get on with it, then. It stinks in here,' said Janie, opening the drawers on a small coffee table. Beyond a couple of remote controls, there was nothing. Ross went into the kitchen, and within a few moments, the familiar oaths and curses could be heard as he searched.

'Fucking shite, load of bollocks,' he mumbled, as the sound of kitchen drawers being opened and the chink of cutlery being moved carried across the rooms.

'Methodical and systematic, Ross,' called Janie, a smile in her voice.

'Ach, stick it up your arse,' he grumbled as something crashed on the floor. 'Shite,' he cursed, at whatever it was that had smashed into what sounded like a million pieces.

They continued to search, but the lounge only had one small

chest of drawers, which seemed to be mainly full of household bills. It appeared that most of the readily movable property had already been taken by the PolSA team.

'There's fuck all here, man. What a boring bastard Jeffries is. He basically owns piss-all,' said Ross, as he walked back into the living room.

Janie was about to agree with him when her eyes were drawn to a plain framed certificate on the wall. She moved closer to it feeling her excitement rising. It was a commendation certificate bearing the crest of the former Strathclyde Police.

Chief Superintendent's Commendation
This certificate is presented to
Sgt 1478 Jeffries for professionalism,
leadership and determination during
Operation McNulty
Presented on 8 September 2005

Janie plucked the certificate from the wall where it hung on a single tack. She flipped it in her hands, looking at the rear, which was sealed with brown tape.

'We should take this,' she said, handing it to Ross, who reached for it while also transferring his phone to his other hand. The certificate slipped and fell to the laminate, shattering the glass and sending shards all over the floor.

'Oops,' said Janie, bending to pick up the fractured frame. She turned it over, and a photograph slid out.

She held it up and felt her heart begin to beat faster in her chest, and the blood suffused in her face. Ross stood next to her looking at the photograph, and Janie could almost feel the tension in her boss's body language.

She recognised them immediately.

Michael Anderson, Tom Jeffries and Gerald McCaskill were

all standing, grinning at the camera, their faces red and their eyes glassy. They were in what appeared to be a sleazy living room.

But it wasn't the sight of the three men that made her synapses fire. It was the semi-naked young woman with them. She was petite and pretty, with platinum blonde, choppy hair, and a slim body. Her face was wet with tears. She looked at the camera, and her expression radiated one thing.

Fear.

Ross's breathing became louder, and Janie turned to face her boss. His face was bright red, his jaw was firm and set, and his eyes were full of fury. 'A nuclear fucking bomb, that's what this is. Mutually assured destruction.'

'Where's McSorley? Taking the photo?' said Janie.

Ross didn't answer, he just continued to stare with blazing eyes at the grainy old photograph.

'Ross?' Janie began.

'I know who that lassie is,' said Ross.

'Who?'

'Her name is Karen Nicholson.'

'Who is she?'

'She was a twenty-year-old Glasgow sex worker who disappeared into thin air on eighth September 2005. She was found in Palacerigg Country Park after almost six weeks. It was unsolved, and she was so decomposed they had to identify her by her dental records. These murdering bastards did it, and this photo, and this commendation certificate prove it.'

'What do we do now?' said Janie.

'We go back to Burnett Road, and we make sure they never see the light of day again.'

94

MAX PULLED UP outside the cottage and switched the engine off. He looked in the rear-view mirror at Katie, who returned his smile. She looked tired and pale, but at the same time serene and happy. Their daughter was in the newly acquired baby car seat in the back, and she was fast asleep.

Katie had spent two nights in hospital, after a little more bleeding than the staff had liked, but she was soon ready to go home.

Lynne and John's door opened and like a rocket, Nutmeg almost exploded out of the house, barking ecstatically at the return of her owners. Max stepped out of the car and greeted the waggy little blonde dog who rolled on her back immediately, her pink tongue lolling in delight. She spun onto her legs and darted around the car to greet Katie.

Lynne appeared at the door and waved, her face wide and beaming.

'Congratulations, you two. Go and get settled and I'll pop round later,' she said, before disappearing back inside. This was typical of their no-nonsense neighbour. No fuss, no getting in the way. She was just there for them, and she'd let them settle before she made an appearance.

Max went to the back door and opened it, looking in at their daughter, whose pink face was relaxed and smooth as she slept, swaddled in a hat and babygro.

Max unclipped the seat and lifted it out, unable to take his eyes off her. She looked like Katie. Even at this early stage he could tell, and his heart lurched at the sight. Nutmeg came up to the car seat, her shaggy ears cocked. She sat down and looked at Max, clearly a little confused at what was required of her.

'Nutmeg, meet Evie,' said Max, lowering the seat for Nutmeg to inspect, her tail twitching as she sniffed.

'Is she okay?' said Katie as she stepped out of the car, wincing a little.

'Nutmeg or Evie?' said Max.

'Both.'

'Evie's snoring; Nutmeg's interested, but respectful.'

'Well, that's a good sign,' said Katie, as she walked around the car and gripped Max's hand.

Katie smiled, her face radiant and beautiful. 'Let's go inside and show Evie her new home. She'll be hungry soon.'

The new Craigie family crossed the small lawn and went inside.

*

Evie began to cry scratchily after Max had changed her nappy, and he handed her over to Katie, who shushed her as she sat on the sofa. Within a minute, Max looked on, his heart full of love as he watched his wife feeding his daughter. A determination gripped him. He was going to be a proper father, and he was going to find a way to balance it with his job. He just wondered how. Was it even possible?

He decided that he'd work out the details another day, but for now, he had a month's leave to get to know Evie.

'Don't just stand there; a cup of tea, and put the telly on, eh? Judging by how long madam takes to fill up, I may be here quite a while,' Katie said, as she stroked their daughter's pink cheek as she fed, her eyes half-closed.

Max chuckled but picked up the remote control and flicked

the TV on, before walking across the open-plan space to put the kettle on.

'Max?'

'Aye?' he said, as he dropped a teabag into a mug.

'You may want to watch this.' She pointed at the TV, her face suddenly serious.

Max moved closer to the TV, picked up the remote and raised the volume. A reporter was standing outside Inverness Sheriff Court, where Max had been just a couple of days earlier, her face serious as she spoke into the camera.

'. . . two men appeared before the Sheriff Court in Inverness charged with multiple offences, including murder and conspiracy to murder following the death of a police officer on a Munro in the northwest Highlands. Tom Jeffries, who Sky News understands is a serving police officer, and Gerald McCaskill, a member of the Crown Office and Procurator Fiscal's office, were both remanded in custody on a seven-day laydown to allow detectives to investigate further into what, I understand, are highly complex matters. Sky News has also received information that both men are being held in connection with the unsolved murder of a woman in Glasgow in 2005. I understand the Police Investigations Review commissioner is monitoring this inquiry closely. A spokesman for the investigative team said the following: "This is a fast-moving and serious investigation, with a large team of officers working day and night to resolve. As the case is ongoing it is inappropriate to say any more at this stage." More information as we get it.'

Max felt his blood run cold as he reached into his pocket and pulled out his phone, which had been switched off ever since the birth of his daughter.

Katie looked at him and smiled. 'Make the call, but promise me you're going nowhere, Craigie?'

'I promise, but I need to hear what's happened.' He powered

up the phone, which sparked to life, and walked out into the garden.

Three WhatsApp notifications pinged up, all from the team congratulating him on the birth of the baby. Of course Ross had added, *Way too fucking lovely to be yours, does she look like the postie?* Max sniggered as he dialled.

'You're on leave, ya fud. Piss off. Congratulations by the way, how's she doing?'

'Katie or Evie?' said Max.

'Evie? Bonny name. Both, obviously.'

'Aye, my granny's name. Both are brilliant. I've just seen the news. What's going on?' said Max, feeling the familiar surge of adrenaline, which was perhaps not the same as usual. He felt satisfied, but did he feel excited? He looked at Evie, her tiny nose, pink face, and fine blond wisps of hair, and he realised that he cared a little less about the job than he used to.

The motivation used to be about the how. Now it was about the why. It was confusing. Max shook his head to clear the cobwebs of fatigue, and Ross's gruff voice dragged him back to the present.

'Before I tell you, you need to know that if you turn up, I'll kick you in the bollocks, okay? You're on leave, and you're there to be with your family.'

'I won't, I just want to hear what happened.'

'Well, I know you, Craigie. You may think you're God's bloody gift to policing, but you're average at best, and it's all in hand. The Chief is preparing for a big statement at some point, and he's conferring with the Lord Advocate right now. This is a big old thing, so I'll tell you.'

'Seriously, my boot in your testicles if you turn up at the office.'

'Fine.'

Max listened as Ross brought him up to date.

'Jesus, so the four of them date back to 2005, where it all began with the murder of that poor wee lassie?' said Max.

'It's all coming together. It turns out that Anderson killed his evil aunt by shoving her down the stairs when he was a lad, which it seems whetted his appetite for seeing women die after falling. Then poor wee Karen Nicholson died after being shoved down the stairs at a rental house in Glasgow, and as every single one of them had raped her before this, they were all in. Captured, and could do nothing about it. Anderson had them all, and somehow managed to draw them all in to his hideous, evil world.'

Max felt suddenly nauseous. 'And they all had a copy of the photo in the commendation certificates?'

'Aye. "Mutually assured destruction", they called it. So, if one went nuclear, they were all fucked. A pissed-up celebration after their commendations for some vice job, led to them picking her up, doing what they did and then ditching her in the woods. I remember the case well, as I was a DS on it.'

'And that led to the desire to kill women on Munros, but why?'

'Jeffries has spilled the beans. He was so pissed off with McCaskill that he unburdened his soul and snitched on the lot of them. It seems like it was group thing that they all got dragged into, with Anderson very much their leader. They'd all stayed in contact over the years, and it all started as sharing porn that quickly escalated from usual type to the extreme. Anderson really seemed to get into it all, and they were all kind of dragged along by it, with the threat that he was willing to go nuclear on it, and finish them all if they didn't do his bidding. He had absolute power over them, as he apparently didn't care about any of the consequences. His focus was all about killing, and if they didn't help him get away with it, he had the nuclear option of finishing them all off.'

Max felt a chill descend on him at Ross's matter-of-fact delivery. 'So they were all in it together?'

'Seems so. McSorley was very much in his shadow, and had begged to be able to do one of the murders, but the other two were all about facilitating. It seems that once Mikey resigned under the big discipline cloud, he went off the rails, and decided that the porn wasn't enough. They wanted to create the films, not just watch them. It morphed into some kind of incel-type badness, which morphed into their making money from it by posting it on the dark web. McCaskill handled the business and sorted the money. According to him, he was being blackmailed after the other three threatened to take the photo with the prostitute to the press, while McSorley and Anderson did the deeds on the Munros.'

'What was Jeffries' role?' asked Max.

'Well, he claims that he was just trying to keep a lid on it, and stop it coming out, but I think he's talking shit, and let's be fair – he's bollocksed anyway, after shoving McSorley off a great big cliff. He's made a decent amount of coin out of it. Fuck him, he can rot in jail with the rest of them.'

'Who's picking up the wider investigation?' said Max, his voice flat and his insides icy. He turned and looked through the open doors, at his wife and daughter on the sofa together. Katie's face was radiant with pure joy. More than anything he wanted to join her, to be with his family, and to be away from the abject horror of this case. He sighed.

'Well, cyber-crime teams across the UK are on it, NCA, FBI, MFI, B&Q, LSD and all sorts of other shite. We're well away from it now, as always. For the best, we can be ready to fight another day, unless we've cleared up all the corruption, in which case we'll be on traffic duty by the end of the month.'

'There'll always be corruption, Ross. You know that.'

'Aye, Chief's just called me to make that very point. He's ready for the backlash, but he has plans for us.'

'What plans?'

'He's had a call from the justice minister. They want to widen our terms of business.'

'How?'

'Corruption anywhere. Military, legal, politics, wherever it is, they want us to get amongst it all. They're even willing to pay for Colin to work with us more,' said Ross.

'I assume you mean Clive?' said Max.

'Whoever. Nerdy hacker mannie from Halifax. We wouldn't have brought these bastards down without him. Now will you get tae fuck and be a family man?'

'Let's not forget Shay. Without him flagging it all up, they'd still all be out there.'

'Aye. Chief wants to give out commendations all over, including him. Load of bullshit, I'd say. Look where a commendation certificate got those Far to Fall bastards.'

'Fair point, well made,' said Max with a chuckle.

'Right, I'm bloody hanging up now, switch ya phone off, ya fanny, and go be a dad. The job will always be waiting for you when you return. Being a dad is the best thing in the world, pal. Me and Mrs F will pop round soon; she's already giving me pelters wanting to see the baby.' The three beeps indicated that Ross was gone.

Max sat on the bench and stared at the phone, turning it over in his hands. His link to his job. His link to The Job. The constant, ever-present tether to another world that could be dark, fascinating, exciting, all-consuming and frustrating, but ultimately, it was just a job.

Max sighed, feeling an uncharacteristic sense of anxiety as he powered the handset down, severing his ties with policing, at least for the time being. Did being a cop define him? Was he capable of doing anything else? Would he ever find the right balance?

'Craigie, tea,' came Katie's soft voice out of the open French doors, pulling his mind from the future to the present.

Max felt his heart soften. He stood up, and went back into the house where Katie was staring at their daughter, her face almost seraphic as she stroked Evie.

Max went to the kitchen, opened a drawer on the low dresser and slid his phone inside, before softly closing it.

'I'm dying of thirst here, Max,' said Katie, a smile in her voice, as she snuggled Evie against her neck, shushing her gently when she began to cry.

'Coming right up.'

Acknowledgements

WELL, HERE WE are again. The end of a Max Craigie book. The sixth. Who'd a thunk it, eh?

I'm so proud of these books, and I am always so conscious that they don't just get written. Books leave an author's computer, and then the real work starts, turning it from a collection of words, thoughts and musings into something approaching a book. The first bit is all down to me, but the rest is a big team effort, and so I have some people to thank in helping me take an idea, and turn it into a proper book.

To my agent, Kerr MacRae, for helping me now to champion the progression of my career – it's great to be working with you.

To Robbie, for working with me on this book and offering good, solid editorial advice.

To all the fabulous team at HQ. This is my sixth book with a top group of professionals, and I've enjoyed every minute taking Max and the team from book one, and hopefully improving the stories at every stage. Massive thanks go to Audrey, my editor. Your incisive grip of the plot, the pace, and mostly importantly, the motivations of the characters have made this book just so much better. It's been an absolute joy to work with you on this book, and I can't wait for the next chapter.

Emma in marketing for making the public aware that the books exist and that maybe they should buy them. All the PR cool dudes, Sian, Kom, Natasha and Sophie. The fantastically observant Eldes, who was eagle-eyed during copyedits, and stopped my inevitable red face that would have ensued had all the silly typos slipped through. Also Jon Appleton, who did another pass, just to make sure. Yeah, he found stuff.

There are also plenty of people that I know work hard on the books, but I never get to meet. So big props to all the geniuses in sales and marketing, analytics, cover design, typesetting and all that stuff that really matters.

To the head honchos of the team, Lisa Milton (Boss), Kate Mills, and Manpreet Grewal, who are really pushing the imprint and are just so supportive of me. You've built a tremendous team, who are knocking it out of the park. (Does this make me a suck-up? God, I hope not, but I have to thank the people, and I reckon the guvnors often don't get the thanks.)

To my very good friend Simon Hammock, who is chief pilot at the Inverness-based Coastguard search-and-rescue team. These guys are on call 24/7, ready to come to the aid of those who need rescuing, whether at sea or on the many Munros in Scotland. As always, I'm in awe of the skill and expertise of you and your crew, dedicated to keeping people safe on the hills. I also appreciate you helping me to keep the book procedurally tight, helicopter-wise, and also giving me some good pointers on the best places to shove people off cliffs. (Not that I'd ever do that. It's just a story, dudes.)

To all my writer pals. Heaps of you, who help keep me sane, are always an amazing source of advice, and laughs. Special mentions go to Tony Kent, Ed James and Colin Scott. You guys rock.

To Clare. Always and forever x

To my kids, Alec, Richard and Ollie. I do it for you guys!

I've never been able to write this before, but . . . to Eddie, my wee grandson, and apple of my eye.

Of course, to all the booksellers, reviewers, bloggers and people who shout loud about the books.

And last but not least. You. The reader. You're the one that matters. I really hope you enjoy these books, because you're the reason they exist. If you don't buy them, I won't be writing them anymore.

Peace,

Neil.

Discover the Max Craigie series.

DS MAX CRAIGIE:
THE DARK SIDE OF CRIME.
THE RIGHT SIDE OF THE LAW.

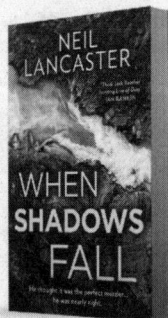

Keep reading for an exclusive first look
at Chapter 1 of *The Dark Heart*,
the next book in the Max Craigie series.
Available to order now!

1

DR DANIEL SOLOMON stood and waved self-consciously, as he accepted the warm applause in the bookshop in central York. The place was packed to the rafters with readers eager to hear him talk about his inspiration for his new book, *An Iman, a Rabbi, a Priest, and an Atheist Go Into a (Juice) Bar: How Religion and Secularism Can Peacefully Coexist.*

The book was his life's work. A polemic forged by his experiences, beginning in Israel, formed in the University of Alberta in Canada and then crystallised while getting his doctorate at Edinburgh. This was his passion. Social cohesion in a polarised world. Unlike many others, he could see a way out of it, and his driving force was to broadcast it to the whole world.

And how he'd succeeded. Against all odds the book had been an instant, massive success, topping the *Sunday Times* and *New York Times* bestseller lists for weeks and weeks on end. For once, a narrative had been delivered that was not polarising, quite the opposite. He preached to all faiths, and cultures came together with a shared vision, and it had landed on the public like nobody could have foreseen.

He had read from the first chapter, which he had performed with all the vigour of a member of the Royal Shakespeare Company at the Rose Theatre. His voice was rich and sonorous, and had carried to every inch of the space, and into each and every listener's heart, as he espoused his vision of unity amongst all faiths.

His final sentence had captivated the audience, his soft voice accented with a curious mix of Israel, Canada and Yorkshire. 'My friends, this is my message. As communities we must stand tall against the scourge – the pernicious scourge – of the racism and bigotry that we all face. We must do it steadfastly, honestly, with courage, humility and open hearts. How can we succeed? We must unite, as friends and faiths together, whether believers in a higher power or not. We are all the same, friends, and our differences must unite us, not divide us. As one, we can form a world where the overriding agenda is not one of want, of avarice, but is one of service. To serve all by being part of one community of all faiths. We must not fail. We cannot fail.'

The rapturous applause of the fifty listeners could have been a hundred-strong, such was the enthusiasm with which it was delivered.

Daniel was a scholar of philosophy, an academic, and a former soldier, in that order. He had seen evil up close, and knew that there was only one solution to overcome it. Acceptance, cooperation and understanding.

The line of readers, all clutching copies of the book, snaked towards the back of the shop, and Daniel spent time with everyone, shaking hands, posing for selfies, and signing and dedicating copies.

He felt giddy with excitement as the queue began to dwindle and the last customer arrived at the table, book in hand, a wide smile across his face. He was a short and stocky man, with huge eyebrows and thick spectacles, and he wore a heavy raincoat, despite the hot, sultry day. 'Hello, Dr Solomon, I loved your talk. Please would you sign my book?' he said, grinning inanely.

Daniel smiled. 'Sure, what's your name, my friend?' he asked.

'Lionel,' he said, showing stained and uneven teeth that were framed by a wispy moustache and beard. His pale, spotty face was covered with a light sheen of sweat. Daniel enjoyed book signings, but you did attract the occasional odd-bod, and it seemed Lionel was one of those.

A quick squiggle in his book, and a pause for a photograph, and he was done.

'Thank you very much, Dr Solomon. I very much loved your descriptions of life in Israel in the Eighties, very interesting.' His voice was high-pitched, monotone and flat.

'You're welcome, my friend, now if you'll excuse me, I really must get going.'

'Of course, shalom, doctor,' said Lionel, studying the dedication and signature rapturously.

There was a brief pause while Daniel thanked the staff at the shop, and very soon he was emerging into the bright, early evening sun, the rays warming his face after the air-conditioned interior of the shop. He sighed, satisfied about a great talk and a good number of hardbacks sold, which would all add to his chances of staying in the *Sunday Times* top ten.

He was excited to get back to his home in Leeds, where his wife, Abigail, would be waiting, eager to hear all about his first big event. Hopefully there would be something nice cooking in the oven. A story with the kids, and then he had a book he was wanting to finish, perhaps with a nice glass of something chilled.

It was as he was leaving the shop and walking along the narrow, twisty York streets that things changed forever.

His phone buzzed in his pocket. Pulling it out and looking at the screen, he saw it wasn't his wife, as he'd expected, but a private number.

'Hello?'

'Dr Solomon?' A well-educated voice, with shades of public school, tinged with a hint of Scotland.

'Yes, who is this, please?'

'It doesn't matter who I am, Dr Solomon, but you are in danger. You need to hide; you must get away and hide.'

He felt his insides chill as he slowed his pace. 'I'm sorry, but who are you?'

'Never mind who I am. Listen, there are people out there who hate you. They hate you and they want you dead. Your book is the final straw to them, and if you want to live, you must get away.'

Despite the absurdity of the words, he felt the hairs prickle on the back of his neck. Who could wish him harm? He was just a lapsed Jew who preached social integration and peace. 'I'm sorry, I think you have the wrong person, I'm just a writer.'

'No. Look, listen to me, Dr Solomon. You cannot go home, they'll be wait—'

Daniel hung up and quickened his pace, looking behind him. The streets were busy, bustling with early evening revellers.

'Nutters,' he whispered to himself, trying not to break into a jog as he crossed from Parliament Street onto Piccadilly towards the Coppergate Car Park, feeling the colour draining from his face. 'Ridiculous,' he muttered, as he risked a glance behind.

And then he saw him.

It was Lionel, from the shop, his hands buried beneath his thick coat. He was matching the pace of Daniel's stride, about thirty metres behind, head down, his slightly knock-kneed gait giving him a curious rhythm. A cold hand seemed to grip him.

Feeling his stomach clench at the sight, he quickened his pace, pushing the doors to the car park open. He quickly validated his ticket at the machine in the stairwell, hands shaking as he poked the piece of card into the slot, and then tapped his payment card against the reader.

Within a minute, he was blipping the lock on his Jaguar, and sighing with relief as he settled into the cosseting leather. He just sat there, breathing easily, as he regained his composure. He reached down and grabbed his insulated metal water bottle, and took a swig.

It was as he was screwing the lid back on that he saw him again.

Lionel was walking slowly towards Daniel's car, his hands buried in his pockets, head down, a half-smile on his face.

'Oh, shit, no, please,' he said, as he fumbled for the start button, his finger trembling.

Lionel reached the car, his hands moving from his pockets, almost seeming to be in slow motion, a copy of the book in his hand. 'Dr Solomon, you forgot . . .'

As Daniel pressed the car's starter, the world seemed to shift on its axis, and his only conscious sensation was of massive, overwhelming pressure, just for a microsecond before the explosion from the device under the car threw it up in the air, smashing the roof into the low, concrete ceiling, before ripping both Daniel and Lionel into pieces with its devastating force.

Dear Reader,

We hope you enjoyed reading this book. If you did, we'd be so appreciative if you left a review. It really helps us and the author to bring more books like this to you.

Here at HQ Digital we are dedicated to publishing fiction that will keep you turning the pages into the early hours. Don't want to miss a thing? To find out more about our books, promotions, discover exclusive content and enter competitions you can keep in touch in the following ways:

JOIN OUR COMMUNITY:

Sign up to our new email newsletter: http://smarturl.it/SignUpHQ
Read our new blog www.hqstories.co.uk
𝕏 https://twitter.com/HQStories
🄵 www.facebook.com/HQStories

BUDDING WRITER?
We're also looking for authors to join the HQ Digital family!
Find out more here:
https://www.hqstories.co.uk/want-to-write-for-us/
Thanks for reading, from the HQ Digital team

Fern Britton
Picks
Exclusively for
TESCO

EXCLUSIVE ADDITIONAL CONTENT

ncludes a Q&A with Neil Lancaster, questions for your book
club and details of how to get involved in *Fern's Picks*

Dear lovely readers,

Prepare to be completely gripped by this intense and absorbing crime thriller by Neil Lancaster. *When Shadows Fall* will take you on a harrowing journey through the dark underbelly of crime, where betrayal and corruption lurk around every corner, and the stakes have never been higher.

DS Max Craigie investigates a series of deaths on the Scottish Highlands which, on the face of it, appear to be tragic climbing accidents. But there's something wrong: they were all women, experienced climbers, and alone when they died. The more Max investigates, the more he believes that they are dealing with something much more sinister. With five victims and conflicting clues, how do you catch someone committing the perfect crime?

The characters in this story are as complex as they are compelling, each grappling with their own demons while navigating a world rife with danger. Every page is packed with action and suspense, keeping you on the edge of your seat as the plot unravels bit by bit.

I can't wait to hear your thoughts on *When Shadows Fall* and how this thrilling tale resonates with you.

With love
Fern x

A Q&A with
Neil Lancaster

Warning: contains spoilers

What was the starting point for *When Shadows Fall*? Which part came to you first? The characters? The crimes? The criminals?

The idea came to me when my good friend, Simon Hammock, told me about a particular case he'd been involved in. Si is a search and rescue helicopter pilot working out of Inverness, and had collected a victim of a fall from the bottom of a cliff in The Highlands. Now, they don't normally use helicopters to collect the dead. It's a risky operation, and is normally undertaken by the mountain rescue team on foot, but as they'd already deployed the winch paramedic down, they took the casualty back to their base.

He told me how the local police were called, as is normal in cases like this, as the Procurator Fiscal will undertake a fatal accident enquiry, and the police need to provide evidence to support this. Si made the point that really, there was no actual evidence either way. It was just a lone walker, appropriately dressed, and in good weather who had fallen. Now, as a crime writer, this got me thinking. (Crime writers do this, and it makes our friends and families worry about us.) I just thought, 'what if a serial killer was stalking the Munros of Scotland?'

I then thought, what if the killings weren't random? I did some perusal of Munro bagging forums, and was struck by the fact that a number of first-time prospective climbers (often women) were seeking experienced climbers to go out on the hill with. This struck me as really risky. I mean, how do you know who these people are?

So, I had my idea. A serial killer using social media to find lone walkers to shove off cliffs.

I had my 'how it happens,' for the plot, but I didn't have my 'why it happens?' Crimes always have motivations, so what was my killer's reasons for doing what he does?

Then it hit me. One of the curses of the ages. Male violence against women. A really troubling, and important topic. It's a privilege of being an author that you get to talk about, and shine a light on subjects that you think are important and need to be discussed. I'm not so self-important to think that I can change things, but maybe fiction can be part of a vehicle to keep people talking about these important issues. This got me deep diving into the issue, and what I found was really troubling. I assumed that the 'incel culture' was hidden in the dimmer regions of the internet, but I was wrong. Within 1 minute of searching for incel related material I was flooded with forums and websites that chilled me to my very core. I really don't want to go too far into this, as it is genuinely shocking and disturbing, but suffice to say that a certain community of these, so called 'incels', hold the most hideous views on women, and I decided then and there that this was a subject that needed further exploration.

The Scottish Highlands serve as a beautiful yet treacherous backdrop for *When Shadows Fall*. How did you choose this setting?

Height! Obviously, I needed a dangerous environment for my killer to operate in. The Munros of Scotland are the roof of the UK. They are stunningly beautiful, but they can be very dangerous to the inexperienced. I have lived in The Highlands for over a decade now, and it is a spectacular place, and I have used it in all of the series almost as another character. I love speaking about my home, and shining a light on it, but it can be hazardous. I think the scenery can add atmosphere and tension. One second the highlands can be as beautiful as anywhere on the planet, but within a few moments, the weather can change, the clag can descend, and you're lost. Or the midges can arrive, and you're suddenly being eaten alive, or the light can change, and the hills change from spectacular and beautiful, to dark and brooding. Sometimes the scenes just write themselves.

When Shadows Fall – like many of the books in the Max Craigie series – features corrupt police. What inspired you to explore themes of corruption within law enforcement?

Corruption is thankfully rare in policing. Most cops are honest, and just want to do a good job, but it does happen. I'm fascinated as to how a police officer crosses the line from honesty to corruption. What causes them to cross that line? Organised criminal networks have been known to plant a 'sleeper' into the police. So, an individual will be encouraged to join the police in the hope that in years to come they will be of value in the future. Some may be put into compromising situations and coerced into corruption, others may just be opportunists who, in a moment of weakness, succumb to temptation. One thing is sure, in the same way that you cannot be 'half-pregnant,' you cannot be 'half-corrupt.'

Corruption exists. Big, organised crime cannot exist without corrupt individuals, and I think it's something that is worth writing about.

Final point on this subject. It's always good cops that catch bad cops. THAT is the most fascinating thing for me.

What was your writing process like for this novel? Did you have a specific routine or method that you followed?

Chaotic, as always. I don't have a routine. I just write when the mood takes me. I have only a vague plan, and I let the characters tell me which way to go. Being more established in the series now makes it easier. I know Max, Janie, Ross, Barney, and Norma well now. They always let me know which way to go.

Were there any significant plot twists or developments that changed during the writing process?

Always. Sometimes an idea can hit me out of nowhere, and I'll just decide then and there to change the whole direction of the novel by killing someone, having someone escape, or doing something even I wasn't expecting. It's not the most relaxing way of writing a 100,000-word book, but it does make it fun.

Which other authors have inspired your writing?

Lots. Ian Rankin is the master, and he's now a good mate. I also consider myself to be something of a frustrated thriller writer, to the extent that I've started a thriller series under a pseudonym (Max Connor.) I grew up reading the novels of Desmond Bagley, Alistair Maclean, Len Deighton, and they all planted in me a deep love of thrillers. I'm also a huge fan of many other contemporary writers, such as John Niven, Tony Kent, Ed James, Tony Parsons, Gregg Hurwitz, Lisa Jewell, Imran Mahmood, and too many others. I wish I had more time to just sit and read, but novels don't write themselves!

What do you hope readers take away from this story? Is there a particular message or feeling you want to convey?

In reality, my priority is to write a gripping, fast-paced story that will keep the pages turning, and maybe make people laugh at times. I think my favourite review was when someone said, 'starting a new Neil Lancaster book is like meeting up with old friends.' That made me really happy. The stories are one thing, but I hope that it's the characters, with their peculiarities, eccentricities, and values that keeps readers coming back. I hope that the themes I choose to talk about get people talking, and maybe make people think, but I'm not writing social history, or commentary. I hope I'm writing a good rattling read.

Can you tell us more about what you're writing next?

As always, I'm juggling projects. I'm currently writing the 8th Max Craigie novel, which will be out in 2027. It's early days, but I'm really liking the way it's panning out. I'm discovering a few new things to talk about, but I don't want to give too much away yet. Suffice to say that it turns out that I'm giving social media a bit of a bashing, which I didn't actually expect, but it's fun.

I've just finished all the final touches on Max Craigie 7 which will be out next year. I'm absolutely delighted with it, and can't wait for that one to come out. I really have thrown Max a few curve-balls in this one. Watch out for news on that front.

As Max Connor, I've just finished the third in the new series, which also will be out in 2027. That will need a good second draft before I deliver that to my publishers. I'm very excited about this one. It's a true spy thriller involving a defection from Russia, with lots of twists and turns.

So, I'm a busy fella, which is how I like it. I still pinch myself every day that after 25 years at the sharp end of policing, I'd end up writing stories about cops in the Highlands of Scotland.

I'm a lucky chap.

All the best,

Neil

Questions for your Book Club

Warning: contains spoilers

- Max often faces moral dilemmas as he navigates the investigation. Were there any decisions he made that you found particularly compelling or troubling? How would you have handled those situations?

- The story explores serious topics of misogyny and violence against women. How did the portrayal of these victims impact your reading experience? Did it evoke any particular emotions or reflections on real-world issues?

- Michael Anderson is portrayed as a deeply flawed character. What were your thoughts on his background and motivations? Did they help you understand any aspects of his character and actions?

- There are many great action-packed scenes, but the characters often come together in dire situations. What scene or moment stuck with you the most? Why did it leave an impact?

- There are some brilliant twists in the story. Did you guess any of them? How did you feel at the end?

An exclusive extract from Fern's new novel
A Cornish Legacy

CHAPTER ONE

North Cornwall, April, present day

Delia squinted through the windscreen, the sun ahead dazzling her. 'You'll see the turning on the right in a minute,' she said. 'Keep an eye out. I might miss it.'

Sammi tipped the last of the crisps into his mouth and sat up a little straighter. 'My eyes are peeled.' He pulled the sunglasses down from his head. 'Will there be some kind of landmark?'

'There's a big metal sign swinging on a post above the gates. Remember? You said it looked like a gibbet.'

Sammi chuckled. 'The gibbet! Yes, of course! Such a welcome.' He sat up straighter, alert. 'There!'

Delia saw the emerging gap amongst the tangled hedge of rhododendrons, with the rusted sign hanging from the post.

'Is that it?' asked Sammi. 'Can't read the name.'

Delia slowed, changing down through the gears. She wasn't smiling. 'Yep. This is it. Wilder Hoo.' The sight of the tatty sign that she had never wanted or expected to see again forced her stomach into a tight knot. Turning, she slowed the car and braked to a halt. 'I really don't want to be here.'

Sammi reached over for her knee and tapped it briskly. 'You're not on your own. I'm here, and those horrible people are gone. Come on.'

Delia put a hand to her chest and took a deep breath to control the old anxiety welling within. 'It's quite late. Let's go and find somewhere to stay tonight and come back tomorrow.'

'It's only half past four!'

'But it'll be getting dark soon.'

'Darling, it's April, not December.' Sammi's voice became soft and sympathetic. 'I know this is hard. But you can do it, and you will do it.'

'I don't want to do it.'

'The past is past. Dead and buried.'

Sighing heavily, Delia put the car in gear and slowly drove the winding tarmacked drive. 'Dead people can still haunt us.'

Stiff clumps of grass and dandelions had forced themselves between the cracked pitch, and in other places, huge potholes housed red, muddied puddles.

'It'll cost thousands just to repair the drive,' she said. 'Look at it.'

She knew that Sammi saw through different eyes. For him, this was an adventure. When Delia had first told him that the house had been gifted to her, he had been ready to celebrate, despite her horror of the whole thing. He seemed to feel only the thrill of an escapade.

Looking out of his side window at the ancient, rolling parkland with great oaks dotted across the scene he said, 'Delia, this is utterly captivating. Please tell me there's a lake. I'm expecting Colin Firth to stride forth in his wet breeches and shirt.'

Delia was scornful. 'If only. No lake, I'm afraid. Just a beach and all these acres of parkland. Do you know, it takes four men with a tractor each an entire week to cut all that grass? When they get to the end, they have to start again. It's a bloody money pit.' Her eyes flicked to the avenue of ivy-clad beech trees ahead, the bare branches forming a tunnel over sodden leaves. 'That ivy needs cutting back too. Argh. Who can afford all this, I ask you!'

Sammi was not listening. 'How long is this drive again?'

'It's 1.2 miles.'

'Very specific.'

Delia sighed. 'My father-in-law preferred to tell everyone it was two kilometres because that sounded longer.'

'And all this land belongs to the house?'

'Yup.'

Sammi was grinning. 'I'd love to jump on a tractor and spend a whole summer mowing all this.'

'You really wouldn't. Back in the day, there were sheep and deer to crop it.'

'Sheep and deer! Delia.' Sammi laughed. 'And all this is actually yours!'

She shrugged. She was weary and wretched. 'Not for long, I hope.'

They rattled over a cattle grid and onto a sparsely gravelled drive.

'OK. Here we go.' Delia swallowed hard. 'Round this bend, you'll see the house.' She took a nervous breath and added, 'I couldn't do this without you.'

Sammi tutted, 'I wouldn't let you come on your own, would I?'

Delia steered the last curve – and there, suddenly, was Wilder Hoo.

Available now!

The No.1 Sunday Times bestselling author returns

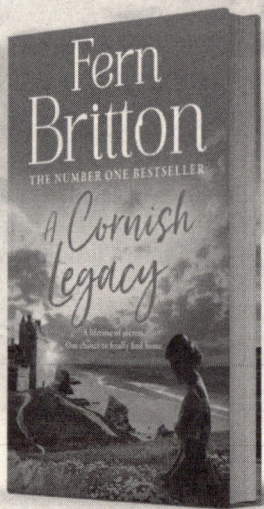

FERN BRITTON

THE NUMBER ONE BESTSELLER

A Cornish Legacy

Wilder Hoo house holds a lifetime of secrets.

When Cordelia Jago learns she's been left the crumbling manor house
Wilder Hoo, perched high on the Cornish coast, she wonders
if it's one last cruel joke from beyond the grave.

Having already lost her marriage, her best friend and her career, she's at rock-
bottom. Now she's inherited a house she hates, full of unhappy memories.

But as she fights with its echoing rooms and whispering shadows, the house
begins to exert a pull on her. The wild Cornish landscape, the stark beauty of
seagrass and yellow gorse against the deep blue sea, begin to awaken
a connection Cordelia thought she'd buried forever.

Could she turn around this monstrous wreck of a house – and, along the way,
let go of the secrets of the past and heal her heart too?

AVAILABLE NOW!

Our next book club title

THE CHRISTMAS TREE FARM
THE MAGIC STARTS HERE...

LAURIE GILMORE
THE *SUNDAY TIMES* BESTSELLER

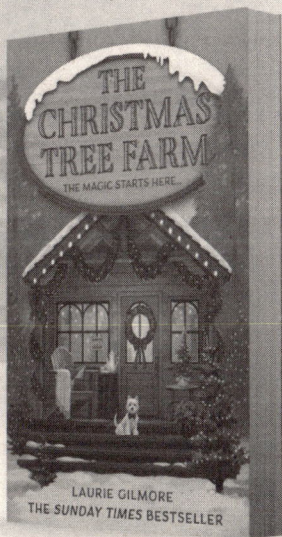

Kira North hates Christmas. Which is unfortunate since she just bought a Christmas tree farm in a town that's too cute for its own good.

Bennett Ellis is on vacation in Dream Harbor trying to take a break from both his life and his constant desire to fix things.

But somehow fate finds Ben trapped by a blanket of snow at Kira's farm, and, despite her Grinchiest first impressions, with the glow of the fairy lights twinkling in the trees, and the promise of a warming hot chocolate, maybe, just maybe, these two lost souls will have a Christmas they'll remember forever…